NANCY THOMPSON was born in Middlesbrough in 1915 and spent her childhood there. At the age of sixteen she joined her parents in the U.S.A. where she studied music at the Boston Conservatory. When she was twenty she returned to England and trained as a teacher. She taught throughout the war years in Liverpool and Wirral, specialising in music.

In 1947 she took a village school headship in North Yorkshire, and subsequently taught for an aggregate of twenty-five years in Wensleydale schools, while also undertaking freelance journalism. Widowed in 1973, she has two married daughters living in London and two grandchildren.

Also by Nancy Thompson
and published by Futura

AT THEIR DEPARTING

On Their Return

A Childhood Memoir

by

NANCY THOMPSON

Futura

To the memory of my Parents
and
for my American sister, Monica,
and
newly arrived grandchildren,
Susanna and William

A *Futura* Book

Copyright © 1987 by Nancy Thompson

First published in Great Britain in 1987 by
Hamish Hamilton Ltd, London

This edition published in 1988 by
Futura Publications, a Division of
Macdonald & Co (Publishers) Ltd
London & Sydney

ISBN 0 7088 3979 7

Printed and bound in Great Britain by
The Guernsey Press Co. Ltd, Guernsey, Channel Islands

Futura Publications
A Division of
Macdonald & Co (Publishers) Ltd
Greater London House
Hampstead Road
London NW1 7QX

A member of Maxwell Pergamon Publishing Corporation plc

Chapter One

On the twenty-ninth of October, 1924, Ellen Wilkinson became the first Labour Member of Parliament for Middlesbrough. Amongst the consequences of this event, both immediate and far-reaching, is a small one significant only to me. The date is the trouble, for it casts a doubt upon the chronological accuracy of my recollections: it gives a twist to the chain of events in my memory that is not easily explained, because I have always linked with Ellen's name that of my cousin, Robert Davison, known until the time of our grandfather's death as Robbie, and thereafter, except to my Aunt, as Bob. This unemployed nineteen-year-old saw Ellen Wilkinson as the panacea for all the troubles of the town. He swore by her, though never in the presence of our Aunt. If she were elected, then the borough would immediately enter upon a new age, a paradise, a kingdom of heaven on earth; so that I felt bound to ask him the question, 'Is she like Jesus, feeding the five thousand?' I received a sharp rebuke, 'That's enough of your cheek. And if I hear you call her by that daft name again, I'll slap you.'

He did not mean the name Jesus, but Wilkie, because when I had marched with an assortment of children at the tail end of a procession singing,

> Vote, vote, vote for Ellen Wilkinson,
> She's the champion of the poor,
> La-de-da-de-da-de-da,
> La-de-da-de-da-de-da,
> And no one will go hungry any more,

then I had insisted that Wilkinson had one syllable too many for what I considered a pretty poor tune anyway, and I had changed it to Wilkie. He thought I was making fun of her, and was too old to shrug it off as being of no consequence. But I was still eight, knew I wasn't mocking her and young enough to see it didn't matter if I was. But

1

October the 29th matters because by then Bob had been left the town two months and was on the other side of the Atlantic. Yet all these things are firmly and clearly planted in my memory: the fuss he made about her, the marching and singing through the long, straight streets, the confusion of turning corners at sharp right angles, the stirring of things that had slept a little since the War – the anger of fathers, the ferment bubbling up amongst brothers – a throwing off of memories, like tattered clothes; a forward look. Even we children felt it in the air around us, though our private predicaments did not always keep up with it.

There is one thing my memory has no record of – the Christmas of 1923, a week exactly after my grandmother died. The Christmas before and the one after are etched in detail. But Christmas 1923 is a blank.

Bob was more brother than cousin. Our maternal grandparents' house at 85 Park Lane, Middlesbrough, had been his home before it was mine. It had also been his mother's but death had removed her from it only a week after my own mother had propelled me into it by giving birth. My father had been admitted a mere few months before. He made up for this lateness on the scene by fathering two more daughters so that, by 1920, the house was home to eight people. Then, the following year, it began to empty. In 1921 Grandfather left for his grave; in 1923 my parents and sisters left for America; then, eight months later, Grandmother followed her husband. She had meant to do so, I knew, from the day my mother left her.

Throughout these changes, however, a thread of continuity had been maintained in the person of my mother's sister – unmarried – who, from the moment the house had been bought in the 1890s, shuttled between it and her work which lay in other peoples' houses, and, as she repeatedly informed the world at large, had kept things in some sort of order. The shuttling came to an end in April 1923 when she was obliged to take up her abode in the house and the care of three people, one old, one adolescent and one just eight. Now there were two, Bob and me, and, as I soon came to understand, we presented her with the knottiest of the many problems she had previously had to

2

tackle and certainly reduced her time for dwelling on political issues. In any case, she had no time for Ellen Wilkinson.

'And what would happen,' she would demand to be told, 'if this woman did get into Parliament? One thing is sure, your grandfather would turn in his grave. A Liberal all his life and her a woman with shingled hair! And red, into the bargain, as well as being such a shrimp. No one could see her standing up to a lot of men. The least she could have done was to grow her hair and coil it on top to give her a bit of height. She'll not get the support of the Wesleyans, I can tell you.' And to this strange view she held despite my cousin's efforts to hammer home Miss Wilkinson's credentials, her strong Wesleyan background and her brother a Chapel minister. As for me, all I wanted to know was whether Ellen would go round distributing baskets of food and, if so, how I could prevent our Aunt from slamming the door in her face. We might not belong to the real poor but facts must be faced, one being a noticeable shortage of food in our household since Grannie's death. And, if this were not remedied, of what use was a confrontation with a lot of men in a big house called The Commons? These things were discussed and I must be content with some flexibility as to the time of their discussion.

January is a dark month but, in retrospect, the darkness of January 1924 seems intensified. It was as though daylight, too, had left the house. I noticed it mainly at teatime when we ate our tea in the murk crouched over the small, round bentwood table drawn well up to the hearth. It reminded me of a giant toadstool but was much prized by Auntie who protected its top and looped legs with a white cloth. When the day would arrive – and she reminded us daily of its imminence – on which we should be turned out with nowhere to go but the pavement, this table was one thing which would go with us because it belonged to Auntie. I had heard many times how she had come by it during the year she had nursed a certain Mrs. Blackburn through a strange and nameless illness. Mrs. Blackburn had received the table from Mr. Blackburn after his absence for a whole week in London. 'A nice little bedside table for you my dear,' he'd said, and planted it there at her bedside, upon which, according to my Aunt, Mrs Blackburn had screamed, 'I don't want it, and I won't have it. Take it away, Blanche, just take it away,'and my Aunt had obliged. In a similar fashion a few lesser items had been acquired from Mrs Blackburn who clearly became violently disturbed at the sight of gifts from her husband.

Lucky for Auntie, I reflected, munching my second and last quarter of apple, because otherwise she might have had nothing to call her own. And all because of the will, or rather, the lack of one. She was on about it again. I supposed it was a subject you couldn't avoid.

'You don't like talking to someone about making their wills, especially if it's your own mother. It's a thing you can't do.'

There seemed nothing one could say, so Bob remarked that the fire was on its last legs. Also he couldn't see what he was eating. (We neither of us liked the topic of the will.) 'Shall I get a bit of coal and light the gas?' he went on, but Auntie said it was only five o'clock and we knew what there was to eat and we knew that she always saw to the fire herself. This was true. We were not allowed even to poke it. She would lay across a thin layer of embers some wood chippings from Uncle Watson's sack. (You keep it like the widow's cruse of oil, I told him once, watching its being replenished.) Then, when the sticks had taken hold, she would dampen them down with a thin covering of slack.

'I don't know anyone else,' she was given to repeating, and did so now, 'who can keep such a low fire going.'

'All I can say,' said Bob when she had departed with the shovel, 'is that her fire's cold comfort. No one would mind the price of coal if the miners were getting a fair share of the profits. But we know where it all goes . . .'

His tirade was similar to those I had heard before. It went in one ear and out of the other as I chewed thoughtfully on a mouthful of bread. I was not concerned with generalities: our personal plight was too pressing. The half apple with bread and butter for tea was one item in Auntie's budget to make ends meet. She held strongly by the nutritional value of the apple basing this, as I now

4

suppose, upon the popular adage about the apple keeping the doctor away. But the butter, she had told us, would soon have to be margarine, and I knew you couldn't get much lower than that. Several items in the food line were outside the bounds of respectability, margarine being one, and I could see us soon belonging to the lower not the upper half of the Lane. Our house and the Bonsils next door were the only double-fronted houses in it: they stood in the middle like a watershed.

Our predicament arose because along with Grannie had gone her pension of ten shillings a week. This left Auntie distressed on two counts, first the loss of income, then the fact that this loomed larger in her thoughts than the loss of her mother. As I heard her say to Minnie Gatenby, 'It's terrible to be thinking about her pension when you've just lost your mother. You have only one mother.' I considered this now, Grannie's failure to make a will and Auntie's failure to persuade her to do so and the resulting fact that we should have no house because ours now belonged to Uncle Watson who would then have two, and all because he happened to be the eldest son.

This strange fact had first come to my notice when Auntie told it to Minnie. I was busy with homework in the usual spot, sitting at the desk in the recess between the kitchen range and the front wall of the house. Five sentences each containing an adverbial clause of reason had to be compiled and I had written one. 'The great god Pan killed the reed because he wanted to make sweet music.' This was a reference to the latest poem by E.B. Browning which we were learning at school.

'So there it is,' came my Aunt's voice as my mind dwelt on the next sentence. 'I talked to Mr. Outhwaite all yesterday afternoon. He's a good solicitor and I have great faith in him, but he can't get away from the legal position. Watson is the eldest son and the house is his in the absence of a will to the contrary. Those were his exact words.'

I scribbled with a pencil in rough, 'Jack must have the house because . . .' chewed the end of the pencil, scribbled through what I'd written, then turned it into the negative. 'Jack does not want the house because . . .' I don't know why Minnie then turned her attention to me. Perhaps my

5

Aunt's words had a flat finality to which there was no reply. She said, 'What's your homework about, Martha?'

'Clauses.'

'Oh. We didn't have those when I was at school. What are they?'

'Well, I've just written, "Jack does not want the house because . . ." and I have to add an adverbial clause of reason.'

'What will you put?'

'The easiest clause of all, "because he has one of his own".'

Minnie lifted her hands, clapped them down on her knees and laughed with glee, as I'd heard somewhere that a child does though I did not believe it. I had never heard one do so and I had never done so myself. I wished I knew what made Minnie laugh, with a husband slowly dying, Auntie had said, of tuberculosis. The laugh drew a map of creases across her face as she regarded me through grey unspectacled eyes.

'Did you hear that, Blanche? She's hit the nail right on the head, although she has to call it by that peculiar name. Ad-something clause. I'd never remember such like. I'd have to think of Santa Claus! But you must see how right she is. Watson will never take your home because he has all he wants.'

'He has more than he wants in Gertrude.' She was wrapping a jar of calves' foot jelly in brown paper, deftly turning in the ends top and bottom and making a very neat job of it. The jelly had been bought for Grannie. Now it was being given to Minnie for her husband. 'Gertrude twists him round her little finger. He'll have no peace until she gets her hands on this house. Of course they won't live in it, theirs being the better one. They'll let it. But I shan't be able to pay them a rent.'

'Why is it a better one?' I asked with a stirring of resentment. On the way to Grove Hill the houses stood in pairs and each pair was separated from the next by a narrow grass verge, a path, some twisted iron railings with caps and a gate. Each front room window was a large bay. Still the houses were not double fronted and I saw no reason for my Aunt's unfair comparison.

'Your Uncle Watson's house is on the outskirts of the town. A more valuable property, as they say, and the mortgage on it causes Watson to work his fingers to the bone. But what has that to do with anything? Your mind should be on your homework, Martha. Which it is, as a rule.'

Which it was, I supposed, though one part of my mind must have heard without knowing it heard; because in the middle of the night when lying awake beside Auntie who purred her way through sleep, my thoughts would take a leap and land on something they'd said, something I was not conscious of hearing at the time. As when Auntie had been talking to Mary Kitching about the will, or rather, its non-existence. I was familiar with Mary's photograph some time before I saw her in the flesh. She and Auntie shoulder to shoulder each in a frilly white high-necked blouse and wearing a string of beads wrapped twice round each neck. Dressed identically, like twins, and taken, Auntie had said with a heavy sigh, a long time ago. Yet when I saw Mary in the flesh, I recognized those huge dark mournful eyes like the eyes of a large sad dog.

'I'm not surprised, not in the least surprised,' came Mary's voice out of the darkness. 'You have to admit, Blanche, that your poor mother had no will to call her own throughout her married life. Not that your father was any worse than the rest. Their own comfort and pleasure is all they ever think of. But women mustn't think at all. As far as I'm concerned, John's not getting away with it. He can sleep downstairs in the armchair if he wants to, and if he can't sleep, then let him sulk. He'll not make me call him back to bed. From what I know of Watson and Gertrude, I should hate to raise false hopes for you about keeping this house. Women with a bit about them can bring any man to heel.'

Intriguing, like so many grown-up speeches, I thought; then had a sudden clear picture of John, whom I had never actually seen, sitting in his chair in the dark, unable to sleep and perhaps seeing strange things stir in the darkest corners, as I did. 'Don't be afraid, John,' I said mentally. 'The night doesn't stand still. It moves on and grows into morning.' Then I flung myself over sideways away from

7

my Aunt and muttered to myself, 'I don't care, I really don't care which of them is right, Minnie or Mary. Perhaps I hope it's Mary.' To be on the street might be a great adventure, and you didn't need much to survive. A real version it would be of those nightly sessions in the back yard W.C. with the candle casting moving shadows about the imaginary loaf, knife, pail of water and a mug, while outside the world stretched without end in a flat, arid desert. There was an excitement in struggling to survive against all odds, and also a strange comfort. I was wrapped in it, on the edge of sleep, when a new thought intruded, a new picture really, of those men sitting in Victoria Square. Not in armchairs, like John, but on benches. Did they stay out all through the night? When you crossed the square, the benches looked full with no spare room between the silent figures. Sometimes their eyes were closed, sometimes they followed you if you looked, sometimes their faces gave thin smiles. And I'd seen some dipping their hands, furry with bits of woollen glove, into brown paper bags and chewing what was taken out. Surviving, I supposed.

A lot of men on the streets. A thousand men. The grand old Duke of York, he had ten thousand men. Ten thousand men unemployed in Middlesbrough was what the Labour people had said, according to Bob. It was too many to think about. A hundred was bad enough. I could not even think about – a hundred. But if *they* were turned out, then I did hope Minnie would be right.

Chapter Two

Hannah Kneeshaw, my mother's friend who lived at 112 Park Lane, had received a letter from Mother written after the news of Grannie's death had reached her in Lawrence, Massachusetts.

'She really is devastated, Blanche.' This long word interrupted my calculation of rods, chains, furlongs, miles. Hannah could be relied upon to gain my attention with her long words. Auntie was ironing a sheet, so it must have been Tuesday. Faintly, like the beat of an elfin tattoo, there sounded through the scullery from the greenhouse Tom Henderson's rhythmic hammering on the sole of a boot. It reached us in the kitchen where the week's ironing was always done because of the fire. This was the one time when it must be made up. Cinders must glow the height of the iron as it rested upright on a bar and faced the glorious redness. A smokeless fire, because the irons must not be blackened. So Tuesday night was the most comfortable time in our house and we always had toast for tea. That evening Bob and I had taken turns with the long toasting fork, holding it at arms length before the incandescent wall of embers and letting the bread brown gently. It required skill and concentration otherwise the fork prongs enlarged the holes and the slice lost its balance. Toasting improved with practice and I wished I could practise more often than once a week. That tea time our toast had been smeared with a thin covering of Bovril which made you thirsty so that now I was hoping Auntie would soon make a cup of tea.

As long as she had some tea to sip, her sitting at the table was all right, but I could not bear it when she sat supporting her chin on her thumb, denting her cheek with her forefinger and resting her middle finger on her lower lip. The first time this mannerism had jangled my nerves was at the Chapel memorial service for my Grandfather when I was six. And from then on, going to Chapel with her had upset me, for this was her praying position, one elbow on her knee. Since the prayers were long, I suffered agonies and was very bad-tempered afterwards. At home she was hardly ever still. She talked as she worked or sang one of her favourite hymns, 'Work for the night is coming, when man's work is done.'

'Well,' she said in answer to Hannah's statement, 'I suppose she's young to lose a mother,' plainly making one allowance though a little grudgingly. 'But she must have realised that she would never see her again. All that distance, and Mother seventy-five. She's got Harry and the children though that's not saying much. She was never strong enough for all that. And a bit spoilt, being always the favourite with Mother. It's to be hoped she can make something out of those expensive painting lessons she had with Mr. Scupham.'

'Oh, I'm sure she will. Did she tell you she's painting some lamp shades for a firm in Lawrence? And Harry has some kind of work. She was determined to save gradually and return towards the end of this year to see Mrs Drinkhall again. But it wasn't to be. You must see her difficulties, Blanche.'

'We're all in the same boat, as far as that goes. Rob should help them. He was the first in our family to be smitten with this emigration fever, leaving out Joe Davison who doesn't count. Monnie daren't have gone if Rob hadn't been there. While they were still at home and I was out nursing, I did all I could to help. But what can I do now, with Robbie and Martha and everything? Just tell me what I can do,' and she changed irons, balancing the cool one on the bar, cleaning the hot one vigorously and then spitting on it. The spit broke into globules and raced in different directions over the upturned surface. I saw this marvel because I had stopped dividing one thousand, seven hundred and sixty by five-and-a-half to find the number of rods in a mile. I stopped because I wanted to hear if Hannah had a solution to our problem, if she could tell my Aunt what to do.

Hannah said, 'It might be as well, Blanche, if you took the leap.'

'And what might that mean?'

'Well, I suppose you might call it a leap in the dark, but I think you're the type who could do very well in America with your nursing experience. Surely there must be some illness about, despite all that sunshine and dry air. People can't live on it forever.'

'I'll look long before I take such a leap. Though I must say the water's the main problem. I couldn't face it. Not after William Henry and the *Titanic*, to say nothing of the *Lusitania*. All the time Monnie was crossing that ocean I was saying, "How could she risk her life like that and be carried every day farther away from her own mother and child?" It wasn't natural.'

'But, Blanche, only one boat was lost. The other was torpedoed. And boats sail every week from Liverpool or Southampton.'

'I'll wait though, until there's another way of getting there. Which means never. All those miles!'

I supplied the missing figure. 'Three thousand.'

'Get on with your work, Martha.'

'Do you want to know how many furlongs? Twenty-four thousand. That sounds further still.'

'You heard what I said,' and she drove home her words with a thump on the sheet. Hannah intervened . . .

'Has Monnie told you they're not doing too badly though they're still in that top floor tenement which is bitterly cold at present? Such severe winters! They are having to use a paraffin heater. Kerosene, they call it. I can't understand why they don't build more solid houses to keep out the elements. Why wooden houses? Perhaps they can't make bricks. But she knows some poor people – emigrants – who have fared much worse. She says she took the children to Boston by train and tram to visit a family they'd met on the boat. The father had been a German prisoner of war and was consumptive. Has she told you about it?'

'No. She tells me very little of their affairs.'

'I'll read it to you, then.' and Hannah opened her large black handbag and took out the letter.

'Don't read it unless you want to.' My Aunt much preferred telling a story to hearing one. But Hannah liked reading aloud. She often read aloud to her Mother, from a suitable book, of course. Once she had told me why. It diverted her Mother's mind from finding fault with everything. In that case, the reading aloud, I thought, was an excellent idea. It wouldn't work with Auntie, though, for several reasons. Hannah found the place and started.

'"I was absolutely shocked. Their home was an appalling wood-framed house, one of dozens in a crowded, smelly slum and I'd expected Boston to be a lovely city. They call the houses fire-traps, two or three storeys high with four or more families to a floor and only one W.C. for all those people. I had to take the children in there and was nearly sick with the stench coming up from it mixed with the queer smell of all kinds of food cooking over kerosene stoves. At least we have an electric cooker which is safer than our gas at home. I thought they lived by the sea and I'd bought the children pails and spades and one of each for their little girl called Frieda. But there was no sand, no soil, not even any dirt, only old tarmac and filthy cobblestone streets. They tried to dig between the cobbles, but the tin spades bent. Worst of all, it was such a long way that we had to stay the night which I spent swatting mosquitoes from the children with a rolled up newspaper and even brushing off bed-bugs."'

Hannah looked up and a trickle of saliva ran down her chin. She fumbled in the bag for a handkerchief.

'It's hard to believe, isn't it? She says she'd have told me before but she didn't want Mrs Drinkhall to hear about it. Not that I'd have mentioned it then. Whenever she's depressed, she thinks about it and counts her blessings.'

Auntie held a folded sheet at arm's length and placed the two folded ends meticulously together. Somehow it was comforting to see her do this orderly thing. She let down the clothes airer, hung the sheet over one of the slats and hoisted it ceilingwards again. Only the squeal of the pulley broke the silence and shattered a picture of my Mother on Redcar sands using a wooden spade to pat down firmly the sand in a painted tin pail while I searched the sea for a glimpse of America. My thoughts clung to the sheet.

'It's as bad as Cannon Street, if not worse,' Auntie commented. She stood the second iron inside the fender to cool. That was finished for another week, and she chose to conclude her comment with, 'Germans deserve all they get.'

There was another pause before Hannah said, as if pondering this statement, 'I suppose so. But they're not all Germans. Monnie says that the school Bessie attends, when she can get her there, is full of emigrants from all over Europe. They speak only a few words of English and the teacher gets impatient and concentrates on the two pupils who are born Americans. Rob's little boy is one of them. Monnie is angry because Bessie is classed with the foreigners although she can speak better English than the Americans when she chooses to speak at all. And every child in the school has to salute the Stars and Stripes each morning and recite something about the American state and the President. That's instead of prayers.'

'So Harry was right. I remember a row they had about it. A godless place, he called it, though where he got his ideas from I don't know. Some Americans he met in the war, I suppose. He always said Martha should stay put and get on with her education here and, if you ask me, there's much to be said for staying put.'

'But Monnie intends to come back for her. I'm sure she will. Sometime.'

On that subject, at that time, I did not dwell, despite an awareness that whether I should be in England or in America was a constant, glued to me like my shadow. It could loom large at times of crisis like the present, then dwindle to almost nothing. I completed the last sum, a reduction of miles, furlongs, chains, yards and feet to feet, set down and worked through in the required manner. The answer came to 20,131 feet. For a split second I wondered about the sense of working out such a sum, then brushed the intrusion from my head, knowing that of course it was sensible. You worked through it according to the rules and, with care, would reach a correct answer which was sufficient reason for doing it. The only reason for not doing a sum would be if it had no answer.

Around the time that my mother, on the other side of the Atlantic, was having words with Bessie's teacher about her being ignored and taught nothing, on this side my Aunt had had a brush with Miss Byers about my being

13

taught too much, that is, too much of a peculiar nature. 'Peculiar' was her expression for anything even slightly beyond her understanding. Her visit to school was the result of my hearing noises between half past eight and midnight when I had the bedroom and the bed to myself. Being alone in a bedroom was a new experience because, from the time my parents left England until my grandmother's fall in the backyard, Grannie had always gone to bed at the same time as I did. I had known how she'd felt the day to be long enough with Auntie's nervous energy keeping us all on our toes. Now I lay alone in the vast expanse of bed and heard something move behind the wardrobe. There was sufficient space for movement because my Aunt stood any wardrobe, no matter how space-consuming, diagonally across a corner.

'Why weren't you asleep when I came to bed?' she asked one morning while I toyed with a tablespoonful of grapenuts. So she knew that I wasn't asleep. I'd always pretended to be, turned on my side facing the wash-stand. You must look different or sound different when you're really asleep. Now I began to think about it, I realised that there *was* a difference. I could always tell when she was asleep.

'I don't know. I can hear things behind the wardrobe.'

I was questioned no further, my Aunt having jumped to her own conclusions. That day the wardrobe was pulled out and its back, together with the wall and floor behind it, were first scoured and then generously sprinkled with a greyish powder.

'I'll not have a beetle or a cockroach in this house,' she declared and re-told the tale of the swarms which had scurried every night from behind the skirting boards of Mr Carlin's house in Marton Road. Her campaign to rid the house of them had lasted four years. Since she was born with a gift for moving heavy wardrobes, the scouring and powdering went on for a week and two mouse-traps were set. Still I complained of noises, though no dead beetle or trapped mouse was ever found.

'I don't think it's those,' I told her when she admitted she was baffled. 'It's more like a sigh. Or a lot of sighs.'

'Beetles can make a lot of noises and all of them

14

different. You'd be surprised.'

'But they wouldn't call my name,' I argued, 'and I heard it last night. Quite plainly while I was practising in my head Mark Anthony's speech. We have to recite it today. Just as I finished, "The evil that men do lives after them, the good is oft interred with their bones. So let it be with Caesar," I heard my name from behind the wardrobe. Then a long sigh.' Auntie's glasses gleamed at me. In the dim light I couldn't see her eyes but I felt her gaze penetrate mine. She was angry.

'Would you believe it? After all the slaving I've done this week, it's neither mice nor beetles, just the stuff they're teaching you at school. Well, I'll make it my business to see Miss Byers today.'

And she did, causing me to quake through the afternoon waiting for Miss Gibson to be called from the room, which was what sometimes happened when a distraught mother of a Standard Six girl arrived. But no call came, and back home, after school, no word on the subject was spoken by my Aunt. At tea time Bob said, 'Well, how did it go with Miss Byers?'

'Oh, she was very nice. We had a talk. It seems the girls have to learn this stuff if they're going in for that scholarship. Naturally, I don't understand why.' She turned to me. 'Miss Byers thinks you're still upset about Grannie and, for a while you should go to bed when I do. You'll be short of sleep, I can tell you. I can't give up and go to bed at eight. Goodness knows how we'll get on!'

Her doubts were justified. By the time we got to bed, she was in her 'nervous wreck' state through having to rush the evening's jobs, and I was ready to be irritated by everything she did, such as unhook her Spirella corsets, use the chamber pot and kneel to whisper the Lord's Prayer. I had been much less upset by voices from behind the wardrobe. Yet when I asked if I could sleep in the other bedroom which had been my parents' and then hers, you would have thought I was asking if I could go on the next boat to America.

'Whatever will you be asking for next? Children don't sleep alone unless they have to, like poor Laura Burt. And there's your headmistress thinking you shouldn't be alone

15

in a bedroom for a couple of hours.'

Nor did Miss Byers' suggestion have any effect upon the intermittent occurrence of the Thing, a name I had to use in the absence of anything more suitable. As I tried willing sleep to come, often the Thing came instead, swooping down, scooping me up and swinging me out into empty space. I was whirled at a terrifying speed in ever widening circles, my ear drums pounding with an ever increasing roar, my heart hammering at an accelerating pace. I was intensely aware of my solitary helplessness in the grasp of a malevolent force which, for want of a better word, I told myself was witchcraft. Somewhere in the spatial distance was a tunnel that seemed to be our goal. If we reached it, I knew there would be no return and that possibility was ever present. I could do nothing but wait and struggle to keep on breathing which I felt would somehow keep me in touch with earth. The return was as if a brake had been applied to the giddy revolutions, a slowing of the heart beat and a final stillness as I sank back into the bed, my nightgown drenched with sweat. I told no one about this.

Chapter Three

Although we still had a roof over our heads, our predicament, as far as I can recall, remained unchanged as the February days lengthened and we managed to eat our apple and bread in what was real daylight. My Aunt continued to predict that we should end up on the pavement and I have sometimes wondered if I really did take that statement literally because a picture of us sitting there materialized one night in late December, 1940, when my Aunt and I sat under the stairs while bombs rained on Liverpool. Bob, she and I were in front of our Park Lane door with blankets, an umbrella, a knife, a loaf and a pail of water. I saw the aged Bonsils from next door step deliberately off the pavement and pass us by on the road, taking care to look straight ahead until they could limp up the curb again. I saw Aunt Gertrude come along and cross to the opposite pavement which was narrow and not in general use being bounded only by the wall enclosing the Nurses' Home. The Levite, I thought.

Occasionally I took in the real situation. In fact it forced itself upon me. Apart from Bob's dole money, my Aunt relied on Tom Henderson's rent for the greenhouse where he repaired footwear. His rent came spasmodically and seemed to be the main cause of her rows with him which, in their turn, caused much turmoil in the lower parts of my body as I ran home from school. I tried various ways of averting these rows, methods ranging from prayer to magic. I didn't expect much from prayer, having found how it could let you down. Still, I did repeat many times, 'Please God, please God, don't let there be a row,' then reinforced this plea by not treading on the lines between the paving flags. When this didn't work, I tried treading on every line between them which was so exhausting to maintain all the way from Victoria Road that I was sure it must produce results. Magic proved no more efficacious than prayer. Ten minutes past four seemed to be her time for bombarding him with verbal abuse while he cowered in the doorway between the scullery and the greenhouse stuttering about Mrs Dick or Mrs Dodd who had had to pawn their decent boots to buy a loaf of bread and still couldn't pay him for having repaired the same. Auntie would then yell that he had been paid yesterday by Mrs Dawkins and don't ask her how she knew, and where had Mrs Dawkins' money gone? Straight to the George and Dragon. Meanwhile, there was I in the doorway between passage and scullery, not daring to duck through the firing line to reach the W.C. and steadily soaking my home-made flannelette knickers.

It happened, however, that one wet day in late February I did not fly home anticipating a row. At playtime that afternoon we had been herded miserably under the shed enduring the long wait for the bell to summon us back up the steps, into the cloakrooms and through the long tiled corridor to our respective classrooms. Miss Gibson's after-noon timetable was flexible, depending on what she thought was urgently needed in our progress towards the scholarship examination. But that afternoon, to our aston-ishment, we saw the piano being wheeled in by four monitors. Excitement kindled at this innovation on a Thursday afternoon. Miss Gibson was not there but we moved quietly to our desks and stood waiting.

'Sit,' ordered Dorothy Morton, the head monitor, and we sat. 'Miss Gibson is not very well so Miss Byers is coming to take you for Music.'

An upsurge of pleasure attacked me and I stifled it. I was suspicious of such a feeling. Our headmistress, gravely dignified in a dress of navy blue, came through the doorway carrying a sheet of music and a roll of paper.

'It's a dark afternoon,' she announced, 'so I think we could all do with something to cheer us up. Music can do this. It can take us out of ourselves. I'm going to play you an ancient melody, in fact one of the very oldest tunes we know. We're not quite sure, but we think it might have come from Ireland. We have one or two girls whose parents came from Ireland. Let's see who they are.'

We all looked round to see three hands being nervously raised. I remembered the foreigners in that American

18

school. Miss Byers was not like that teacher. I felt proud of her as I watched her place the roll on the piano top, open her music and sit down on the stool.

'Listen carefully, because after I've played it I shall try to tell you why it is a good tune. We'll talk about it, then we'll learn to sing some Irish words written for it.'

No one moves as the tune begins at a strange low pitch. The notes take on their own life and flow into mine. I close my eyes not caring who sees me do so, because I know what it's about. There's a deep pool and a salmon leaping to get out of it, leaping to get over the top of a high waterfall. Like the one Bob showed me on a cigarette card and we both said how we'd love to see one really leap and really make it. Because a lot of them don't. The fall is too high and they drop back exhausted – just like the tune. And the pool has a name. It could be Pain. What a lovely note on top 'me'. A long, longing note. But it can't stay up there. No, I was right. Down it comes, right back to where it began. It's lifted itself for the last time. I know because it's weaker, like the salmon. It's slowing down, and there it goes, wrapped in a sad, strange chord – not one I know – as it sinks into the pool. And now it's gone.

Miss Byers waited a moment, took the music in her hand and stood up.

'Did you like that, girls?'

'Yes, Miss Byers.' I suppose they all joined in, except for me. I kept my lips clamped together as she proceeded to explain and demonstrate with one hand at the keyboard, how the notes rose and fell, rose and fell again with a small difference. Could we hear the difference? Then came the second half of the tune with the same rise and fall, but where is it now? In the upper half of the scale, climbing higher still until, reaching the highest note of all, it lingers, then falls in little loops and heads for home.

'Listen,' she said, 'to this curious ending called a cadence.' We listened and were quiet for a while. She was very good at that, knowing when to allow silence to take over, a silence when each of us could think our separate thoughts. She broke it by asking who would like to give some reasons why this tune could be called a good tune.

I make myself small, as small as possible by contracting

muscles, hunching shoulders, squeezing arms to my sides – not folded, which is forbidden – eyes cast down and catching sight of my protruding lower lip. I will myself out of sight. Someone else has to answer. Someone else must. Because I won't. The silence now is not as before. It is uncomfortable, upsetting, then shattered as I hear, 'What about you, Martha? I'm sure you'd like to say something.'

How can grown-ups be so stupid, even Miss Byers! Now I have to look at her and drag myself to my feet and recollect with agony what to say and what I will not say.

'The tune rises and falls. It repeats itself, though a bit different. Then the second half rises from soh to top doh and falls back. Then it reaches top 'me' and stays there, then drops in loops to bottom lah and goes through a cadence to doh.'

'Exactly. You've followed that very well indeed. But is there anything else you'd like to say? Anything which makes you think it's a good tune?'

Anything else? Anything else? What else does she want?

With extreme reluctance I mutter, 'Well, the tune leaps and falls back like a salmon leaping at a waterfall.'

This was too much even for disciplined pupils. A titter was heard from here and there, then quelled by a single look. She turned to me and said, 'So you've heard the song before, Martha?' To which I could truthfully reply that I had not.

'But I think you have heard some of the words. Perhaps your cousin has sung them. It's a well known song. When we come to the words, you'll see that the second verse begins with two lines about salmon leaping over the weir.'

I felt uneasy. Surely Miss Byers didn't think I was telling a lie and for no reason. Didn't she realise that I knew too well the consequences? So I told her again that I really could not remember hearing this song before. She looked at me intently, then said, 'It's a strange thing, what we can hear without knowing it.' Then she took the roll from the top of the piano and handed it to Dorothy Morton. 'Will you please clip the words to the blackboard, Dorothy? Now we'll read it together,' and we chorused along with her,

In Derry Dale, beside the singing river,
So oft I strayed, ah many years ago,
And culled at morn the golden daffodillies
That came with Spring to set the world aglow.
Oh Derry Dale, my thoughts are turning ever
To your broad stream and fairy-circled lea,
For your green isle my exiled heart is yearning,
So far away across the sea.

We finished the second verse and she told us about the lovely, unhappy country with its potato famine and bread too dear to buy and how those who could had to leave it and find new homes in America, though some of them came only as far as England. Naturally, she said, they were sometimes homesick and longed to see their native land again.

I ran all the way home, pelting through the puddles and splashing my stockings to the knees. I wanted to be at the organ. I wanted to play the tune. I wanted to sing the words,

Oh tarrying years, fly faster, ever faster,
I long to see the land I love so well . . .

Was that how they felt, in Lawrence, Massachusetts? Could it possibly be that my mother longed for Middlesborough with the iron and steel works, the shipyards where no one could get work, the Transporter Bridge and the streets of houses built of solid brick, not wood? Did my father wish he'd never gone there, though he hadn't liked Middlesborough much either? A place so unlike the lovely one in the song with its daffodils and broad stream and salmon leaping over the weir. And what about the Irish girls' mothers? Were they homesick for Ireland? Was everyone homesick for somewhere? Sick for home?

I don't think I realised how silent the house was as I closed the front door behind me. I was heading for the organ in the front room though first my wet coat must be hung on the scullery door. But for that, I wouldn't have seen her sitting by the grate in the kitchen, doing nothing. I noticed her just as I was struggling out of my coat beside the kitchen doorway. Her elbow rested on the bentwood table, her chin was supported on her outstretched thumb and her forefinger lay along her lower lip. My left arm stayed in the sleeve of my coat which dangled on the floor while spasms of nervous pain shot through all my body.

'What's the matter, Auntie?' She looked up, removing her hand but keeping her elbow on the table. 'I'm just wondering what we can have for tea.' It was unlike her to sit just like that, wondering.

Another spasm attacked my stomach. Was she hungry? We'd had only a pancake for dinner, I recalled, and a piece of bread and butter for breakfast. Her round glasses with their thin metal rims seemed to look at me reproachfully in the grey light.

'There must be something in the pantry.'

'Nothing, really.'

'Can't we buy something then?'

'I've no money, Martha. Do pick up your coat from the floor. The gas bill had to be paid. I couldn't keep it unpaid any longer and Tom Henderson has given me no green-house rent for three weeks. He persists with this story that people can't pay him, but he drinks what he gets. The next thing we'll hear is that he's been turned out of his bed at Sidaway's. And I'm not going to ask Watson for help, not as things are with the house. I just don't know what we can have for tea, unless...'

'Unless what?'

'Well, I declared I would never part with it because it was all she had to leave. The half-crown in Mother's purse. I don't want to spend it.'

Then I saw what her arm was protecting. I crossed to the table and picked it up. Grannie's little purse with the three pale brown buttons which were not buttons but studs to open different compartments. I remembered Grannie showing it to me, pointing with pride to the inscription in a tiny decorated framework, 'Warranted real velvet calf'. 'It looks more like polished wood,' I'd said and she'd replied, 'That's how it goes with so much handling. Harder, stronger with wear. You can't wear it out. Your Grandfather gave it me when we were married, for housekeeping, you see.' 'It wouldn't hold much,' I'd said bluntly. But when she had unfastened the studs, grasped both ends, then gently extended it, the purse had opened wide like that concertina Jack Smart had just bought. 'Count the compartments,' she'd said, and I'd counted six. She'd smiled. 'It will hold quite a lot, you see,' which made me ask, 'Was it ever so full that you couldn't fasten it?' and, still smiling, she'd shaken her head. 'Not really. I keep only threepenny bits inside it now,' and I'd looked at the two tiny coins nestling in the middle pocket. 'It's as light as a feather, Grannie. But wouldn't it be heavy with pennies and florins and half-crowns?'

It felt heavy now, with its one half-crown. As heavy as lead to me at that moment.

'How did it come to be there? A half-crown?'

'I'm sure I don't know.' Her voice grew irritable. 'Martha, your coat is still trailing on the floor. I found the purse in her drawer when I had to clear things out. I used to collect her pension. You know she hadn't been out to spend any money herself since your mother went. I got what she needed. That's all she left and I wanted to leave it there, silly as that might seem to some people.'

It didn't seem silly to me, but still . . . I took the half-crown out of the purse and snapped the studs together to close it. I said, 'Never mind, we'll still have the purse, and it's the purse that matters, isn't it?' She rose and kissed my cheek and I'm glad she didn't seem to notice my instinctive recoil.

'You're a good girl. Get into that coat again and come with me to the shop.'

I never really knew why we went through the late wet February afternoon all the way to a shop at the far end of Aubrey Street. I never knew why she bought three meat pies as well as a loaf of bread. For she scorned shop pies of any kind, just as she scorned shop-fried fish and chips which she often said Tom lived on. I only know with certainty that, as I walked the long street close to her side to keep under the umbrella, a black sheet dropped over me and I was somewhere else – an alien in a hostile land.

I returned with the clanging of the bell above the shop door. It was an unfamiliar shop, but it felt like home.

Chapter Four

What was she doing there, the unknown figure at whom
we were all staring from the moment we lined up for
Prayers? With all those eyes upon her, no wonder she kept
hers lowered. She could not be a new girl or she wouldn't
be standing with the teachers. Yet surely she wasn't a new
teacher – she was far too young and pretty. She might, I
thought, be just slightly older than Dorothy Morton who
was fourteen and would be leaving at Easter. People's ages
interested me. I decided she must be older than that
because of her hair. It was not in plaits, but gathered into a
heap at the back of her neck and held there apparently by a
brown ribbon tied in a bow. My hair would never be held
in place just by a ribbon, so hers must be thick. Then there
was her dress. Peculiar, my Aunt would have called it,
because the cream blouse was neither drawn in tightly at
the neck nor at the waist. Instead, it had a wide, loose
collar and was pulled in at her hips. It distinctly reminded
me of the blouse worn by Dick Kneeshaw in that photograph taken when he was ten, and from the side her skirt
looked like his trousers ending a few inches below the
knee. In this instance I would have agreed with my Aunt,
her dress was peculiar.

Even when Miss Byers said, 'Good morning, teachers.
Good morning, girls,' this newcomer did not raise her
eyes. She looked frightened, her profile like that of the
princess in the story of the frog prince. Facing some kind
of ordeal was the impression she gave. But, I thought,
people often made a great fuss about nothing. What was
wrong with a harmless frog eating its dinner off your plate
or even sleeping in your bed?

We sang 'New every morning is the love' and, since I
knew all the words, I kept my eyes on her. She kept hers
on her hymn book and not once did she glance up
although I willed her to do so. Well, I thought, as we
recited the Lord's Prayer, it must be dreadful to have

24

almost a hundred girls staring at you.

When we opened our eyes and relaxed our hands from their position of prayer, Miss Byers introduced her as Miss Sykes, a pupil teacher. This came as a shock in view of my speculations that she could be neither. In any case, how was it possible to be both? It *was* possible, it seemed, because Miss Sykes, we were told, would be learning how to teach. I was no less puzzled than before for the simple reason that I had imagined teachers to be born, not made. Certainly a race apart. The strange business quickened my curiosity. I was eager to see how a person was taught to teach. It began with Miss Sykes sitting in a corner by the cupboard, pencil in hand and a copy book on her knee. During Scripture, as we chorused David's lament for Saul and Jonathan, 'The beauty of Israel is slain upon thy high places; how are the mighty fallen,' I was aware of the beauty of Miss Sykes. Her cheeks were the colour of Caroline Testout, a pink rose on one of my cousin's cigarette cards, and hazel was, I believed, how you would describe her eyes, though whether after the twig or the nut I was uncertain. But I had called my doll Hazel. After Scripture she was told to observe how Miss Gibson gave a lesson on Stocks and Shares. We began with some examples after having been carefully instructed in the difference between Stock and the money which bought it. Miss Sykes passed up and down between the double desks marking our answers with a pencil. She was about to come down our aisle when the door opened and Miss Byers called her to proceed to Standard Five. She must first get a general impression of the whole school.

I saw little of her for about a week, but enough to have established what I believed was a communication between our eyes. This occurred in assembly, in the playground where she paced back and forth, and sometimes when she passed a few of us in the corridor. I anticipated her glance at me, but then flicked mine away so that at least I could imagine it had been meaningful rather than accidental. This supposed interplay lent colour to the school day but, as yet, I did not dwell on it at home.

Then came a day when she settled down in our class. She would, Miss Byers explained, be taking us for a lesson now and again. Our expectations ran high; we were tensed up as she began to write on the blackboard according to Miss Gibson's instruction. She had written four words when Miss Gibson rose from her desk.

'Good gracious me, Miss Sykes, that writing will never do. I cannot believe they have not taught you to write correctly,' and her disbelief gave a querulous tone to her voice as she grasped the edge of the poetry book from which Miss Sykes was copying Wordsworth's 'To a Cuckoo'. For a moment Miss Sykes clung to it as a startled dog will cling to its bone. Then, of course, she let it go.

'I should have thought,' declared Miss Gibson, striding back to her desk, 'that correct handwriting was a prime requisite for entering the teaching profession. A good style in that respect runs parallel with clear thinking. You don't have one without the other. And really, I do not expect to be teaching handwriting in Standard Six. I'll write you a copy of the verse and then you can practise it at the table. We want the looped cursive style with no fancy curls or flourishes and no breaks between the letters in any one word. The downstrokes must be heavy, the upstrokes light and the writing needs a slightly forward slant, certainly not as if it were collapsing, but as if it knew where it was going. That, in fact, applies to any subject you teach. You must have a sense of direction; you must know where you're going. Most of the time this lot,' and, with a sweep of her left arm she indicated us, 'don't know where they're going. They wander in circles, as if in a fog, and end up where they started.'

In silence we acquiesced.

So Miss Sykes practised handwriting while Miss Gibson took us for quick mental arithmetic to sharpen our sluggish wits. When they were edged to her liking, she returned to Miss Sykes and examined the results of her efforts.

'Well, that's slightly better,' she conceded, 'but correct those r's. You're not writing Greek you know.' I was astonished at Miss Gibson's familiarity with Greek. I'd been in Standard Six since last summer without having heard of this accomplishment. As a learned person she had always ranked pretty high with me; now she rose a degree higher. At the moment she was clipping the copy she had made to the top of the blackboard which had been turned over so that Miss Sykes could use the side with lines. 'You'll have to keep to lines,' she was being told, 'until you learn not to write diagonally across the board. And take your time because I certainly don't want any bad habits creeping into their handwriting. Children are prone to imitating whatever is incorrect and I have enough to do as it is.'

Miss Sykes began on the third line with the copy well in sight above it. No sooner had she written the first word than, with an audible crack, the chalk broke and one piece fell to the floor. A girl tittered. Within a moment came the sharp reprisal, much louder than the breaking chalk. She nursed her stinging ear with one hand. During this brief duo Miss Sykes had retrieved the fallen chalk and planted it in the groove of the nearest desk which happened to be mine. I stared at it. So did Miss Gibson who stalked across saying crisply, 'At such a time it is not sacrilege to quote from the Lord's Prayer. After all, the Bible is there for our daily use.' And she picked up the chalk daintily and held it for Miss Sykes' scrutiny. 'Lead us not into temptation, Miss Sykes. If you put chalk within their reach, how can you expect them not to decorate pavements or even lavatory walls?'

The two stood in front of my desk, the chalk between them with Miss Sykes' eyes glued to it. I could see her flaming face and her small quivering chin. A rush of conflicting emotions bombarded me, the uppermost being acute embarrassment. 'Please don't let her cry,' I prayed automatically. It would be dreadful if Miss Sykes were to drop a degree in my esteem. Rarely did Miss Gibson produce a tear from any one of us. We were not hot-house plants. We were hardened.

'Carry on,' said our teacher who believed in the hardening process. 'And don't press so hard. You might manage better with the short piece. You might have more control. It's the same with handwriting as with everything – direction, then control.'

In an obvious effort to exercise both, Miss Sykes' scrap of chalk laboured across the board and after some time produced –

While I am lying on the grass
Thy two-fold voice I hear.
From hill to hill it seems to pass,
At once far-off and near.

The f's had to be erased and corrected, otherwise it seemed
that the writing would do for the time being. 'They are
learning this poem,' said Miss Gibson, 'and it will serve
for a lesson in analysis. I'll lay out the plan for you on the
other board.' And she did so by drawing a horizontal and a
vertical line which divided the board into a narrow space
above which she wrote Subject, and a wide one with the
heading Predicate. She then subdivided Predicate into
Verb, Object and Extension by means of two more
vertical lines. Miss Sykes' enormous eyes watched the
deft, practised chalking, the lines dead straight, the per-
pendiculars accurate, the writing impeccable.

'Now,' said Miss Gibson, 'this is the method they have
been taught. They understand it. Ask them to supply
words under these headings. Write them in if correct; if
not, ask suitable questions to show where their reasoning
has gone wrong. Analysis of sentence structure is a fine
foundation for reasoning as well as for the correct use of
the spoken and written word. Be firm, make them think,
stand no nonsense,' and her lips, no thicker than two
pencilled lines, tried to lift in an encouraging smile. They
failed. She wouldn't have been Miss Gibson if she'd
smiled. We always knew where we were with her – a two
way traffic of teach and learn and nothing else. We
accepted her methods of getting things into our thick
skulls just as she accepted their density and found means of
penetration. The moves were all predictable. But, of
course, this was not so with Miss Sykes. Uncertainty
made us alert and wary as she replied meekly, 'Yes, Miss
Gibson,' and then faced us.

'Will you read out the verse together, please?'
We obliged.
'Now, shall we take the first two lines only? How many
sentences are there?' Hands shot up.
'You, yes you. The girl in the green jumper. Marjorie,
is it?'

'Yes Miss. Two Miss.'

'Good.' Miss Gibson, marking at her desk, looked up sharply.

'Will you please read them out, Marjorie?'

Marjorie read out each of the two lines.

'Thank you. Now which is the principal sentence?'

'While I am lying on the grass.'

I shot up my hand and waved it furiously. But, if she noticed, she chose to ignore it.

'Now we must look for the subject of that sentence.'

'I think not, Miss Sykes,' interposed Miss Gibson, 'because Marjorie Hewitt gave you the wrong answer. In fact she's given you two wrong answers. What's the matter with you, girl?' and Miss Gibson strode between the desks to administer the corrective.

'Marjorie ought to know, and I believe she does know, that there is one sentence, not two. One sentence with a clause and the sentence is *not* the first line.'

Again Miss Sykes' face flamed beneath the straight dark eyebrows.

'Oh, of course, I'm sorry,' and she stumbled over her words. 'Shall I begin again?'

'As long as you know what you're doing.'

She didn't. I knew, and Miss Gibson knew but was reluctant, I sensed, to interrupt her routine a second time to teach Miss Sykes Analysis. I could see all this in the set of her lips and irritated glint of her eyes behind the rimless glasses. And seeing it, I knew what I must do. I must reach out and go to the aid of poor, lovely Miss Sykes. Protect her from Miss Gibson's hurtful sarcasm. I did not know why except that she was Irene Wilson, Nellie Bessant and even Fanny Barnston with her flaming hair and red bare feet. She was all these rolled into one, but more compelling. Pity drenched me. My hand waved under her face before she had managed to repeat her questioning. I had one eye on Miss Gibson and saw that she had at least one eye on me. I breathed hard, clenched my other fist and willed Miss Sykes to give me a chance to answer. And she did.

I rose, controlled my breathing and my voice. Then I said deliberately and with full use of pauses so that she might take it in and transfer it to the board without forgetting, 'The principal sentence is "Thy two-fold voice I hear." "While I am lying on the grass" is a subordinate clause of time to be put in the extension of the predicate. "I" goes under Subject, "hear" under Verb and you put "thy two-fold voice" under Object.'

'Thank you,' she said faintly, while both Miss Gibson's eyes had me transfixed.

'That's enough, Martha. Don't dominate the class.' That, of course, was exactly what I intended to do from thenceforward as far as grammar lessons with Miss Sykes were concerned. She couldn't analyse any more than she could write correctly but, whatever happened, she must be saved from further humiliation. Moreover, it was I who would save her. At least four other girls in the class could make no mistake in Analysis. Miss Gibson had so trained us in her favourite subject that she could count on our scoring full marks in that examination question. I told myself I didn't trust those other four. The pleasure of seeing a pupil teacher in trouble might outweigh the pain of a boxed ear. But this was devious thinking, the plain truth being that I wanted no one else to save her. I wanted that job and I wanted her to know I was saving her as clearly as if I had wrenched her, in the nick of time, from beneath the wheels of an oncoming motor car.

That playtime we did more than exchange tentative glances. I made a bold approach, my heart turning somer-saults.

'Please, Miss Sykes, may I walk with you?' (Madam will you walk, Madam will you talk, Madam will you walk and talk with me? ricocheted in my head.)

She looked startled, like a fawn, I noted mentally, having had that creature's name for homework in a list of similes. I also noted her enlarged wet eyes but felt no scorn at the sight though it seemed likely that she had been crying in the teacher's W.C. I searched my mind for something to say but, since common sense restrained me from blurting out 'You're the loveliest person I've ever seen,' I was silent and in silence we paced the yard twice. Then she said, 'I don't think I'll ever make a teacher.'

'I don't think so either,' and having said it, it couldn't be unsaid, to my abject shame and remorse. I hastened to mend matters. 'I mean, not a real teacher, like Miss Gibson, but a Sunday School teacher, yes.' Something seemed wrong with this, too, Sunday School teaching being in a different category, unsuitable for comparison. 'Or a head mistress like Miss Byers. She's lovely,' but simply could not add, 'and so are you.'

However, I looked hopefully into her face and met a ravishing smile which melted all my caution. I put a clammy hand in hers well aware of the arrows of ridicule shot at me from various quarters. I didn't care. It was easy to remove us from the school yard and drop us in 'The Wood at the End of the World', the name of a picture I'd found folded inside one of Aunt Annie's music books. That's where we were, she and I, clothed in transparent fragments of gossamer, holding hands with other maidens similarly clad and blissfully encircling an ornamental tree dropping ripe pomegranates on our heads. In that ecstatic state I remained until the bell rang. Neither of us had spoken another word.

After tea I sat at the organ and learnt a new song, the one with the queer words which were Scottish, according to Bob, and written by Robert Burns – no relation to his pal, Fred Burns, he had hastened to add.

> O, wert thou in the cauld blast
> on yonder lea, on yonder lea,
> My plaidie to the angry airt
> I'd shelter thee, I'd shelter thee
> Or did misfortune's bitter storms
> around thee blaw, around thee blaw,
> Thy bield should be my bosom
> to share it a', to share it a'.

I found this so apt in the present circumstances that I continued to sing it until bedtime, several times trying out 'shoulder' as a substitute for 'bosom', a word which embarrassed me and which I thought Robert Burns should not have used. Besides, my shoulders, I liked to imagine, were broad like my father's; my coat always seemed too tight across them, whereas there was nothing at all in the other region.

A few days later, after dinner – which was Auntie's speciality, herrings gently fried, so Tom must have paid some of his greenhouse rent – I stepped into the Lane, closing our front door behind me, and received a paralysing shock. On the opposite pavement was Miss Sykes sailing along, case in hand.

'Hullo, Martha,' she called and crossed the road. 'So this is where you live.' She reached out her free hand and took mine into it. Hers felt cool and moist, mine hot and dry. I stumbled into step with her.

'I live in Clairville Road.'

'Oh.' Better houses even than Uncle Watson's, with a wider front lawn and ornamental gates and a clear view over an open field to the Park. A profound sense of inferiority tied my tongue. It was different being with her out of school. I had nothing to offer, nothing to say. As we approached the school gates, I muttered thickly, 'Please let me answer if we do grammar today,' and I suppose she did for I continued to help her out of this difficulty for what seemed like years. That afternoon I waited, wondering if I might walk home with her, but as she emerged from the playground she waved and turned in the opposite direction up Victoria Road and I went on my way alone.

That night I asked Bob if I might borrow his cigarette card Roses. The collection and exchange of cigarette cards was all the rage. Apart from the pictures and information on the back, there was the incentive to be the first to complete a set. I had seen the way Jack Smart opened a new packet and extracted the card. Like the gamblers I had heard about at Redcar races. Bob had no money to spend on cigarettes but he was given those cards which were not so popular with the rest – Roses, Wild Flowers, Gardening. The most highly prized were Motor Vehicles, Railway Engines, Battleships and Weapons of War. The latest thing in transport, air-borne machines, had just got themselves into print on the cigarette card.

My request was granted and I spread the cards over the desk. Lady Roberts, a slender, flame-coloured lamp. Caroline Testout, full blown like a pink pin-cushion. Mrs Henrietta Morse, an open goblet of glowing gold. Then the dainty pale-pink delicacy of a Dorothy Perkins spray. Both their appearance and their names conjured up a vision of regal ladies I had not known existed. I spent a long time weighing their respective merits before deciding which one was Sylvia. For that was her astonishing name. Miss Sylvia Sykes. No name could be a higher tribute to her beauty! A couple of Bob's recent songs circulated in my head. I supposed he had Doris Mould in mind when he sang them, though goodness knows how he managed to compare *her* with a rose. 'Oh saw you not my lady out in the garden fair, rivalling the rose and lily with a glory of golden hair.' Sylvia's hair was brown I had to admit, but still . . . I hummed the other song, 'No rose in all the world until you came,' and changed round the cards placing Dorothy Perkins at the top. She was best suited to Sylvia, being tender and girlish, not proud and stately like the rest. I was quite lost for words to describe Sylvia.

'Oh rose bloom ever in my lonely heart.' My voice sailed over to my cousin sitting at the table biting a pen in his struggle to compose a letter to my mother asking if they had found any prospects for him in America.

'Shut up, Martha. What's the big idea?'

The big idea! It struck me like a lightning flash. I pitched off the desk stool and stood at his elbow.

'Bob, there's the most wonderful girl, well, lady, not quite either really. She's a pupil teacher at our school. Sylvia Sykes. Don't you like the name?'

'Well, what about her? I want to finish this letter.'

'I just want you to see her. If your could just see her, I know you'd prefer her to Doris. If you could bring her to tea some time and tell her how you expect to go to America, she might go with you instead of learning how to teach. She's not particularly good at that anyway. But she might be one of the family, then I shouldn't have to lose her.'

I took a deep breath while he stared at me. I breathed too deeply. The room spun round and I sat down again. He got up.

'Is there something wrong with you?' he asked. 'It's none of my business, but I'm going to tell your mother they should never have left you. Look at you now, white as a sheet! You'd better get off to bed. Aunt Blanche is across at Burt's. I'm going for her.'

It wasn't easy to look at myself, for Grandfather had banned mirrors as objects leading to perdition and, even now, I knew of none in the house but the one Bob used for shaving which he had taken to leaving on the wall beside the scullery sink. The idea of looking like a sheet was sufficiently intriguing to send me into the front room for Grannie's embroidered footstool on which I had stood as a toddler to reach an organ key. I now used it, rearing unsteadily on the padded surface, to take a first look at myself. What I saw was unforgettable – a pallid shape with dark, smudged eyes and over prominent teeth. Instantly I removed myself, carried back the stool and climbed the stairs drained of elation. Mirror, mirror on the wall. It doesn't lie. I am not myself, or rather, not what I thought I was. But that is how *she* must see me. An awful thought.

When Auntie strode into the bedroom, she took my temperature. It was by no means the first time this slender glass stick with its hidden magic had been stuck under my tongue, but the purpose and the result were guarded secrets. My Aunt had trained as a nurse and whatever the thermometer did or told her was never divulged to the patient. I had learnt to submit to the routine with the same detachment as I would let her re-tie a loosening ribbon in my hair, and did so that night.

But my face, white as a sheet, was a different matter. I acquired a new morning habit just before going out to wait for Sylvia. I would hold each cheek over the fire, or, if the fire were so low as to be useless, then slap each cheek with a flannel soaked in icy tap water. The burning or the smarting was a sign, I thought, that colour was forming there – some rose pink, like Sylvia's. But Sylvia did not always round the corner of Nazareth House, at the bottom of the Lane, by half-past eight; and, if I had to wait time without end for her arrival, then I knew that my efforts to defeat nature had been in vain and that my face was again the colour of a sheet.

Chapter Five

In reply to Bob's letter, my mother's, addressed to Auntie as it always was, held out enough hope to elate him. What they must have, the letter said, was a decent house to live in, so they were now on the look out for work on one of several small estates beyond the suburbs of Boston. There was usually a house provided and, hopefully, some gardening work would turn up for Bob. No rose gardens, my mother said, like the ones some people had in England. The soil was too shallow and the climate too extreme; but there were lawns to be looked after and greenhouses, while tomatoes, melons and pumpkins all grew outside. She felt sure there would be an advertisement before long. Also, she had been told that the people in the area liked to employ the English.

To be a gardener was my cousin's ambition. No one knew why, since he had had little to do with gardens. He would have helped more in Uncle Watson's allotment had it not been for the incident with a snooper from the Labour Exchange. Either you were in employment earning money or you were on the dole doing nothing. If you happened to be digging someone else's garden, then they should be paying you and your dole proportionately cut. Bob had grown pansies and polyanthus in the two tiny beds of soil built up on the concrete of our back yard. To grow gladioli and chrysanthemums was his aspiration, but melons and tomatoes would certainly do – you could tell by the way he now chattered on about passports, visas, consulates and liners. Already he was half way through the process of getting to America. Regarding liners he turned out to be surprisngly knowledgeable, almost as though he had memories of being on one. (Later, I was to learn that he had been; that he had crossed the Atlantic and back again twice during a period of his boyhood that had been sealed off from all reference.) He talked about port and starboard, prow and stern, the bridge, the cabins, the boat decks, the hatchways until you would have thought he was already on board. In so doing he pushed to the back of his mind the matter of the twenty pounds needed to pay his passage though our Aunt quickly pulled it forward when he mentioned taking Doris Mould to Liverpool to see the boat sail.

'And who, pray, will pay her fare to Liverpool? You've your own fare to sort out first, all the way to New York.'

Some of his enthusiasm and all his talk about liners brushed off onto me. I felt I knew a liner better than a motor car, a few of which were now being driven along the main streets while boys jotted down numbers in little notebooks. It was unlikely that I should ever ride in a motor car, but I might conceivably sail in a liner. Or I might watch one sail. And this idea took root and grew. Doris was soon disposed of, a giggling girl who had once played a silly trick on me. Into her place stepped Sylvia who would love to go to Liverpool, and there ought to be no problem about *her* fare. For where would she have been without my help in grammar lessons? She would surely pay her own fare in return for that. Besides, Clairville Road people could afford such things. As for my own fare – we were to go together – I would have to save it. My weekly income was threepence; a penny from Tom, one from the butcher and one from Auntie or Bob whoever had it to spare. The fare for a child I estimated as five shillings, so it would take twenty weeks to save it. Was Bob likely to depart before then? Remembering that he had to save twenty pounds at least, I decided not.

In bed, in the darkness, I saw the three of us climbing the gangway of the great liner as she lay with her port side to the quay. I'd been glad to learn that a liner was known as 'she'. I saw us descending the companion-way in search of Bob's cabin. But no, that must not happen because the cabin was on the steerage deck, a fact which Bob has tried to forget. I think I ought to see it, but Sylvia must be left on deck to admire the view over the river. (Imagination fails me here. I don't know what that river looks like.) We join her again as the ship's siren blows a harsh continuous note while an officer, uniformed with gold braid, swings along the deck calling, 'All ashore who's going ashore,' and

36

the three of us then form a little knot saying things like, 'God be with you till we meet again,' and Bob, whose voice I hope he'll control, will say, 'The next time, Sylvia, you'll not be going ashore. You'll be coming too,' with a glance for me and three words, 'Martha as well.' Then Sylvia and I walk down the gangway and watch the boat being eased from her mooorings, so slowly that we still see Bob leaning over the deck rail for a long time and waving. In fact we see a streamer, not thrown by us, twist round his neck as though to hold him to us. But the tugs are at work and the boat has moved out into the deep channel and turned, so that we lose Bob until he reappears on the starboard deck. And now the pilot has taken over to steer her down river and Bob's figure has merged with the rest. Still we watch for quite a while until the liner herself is no more than a smudge on the mouth of the river beyond the sandbank. A smudge on the wider horizon of sleep.

I clung to this nightly adventure for days or weeks, and not even the proximity of Doris Mould tripping in and out of our house could quite dispel my faith in its reality. Meanwhile, Bob lived for the next American letter and Auntie continued to cope with our predicament, reminding us that if Bob left, his dole money would also depart leaving an empty bedroom which somehow must be filled. Tom's name was mentioned more than once to neighbours and by neighbours, and also Mrs Sidaway's, the woman from whom Tom rented a bedroom. The fate of the house was shelved, I understood, pending a resolution of Bob's fate and mine. These were grave matters but were transformed into airy nothings by an event that steered my thoughts in other directions leaving Sylvia and Bob to their own affairs.

I was summoned to Miss Byers' room and covered the long corridor between Standard Six door and hers almost at a run, as if the quicker I met the blow, whatever it might be, the better. Had my Aunt paid another visit to our headmistress? I couldn't imagine why, but her actions were unpredictable so I tended to be on the alert for signs. I knocked and heard the call 'Come in.' My heart missed a beat and slowed down as Miss Byers smiled at me with her usual serenity. She was wearing a lavender coloured morocaine dress, the same material as the good one possessed by my Aunt though not the same colour. I could never understand Auntie's addiction to brown. I stood to attention in front of Miss Byers' desk.

'I don't suppose, Martha, that you've ever been to a concert in the Town Hall?'

She was correct in her negative assumption. I had never even envisaged an interior to the Town Hall. For me the place was an immense building with arched doorways and windows, a steep roof, a tall, thin clock tower and a flight of steps so high and wide as to lift the place, I thought, between earth and heaven. It was not the sort of building you looked at when you were just approaching nine – altogether overpowering, as the station had seemed a year ago. As for concerts, yes, I had had a certain experience of those. I had sung and recited and listened to other children doing the same at Chapel concerts. I had been a fairy and a sunflower and once even a cat in Miss Swales' productions in the social clubroom attached to the Chapel. I didn't known whether these counted, but I could certainly say, 'No, Miss Byers,' regarding concerts in the Town Hall. She then supposed that I'd never even *heard* of the Felix Corbett Celebrity concerts and I was able to say she was right in that supposition, too. I had not even heard the name Felix except in association with a cat when some girl was talking, I think, about the Pictures at the new Cinema to which I was not allowed to go. I tried to gather into my head all the information I could recall in order to keep abreast with Miss Byers' odd questions.

'Felix Corbett,' she said, 'is our town organist, but he is just as famous, perhaps more so, for the concerts he inaugurated twenty–five years ago and has kept going ever since. Celebrated musicians from all over the world have played at his concerts in the Town Hall and next Wednesday there is to be a famous pianist, Miss Myra Hess. I've sent for you, Martha, because each school receives one free ticket to give to the pupil most likely to benefit. I've always thought it a pity that you couldn't have had piano lessons, but this is a chance for you to hear a piano played properly.'

38

She paused, as if struck by another thought. I took my courage in both hands and said, 'But Miss Byers, you play the piano properly, don't you?' She laughed and said, 'I love the piano, but I'm not a pianist. When you hear one, you'll know the difference. Only one thing worries me about your going. It's rather like throwing a learner swimmer in at the deep end. I hope it won't be over-whelming. Too much for you, perhaps. Still, there it is. I've had you in mind and I'm sorry I can't take you myself. I've always wanted to hear Myra Hess play, but unfortun-ately there's a meeting that night which I must attend. As it happens, Miss Sykes is going and she is prepared to take you. She plays the piano though she's no pianist either, but at least she'll be able to tell you about the programme. After all, these concerts are supposed to encourage musical talent as well as attracting peole who can afford to attend them, sometimes for reasons which have little to do with music.' And her bare eyes, visible above the glasses perched low on her nose, seemed to twinkle at me as though we shared a joke.

We didn't. How could I think of jokes in a stunned, numbed condition? To go with Sylvia to the Town Hall! It was all very well going to Liverpool with her in imagina-tion, but to walk beside her in actual fact up the Town Hall steps, then sit down at her side for a whole evening, that was beyond imagining. Miss Byers was right. It would certainly be too much for me, though not in the sense she implied. She seemed oblivious of my dismay as she briskly handed me a sealed envelope saying, 'Give this to your Aunt. There's a note inside with your ticket. Miss Sykes will call at your home and answer any questions Miss Drinkhall might care to ask.'

She called, and the very fact of seeing her sitting in our front room chatting to my Aunt was enough to unhinge my mind. It was hinged again when I realised that Auntie had only one question to ask, that being what was I expected to wear? But, during the next day or two, other questions were asked of Auntie especially by Mrs Burt who wanted to know why a girl who hadn't had a single piano lesson should be afforded this privilege. Dear me, their Laura was practising the piano for an examination!

To my astonishment, my Aunt then displayed a hitherto undisclosed knowledge of our family's musical propensity which, from what she said, stretched back through generations! Hadn't her brother, Rob, and sister, Annie, both bought organs, not to mention that Welsh harp thing or zither or whatever it was called? And William Henry, had he lived, would have shone with his trumpet in a York brass band. One of her uncles had owned a violin, and she, herself, had always been told that something might have been made of her voice. And look at Robbie with the organ. Being able to play *without* music saved a lot of expense. Never before, in my hearing, had she gone on so in the music line; and Mrs Burt was silenced. Mary Kitching said one had to remember the poor rate payers; these free tickets came out of their pockets, her own included. Minnie Gatenby said Blanche must be proud; Mrs Kneeshaw that she had never heard such nonsense; Hannah that it was a wonderful opportunity; and Bob, sounding oddly resentful, said that he had no recollection of free tickets being dished out when he was at school and what good was it going to do me, he'd like to know, hobnobbing with the top knots?

From the moment that Sylvia tapped delicately on the door that Wednesday night, I suffered a dislocation of mind from body – a reversal of the Huck-a-Back experience soon after my sixth birthday; that early morning in bed when, out of a nebulous existence, self-awareness had penetrated my consciousness and told me who I was. Now it left me and watched with detachment the girl climbing the Town Hall steps dressed in a home sewn coat, velour hat, black stockings and shoes and a pair of gloves knitted hurriedly by her Aunt. Beside this girl climbed a young woman in more spectacular attire – a red coat that ended below her knees, a tight, brimless hat with a little feather waving from it, and such high-heeled shoes on her dainty feet as to suggest, overall, an unsteady mast blown in the wind that gusted from the river.

I saw myself inside the Town Hall, a place reminiscent of our Chapel only longer and with no communion rail. Where that should have been was a platform and, rising behind it in tiers, seats like those for our choir. I looked the size of Tom Thumb because everything was so large, especially the organ which broke through the ranks of seats and flaunted its painted pipes. Not like our Chapel organ hiding modestly behind the choir.

There we are in our seats with me staring at an object occupying the centre of the platform, a thing like a huge black shapeless box standing on three legs and one other vertical contraption. Its enormous lid is open. It has caused a stir in my memory; a brown box on three legs in Miss Johnson's drawing room at Nunthorpe, but with no lid at all and everything locked. 'What's that?' I seem to be asking my Aunt as she dusts another nameless piece of furniture. But it is Sylvia's voice that answers with a funny laugh as though she can't believe her ears.

'It's the piano, of course.' So I don't ask about the lid because she must not know that I know nothing. Which is true, I realise. Nothing about anything here. I shall not risk asking another question to show my ignorance.

Now the chattering is changed to clapping and I can see myself joining in and clapping like a clockwork toy and looking round to see why it has all grown dark except for the platform. There, under bright light, a lady in a black gown is sailing towards the piano where she stands, bowing and smiling. She bows frontwards, sideways and even turns round to bow backwards to the people in the rising seats who seem to be going mad. Around Sylvia's seat and mine, the people clap more limply. For a moment I imagine myself to be that lady, though I would wear a purple gown, not black. Now she is on the stool fiddling with its sides; now rubbing her hands together slowly, not at all as Bob does when he's cold but as if she had all the time in the world to warm them while the people sit and watch her, quietly waiting, as if they too are prepared to wait all night. But, at last, she lifts her arms, which are bare, and holds them in front of her for a few seconds, motionless. Then quicker than your eyelid can blink, they pounce, and the piano comes alive, thundering like the voice of God on Mount Sinai.

I saw an image of myself, petrified in the midst of all that sound, of blastings and hard hitting rain striking roofs and pavements and windows. How could anyone buffet a piano so, or play so many separate keys in so short a time? And what could be made of those great blocks of sound, some of them striking your ears unpleasantly; then all that running up and down, up and down the keyboard? It was a long time before a tune could be found, at least by me, and I could see myself beginning to wilt with the exhaustion of hearing all that noise. Then, after the second outbreak of applause, with a few people on the platform seats stamping their feet, the pianist, as Miss Byers had called her, sat on the stool again and began to stroke the keys. She stroked them tenderly, her arms lifting gently first one way and then another, and the hall was filled with a quiet rippling sound which I remembered hearing when those little waves came running up the Redcar sand from the empty sea. And now a tune arose amongst them like a mermaid with seaweed hair, lifting herself from the shallow water to look across the land where she could never live. It was beautiful, I thought, but sad, and when it came to an end, very slowly and quietly, there was a storm of clapping as if they were going to make her play it all over again. I wouldn't have minded if she'd done so, for the tune was still singing in my head to the sol-fa names. But she left the platform after the second lot of bowing, and people were rising and shuffling along our row and the one in front, and Sylvia's voice restored me to my severed consciousness.

'How did you like that, Martha?'

'Yes, thank you,' was the absurd reply I gave.

'That last piece is her famous one, a piano arrangement of "Jesu, joy of man's desiring," by J.S. Bach.'

'Oh,' I said, but refrained from mentioning the ridiculous image I'd seen as I had listened to that music.

The row in front had emptied leaving in view a line of girls all wearing panama hats with striped bands of red and navy blue. Movement and chatter hummed along it, a bright current of perpetual noise and motion. Then, at the far end, a tall girl rose and made her way along the empty row. Her hat was pushed to the back of her head leaving bare a straight, short bob and a fringe. She reached Sylvia and stopped.

'What's the verdict?' and laughed, her eyes disappearing

at the same time as her beautiful, even teeth came into sight. 'Fun, isn't it? Quite fun including the bare arms, bosom and all.'

'That's enough of your nonsense,' said Miss Sykes, a note sounding almost like a warning in her voice. 'A bit tedious, I thought. Still. . . . Oh this is Martha, and this, Martha, is my sister, Ethel. She's with the High School girls. That's where I was, you know, before my pupil-teaching year. Wish I were back there!'

'Idiot,' said Ethel, 'Wish I were left.'

'Don't be so off-putting. Martha has it all coming to her. She'll get in on a scholarship.'

'Oh,' I was surveyed appraisingly. 'One of those, are you?' and clearly, no answer was expected.

'You all right? asked Sylvia, also surveying me.

'Looks peeky,' said Ethel.

'She's always pale, but you could get her some tea or something. I'll have one, too. Better come with you to help cope with the mob. Must be getting to the end by now. Stay there, Martha. We won't have to be too long, anyway.'

'When are we going home, please?'

'Oh, not for ages, I fear,' groaned Ethel. 'We're only half way through. There's another lot to come yet, worse luck. This is just a breather to help us renew our strength. You're all right, aren't you? Don't want to go yet?' This was more of a statement than a question. I said I was all right.

But when the tea came, I sipped it slowly. I had been watching the row of hats and couldn't take my eyes off them even while sipping tea. Their owners had stayed in their seats, but the hats were on the move continuously and spirited chatter rose from beneath the brims. Sometimes one was turned right about and I caught sight of a lively, laughing face. Like butterflies. Red Admirals on cigarette cards. Red Admirals with dark jagged edges like little sword marks pointing to the dark oval patch in the middle. I'd seen a real one once in Uncle Watson's allotment. It was poised on a marguerite. I'd seen it clap its wings together, then open them and flit away. 'Why does it do that?' I'd asked, and he'd replied. 'To attract attention, I shouldn't wonder.'

'Please, Martha, finish your tea. The interval's over. It's the famous Chopin Polonaise, now.'

The hats had vanished one by one as the row in front of us filled. The music began again and this time it hammered its relentless rhythm deep into my head. It was a tune I understood, a tune which Miss Gibson would have understood despite the fact that she couldn't teach music. For it was a tune that had quite made up its mind where it was going and it brought me to a similar state of resolution. Other items followed, but I scarcely heard them. The pianist had played the one I would remember.

The concert ended with her returning twice. Here and there a few enthusiasts tried to bring her back a third time, but most people were on the move and so were we. At the top of the steps we joined the High School girls who were still chattering.

'Not bad. I liked that Brahms Intermezzo.'

'I preferred the Chopin and that Rachmaninov thing. He emigrated to America. Who wouldn't, from Russia?'

'Oh, I'm for a bit more romance. You know, with a capital R. I wanted to shout, "Encore, encore." Give us the Liszt Liebestraume or something like it.'

'Oh love, love, love,' she sang on one note and this attracted a chorus of giggles.

'Well, I think we must tell old Felix we prefer a male soloist.'

'No, not just one, but a lot of men. A whole orchestra like the one we had last year under Beecham. Do you remember how we all chose that cellist? The way he attacked those strings was. . . .' They all seemed to hold their breaths. 'Well, what can you say?' she finished lamely leaving another voice to take over.

'An orchestra's expensive. The borough can't afford one often, my father says.'

'Well, what about one of our own? What about your father's orchestra, Catherine?'

The one silent girl, or so it had appeared, was smaller than the rest, being about my own height but with a rope of black hair falling down her back and beyond the lower edge of her blazer. She turned to look at the speaker, and

44

her eyes, grey and grave, happened to encounter mine. The question evaporated, unanswered, because Catherine just smiled.

'Anyway, if you ask my opinion, Felix himself can bang away on the piano nearly as well as Miss Myra Hess.'

'Maybe, if only he weren't stuck with one lot of banging. Billy Boy! Will he ever start the singing lesson with anything else?'

'Not he. But I bet you I'll tell him on Friday that we want a Billy not a Nancy at his old concerts.'

'You wouldn't dare!'

'Oh yes, I would. And not a pianist either. No one but a gorgeous black haired tenor like Caruso to sing excruciating things from fantastic operas,' and the girl clasped one hand over the red shield on the breast pocket of her blazer and threw out the other towards Albert Road. Laughter bubbled about us until a girl with the voice of a teacher said, 'That's enough, you lot. Make your way out more quickly and quietly. And remember your arrangements for getting home. Gloves on, Rita. Gloves on, everybody,' and the hats and blazers fell into some sort of order and proceeded down the steps into the gas lit dusk.

Chapter Six

That night I had a prolonged fight with the Thing. It scooped me out of bed into a vortex of giddy revolutions and it was Auntie's voice which told me I had won. I came to rest as a spinning top does and heard, 'Martha, your nightgown's soaked. Come along, let's have you into a clean one. Robbie, put the kettle on for a hot water bottle.'

'Polly, put the kettle on,' revolved in my head as if stuck there while outside Auntie's voice hammered on, 'No more concerts for you. I should have known better than let you go. And no school tomorrow, either.'

I argued mentally about this but, when morning came, I found she was right. I got up, but had trouble crawling back. I lay still and played optical games with the nearest carved protuberance on the marble upright of the fireplace. By some trick of focusing your eyes, this object could either be a circular hollow surrounded by a banked up earthwork, or a hill encircled by a ditch. It passed the time until Bob appeared muttering about what I had once done to sever all connection with the medical world.

'I don't suppose the doctor would come if she called him. I wouldn't if you'd slapped my face. As soon as I reach the States, I'm going to see that you're sent for. It's too much for Aunt Blanche to deal with.'

In case he should do this, I wrote my letter that afternoon after sitting up and waiting till my head stopped spinning.

Dear Mother and Father,

I hope you are all well. Bob is longing to come to America so I hope you will soon find some work on an estate. But don't worry about me because I have made up my mind to go to the High School. I saw several High School girls at the Town Hall last night. They are different from us. They know so much and I want to be like them. I can get there without any money so no one has to pay for me. The daffodils in the grounds of the Nurses' Home have been lovely and I hope there are daffodils in America.

    With love,
      Yours sincerely,
      Martha.

I read the letter as through the critical eyes of Miss Gibson and could hear her exclaim impatiently, 'Don't you know there's such a thing as the English Language which happens to contain several thousand words and you can't find one word for 'made up my mind' but have to use the language of a two-year-old?' I could also hear my reply. 'Determined is all very well but it doesn't mean your mind is so made up that it won't change. And mine is. I know now what passing the scholarship means and I'm staying here to pass it.'

The fact is I hadn't known before, during the years I'd been propelled in that direction. I knew some grown-ups would be proud if you passed this thing and others would wish you hadn't. That it would take you amongst girls like these who knew so much even though they might fall short in handwriting and analysis, and who were so unaccountably merry (I'd searched for the right word, light-hearted, gay?) – that this was what a scholarship meant was enough to give my own nebulous ideas a shape. I folded the letter, manoeuvred it into an envelope, licked the gum and, finding my mouth very dry, I had to bang the letter hard on the commode in order to seal it.

On Friday my throat was sore and I was sitting up in bed, my neck clamped in one of Grandfather's socks stiff with goose-grease when Minnie Gatenby walked in. She fingered the sock, pulled the edge away from the neck and peered into the space between.

'Swollen glands and no mistake. But, Blanche, I swear by a sweaty sock. There's something in sweat that draws the inflammation.'

'The same thing as there is in goose fat. I'm not having the smell of sweat about her.'

'Only one smell is worse than that of goose-grease,' I croaked, 'and that's the smell of gander-grease,' which did not amuse my Aunt but brought a show of mirth from

Minnie. This ceased as she picked up a sheet of paper, one of many strewn across the quilt.

'Gracious me, Martha! Whatever are you on with?'

'Just a bit of scholarship work.' In spite of the croak, I hoped this would sound airy and off-hand.

'What, have they sent you some from school?'

'No. It's just a list of things we might get. I'm ticking off the ones I can do and putting a cross beside the others.'

Minnie voiced her amazement. 'What's all this? Deer, doe; fox, vixen; duck, drake; gander, goose; duke, duchess; marquis, marchioness; sultan, sultana?'

'Feminines. I'm not sure about the last one. It sounds silly. And those,' I proferred another sheet, 'are plurals – exceptions that prove the rule – deer, deer; ox, oxen; narcissus, narcissi. And those are the names of young like hare, leveret; eel, elver; swan, cygnet.' My voice grew strident as I slapped the quilt. 'And that's a page with a lot of similars and that's one with a lot of opposites. And those are proverbial opposites like "Look before you leap," and "He who hesitates is lost".'

'Clever beyond words,' applauded Minnie. 'But where is it likely to get you?'

'To the High School. That's where!'

'To learn some more things like that?' Minnie's amazement had reached its peak as my mood plunged. I sank into the pillow muttering, 'I think I'll read *Chatterbox* for a bit.' The thick, smooth paper and large print of this popular Annual, not to mention the contents, made it easier to deal with than *Ivanhoe* which was our current reading matter at school. Illustrations abounded, my favourites being of the Dinosaurs in their millions-of-years-ago world. Their grotesque sizes and shapes, absurd embellishments, their jocular, toothy faces and, above all, the human speech with which the story endowed them had a sense of the ridiculous missing from any book I'd ever opened. Still, it was evident that these creatures had actually been real – though without the power of speech – inhabiting a world of peculiar plants which they spent their time devouring. This was not so with the Woodenheads. Their story ran through the Annual serial-wise with pages of other material separating each episode. They belonged to science-fiction and were a foretaste of things to come.

The tale began with a boy, his sister and their dog, Tim, waking one July morning to find themselves the sole survivors in a changed world. Overnight, winter had arrived, snow-covered, ice-bound, weird, with no sign of a living creature but themselves until they sighted the Woodenheads. These came in single file, seven of them, gliding with silent menace over the virgin snow which, the children noted with horror, kept its virginity as they passed on. Six feet high, encased in ice, limbless, feature-less and shaped like possing sticks without arms, they were the stuff of nightmares. Their sinister purpose was to finish their job, the extermination of the human race. I could never discover why they hadn't done so already. Then I reasoned that if they had, there would have been no story. After many adventures, it was Tim who unwitting-ly demonstrated the secret of their power. A diminished file of five had managed almost to surround the little terrier, but not entirely. His tail, beating time to his vocal fury, happened to remain outside the circle and, as the Woodenheads glided away in the belief that he'd been liquidated, behold, the tail in mid-air, attached to nothing.

I read as far as that, then allowed the book to slip from my fingers. I had read the story before and knew that, by some absurd stratagem, the Woodenheads themselves would be routed and the world restored to normal. I felt curiously relaxed, content almost, to be convinced that the world would not end, though I had to concede the prevalence of this theme right through from the Bible down to *Chatterbox*. Almost as if people wanted an End, and many, like me, had been brought up on the idea, expecting the End any day. This was the first time I had sat, or rather lain, and considered the subject. If there had been a beginning with Adam and Eve, and there was to be an End with the angels, then things must move in a straight line with one experience slipping away forever while another took its place. So what about Huck-a-Back which had not left me, which was always there. A straight line was wrong. Circles perhaps were better. The earth was all circles; so were hats and clothes fitting round you and lots of playground games like Ring-a-ring of Roses,

Poor Mary sat a-weeping, In and out the Window. And the Woodenheads needed circles to destroy you. A circle had no beginning and no end. But what if people wanted a beginning and an end because they hated what was in between? Like Auntie who was always saying she had one foot in the grave which made you wonder if she wished all of her were there. Though I had to admit that the grave was not quite the same as the End when all the millions who had ever lived and died would be accommodated with those still alive. All together again in either heaven or hell. But where, for goodness' sake, was there space?

I sat up and my head felt clear. A decision was needed because you could not stay wondering forever. I would throw out the End. Expect it no longer. I would live in a world *without* end, and I felt almost gay, as if I had been admitted to the High School here and now.

That night I slept. A long, deep sleep it must have been because when I woke, a high sun was flooding the room with unusual brightness and the looped lace curtains hung against a backdrop of blue sky. I lifted the bedclothes, put my feet to the floor and waited till the bubble on my neck grew solid. Then I reached the chair by the window. Over the top of the brick wall opposite lay the lawns, trees and paths of the Nurses' Home. I always saw it as a garden staged specially for ourselves and the Bonsils for no one else could claim this view of it. At the back, to the right, rose the building of worn red brick with jutting gables, long blank windows and an army of tall chimney pots. Until recently, I had heard, this had been the mansion home of an iron and steel magnate who had made a fortune but paid his workmen very little. A figure came into view, a nurse in white head gear and a navy cloak, crossing at a steady pace towards the door. Everything was starkly clear, even the daffodils with their strong thick leaves and withered trumpets. They had come and gone since I'd sat here looking at the rain while Grannie died. A lot of things had gone since then; her chair and sofa that took up too much space for Auntie's liking and too much time to beat the dust out of them. My ninth birthday had come and gone leaving me with three large books – *The Complete Works of William Shakespeare* bound in olive

50

green, inscribed in gold, though Bob, who gave it me, said not gold, just gilt, in case I thought it had cost too much and *The New Gresham Dictionary* similarly bound, from Tom. 'It's to help you get that scholarship,' Bob had said, and Tom, 'You can use it for crossword puzzles, you see.' He liked doing these puzzles himself and had already borrowed it The third book was from my parents and had arrived late. It was a bulky parcel with loops of string straying loosely away from the corners and the brown paper unfolding itself. 'Just like your mother,' was my Aunt's comment. 'She never could pack a parcel properly. I don't know how it's got here.' It turned out to be a large book of Bible stories bound in silver grey with lettering which I now knew to be gilt, and inside, one story on each page with a full sized picture – a steel engraving, Tom said – facing the story. It was a beautiful volume, not new, according to Auntie, with pictures quite different in character from those in our Family Bible. I liked the pictures but found the stories, to use Auntie's word, peculiar. For instance, 'Consider the lilies of the field' was changed to, 'Look at these beautiful flowers growing round you'. What right, I thought, had people to change the words which Jesus had spoken? My Mother's letter said they had applied for an estate job advertised in the *Boston Herald*. The winter had been dreadfully cold with deep snow but now, all of a sudden, the lilac was out, with great heavy heads weighing down the bushes. Winter had changed to Summer with no real Spring in between. She wished she could see the daisies in the Park because no small, pink-tipped daisies grew over there.

'Is she homesick?' I'd asked Auntie who was casting off the thumb of the second glove for me to wear to the concert. Her only answer was, 'It's no use wasting time thinking about daisies.'

Well, the daffodils had gone quickly too, I thought. Like Robert Herrick's poem which we'd been learning at school with Sylvia. William Wordsworth's, too. Strange that daffodils should fill his heart with pleasure yet make Robert Herrick weep with pain. I had raised my hand on an impulse to mention this odd fact, but Miss Gibson had asked brusquely, 'Do you wish to leave the room?' which brought a hasty 'No, Miss Gibson,' and that was the end of that. It was even stranger, though, about Sylvia, who had for weeks filled my own heart with both pleasure and pain. Then, in the twinkling of an eye, these had gone. Had *she* changed, or had I? Whatever the explanation, I had not willed it so.

It was pretty in the garden. Another figure was crossing the lawn, heading for the clump of trees. If she wore a uniform, it was indistinct, like the reflection of a swan swimming on the park lake. 'Surely you saw my lady out in the garden fair.' It passed out of sight under a tree and a lot of birds sang. No sore throats, I thought, and then heard a faint plop on the painted window ledge. I dashed my nightgown sleeve across my face.

That night, being Friday, I was soaking in half a poss-tub of soapy water planted in the middle of the scullery floor when the door knocker gave three diffident raps. It could always tell you something about the person who was rapping.

'Botheration,' said my Aunt, 'Now who can that be?' knowing it was none of her circle who came in without knocking. 'Wash your neck well, even if it hurts a bit. We must get rid of the smell.'

My half-hearted attempts to obey instructions were arrested by a lilting voice. My hand, holding the sponge, stayed on the back of my neck.

'I'm so sorry she's not well,' I heard. 'I do hope she didn't catch anything at the concert, Miss Drinkhall.' Then Auntie's voice, 'Oh no, I shouldn't think so. She's prone to sore throats.'

There was a pause, while shame, like a shower of ice-cold water, fell over me. Even in the warm soapy tub water, I shivered.

'I can't ask you in to see her, I'm afraid, She's having a bath.' Oh my tactful Aunt! Say no more! Let her think I'm in a proper bath. Not that I knew anyone who had a bath with a tap fixed to it. But some people did have long tin things shaped specially for taking baths. They were not immersed in barrel shaped poss-tubs.

Sylvia's voice said she was sorry. She'd like to have seen me to ask how I'd liked the concert. My Aunt said she was sorry, too, but no more than that. She was not going to be drawn out about the concert. Then I heard the voice I'd adored say, 'Will you give her these flowers, please?' and Auntie's saying thank you, she would, and then the closing of the door.

It took me a long time to recover from that. The flowers were tulips mixed with those white, orange-eyed narcissi which come in the wake of the daffodils. Auntie put them in her best narrow-waisted, wide-brimmed black vase and they looked lovely. I extracted two of the narcissi and carefully pressed them in a folded piece of blotting paper from my arithmetic book, then placed both between the pages of *A Midsummer Night's Dream* and made a vow that there they would remain until Bob married Sylvia. And although I did not prick my finger to seal the vow, and although I used the Shakespeare a great deal, there the flowers remained for about fifty years.

On Monday I left the house soon after eight. The weather had changed and a grey fog obscured the sky. Everything looked dirty, but birds were still singing from somewhere behind the high brick wall. I didn't wait for Sylvia. It was much too early. Within two minutes I was crossing Victoria Road where I should have turned left. Instead I headed straight on up Woodlands Road and turned at the corner of Clarendon Road. I kept to the left-hand pavement and did not stop till I was opposite a high wall surmounted by a row of tree tops in their first flush of green. Behind that wall lay the Palace Beautiful of my inward vision while outside it my body was clamped to the grey pavement and my eyes glued to a small dirty looking wooden door. Mentally I excused its appearance. It was, after all, the back door. The front entrance, I knew, was through impressive wrought iron gates, then a double door under a clock tower. They were much further away, at one end of Albert Road, a road that began at the station, then ran, straight as an out-sized ruler, to the school gates as if these were the destination of every passenger who alighted from the trains.

This grubby door, with a few locks of ivy trailing untidily from the wall above it, was shut, and no one was in sight either way. There was an absence of life as though a spell had been cast, a weird winter without the snow. Again, I glanced in both directions, one part of me expecting the sinister Woodenheads to appear. They didn't, but the road remained empty. I crossed it and pressed down the sneck of the door which I now noticed was dull green and much in need of painting. It was bolted.

I was locked out. Like that time when I was four and locked out of Victoria Road School. Only now the frustration could find no relief in a vocal tantrum. I was too old for that. Instead it tied knots in my chest which hurt. The situation was beyond understanding. Time must be getting on. Girls must be coming to school. Things must still be happening. But nothing did, so I must conclude that the school had closed. No other explanation presented itself and a frost within me spread to numb all my senses. I was unaware of moving away or of turning to cross the road. But my eyes took in the ham facing me on a hoarding high on the opposite wall. Its size and blood red bulk were startling and some of my senses returned.

A narrow margin of white fat half encircled this eye-catching shape, and the fat was bordered by a line of brown crackle. Blobs of glistening liquid spattered its blue-edged dish, and underneath all ran the slogan, YOU CAN'T BEAT NEWBOLDT'S HAM. JUST EAT IT. After reading this twice, I felt sick, or hungry. It was hard to say which. I gripped tightly my Aunt's note to Miss Gibson as a link with the commonplace while making my way back to Victoria Road.

At playtime Miss Sykes approached me.

'Hullo, Martha. I hope you didn't catch your sore throat at the concert.'

'Oh no. No.' I tried to be coherent. 'Thank you very much for taking me.' I had already thanked her once on the way home and Auntie had thanked her when we had parted at our door. But I had to have an opening to what I wanted to ask. 'And thank you for the flowers, too. They were lovely. There's something I want to ask, please.'

'About the concert? Well, I can't promise an answer, but I'll do my best.'

'No. It's not about that. It's about the High School. Do you know if it's closed?'

'Closed? What on earth do you mean? I don't under-stand.'

'Well, the back door was bolted, and nobody was going to school.'

'Goodness, I didn't know what you meant. It's closed today and tomorrow for half term. You don't have half term at this school. They go back on Wednesday.' She laughed, then said, 'I can't see the High School ever closing, any more than this school. There'll have to be a blue moon first. Come on, you'd better walk a bit. The wind's chilly for standing about, and I'll get into trouble for not supervising.'

After play we were told to write an essay on Advertis-ing. This was an avant-garde subject for those times, one of the signs of a progressive school. We had to invent and use at least one slogan, Miss Gibson told us, at the same time expressing the hope that we knew what a slogan was. Miss Sykes would walk round and supervise and even help us with difficult spellings. But under no circumstances must we take advantage of this, as she knew full well we would attempt to do, by asking for simple words like 'hoarding' and 'illustration'. On the other hand, the school was allowed only its ration of red ink. She did not wish to use all of it correcting the essays of a handful of girls.

I was not inventive as regards slogans, but I had a shot at the ham. I described it and used the slogan, NEWBOLDT'S HAM. THE BEST HAM SINCE THE DAYS OF NOAH. I thought it an improvement on the one I'd seen and I gave the Bible credit for coming in useful at times. I glanced up at Miss Sykes' face as she read over my shoulder. She looked perplexed. It didn't matter. I knew that Miss Gibson would see the point.

Chapter Seven

The postman's knock was unmistakable; three sharp self-evident raps heralding news and producing a tightening of all your muscles. My throat, trying to swallow small mouthfuls of shredded wheat soaked in water, refused to function at all. If the postman judged the envelope's contents to be a bill or something as commonplace, then he shot it through the slot on to the doormat. But otherwise, and especially if it bore a foreign stamp, he waited a full minute for the door to open.

'Morning, Miss Drinkhall. Letter from America.'

Across the small area of the bentwood table my cousin and I stared at each other, frail hope struggling with more powerful fear. There was a letter, but would it contain anything? Anything we wanted it to contain? Time stopped as she came through the kitchen door and stood examining the envelope. 'It's taken long enough to come,' she said.

'For goodness' sake get it opened.' Bob's voice was strident. He saw no reason why a letter intended for us all should be our Aunt's exclusive property even though the envelope bore her name. My share of the contents was usually a single sheet from Mother saying, 'We are very pleased to hear of your progress at school. Your father says work hard and it will be worth it. If he'd had your opportunities, he might have been somebody.' This did not make me see him as nobody. It blew up my pride in him. But for circumstances, he would have been rich. And now, in a land of different circumstances, he had taken on a new image in my eyes. I chose to believe that he was earning money rapidly, a fact that I was not slow to impart to the girls at the school.

Our Aunt slit open the envelope and drew out a bundle of sheets folded once downover and then across. She unfolded them and no dollar bills fell out.

'She must have something to say in all that lot.' Bob

clung to his hope as I let go of mine and the silence was heavy as her eyes dwelt on my mother's writing. Information was dealt out in fits and starts.

'They're moving. They've got this job on that estate. There's work for both of them and a house, and she thinks the people on the next estate want a gardener. It might suit you. . .' His leap from the table dragged the cloth. His tea spilt over the clip mat.

'Don't worry, I'll clean it up.'

'You'll do no such thing. There's nothing like tea stains,' and the letter went with the tablecloth as she departed for her stain removing equipment.

'It's great,' he rejoiced, returning the cup to a saucer slopping over with tea. 'A gardener's job! I'll be able to grow flowers for shows in my spare time.' I tried hard to feel at one with these high expectations.

'I'm never done, never done,' Auntie complained, scrubbing furiously at the grey clips and I thought, why do little things upset her so? The absence of dollars is much worse, and said, 'I wish there'd been some money.'

'That goes without saying.' Her voice was taut and tart. 'They've been no better off in Lawrence than they were here, and time alone will tell what this next move will bring. Your father's swollen with mosquito bites.' She's beating about the bush, I thought. Holding something back.

'What sort of work will they be doing?'

'You may well ask.' She rose from her knees, took the letter from her apron pocket, smoothed it out and began to re-read it. I looked at the clock. It was a quarter to nine.

'Please tell me, Auntie. I'll have to go.' I had collected my homework from the desk and stood ready.

'Well, if you must know, it seems that your mother is going to do all the laundry for the big house on this estate.'

'Laundry? What's that?'

'A fancy name for washing, that's what it is. Why can't they call a spade, a spade? Washing clothes, bed linen, table linen, body linen, everything.'

I could not believe it.

'But she can't do washing. At least, she never liked it. It was too much for her.'

'A lot of things were too much for her! Getting married was too much for her and all that went with it. Never would she have been driven to do washing for a living here. No one would catch me doing it.'

'But Auntie, you *can* wash. You can wash all day.'

'Of course I can, and have to, but not for a living. Wait until Gertrude and Lena hear that piece of news. And your father's not even doing proper carpentry. He's to do anything that turns up on this place. Much worse, in my opinion, than making first class coffins for Mr Whittingham.'

'Let's see.' Bob snatched at the letter. 'There must be a mistake somewhere.'

She let him read it and took her cloth and pail to the scullery.

'Is there? A mistake, I mean?'

'Not exactly. But she's not exactly right either. Your mother says laundry work is quite different from washing here. She'll have a special room fitted with machines. Machines to wash, dry, mangle and iron, all of them worked by electricity. There's nothing like it here, she says. Even heated rollers to iron the sheets and radiators fitted round the room and no steam at all. It's a nice house at the bottom of a hill that's covered with pine trees and a log cabin at the top and an orchard of peach trees below sloping down to the River Charles. There, it sounds great, doesn't it? And she's going to write and tell you all about it.'

I said I supposed so as I let myself out of the house and ran through an unpleasant drizzle along the Lane. But I knew I would not relate the contents of this letter to the girls at school any more than my Aunt would to Gertrude or Lena. Somehow those contents seemed a far cry from the process of acquiring wealth.

While my cousin's thoughts grappled with ways and means of producing his fare to America, my Aunt's dwelt on what *she* would do when he found it and left her without his dole money. On a Saturday morning in early June she was opening the door of the kitchen oven and lifting out a covered pot of stewed rabbit. Grannie and Mother had always used the gas oven in the greenhouse but Auntie considered she could do a slow stew more cheaply with the low kitchen fire than with the low gas. It wasn't the month for stews, but rabbit was cheap and nourishing and what was left could be made into a pie for Sunday dinner. After prodding the rabbit and replacing it in the oven, she said,

'Robbie, since you expect to leave for America in the not too distant future, I think we'd better be selling this old organ. Mr Burt knows a man who'll buy it and put it into working order. It's no use as it is.' Bob lifted his eyes from some documents which, I understood, had to do with his visit to the American Consul in Liverpool.

'Sell my mother's organ? Never!' and he brought his fist down on the table. I was startled to see what I had never noticed before, a likeness to Cousin Liz; his coppery face, and cheek bones, and jutting jaw. That's why he must work on the land like her I thought. Not down on the docks or in an office.

'Don't be childish,' said my Aunt. 'How can I be lumbered with organs left by people who go to America? The one in the front room was left by Rob who said he was coming back and didn't. And if you come back, it won't be for the organ. I want to bring my mahogany dining table and chairs out of store and put the table where the organ is now. Lodgers will need to eat, not play organs.'

'Lodgers?'

'Yes, lodgers. I'll have to take them in, won't I? There's nothing else for it.'

'But you can't take lodgers!'

'And why not? It's better than taking in washing. I've kept Monnie's room free with that in view. And there'll be your room when you go, and even the boxroom. It's large enough for a small bedroom.'

'Do you mean that, with only you and Martha here, you'll take in MEN?'

'What's wrong with men? You're one.' I was told to hold my tongue. Then Auntie said, 'Who else? I've never heard of women lodgers. Women are always at home or, if not, they're working in other people's houses. They can't afford to board.'

'What about teachers?' It seemed helpful and I thought most teachers were women.

Auntie shovelled some powdery coal from the scuttle and scattered it over the low fire. Her movements were slower than usual, as if she were thinking.

'I suppose some of them board,' she admitted eventually. 'But I don't think I should get on with them. I've worked for both men and women and I've always found men easier to satisfy.'

Bob said, 'Have you asked Watson?'

'Why should I? He has sense enough to know we can't live on nothing as you seem to think. He might know someone through the Prudential. Or I'll write to the Borough Council and the Education Authority. There must be some decent men who'd be glad of good board and lodging.'

'What about Tom?'

'Oh, him. . .' It sounded as if she had flicked away a fly.

So Aunt Annie's organ had gone and in its place was installed the mahogany table. It was square and supported by four very stout legs. We saw the reason for their stoutness when the table was extended, a process which she demonstrated many times for the benefit of the neighbours, always commenting on the particular smoothness of the action which depended on a giant screw underneath. When this was turned by a handle, the table split in the middle and the two halves moved in opposite directions far enough to admit one or even two leaves. I recall Hannah, Mrs Grayson and Mrs Burt watching this wonder as Auntie triumphantly turned and kept on turning until they had to skip out of the way of the advancing table top.

'How many people are you planning to seat, Blanche?' asked Hannah.

'That remains to be seen,' was the reply and Mrs Burt murmured to Mrs Grayson that there wouldn't be room for much else.

It was during this hectic interval that she and Mrs Burt had become firm friends due, I think, to Mr Burt's being an upholsterer. Their tiny front room in Muriel Street was furnished with a three-piece suite upholstered in geometrically designed green and fawn plush, a covering which had immediately caught Auntie's eye. The suite had been covered by Mr Burt during the moments he could spare from covering other people's and Mrs Burt had told Auntie she had not expected to see it done in her lifetime. They were discussing this achievement one day and Mrs Burt said the material had been tucked away, waiting, for years.

'Does there happen to be a scrap left?' asked my Aunt, as though, I thought, she were thinking of a kettle holder. 'Because I have six leather seated dining chairs which match the table and would look very well covered in that.'

Mr Burt had measured up and found it could just be managed at a pinch, and Auntie had to pinch, too, and use the proceeds from the sale of the organ in order to pay for them. Ever afterwards she felt it had been worth while. The table and chairs had been bought from Mr Carlin and stored against the time when she could set up home.

This was how I became acquainted with Laura. I was not insensible of the strong maternal and paternal qualities of her parents. Mrs Burt had a great sympathy for me, informing me often that she didn't know how my parents could have left me as they had, and she was as often inclined to remind me of my debt to my Aunt with the words 'But you don't know how lucky you are to have Auntie.' (It seems to me now that it was Mrs Burt who began the cult, which grew, of calling my Aunt by this diminutive so that, through a gradual metamorphosis, she lost both her christian and her surnames and became known to friends as Auntie. Clearly, I played a part in this change.)

Mrs Burt would invite me into their front room to listen to Laura play her 'piece'. 'I don't know how they manage it,' my Aunt had said to Minnie, 'but they have to do something for her since they can't give her any brothers or sisters. So they pay for piano lessons and are planning to buy her a bicycle. Then the three of them will cycle off into the country on Sundays. I'm not altogether in favour of that. They don't go to Chapel.' And Bob had said,

61

'They believe in cycling and in the Co-op and Dividends as we believe in God. It probably does them more good,' It was a remark he would have given worlds to have left unsaid when his Aunt reminded him of his dead mother and her ever watchful presence.

At the piano Laura sat sternly upright, the thin book containing six Associated Board pieces balanced between her and her reflection. Her hair was wrenched back from a broad forehead and fastened tightly into two long plaits. She played carefully, distinctly separating each note or chord so that a tune was difficult to follow. At no time did I finger the piano to discover its potential or the purpose of the two pedals which her feet never touched. The organ, I decided, was superior in that respect – one note flowed into the next. Then recalling the concert and Myra Hess's 'famous piece', I felt there must be some way with a piano of joining one note to the next.

My Aunt's plans for taking one lodger suffered a temporary setback due to the imminence of the Sunday School Anniversary. The removal of furniture in and out of the kitchen had caused her to overlook this until Aunt Gertrude, calling to see what Blanche was doing with the house, had asked her with forced casualness if I was going to perform at this event.

'Of course she's going to perform. Hasn't she always done so?'

Her vehemence suggested long preparations whereas, in fact, she had to start thinking what I should wear and had a mere fortnight in which to concoct something. I, myself, was not sure how often I had participated because my Mother had treated it as a normal Sunday except that parents could go if they wished. As for the previous year, Auntie was still too busy settling the household into her ways; I don't think she even attended. For my own part, I was no more stirred by being asked to stand up and sing or recite surrounded by children packed into the choir gallery with a raised platform below it, than when I was bidden to do so from my desk at day school. Many children forgot their words, but I was not one of those; many children wore new frilly dresses, but neither was I among them. I wore my usual Sunday best.

This year it was clear that I was going to be dressed up and Auntie gave the matter her full attention. The result was a quantity of figured white voile taken from her blanket chest. On first seeing it, I'd said a very upsetting thing. I'd asked if it had been intended for a wedding dress and I knew by the blood rushing to her cheeks and slackening them till they almost quivered, that the thing should never have been said. She had set to work on my dress which was shaping, I had to admit, like a thing of beauty with a full gathered skirt, a figured yoke and a length of white taffeta ribbon to tie round the high waist line. I think she had forgotten my unpleasant question and was delighted with her work. She kept saying how well it suited the hymn and the poem which Miss Swales had given me to prepare and which Auntie had asked to see.

The more she talked of the event, the more I withdrew from it. To be truthful this was due to neither perverseness nor to nerves but simply some vague premonition that it wouldn't happen. I could not anticipate it. So that, on Friday night, with supposedly eight days to go, the fact that I chose to say something about it must have sprung from contrariness. I was to sing, 'By cool Siloam's shady rill' and to recite, 'An old-fashioned garden'. 'It's a lovely poem,' Miss Swales had enthused. 'But not many children can memorise anything as long as that.' It had four verses with eight lines in each. When my Aunt had read it, she'd said, 'You should be a star turn reciting that.' From the depths of the tub, lather from my soaped hair covering my shoulders and getting into my mouth, I mumbled, 'I'm not going to say that poem.' I had to repeat the sentence in answer to her 'What?'

'Don't talk such nonsense.'

'The first verse is all right about ordinary flowers though it's silly calling daffodils and roses old-fashioned because there they are, every year, just the same as before. But I object to that part in the second verse, "Would you ask me the names of those flowers, they are kindness and sweet courtesy, and tenderness, too, and affection," and also the line, "In the heart is that old-fashioned garden," I won't say that because it isn't true. How can a garden be in a heart?'

The question was flippant, of course. I was well aware of that. It had nothing to do with my dislike of the poem. Auntie rinsed my hair in a stunned silence using a ladling tin of clean water. Finally she transferred her feelings to the drying of my head which had a rough time of it. Then she said, 'Whatever am I to do with you? You're so peculiar. It's a very nice poem and Miss Swales chose it specially for you. What am I going to say to her?'

I threw my left leg over the edge of the tub and she threw a towel over my shoulders. I dried myself in a silence which I found disconcerting. It was I who had to break it.

'Listen, I'll tell Miss Swales. I'm sure it doesn't matter because there's one we've learnt at school about daffodils. It's a famous poem. I'll say it to you.' And, wrapped in the towel, I started immediately lest she should refuse to listen.

> 'Fair daffodils, we weep to see you haste
> away so soon;
> As yet the early-rising sun has not attain'd
> his noon.
> Stay, stay, until the hasting day has run but
> to the evensong;
> And, having prayed together, we will go
> with you along.
>
> We have short time to stay as you, we have
> as short a Spring;
> As quick a growth to meet decay as you or
> anything.
> We die, as your hours do, and dry away
> like to the Summer's rain;
> Or as the pearls of morning's dew, ne'er to
> be found again.'

'You're not likely to be dried away at this rate.' She stood with my nightgown on her arm. 'Be quick now, and finish yourself off.'

'Don't you like it?'

'It's peculiar like a lot more things you learn at school. People won't understand it. It's not a Chapel poem at all.

There's nothing in it about God or behaving well.'

'There's the bit about praying.'

'But flowers don't pray any more than they grow in hearts.'

There was no answer to this. She had scored on a technicality. Yet I knew there must be other arguments against the one poem and in favour of the other though I was unable to formulate them. The only argument I might have voiced was that the High School girls would accept 'To Daffofils' and reject 'An Old-fashioned Garden'. I must try to compromise. I sat on the towel to dry my feet. 'Well, if you like, I'll say Psalm 103. It has twenty-two verses and two of them are just like that poem.'

> As for man, his days are as grass;
> As the flower of the field, so he flourisheth;
> For the wind passeth over it and it is gone,
> And the place thereof shall know it no more.

'There. What's the difference? And you can't call a Psalm peculiar.'

'Here's your cocoa. Drink it, and get to bed.'

I really thought I could reconcile Miss Swales to the Psalm. She taught elocution and must have been almost a hundred. As it turned out, though impressed by the length, she raised an unexpected objection. The Psalms were really Church of England. They were not exactly suited to Chapel except, of course, the twenty-third.

Chapter Eight

The following Friday morning I went to school with a light head, heavy legs and pains all over me. My shredded wheat was left untouched, there being no room in my throat to swallow it. My cousin put it down to nerves. All the kids in his class were nervous about Sunday, he said, and this was sufficient to divert Auntie's attention from me to the shortcomings in his speech. His use of slang, she said, was beyond all reason; whatever would his mother have thought? (I'd heard her once tell Hannah that poor Annie dead held him in a firmer grip than she would have done alive.)

There was no point in mentioning my aches and pains. Many children had them and mostly they were attributed to growing. Besides, I was obliged to go to school that morning because Standard Six had earned a merit holiday in the afternoon; a holiday for full attendance throughout the week providing the register contained no noughts on Friday morning. This did not happen often. Had it done so, then the reward must needs have been withdrawn, for no one could contemplate a half empty school each Friday afternoon. I don't know whether Miss Gibson was likewise rewarded, but she certainly viewed the hundred per cent attendance as a feather in her cap.

If a child was in school until playtime, then its attendance was not cancelled. Therefore it was playtime before Miss Gibson sent me to Miss Byers' room where I was given a note for my Aunt and told to go home. I saw the opened note on the kitchen table when Auntie went to fill the kettle for a hot water bottle. It said I wasn't fit to be in school and might be infecting other children with whatever throat ailment I had. It might be wise to call a doctor.

I need not dwell on my Aunt's reaction, especially when she discovered that my voice had gone. She planted the thermometer in my mouth with instructions to keep my lips closed and not bite it – no easy matter with my protruding teeth. As she filled the three-sided iron bottle, I thought for the second time in two weeks that she was about to cry. But she wasn't the crying type and she soon controlled herself.

In bed I plucked at the sock round my neck. It enclosed a generous application of Musterole in place of goose grease. Musterole was an ointment which burnt your skin and gave off an evil smell. It was so widely advertised as a new remedy for colds, throats, chests and all other aches and pains that poor people saved hard to buy a jar. I did not feel like inventing a slogan for it. Instead I blamed it as well as the sock for the strange sensation of floating up to the ceiling to join a bluebottle that already clung there. I blamed both these unpleasant things, but I could not complain because suffering them was nothing compared with her disappointment. Mentally I repeated her words, 'Your throat is nothing but a nuisance,' and then recalled her expression as she read the thermometer. Only last night she was at Mrs Burt's receiving on my behalf Laura's white socks and shoes, the loan of which had been offered to save Auntie having to 'stretch the pennies' as Mrs Burt put it.

I had capitulated on the subject of the recitation. 'An Old-fashioned Garden' I would recite, if I were to recite anything at all, clothed in a voile dress that made me look like a fairy. Not Peaseblossom, Cobweb and company. You couldn't see them in voile. But the fairy with a wand. I know my Aunt thought I had got over my silliness, that I had been showing off at the expense of Miss Swales or something like that and I was not surprised at her inability to take me seriously. For how could I have explained the curious certainty inside me that I should not be reciting *any* poem at this year's Anniversary; that something blocked the way. Yet here I was, almost voiceless and filled with remorse about that dress.

I considered the dress. It was all I could do, consider. The second time her beautiful figured voile had missed its mark. I had seen brides in Aunt Gertrude's fashion magazines and was now certain that the voile had been intended for a wedding dress. Once I had seen the name Arthur written in the front of her Bible. I turned my eyeballs, it hurt to do so, and looked towards it lying with her own and Grannie's hymn books on top of the chest. Its binding was intriguing, mottled leather with the margins bent frill-like either to protect the gilt edges of the leaves or to conceal a secret. I thought it would be cool to hold between my hot hands, but reaching it was the problem. What was involved in the business of reaching it? Stepping out of bed, stretching up my left arm, grasping the Bible and falling back into bed. I went over the process a few times in my head. It seemed impossible. But if I were to *try*! I did try and there I was, back in bed with the book lying on my ribs until things settled inside me. After a long time I lifted it. The front opened at a tasselled book-marker, a stretch of yellowed, papery ribbon. I could make out the four words at the top, four words in two rows, red, green and purple, and, by rubbing a finger over them, I knew they were embroidered. The Old Arm Chair. And there was the picture of it beneath some very tiny print which I couldn't read. I fingered the tall chair with its green cushion and red Bible propped against one arm. It was all embroidered. Then my gaze shifted to the sloping handwriting on the nondescript brown page oppo-site. I could read that, although the ink was smeared on two words. 'The Lord watch between me and thee when we are absent from one another,' and underneath, Blanche from Arthur, Christmas 1902.

I was glad to let my eyes close and just have those words circling in my head. Poetry, lovely but sad. Separation and long night watches. I tried to calculate. How many from two up to twenty-four? Take two away. It leaves twenty-two. That's how many years, twenty-two which I tried to hold on to while thinking of the days in a year. Even when I managed to bring those to mind, there was no way of working out the sum except on paper. God must have made twenty-two times three hundred and sixty-five night watches between this man, Arthur, and my Aunt and that was not counting the extra day in each leap year. A formidable number but, I supposed, not long for God.

Now, here was my Aunt, lifting me under the armpits into a sitting position, plumping up the pillow and straightening the bedclothes, all exactly like a nurse. She shook out a square of flannel, arranged it under my chin and spooned into me a dose of cascara. The thick, dark brown liquid tasted, I always thought, like rotting leaves though I knew the taste of these only through their smell in the park. Like the majority of her generation, she still clung to the Victorian remedy of bowel-purging for most complaints.

'I just don't know what to do about a doctor,' she said. 'Hannah tells me there's a new one come to the bottom of Southfield Road. A Scots name and a broad Scots accent. But he's disinclined to give medicines, so what's the use of that? You can't pay him for nothing. He won't give Mrs Kneeshaw any bromide which brought me through my nervous breakdown under Doctor Howell. He told Hannah that far too much of the stuff had been in general use. It was all right for soldiers at the front. I don't see the point. I suppose civilians can suffer from the same complaints as soldiers. He'll not get patients that way, though Hannah seems to have taken to him. Now, you'd better get some sleep. I must find the time to write to your mother. We can't go on like this. She'd better come back and see what's to be done.'

I must have dreamed, or how did I get here again swallowing Fennings Fever Cure? But if it had been a dream, it was still more real than the bedroom, its furnishings and my sore throat. Everything about it was larger than life and clearer than vision. The mass of bricks where the backyard wall had collapsed was enormous and the bricks themselves were pulled into bizarre charred shapes. One flower bed remained but, instead of its normal modest size, it stretched away into the far distance and there sent up a row of elongated trees whose branches spread across the sky towards us, letting down pendulous leaves which just cleared our heads and a pool that lay between us, Bob and my small sister on one side, I on the other. They each stood on a rosette of London pride leaves the size of stool tops. The sawed edges were dark and sharply etched and the centres floodlit from below, a lurid green.

We were staring into the pool's extreme depth. This was

not a depth that disappeared, merging as with an ordinary pond into murky obscurity. From its bed to its surface the pool was as transparent as a polished mirror, and as still. This brilliant translucence suggested a synthetic substance made to resemble water but motionless because it lacked liquidity, and outside the laws of light since there were no reflections. The whole scene emanated a curious vitality beyond our normal concepts of life.

We stared through this water to where, half embedded in its sandy bottom and forming three concentric circles, were what I took to be some massive onions raising their pointed papery tops in our direction. My sister clapped her hands and jigged up and down on her leaf of London pride.

'I planted them. I planted them,' she piped.

'What are they?' My own voice was sepulchral.

'They're bulbth, bulbth,' she lisped, and I noted she was still without her s's.

'You couldn't have planted them,' I argued. 'You couldn't reach down there.'

'I could. I did. My arm grew and grew. It grew downwards.'

'They won't grow,' I croaked. 'They can't grow all that way up to reach the air.'

'They're water lilies,' chided my cousin. 'Lilies that grow in water. You ought to know.'

'I don't. I don't know how they'll ever reach the top.'

'Long stems is the answer. They could grow from the middle of the earth and still spread flat leaves on the water top. It's clear enough,' and they both laughed in a demented sort of way.

The Fennings Fever Cure was drying up my mouth. I slept again and had the same dream. Unless I had not been able to separate afternoon from night, or one day from the next.

The grandfather clock in the hall was striking when I knew myself to be awake. Bob was holding out a steaming glass of lemon drink. As I pulled myself up to take it, I saw a slice like a yellow sun decorating the surface.

'How's your throat?'

I didn't know but tried to say a bit better and what time was it. It hurt to talk.

70

'Just struck nine. Aunt Blanche has gone to the butcher's to be there when he opens. Hard luck about the Anniversary, but I don't suppose you mind, being not keen on the poem and all that. Lie still. You'll get better more quickly that way, though I still think she's mad not calling a doctor. Can't understand the woman.'

I thought least said, soonest mended on that score. So I shook my head and took a sip of the lemon. It burnt my top lip. It was no use his just standing there and I was relieved when he went. From my propped-up position I noticed the bevelled edge of the wardrobe mirror take on the colours of the rainbow. Once before I'd been curious about this and had asked why. I was told it was caused by the sunlight striking the sloping edge of the glass which was evident and no explanation at all. I considered it again. There was nothing else to do. My eyes ached too much to read and the growing pains affecting all my joints refused to be ignored. Thankfully there would be some point in the future when I'd stop growing and be done with the pains. Minnie said you grew faster when you were in bed, which was a comfort at the moment. I wondered if the rainbow in the glass might be one of those things you learnt about at the High School and this thought dredged up into my consciousness the horrible word IF. Often things seemed to lie in the bottom on your mind until something, like the colours in the glass, made them surface. Before I had resolved to become a High School girl, the process of 'passing the scholarship' had been taken for granted like knowing that you would grow. Since then I hadn't been so sure. What if I didn't pass?

I pondered the matter. Plainly, I was prone to disappointing people. I had disappointed my Aunt with regard to the Anniversary and my mother, I supposed, by refusing to go with them to America. In a way too terrible to dwell upon, I had disappointed Grannie by not being Bessie, and Mrs Burt often alluded to the invalids Auntie would have been paid to nurse if she hadn't had to look after me. Then there was Sylvia. It was hard to know why she was disappointed because I had ceased to adore her, but something in her behaviour suggested that it was so; and if I didn't pass the scholarship, then that would be the biggest disappointment of all to Miss Gibson and Miss Byers. These things were hard to bear. I felt I couldn't bear them and tried to forget by gulping down a large mouthful of the lemon drink and scalding my throat which was easier to bear.

'Your Great-Uncle Watson has descended on us out of the blue. Why he couldn't have sent a postcard is beyond understanding. They're cheap enough, though not for his pocket, it seems. When I came in from the butcher's there he was in the greenhouse chatting to Tom Henderson and keeping him from his work. It means I'll have the Sunday dinner to cook today which puts everything out of joint for the week. Here's your Bovril to be getting on with. He's catching the five o'clock train back to Ayton. I neither know why he's come nor which way to turn.'

All I could think of replying to this long speech was, 'Is he old?'

'Who?'

'Great-Uncle Watson,'

'He'll be seventy. You've seen him. The day of your Grandmother's funeral.'

'I don't remember.'

'Well, I suppose he'll come up to have a look at you though he never has liked children. He didn't have any.'

She swept up the glass with its slice of sucked lemon in the bottom and departed. I rested my upper lip on the Bovril and blew over it, ruffling the surface. I wondered for how long I'd been away and glanced at the wardrobe mirror. The rainbow hues had gone and the sunlight was slanting down on the table in the window, the one with the small, rectangular tip-up top, delicately carved pedestal and three spindly ankles and feet. It was her pride and joy and, although it would take sixty years before I learned that it was Georgian, I never did learn how she came by it. Of course, its surface was shielded by a cloth whiter than any fuller on earth could white it. I spilt a drop of Bovril in my impatience that the Bible should toss another sentence into my head. It did not let you go easily, and I recalled the copy on which my knees happened to be resting. I must put it back where it belonged.

The cloth had a deep edge of heavy crochet work. Long ago she had actually had time to crochet. I had learnt this once on asking the purpose of a hollow spherical object, prettily designed, which opened into two halves and had a small ivory-edged hole at the top. It was to hold balls of crochet cotton and, one Saturday night, I saw her use it, the thin, white string emerging in jerks from the painted ball while the patterned work falling from her hands into her lap seemed not to grow at all. She never hooked a wrong stitch to be taken back as I did with knitting. She was careful and patient, just as she was when snuffing blackcurrants which Uncle Watson, who had once brought her some, called a waste of good time. 'They're not like gooseberries,' he'd said. 'There's nothing on them to snuff. But snuff them by all means, if you're looking for something to do.' A remark which would have raised a storm if anyone else had said it.

Time must once have been kind to her to let her get all that crocheting done – the yards and yards wrapped in tight narrow bales and stacked, as I had seen by chance, in the top half of the chest of drawers – the grained yellow chest with the eight glass knobs, the four top ones being fakes because behind them, instead of a long and two short drawers, there was nothing but a cavity with a lid. I had run upstairs to find Hannah and had seen her propping up this heavy lid against the wall. Auntie's head was in the chest and I grasped one edge and peeped over. The crochet work was stacked at that side on top of some white sheets.

'Goodness,' I'd cried, quite astonished at so amazing a deception in furniture. 'They're not really drawers at all, only a box.'

My Aunt appeared unaware of me. When her mind was on other things, she often treated me as a piece of furniture.

'It was my bottom drawer, Hannah, years ago of course. But times change and it's come in handy for another purpose. I thought you ought to know where to find them. The sheets are there and the rest is here,' and she lifted out a large, flat cardboard box decorated with green and gold stars. She untied the binding string and put the lid to one side, then drew out, one by one, two folded damask towels, a smaller one with three rows of scarlet running stitch across its end and a mammoth sized serviette all of which had been treated, it was obvious, with a bag of Reckits Blue then starched to stiffness. Next came a folded nightgown with broderie anglais round the high neck and three linen buttons, a lock knit vest and finally two pairs of white stockings, one thin and one thick. The latter pair she held aloft by the toes. They were of great length.

'Took me a while to knit those,' she said, 'but I'll be longer wearing them,' and laughed. 'When anything happens, you'll know where they are and I know I can rely on you to see to me. My sisters-in-law would be useless. Strange how squeamish women are getting about it. Someone has it to do.'

'What's that piece of coloured stuff?' I'd asked. It was folded in four and, apart from the red stitching on the towel, it was the only coloured object in that white interior.

'Oh that.' She shook it out, and it quite took away my breath, the most magnetic square of material I had ever seen. Rich, regal velvet with sheens and shades of a colour I had no word to describe.

'Please, please let me feel it,' and I stroked it with delight. Hannah shuddered. 'It's queer, I can't bear the feel of velvet.'

'Like me with buttons,' I said, though still spellbound. 'It's like a piece of a king's robe. What's it for?'

'A scrap someone gave your Aunt Annie. She liked to make patchwork cushions with bits of velvet. She sewed them together with a feather stitch in gold thread. And a perfect feather stitch she could do, too.'

'What do you call that colour?'

'I don't know. She called it puce. A cross between plum and cherry, I should think.'

She folded it again and the velvet side was hidden. 'Poor Annie. I've known the time when she would sit with her patchwork and me with my crocheting. We'd talk, though I know we didn't always see eye to eye. Making plans. Little did we guess . . . That's why I'm showing you, Hannah. No man knoweth the day nor the hour.'

'Make it into a cushion, Auntie,' I pleaded. 'Put a piece of

74

lining on the back to make a cushion cover. Don't put it away with those other things. It shouldn't be with them forever.'

'We'll see. When I have time. I do want to get my crochet work used on something, though goodness knows what.'

I was a fly on the ceiling with eyes in the back of my head. I watched the two women facing each other seated in wooden armchairs with tall backs and holding between them a strip of white linen. They were stitching a border of crochet work to each long edge.

'What's it for?' I called, apparently having human speech. And because there was no reply, I called again. 'What's it for? I demand an answer.'

'A tablecloth for the bridegroom's feast,' chanted one without lifting an eyelid.

'Which feast? Which bridegroom?'

'You ought to know.'

'I don't know the bridegroom. Only the bride.'

Both women stopped stitching and stared knowingly at each other.

'You're wrong,' I cried, quite put out by the secret they shared but not with me. 'It's not wide enough for a tablecloth. It's not wide enough for anything but a coffin. It would fit a coffin, I think, and that's what it's for.'

'And what's all this, girl? In bed on a day in June?'

All my senses strained to bring things into focus, withdrawing telescopically from a far off view to settle on this figure within arm's reach. This Moses of the commandments out of Blomfield, with his beard, his intense and startling features, his eyes glinting with Thou shalt and Thou shalt not, and his rod that had riven a rock now poking the bedclothes above my leg. The Bible, I thought, he's after that, then felt hands grasp my armpits and hoist me again into a sitting position.

'Great Uncle Watson come to have a look at you.'

Sitting up I almost lost him again. His figure collapsed into shapeless curves, but I could hear him.

'You should be ashamed of yourself, lying here like a

broken reed. A girl with Watson blood in her! You should be up and doing, running round the Park a few times a day. Look at me, fit as a fiddle at seventy. Climbing Roseberry in twenty minutes and returning at the run, clearing a few boulders into the bargain. Look at your Aunt here. Look at your Grandmother. Look at Lizzie still farming Huck-a-Back on her own at seventy-four.'

'Lizzie? Cousin Liz? Can I go to see her?'

'What, to Castleton? You look like doing that, I must say. Get out of that bed first.'

Feebly, I disarranged the bedclothes with this intention.

'Her temperature was over a hundred this morning, Uncle. Remember, I was a nurse.'

'A nurse! And why have we got nurses? Because people will make invalids of themselves. Which is what you're making of her. My wife all over again. Never moved out of the house since I brought her home from our week in Scotland. Took her to the ends of the earth for that honeymoon because I'd made up my mind to afford it. And it finished her. No mettle in her. Found out after the wedding that I'd taken her for the worse. I've only myself to blame. You can't expect much from poor stock.'

'I'm glad you're honest enough to blame yourself. Isn't it you who's made an invalid out of her?'

'Now what's the meaning of that, Blanche Maud Drinkhall?'

'Well, one hears tales. Things will out, you know.'

'Only if there are ears to hear them. My wife set out to be an invalid and she managed it.'

'Yet, in spite of her invalid state, she's cooked and washed for you and kept your house clean.'

'Aye, as if she were dying on her feet. Never done any shopping. Never gone near the Chapel.'

'Which seems to have suited you, poor woman.'

'I did not come all the way from Great Ayton to take any lip from you, young woman.' (This was a shock. She seemed anything but young to me.) 'And I don't waste sympathy on invalids. You had a try at being one yourself, if I remember rightly. But you've had to mend your ways with no man to support you. The Watson blood had to surface. You'll live to be eighty.'

'That's what you think. And don't forget that your wife's made seventy. A good age for a sick woman.'

'That's right. I've kept her going with that in mind. I married her and vowed she'd reach her allotted span. But there'll be no borrowed time for her. Which brings me to the reason for this visit now that your mother's gone. There was no point in raising the subject while you still had her to see to. The fact is, I could do with you soon, my wife's days being numbered. I can't be seeing to her hand and foot, nor spend my last years seeing to myself. There'll soon be a home for you at Great Ayton and, don't forget, a bit of something for you when I'm gone, which you'll not say no to. But first something must be done about this girl. Get her back where she belongs, with her parents,' and he bent over the bed and playfully slapped my covered legs.

My Aunt asked him what exactly he thought he was talking about and was told, 'Just that. It's where a child belongs, with its parents. What they were doing to leave her nobody knows. Her father shirking his responsibilities. Everyone talks of it. And if you keep her long enough they'll change their tune and say she was yours.'

My Aunt said was that so? And if it was she would do a bit of talking herself for a change. I'd been left in her charge and with her I would remain and people could say what they liked. It was well known what dirty minds some people could have. And I was not changing schools at this point in my education, no matter how much they liked to blacken her character. Here I was and here I would stay, and I felt that she had drawn herself up by a few inches and that there *they* stood, ready for the signal to advance as in the tournaments at Ashby De La Zouche. And while my ears had recorded the gist of this interchange, my eyes had got rid of Moses and had taken in my Great-Uncle – his long nose running past his lips to touch the swell of a white beard that covered half his chest. His cheeks seemed missing too, for his eyes, deep-set like Grannie's, I remembered, were overhung by eyebrows that matched the beard, being white and stiffly curling. And the rest of his forehead was obscured by the end of a silver curl which, I had noticed as he bent over the bed, lay

77

across the middle of his head. Had he put it in a curling rag, I wondered, and left it uncombed when he pulled out the rag? He was surely peculiar enough to do anything! Only as Auntie was bringing her long speech to an end, did I see any part of his mouth, then it was the bottom lip, the pale pink inside of it that slowly came into view as he glared at her. He, too, had assumed his full stature, but his lip, I thought, was like my cousin Margaret's when I didn't want to play her game. When he spoke again he seemed to hammer home his words.

'Education? Education for lasses? Poppycock! She can learn all she needs to know from you, or rather her mother. What do lassies want but a sound knowledge of housekeeping, make do and mend, patch and darn? Don't mention education to me. Money wasted keeping bairns at school till they're men and women. I started with a pick axe under Roseberry when I was eleven and you and your mother were in service at that age. What's got into you, woman?'

'Just this. That things change, and let's hope for the better. I wouldn't want to live my life again, and she's not going to have one like it. She'll go in for teaching.'

'Teaching? Well, well, there's food for thought, I must say. And stay a spinster, will she? Then she *will* be taking after you, Blanche. Certainly not after her so-called mother, or Annie either.'

My Aunt said she would be obliged if he would please catch the three o'clock train instead of the five, and I saw then how it was when two giants are locked in combat and the value, at such a time, of a tactical, temporary withdrawal. My Great-Uncle achieved just that, saying, 'It's the Watson blood in you, plain as a pikestaff,' then turned his attention to me.

'At all events, we'll have this girl on her two feet. I've something here for throats. Always carry it with me in case Ellen gets her hands on it. Can't have her finishing herself off. Now come on, Blanche, remove that sock, please.' My Aunt, thrown off her balance, I suspected, by this change in direction, asked why and he told her. 'When you were nursing in that Hartlepool hospital, did you ever have two rows of patients facing each other and all with socks round their necks? For that matter, did they use socks at all? Hospitals have to keep up with the times, you know.'

Unexpectedly, he had made an ally of me. 'Please Auntie, I'd feel better without the sock. I'll try to get up.'

'There you are, she'll try. That's what we want. She'll try. Get out of the other side, facing the washstand. I'm going to teach her to gargle.'

My Aunt laughed outright – a rare occurrence.

'You've taken on more than you've bargained for. No one's been able to make her gargle. For that matter, no one's ever been able to look down her throat. That's partly why I haven't had her to a doctor. It's the first thing they want to do. But no one's ever been able to.'

'Well I am someone, not no one. Young woman, there is no such word as can't. You can do what you make up your mind to do. And you're going to gargle with the stuff in this little container that saved my life when I had smallpox.'

'Smallpox?'

'That's right. Take a look at my pock marks,' and he pointed to a small patch of cheek above the hair. I looked and remembered those round dints in Miss Burns' face and was compelled, though with some misgiving, to take notice of the unusual impressions in his leathery skin.

'But mine isn't smallpox, is it?'

'No, no. Don't twist things about. I don't know what you've got, but whatever it is, this will cure it.'

With the sock removed my neck felt icy but more comfortable and I had edged my legs out of bed until I sat, sunk deep in the feather mattress, facing the washstand with its mottled marble surface and tiled back. I ached all over. He handed me the grey metal container saying, 'Open that,' which I endeavoured to do but without success.

'There you are. No strength in your fingers. Look!' and I had to admit that the way his tough old fingers unhinged the tight, deep lid of this cylinder seemed like a conjuring trick.

'What is it?' asked my Aunt. 'I have a right to know what you're giving her.'

'Permanganate of potash.' He stood the thing on the washstand, lifted the tumbler from the water bottle and poured in a little water.

'Ever watched a blackbird sing?' he asked.

I hadn't. Not even heard one to know it was a blackbird. Birdsong came from over the opposite wall, but you had no idea which sort of bird was singing. The only birds we were taught about at school were the owl which they said could only see at night, and the cuckoo because of its immoral ways.

'Never mind. A blackbird hops or even runs to the beck for a drink. It has a few swallows, tipping up its beak to let the water dribble down. But the last drop it holds in its beak. It flies to the top of a young ash making sure it can be seen, perches there, throws back its head and blows bubbles in its throat. All it does is keep its beak wide open and blow – ah–ah–ah – and out comes its song, liquid sounding because it's coming through water. You can see its throat working, in and out, just blowing bubbles with its beak wide open. Listen!'

He took a mouthful of water, tipped back his head and opened his mouth, his beard projecting like the bill of a duck. And there came from his gaping mouth a rising and falling scale of bubbling sound; then another reaching a tone higher and yet another higher still, a fascinating performance both to watch and to hear. Then he threw forward his head and spit into the china wash bowl.

'I suppose you call that clever,' said my Aunt.

'Aye. Lizzie Watson taught it me. After Father died of the smallpox. Mother lost a couple of little ones, too. She took us over to Huck-a-Back from Newton, just George and me. Ann, your mother was away in service then. We walked over the top to Kildale. I would be ten, Lizzie fourteen and a rare bonnie lass. Watson to the bone. All Watson was what I came to think later on, her mother and uncle farming there, four miles from anywhere and never a word about who fathered her. Aunt Betsy gave Mother this stuff in this very shaving stick container and Lizzie got both us boys gargling. Said it was like larks singing at heaven's gate. We thought it daft then, but it stuck. Not so many blackbirds up there. They like trees, hedges, low shrubs. But larks galore bursting themselves with song only you can never see their throats like you can with blackbirds and you can't hear the sound the same, like water running over pebbles. Now lass, get busy. Let's see thah try.'

Strange how he'd dropped a little into her speech which drew her ever so slightly out of the mists that had lately hidden her. I took a mouthful of water and, throwing back my head, choked on it. Twice more I attempted, making an awful mess, Auntie said, over everything. The third time I held the water in my throat. I stood on the moor, eyes scanning the sky for a tiny singing speck. I felt myself rise. My throat relaxed, the muscles began to play with the water and I heard the spring outside Huck-a-Back where Lizzie would bend to fill the water pail, one hand on a standing stone to steady herself. I saw the brilliant wet moss and the pricking over of young rushes. I heard the bubbling. I gargled.

'That's the stuff,' my Great-Uncle said as I emptied my mouth. He took a pinch of something from the container and let it drop into the half filled glass. Black crystals sank to the bottom and from them charcoal threads snaked to the surface where they lightened, became the blue-purple of lavender, then the pink-purple of heather, then circulated in a glorious diffusion.

'Now, gargle with that.'

After a few abortive attempts, I succeeded, and all the surfaces of mouth and throat were scoured by the action of the harsh solution, as though, I thought, with a piece of emery paper. After I had spit out, Auntie made a fuss about the bowl where the purple stain turned rapidly brown and would need the scouring powder to remove it. Her Uncle took no notice. He produced a round tobacco box and into it shook a scattering of crystals.

'Keep her gargling with that. Only two or three grains at a time and get her out and about. I cannot bide this invalid business in our stock.'

The stock showed an amazing resistance to the permanganate of potash which, in the more enlightened times to come, was pronounced a deadly poison working through the surface of the skin, so that medical men experimenting in laboratories were warned to wear gloves when handling it. But we of the Watson blood gargled with it safely for three generations.

Chapter Nine

No sooner had I returned to school than American letters began to arrive. The first gave the postman an excuse to linger.

'Morning, Miss Drinkhall. American letter for Mr George Robert Davison and I'm afraid I must ask him for his signature on this here form.'

'Whatever for?' Bob and I heard her say. Then, as he leapt from the table, I heard the postman's voice continue, 'Just a matter of form, Miss Drinkhall. The sender has paid extra postage, considerably extra, to make sure it would be taken special care of all the way by land and sea. If it happens to get lost, then the postal authorities have to pay up. So they're not often lost. Ah, there you are, Mr Davison,' (We were all three there, in fact.) 'If you'll be so good as to sign your name on that line,' and, holding a book of lined pages in front of Bob, he indicated the place with his middle finger. His forefinger, I saw, ended at the knuckle joint. 'That's it, thank you. Hope the news is good.'

Good news? How could my parents, doing washing and odd jobs, be paying a lot of postage for good news to reach us?

'Let me see it,' Auntie ordered, and scrutinised the address in the better light of the kitchen. 'It's as I thought. That's not Monnie's writing. It's Rob's. You'd better be prepared for the worst.'

'You mean – it's a death?' I don't know which of us voiced it, but I'm sure we both thought it. Then I asked, 'Has Mother died?' though the question seemed meaningless, and Bob shouted, 'It's addressed to me' and, snatching it, slit open the envelope and wrenched out the folded contents.

With the first unfolding, there fell on to the tablecloth a single folded dollar bill. No one moved as we stared at it. Then I said. 'It isn't a death, you see. It's only a dollar,' and

Auntie exclaimed, 'Rob must have gone mad, paying all that postage to send a dollar.'

As no one else picked it up, I did. It was money, anyway, and who cared about Rob's madness? Then I said, 'It's not a dollar. It's the wrong colour. It's gold and black, not silver. It's got a different head on it and the figure isn't a 1, it's 100. Look.' I handed it to Bob and heard the clock's laboured tick as he stared. At last, slowly, he said, 'She's right. But there must be a trick somewhere. They can't make a single note worth a hundred dollars. How much is a hundred dollars, any-way?'

'Twenty pounds.' I had already worked it out. It was the sort of mental arithmetic sum we were used to. (Five dollars to the pound remained static during my child-hood.) Such sums of money were common in school arithmetic, but unimaginable in real life. 'Twenty pounds!' echoed Bob in disbelief. Our Aunt said, 'Give me that letter. Rob should have written to me, his sister,' and, since the golden bill seemed to have drained him of resistance, he allowed her to take it. 'You might as well know what he has to say, so I'll read it aloud,' and she proceeded to do so.

'"Dear Robbie,
          This letter is from Big Rob to Little Rob. That is what I wrote on the postcard I sent you when you were four years old showing the tug boats breaking ice in Duluth harbour. You remember the picture you had just sent me from 85, Park Lane of yourself in a velvet suit and gloves, a large hat with a turned-up brim and your cork-screw curls? You were stand-ing on a rug with my over-fed collie, Rover, sitting beside you but nearly as high as you. You were looking after him for me until I came home. I didn't come, as you know, but you came to Duluth with your mother to try to make a home there for you and that husband of hers. I feel responsible for her ever coming to join him, unspeakable scoundrel that he turned out to be."

'Rob should mind his language,' my Aunt interposed.

'"So I'm sending you a hundred dollars which will pay for your fare to the States. It's the least I can do. America has not treated me badly, but I couldn't ask you to make your home with us, not now that I'm married with two children, an adopted girl and, at last, one of our own, another little Robbie. But I know May Monica has been like a mother to you and now that they have a place to call their own, I'm sure that you'll settle there and get some work in the vicinity. It's a good country if, as they say, you have some guts. The climate near Boston is nothing like as severe as in Duluth where you and your mother nearly froze to death that winter.

'"On the emigration forms you'll get from Lithgow's, you'll have to state that you are coming to live with me. An American citizen has to be responsible for you and I became a naturalized American as soon as I could. If you're staying here, there's no point in hanging on to your British citizenship and I don't understand why Harry is so stubborn about this. It is certainly no help to him. Give Blanche my kind regards and tell her to stop worrying."

'What does he know about worry, a man who never had to struggle to make ends meet? And all the help he had from me, his sister by six years.'

'Give it me,' shouted Bob, 'and let me finish it.'

'Be quick,' I pleaded, 'or I'll have to go.'

Bob found the place and read, '"Tell her to stop worrying. It's a pity she doesn't come out. She's the sort who would do well, with plenty of push in her. Give this money into Watson's safe keeping and let me know how you get on with all the red tape. I'm afraid it has to be gone through before you can book your passage. Kate sends her love,
            Your Uncle Rob (Big Rob to Little Rob!)"'

'Well, that's that,' said my Aunt after a pause, 'He's done something for his family at last. And now we'd better get on.' Then, as Bob stood motionless with apparently no intention of getting on, 'What's the matter with you? You've got what you wanted, your fare, yet there you stand, looking as if you'd seen a ghost.' That was how he did look, old and frozen, with a face like a sheet. Only his fist moved, clenching and unclenching over the hundred dollar bill. 'Don't tear it,' I shouted, and then, to my horror, I saw a wetness on his cheek. Thoughts flew in and out of my head, wildly chaotic. These people, where were they all? His stricken mother, her scoundrel husband and the mysterious baby who had been born, had smiled at her, and died. And this American uncle who had the guts to get on and could part just like that with a fortune, yet was silly enough to call my cousin Little Rob. Where, anyway, was this four-year-old in a velvet suit and with corkscrew curls. He couldn't possibly be the man standing here trying not to cry, the man who now shouted, 'I'll find the bastard. If it takes me all my life I'll find him and when I do, I'll kill him. They can hang me, or electrocute me, or whatever it is they do over there. I shan't care. I remember standing beside her looking out over that frozen sea. We couldn't get warm anywhere. I'll find him, I tell you, and I'll kill him.'

Auntie poured a cup of tea. 'I understand America's a big place and, according to the very peculiar postcards Joe Davison chose to send your mother, he'd travelled the length and breadth of it as well as of Canada, another large place. You'll have no time to go looking for needles in haystacks. You want to forget all that and begin to live your own life which won't be a bed of roses, I can tell you. And as soon as you're earning money, take over that insurance policy I've scraped so hard to keep going for you.'

I saw him change. He put the money carefully into its envelope and began to talk about saving and coming back for Doris Mould.

That was a Monday and the following Monday brought a letter from my mother addressed to Auntie but enclosing a page for Bob and one for me. My Aunt's first reaction was one of astonishment that mother had replied almost by return of post to her own long letter stating that I was at death's door; her second of censorious amazement at how casually this piece of news had been received.

'I really can't understand her,' she said to Minnie that night as she sorted through currants and sultanas while I was occupied at the desk making up for lost time on

86

L.C.Ms and H.C.Fs. 'You would think that, with Mother dying so soon after they left,' (was eight months soon? I wondered) 'she would be most alarmed about Martha.'

'But why?' Minnie asked, and I caught sight of her rubbing furiously the end of her nose, which she did, I had noticed, when she was trying to stifle a laugh. She still laughed at times although I understood that her husband's illness was reaching its final stage. Auntie told people that, since Minnie thought the world of her husband, it was inexplicable that she could still find things to laugh at.

'Why, Auntie? Goodness me, your mother was seventy-five and Martha's nine. I see no connection at all.'

'Well, you ought to. Children do die, you know that as well as I do. Look at Willie and all I did to try to save him. Gertrude either couldn't or wouldn't face facts and hospitals so it fell to me to take him and watch all that electricity shot into his poor little body. So much of it that he upset us all by moving after he was laid out. I noticed his arm, but tried to think I was mistaken. It was Monnie who distinctly saw him smile, a real smile, and that after he was in his coffin the morning of the funeral. Monnie fainted, but then she used to faint if she saw a cut finger. When we pulled her round she said. "They mustn't bury him. Don't let them Blanche, because he's not dead. He moved his mouth. I *saw* him smile." We got the doctor, of course. He did some tests but said it was all that electricity still in his body. They were wrong to give it him, experimenting on the poor little soul.'

'A dreadfully upsetting thing to happen,' said Minnie, 'though I've heard of that smile occurring after some types of illness. But that's hardly the point. Martha's not ill. Are you?' she called to me, and I said 'No,' despite feeling queer at that moment. Auntie said thank goodness it was summer – not the usual time for sore throats. There was this cake to be baked and iced ready to go with Bob. Why, in so marvellous a place as America, there was no such thing as ground almonds, was beyond comprehension. Almond paste had always been a favourite with Monnie and, what was more to the point, she, herself, had never baked the Christmas cake.

Bob's letter told him there was a job awaiting him with

people called the Youngs who owned the next estate. Since Rob had sent his fare, he was to hurry along with his medical examinations, smallpox injection, get his passport and visa and try to book his passage on the *Caronia* leaving Liverpool on August the 10th. This gave him a month, which should be enough. Rob would arrange to meet him in New York.

The letter to me was from my Father who, like Bob, only put pen to paper when forced to do so. My Aunt's letter must have applied a small amount of pressure. He said he hoped my sore throat was better. All children got sore throats from time to time. He supposed the examination was drawing near and, if I should pass it, he would send me money to buy a bicycle. This stupendous news had started on its way round the class even before playtime that morning and must eventually have reached the ears of Miss Gibson, probably by way of Miss Sykes to whom I had no doubt imparted it in order to impress her with my father's wealth. That afternoon Miss Gibson gave the entire class, though only fifteen of us were taking the exam, a lecture on the dangers and even the sinfulness of bribes and working for material rewards. The pleasure of work should be the only spur to attainment and, if we should pass an examination, then that was reward enough. So she wanted to hear no more about what had been promised by parents and relatives.

It had little effect on Edith Turnbull who intimated that she also had been promised a bicycle. 'And that's all *I'm* working for,' she finished, but added, 'It's all very well for you. You have another chance if you don't get through this time.'

Miss Gibson's lecture had had no effect upon me. I was too bothered by a few other things. I supposed I had recovered from whatever was wrong with me. I had managed to gargle regularly with the dissolved purple granules and felt proud of this new physical accomplishment, improvising snatches of tunes and making a mess in and around the kitchen sink. The stuff had an unpleasant way of invading everything in the vicinity and the colour did not remain purple. It turned to a dirty brown. I had stood on a stool and stuck out my tongue towards the shaving mirror expecting to see an interesting mat of purple. Instead I saw a thick brown scum which I tried to scrape off with my nails. My teeth were dark brown. I scrubbed them with a piece of emery paper scattered over with salt. Auntie said it would make them decay and when I asked which would, the granules or the salt, she said she didn't know.

Despite the gargling, I didn't feel myself. If I had the Watson blood in me, why didn't I feel as strong as an ox. (This was one of the similes we had to learn though I doubt whether we knew anything about an ox.) I knew quite a lot about blood, having been reared on the Blood of the Lamb and its implications. My Aunt talked freely about poor blood and weak blood and Uncle Rob's wife's sister who had both to a degree of pernicious anaemia and had to live on raw liver. Also, I was used to seeing blood rush from my nose which had caused my mother to faint immediately. What puzzled me was that the same blood could be in different people and could connect them, as Great-Uncle Watson had said, and, being there, could make you either weak or strong according to its type. I came up with no answer, only with a certainty that, if this Watson blood made you strong, then I wanted my fair share of it. I wished I *could* run down a mountain and possess the power of Baysdale Beck in flood. I wanted to be like that Beck, dominating the valley, sweeping away bridges, uprooting alders – but leaving sheep unharmed. Perhaps, I reasoned, I had been allowed a mere trickle of Watson blood, like peat water welling up from wet moss and oozing in slow separate drops down the face of a tiny rock. That was more the way I felt, not strong like the Beck.

The other thing was the pool in the dream. I couldn't completely sever myself from it. That morning Miss Gibson had given us a choice of essay to accustom us to deciding quickly so as not to waste precious time. A choice was the last thing she could agree with. The people who set the papers knew nothing about children. It was typical of children to shilly-shally when faced with a choice. The three subjects given were, Transport, A Walk through a Wood, or Down a Coal Mine. I chose the second one but found myself wandering off to the lily pool. I'd been

89

given several warnings of late not to wander from the point. 'You seem unable to control your scattered wits,' she'd said. 'They run away with you, goodness knows in what profitless directions. You'd better get them reined in. The examination draws nearer not further away.'

The pool seemed ever-present and gave me a strange sense of leading a double life. Like the places I'd been suddenly pitched into when I was younger but now I was half there and still half here, which was a nuisance especially when writing an essay about a wood. I knew when I'd finished that I would get only six or seven out of ten on account of my voyage across the pool on a water-lily pad.

There was also the uncertainty about what might happen to me now that a way out had opened up for Auntie. Most of her friends appeared to side with her Uncle. They said I was too great a responsibility and one that should never have been laid upon her. Mrs Burt held strong views on this. 'Auntie has her own life to live,' she explained to me in my Aunt's presence. 'Laura's Daddy and I would never have dreamed of leaving her with anyone else, not even with her Auntie.'

'They didn't leave me. I refused to go.'

'Then that was very naughty of you. If Laura had acted that way, she would have been soundly smacked. Daddy wouldn't allow such disobedience.' Here my Aunt intervened.

'There was the question of her schooling which her father thought would suffer,' to which Mrs Burt replied that there were more important things than education. Mary Kitching said education was a desirable thing in itself, but Blanche should never have been landed with a child. It was almost as bad as being landed with a man.

I was sharpening a pencil at the scullery sink when I heard my Aunt tell Tom Henderson that she had another home to go to at any time, and, while he went on hammering in nails, two light hammer taps at a time with pauses between to take a couple of nails out of his mouth, all rhythmical and precise, she continued, 'I always said there'd be a way out for me. I've prayed for it and it's come to pass.' And when Tom managed to say indistinctly, 'Is the little lass going over to Harry, then?' she

90

pounced on him. 'It's really no business of yours, is it?' And he'd replied, 'Then why tell me?'

Ominous as this sounded, I still felt she had little intention of shipping me off across the waters, rather that she was rubbing salt into Tom's sores. Where would he find a place to do his work, I wondered, if he could no longer have our greenhouse? Then I remembered her saying, after reading that letter from Uncle Rob which had tried to persuade her to cross the water herself, 'This is my home as long as Watson agrees, and I'll find a way of keeping it together. I'll stick to my guns. It won't be easy, but life isn't easy. Doctor Howell always said my later years would be my best.'

Bob's departure was the main event of that summer holiday. (School was closed for exactly four weeks during August.) When I was five I had gone to Nunthorpe for the entire period; at six it was Huck-a-Back for a long time; at seven we had had that one disastrous day at Redcar; then soon after my eighth birthday, at Whitsuntide, we had had half a day at Fairy Dell. Now I was nine and we went nowhere. So, although it did not strike me at the time, my growing older proceeded in inverse proportion to the amount of holiday away from home. Auntie had all her work cut out, as she put it, making sure that her nephew would arrive in the New World with a decent set of clothes neatly packed. No customs official was going to take *him* for an impoverished European or a slap-happy Irishman. He would be as respectably turned out for stepping ashore at New York as she herself would be on her final journey to another world.

Then there was the Christmas Cake to ice and decorate. Auntie never coated her fragrant, beautifully textured almond paste with white icing which was nothing but a nuisance to cut through. Having made the paste even and silky smooth, she then used a special fork with excessively worn down prongs and rucked up the surface to look like miniature sand dunes except for the circular top edge which she shaped with indentations using an implement which had been Grannie's for shaping the edges of pork pies. It gave a wonderful effect. She had bought from Merediths some preserved violets and angelica and arranged these in a little bunch like one of Mother's paintings and finished the decoration with a bow of mauve satin ribbon. She spent a lot of time and ingenuity packing it in the oval tin hat box to make sure it would emerge in pristine condition. She told Bob repeatedly that it must go in his cabin and under no circumstances in the hold and gave him straps to secure the box to something of an immovable nature so that it would not be skimming about the floor when the boat pitched and rolled. I overheard my cousin say to Bill Smart that the thing was going to be a blasted nuisance – the game was not worth the candle. Besides, what would people think of him carrying a hat box? Bill tried a word of comfort and support. He said the shape and height suggested bowler hats, not women's, but Bob was not so easily cheered. He said what difference did that make? He had not reached the age for wearing bowlers which were on their way out, anyhow.

In the box room he'd found an old case in which to pack a few things needed on the voyage – not much for anyone going steerage, he'd remarked – and then the trunk. This had actually been used by his Mother which kept him from levelling at it too much criticism. It was a strange affair, being neither of tin nor leather, but of a black woven material, quite flexible and held in position only by binding strips of mottled brown leather. The top edge of each side and the lid itself rose in sharp curves.

'What's it made of?' I had asked Bob when they bumped it downstairs and out into the greenhouse where my Aunt proposed to make it presentable.

'Cardboard and old sacking, I shouldn't wonder,' which I'd thought was a joke though it probably wasn't. When the lid was opened, we saw an intriguing lining of blue and white pin-striped material like a man's shirt.

'It's seen better days,' my Aunt had declared while they were trying in vain to make the two sections of the lock meet.

'Worse, I'd say,' Bob had muttered. But for better or worse, the days had undoubtedly warped it, which accounted for the intricate system of strapping with which he was struggling to bind the trunk just after eight o'clock on the 10th. His bed had been stripped and the sheets were already boiling in the copper. His last memory of this house, I thought, will be the smell of wash day, especially the smell of that copper on the boil. And Tom will be moving into his bed tonight – a disturbing thought with its undertones of possible rows, for however was Tom going to afford his bedroom rent? And Auntie would need both rents, for his bedroom and the greenhouse, now that Bob was departing. Uncle Watson had at last told her that the house was to be her home as long as she could maintain it. I heard her tell Minnie this, as well as the reason. 'He said I'd already done more towards its upkeep than anyone else since the very day Father bought it. It's always been my only home, you see.'

In one way I was relieved that Bob did not want me to go to the station. I would have liked the novelty of a ride in the motor cab for which Uncle Watson was paying. But I would rather not be there if Bob should let his voice break as it had done the previous tea time with Doris Mould to tea. It occurred, I thought, because of his persistence on the theme of the little house he planned to set up and then return to marry her and take her back there. Doris had giggled into her serviette, so much so that she couldn't get on with her tea. Then, when my Aunt had remarked that two years was a long time, especially at his age, and no one could say what changes might take place, Bob had said, 'Look here, Doris . . .' and then choked on her name. I was embarrassed, but Doris had lifted her face out of her serviette and transfixed Auntie with her round blue eyes and the look was not one of annoyance, but relief. It suddenly occurred to me that the giggling was connected with this. It meant what my Aunt had just put into words. Poor girl, that she couldn't say it for herself. Sylvia would not have resorted to giggles. But now, as I took in my cousin's features for the last time as I supposed, having heard so often that they never came back, his blue eyes, his ruddy skin which was a riper red than usual, it flashed upon me that, apart from Minnie, any laughter our house had known in my time, had come from him. I did so hope he would meet a girl in America who would laugh with him, but not giggle.

I was worried about the goodbyes. It was hard enough

for me to keep my own face the way it should be, but that was one thing I had learnt from my father. Bob had never known a father to teach him that lesson.

Chapter Ten

During the rest of the holiday after Bob's departure, I was almost driven to playing marbles with the boys and might have done so had Auntie not intervened. She had caught me crouched in the gutter just messing about really with my cousin Donald who never played with the serious marblers. I was asked how I thought she would ever get my dress and petticoat clean and whatever had come over me not playing with Laura, Peggy and the rest? I couldn't tell her that to join them meant skipping and if I skipped, my legs gave out in no time. Just then skipping was at the height of a periodic outbreak. The Lane was full of skipping ropes. In a week or so they would suddenly vanish and tops, whips, wooden hoops or hopscotch would take their place. I wasn't wanted in the house either, because Auntie was papering the back bedroom. I should like to have watched because I could recall none of our rooms being papered before.

'I can't do with you around, Martha. I haven't much time and you're under my feet. As if it isn't difficult enough trying to paper a room with four rolls of one pattern and one and a half of another.'

I saw her point. The paper had come from Mary Kitching who had had a decorator to paper the whole of their house and only a decorator could be so far wrong in estimating how much was needed. Mary had complained bitterly about the surplus rolls. 'Of course the walls will never need patching with the same paper,' which was his argument for having a surplus. 'When I have them re-papered, I shall want a different pattern. And where can I store them? The cupboards are all full, so they'll have to go on top of the wardrobe and need dusting every week.' Eventually, my Aunt relieved her of them.

I removed myself into the front room and played the organ. 'Rocked in the cradle of the deep', 'Eternal Father', 'Fierce raged the tempest o'er the deep'. Thus I followed

Bob's perilous crossing and could have passed a lot more time this way, but for my legs. I happened to mention this to Tom who wondered if the pedals needed a drop of oil. When I told him I would get Auntie's bicycle oil can, he looked thoughtful, then said, 'We'd best leave your Auntie out of this. You have to tread carefully when she's papering,' and his wink in the direction of the ceiling made me smile.

I returned to the front room, memorised some more lines from *A Midsummer Night's Dream*, then drew back the lace curtain and saw Frank Smith leaning against the opposite wall. I went out and over to him and for a short while we stood together, some girls skipping on one side of us and on the other, near the stableyard door, a group of boys bent absorbedly over the gutter. Behind me my hands pressed into the pitted wall. It must have been built long before our block of houses with perhaps a field where they now stood. Their bricks were still smooth and red. In fact they blazed in the light of the four o'clock sun shining obliquely from the bottom of the Lane. They made your eyes ache to stare too long.

Slap – slap – slap – ! The long rope, held by two girls one on each pavement, hit the road with even revolutions. The voices chanted,

> "All in together girls, never mind the
>   weather girls,
> Nineteen, twenty, leave the rope
>   empty"

and four girls left it bounding away from us while one girl, Fanny Barnston, left it coming our way, the tricky method of leaving a turning rope. Fanny could enter the rope from this side, too, a feat shared by only one other girl. It took me all my time to enter with the rope turning towards me, then take my first jump so as not to stop it and return once more to the task of rope turning. As I watched, standing beside Frank Smith, I decided that group skipping demanded the co-ordination of all your muscles whereas marbles needed nothing but your eyes and your forefinger. A boy was there now, poised in the gutter like a statue, his forefinger placed behind a chalk marble, his eye on a glass alley lying two inches from a hole. Four boys stood fixedly, watching. The boy glanced at his marble, again at the alley and his finger touched the marble. It hit the alley which rolled obediently in the right direction, rolled slowly the two inches into the hole. The boy rose, collected his spoils and swaggered off rattling his cloth bag unnecessarily. Well, I speculated, the game of marbles would train the boys to shoot straight and true in the next war already being predicted by several fathers. But how would Frank fare if he had to fight?

'Do you want to skip?' I asked him.

'Oh I don't know. I'm all right.'

Now and again he plucked up courage and skipped. None of us minded. It was hard luck on him that the wearing of caps had gone out of fashion that summer. As long as he could wear a cap, he had played marbles, though not well. But the time had come when to wear a cap had marked him off as being different even more than the square of mouse-like fur on his right temple did when exposed. And exposure was total when crouched there with the eyes of several boys fixed avidly upon him. What the boys made of the patch I have no idea, but I did know they liked nothing that singled you out from the rest. We girls, on the other hand, seemed not to mind, especially regarding Frank's patch. It attracted and intrigued us and at times we were hot on the scent of discovering how he had managed to acquire so unique a possession.

Our curiosity was hugely stimulated by the tale passed from mother to mother, and not excluding my Aunt, that, shortly before Frank was born, Mrs Smith had been terrified out of her wits by a rat leaping from the dustbin as she'd raised the lid. Rats were not common in our part of Middlesbrough which had a high standard of cleanliness, so it may well have been the rat itself which provided the lurid appeal to our elders. We girls had not yet learnt to fear a rat, but we were quick to smell one and we glanced knowingly at each other as one of us, with a tentative finger, would stroke Frank's fur. The connection between him and the rat was not a direct one. Where was he, for instance, when Mrs Smith had been frightened out of her wits? As I put it to Peggy Marwood, taking due care with the latest in grammatical construction, 'By whom or by what means had a square piece of fur been transferred from the rat's body to Frank's temple?' and I had waited excitedly for her reply. She had looked suitably startled and had then replied that she supposed it was a spell. When I had asked the same question of my Aunt, she was even less forthcoming. 'How should I know?' she'd barked. 'And it's not a subject we talk about. Let the poor boy alone, Martha. Isn't it enough that he has to carry that all through his life? If he'd been a girl, they could have covered it with one of those long bobs and a fringe. They look awful, but at least the disfigurement would have been hidden.'

'Come on, you two,' yelled Fanny, her mop of red hair leaving her shoulders and falling back as she skipped. 'Come and be On, then we can have seven girls in. It's more fun.'

'It's fun, only fun.' I heard her voice from a long time ago as Frank and I, the odd ones out, went to take the rope ends from Laura and Peggy. And as we struggled to turn the heavy length – almost as arduous as skipping – I had a side view of Fanny and saw her chest, under the thin cotton dress, jumping up and down as well as her hair. The sight upset me and I recalled the time I had been forbidden to play with her because of her hair. Would this addition to her figure be a second disqualification if my Aunt were to notice? Fanny would be eleven but she would not leave school for three years. *If* I got to the High School, then something else would stop me from playing with her, anyway. Because I had never seen a High School girl playing with girls from Victoria Road School. In fact, come to think of it, I had never seen a High School girl in our Lane at all. Where, I wondered, did they live?

I spent the last days of August in the back yard shed. Tom had brought in a tea chest with one side removed and an old stained stool. I was pleased with the way the tea chest wobbled when I used it as a desk for writing. I could identify with Jo March in her apple loft or with William Shakespeare who probably had nothing better to write on than a rickety table. That man's output astonished me beyond words. One hundred and fifty-four poems on top of all those plays! He must have stuck at his desk all day and far into the night. I read aloud some of the poems which were called by the strange name of Sonnets, and I was aware of two things; first, it was matterless that often I didn't know what he was on about, because simply to read them aloud was beautiful; and second, that, in some obscure way, they reminded me of the Bible on which I'd been reared. I was declaiming number eighteen, 'Shall I compare thee to a summer's day,' perhaps with Sylvia in mind, perhaps because it was less enigmatic than some, when there reached me the sound of Auntie's voice raised in protest.

'I tell you there's nothing wrong with her, Watson. She often recites things aloud, when her throat isn't sore, that is.' I recognised this as another reference to my non-appearance at the Anniversary. It was hard for her to forget that. 'She's all right if she's left alone. It's warm enough and she's out of my way.'

Then Uncle Watson's voice, 'I'm not with you there, Blan. I came through the back door with a sack of sticks and heard her reciting a lot of nonsense. She needs to get out more and be weaned from this school work. For once I think Gertrude's right. Our Margaret's taking this examination too, and she never sticks at books like that.'

'She's not taking it after next Christmas, is she?'

'No. And no more should Martha. Bairns shouldn't be allowed to have two goes at it. It's neither fair to them nor to the others. Gertrude never stops talking about it.'

'That I can well believe. She'd have thought differently if the boot had been on the other foot. If Martha doesn't take it this coming year, she'll be yet another year in Standard Six learning the same things again and that's not fair on her. Besides, if she gets to the High School a year early, she'll get through the teacher training earlier and be able to help me a bit.'

I thought my ears had deceived me. This was the first I'd heard about Auntie requiring any help from me. Often enough she'd been told in my hearing that I was now quite old enough to wash dishes, make beds, lay the table or the fire and clear out ashes. From time immemorial girls of my age had been undertaking much tougher jobs than these in the house. Laura Burt helped with the baking and enjoyed it. To such remarks my Aunt did not reply and I had long ago learnt the futility of offering help, like rolling pastry or cutting shells for tarts, because Auntie would have none of it. 'You'd make me more work than if I did it myself,' was her invariable reply.

Uncle Watson's head appeared through the shed doorway. 'Now then, lass, how are you? Come on up to the house and go with Margaret to pick peas at the allotment, '

I took him at this word, and, when we reached the allotment, I picked peas galore, podded them and ate them. Margaret was aghast.

'He can't have said you could eat all those. He only lets me have two pods to eat. He grows them for dinners and to sell.'

'He told me to pick them.'

'Yes, but not to eat them. You'll see.'

She was right. When he arrived in his old gardening clothes and a pail slung over his arm, he looked gravely at the litter of empty pods beside the row of staked plants.

'Well, I'll be jiggered! Now you'll be ill, I shouldn't wonder and your Auntie will blame me. Besides, we wanted today's pickings, a few for supper and the rest to give to Alf Jackson in return for two or three tomatoes. Alf has one of those new greenhouses.'

'What did I tell you?' and you might have thought it was Aunt Gertrude speaking.

Her father let the matter drop and said he would try a root of potatoes though he didn't expect much. They were sown late because of frosts and then there'd been a drought. He stuck a fork into the earth, dug it well down and carefully lifted it. At the sight of the small pale globes clinging to a mesh of fibrous roots, a sort of simple pleasure stirred in me. I touched the tiniest white potatoes, no larger than chalk marbles. Then he handed me the root and I took it just below its dark mass of fleshy leaves.

'Give it a good shake and see how many drop off.'

The larger ones hit the soil which sent up a strong smell. The tiny ones hung on.

'Not ready to leave their mother yet,' he said. 'You'll have to pull them off,' which took both Margaret and me some time. 'These have no skins,' I observed, 'and the others have skins like babies.'

I spread out my fingers and combed the gritty rootlets and felt the sun still warm on my face although it was almost five. I had the silliest desire, to strip off my clothes – dress, flannel petticoat, liberty bodice, knickers, vest and stockings, and lie in the freshly turned soil and feel the rays of the sun go right through me.

Another root was lifted, shaken and stripped; and now, he said, there would be enough for a good boiling and we children could have all the baby ones which were very sweet.

'Would you like to pick some marigolds for your Auntie? She likes them and they look well in that black vase of hers.'

'Mother hates them,' said Margaret, 'She calls then weeds.'

I asked why and her father replied, 'Because they grow by themselves, I suppose, with no help from me. Not like sweet peas, always needing attention. You'd best pick some of those for your mother, Margie, or there'll be trouble. Here, use these scissors, or you'll have the whole plant down. Even in the picking, you have to be careful with sweet peas.'

I can see Auntie Gertrude now, a beautiful, inactive woman, the antithesis of my Aunt who was never still; and looking discontented just as she looked when we went through the kitchen door that day. She was sitting doing nothing, her arms spread in front of her across the table and, despite her expression, you could not help but admire her brown eyes, shining auburn hair, thick and heavy, and her Autumn tinted skin. It was plain to everyone that Uncle Watson adored her. 'Look,' he said, showing her the potatoes in the pail, tilting it on the table edge.

'Take the dirty thing off the table,' and her voice was startling when you considered her words. It was liquid and lovely.

'Nay, Mother, it's clean enough. What about a bit of supper? These'll need no scraping, just a wash. There's a bit of cold meat, isn't there? Shall Margie lay the table in the dining room?'

101

'You'll not eat in the dining room in those clothes.'

'All right, Mother, all right. If you'll move, the girls will put the cloth on the table here.'

At that time theirs was the only house I knew with a dining room. And a drawing room too. They had three downstairs rooms and so had we. Only the names were different. I seem to remember my Aunt saying that what first woke Watson from his daze to discover the sort of woman he'd married was when Gertrude began to warble on about furnishing the drawing-room. It must have been idle talk for there was nothing in the drawing-room but a cumbersome three piece suite and a plant stand in the bay window bearing an unhealthy aspidistra. In this emptiness Margaret and I sometimes played though only during school holidays. She went to Marton Road school.

Once and only once I saw inside their bedroom, one Sunday afternoon of that holiday. According to Margaret, her father and mother had gone to bed. We were playing with her dolls, a game of fathers and mothers, not a favourite with me.

'Let's pretend,' Margaret had said.

'Pretend what?'

'That we're a father and mother. Which do you want to be?'

'Neither. Why can't we pretend to be the Fairy King and Queen? And the dolls can be fairies. We could act a play.'

'How daft. Fairies aren't real.'

'Neither are we. Not real parents, I mean.'

'No, but we will be one day. We won't be fairies, stupid.'

I submitted, as I usually did when playing in her house, and we washed and nightgowned her dolls and put them to sleep on the sofa. Then, by some odd strategy, we were rolling about on the floor on top of one another with our clothes in considerable disarray. I scrambled up and pulled mine to rights. 'That's not the way fathers and mothers go on,' I felt compelled to say.

'Oh, isn't it? That's all you know about it. Your father and mother aren't here. Well, I'll show you. Come on, we'll go into their bedroom.'

'Whose?'

'Father's and Mother's. Only don't make a sound.'

'No, I won't go. I don't like bedrooms. '

'Come on, or I'll tell.'

'Tell what?'

'What we were doing.'

'But what were we doing?'

'Pretending. You were doing it too, and if you don't come, I'll tell.'

My thoughts stirred. If what we were doing was nameless, then how could she tell it to anyone? I followed her, however, though not exactly blackmailed into doing so, and, as we crept up the carpeted stairs, I noted how much more handsome they were than ours which were covered in linoleum.

Margaret turned the brass knob with scarcely a sound, as though she were well practised, and eased open the door. As I tip-toed after her, a sense of doom fell upon me. A gutteral snore, mounting to a pitch higher than you can sing, came from the bed. It broke in a snort, then there was silence. I remembered Grandfather and that last noise before he died. I made myself look at the bed, and there, nearest to us, lay Aunt Gertrude in a camisole and white underskirt, her bare arms thrown upon the pillow at either side of her head. Her hair was loose and seemed to flow over everything. She lay quite still; only her brown eyes swivelled and stared stonily at us.

'What do you want?'

'Nothing,' Margaret whispered.

There being nothing I wanted either, we just stared. Beside her lay Uncle Watson, also on his back wearing his shirt and some kind of wide knickers, unlike Bob's short pants and certainly unlike Tom's combinations which I had lately seen on the clothes line. Uncle Watson's shirt was loose all the way down. He was beginning another snore, his mouth open, the top set of his false teeth sitting on his lower lip as if he'd spit them out. When I could tear my eyes away from them, I noticed his hands resting on his chest, the finger tips loosely interlocked.

I had seen dead people and, but for the snore, he might as well have been dead. I don't remember asking Margaret, afterwards, if that was what she'd taken me to see.

Chapter Eleven

School resumed with Miss Gibson telling us that we must all work specially hard because this was Miss Sykes' last term with us and fifteen scholarship entrants must work harder still because next term the examination would be upon us. With all this pressure it seemed wise to consider the subject of my evening prayers. Ought I to be saying them, as I had taken to doing, lying on my back in bed, or kneeling in the cold as I had been taught to do and as my Aunt still did. Or would it do to sit up in bed with the bed clothes pulled about you, a position approximating to the one we adopted in Chapel? The whole business of posture when praying had just been highlighted by poor Mrs Grayson's trouble.

She had been converted at a Prayer Meeting to which my Aunt had taken her. There was some secret horror in her life that brought on so much weeping in our kitchen that Auntie had been forced to say, 'Come to the Prayer Meeting, Mrs Grayson. Come along with me. I really don't know of anything else that will help you.'

I knew this to be a last resort because I had never detected in my Aunt that stringent religious observance practised by Grandfather.

'What's the matter with Mrs Grayson?' I had asked after she'd gone, and not for the first time of asking either. I hoped persistence would prevail.

'Her husband. I've told you before.'

'Is he seriously ill?'

'No, he's not. He's a beast.' As usual she was being tight-lipped on the subject.

'What will Mrs Grayson pray for at the Prayer Meeting?'

'How should I know? To be able to put up with him, I suppose.'

'Not to cry so much, you mean?'

This was something I knew God *could* do, if he chose; I

knew from experience, just as I knew there were things he refrained from doing if asked. What he could or could not do was often on my mind.

'Why doesn't her husband go to the Prayer Meeting and asked to be changed from being a beast?' There were precedents for this, I remembered. Beauty and Beast. I reckoned that at least a tenuous connection existed between fairy tales and real life. The beast could be, indeed was, transformed . . . But my Aunt's reply put an end to such speculations.

'Wild horses wouldn't drag George Grayson to Chapel, let alone a Prayer Meeting.'

A few days later I heard my Aunt tell Mary Kitching that, during the Meeting, Mrs Grayson had been moved to give herself to the Lord. 'But I don't think she really knew what she was doing, poor thing. She was weeping again after we left. I had to give her a good linen handkerchief which she'll not remember to return, the state she was in. And do you know what she said? Mind you, I don't think she was fully aware of her words, and it does go to show how she suffers. She said, "I'm only too glad to give myself to the Lord if he can only save me from having to give myself to that brute".'

Mary was silent, so my Aunt went on, 'Clearly, the poor soul does not understand about prayer.'

Still, Auntie was determined to see the matter through and took Mrs Grayson with us to Chapel the following Sunday night. When the preacher said, 'Let us pray,' Mrs Grayson dropped to her knees on the bare floor while the seat tipped back with a bang. People were startled. I suppose they thought someone had fainted. All around I saw their heads lift from the bent-over praying position, and those who could see stared at her kneeling figure. The preacher took no notice. He wasn't our Chapel minister but one of those who can't bring the prayer to an end. When he did, we had difficulty getting Mrs Grayson back on the seat. I had to hold it down while Auntie levered her up. She was rubbing her knees and whispering, 'I'm afraid they've gone to sleep,' and Auntie whispered back, 'We don't kneel in Chapel, you know.'

So the subject of prayer posture was in my mind on the

way home. I had seen people drop off to sleep while bowed from a comfortable sitting position, especially when the prayers were so long and so repetitive. If your knees went to sleep with kneeling, then it wasn't so likely that *you* would drop off. And when, a day or two later, Auntie was telling Mrs Burt, I asked outright why Mrs Grayson had knelt down.

'I suppose, as a child, she'd been to the Church of England. It must have been that, not the Catholic Church, since once a Catholic, always a Catholic. She's nothing, now. But I know they kneel in the Church of England though naturally I've never been to a service there.'

'Then what about their poor knees?'

Mrs Burt spoke sharply. 'Should you say that, Martha? It's hardly good manners. Should she join in adult conversation, Auntie?'

'Oh, it doesn't do any harm. Half the time she doesn't hear what's going on. She's busy with her homework. She has a lot of homework, you know.'

I sensed her resentment at Mrs Burt's criticism and admired her quick parry. Laura didn't have homework. My Aunt was a clever fighter. If only she wouldn't fight with Tom. These clashes were not easy to bear. They had blown up afresh after Tom's moving in from the greenhouse and seemed to be one of the things to which I could not grow accustomed – not like the quarrels between my mother and father which had struck me as being like children's. Auntie tended to become distraught, even violent as in the row involving the plates. I had raced home as usual, using every strategy of prayer and magic as a preventative, and burst through the hall to the scullery doorway in time to see her throw a plate at Tom. He dodged it and it smashed in pieces on the greenhouse floor.

'And don't expect me to wash any more of your filthy night-shirts,' she declared. 'You can take them back to Sidaway's.'

'Blanche, Blanche, just mind what you're saying.' Tom's voice was less of a dither than usual – a bit firmer.

'I'm minding what I'm saying. I'm stating a fact. You know as well as I do what makes them like that and they'll not go into my copper with decent clothes. And if ever I find your sheets in that state . . .' Her voice had risen several tones, becoming like a shriek.

'Shut up, woman. Have a thought for that child in the doorway.'

She turned, stared at me as if I were a stranger with no right to be there, then picked up another plate and hurled it at him. 'Very well. If you don't want it in plain words, you can have it this way.'

'Auntie,' I shouted, 'what about the plates?'

'What about them? What do I care about them, or anything. If your Mother hadn't left you behind, I'd not have been here to put up with his insults,' and she turned, gripped the scullery table and I saw the tautness flow out of her body leaving it limp, defeated looking, which upset me far more than even the plate-throwing had done. But when she turned and told me to hang up my coat, I saw no sign of wetness on her face.

A few nights later, climbing the stairs towards the gloom of the landing – it was just light enough outside to allow the border of the window panes to glow darkly red, a colour which made me think of hell, I was stopped midway by a voice. 'Blanche, please Blanche.' It was Tom's, but the tone would certainly have been labelled as peculiar by my Aunt, or so I thought. Soft, beseeching, as if asking her for something she might be persuaded into giving.

Then her voice, 'Stop it, stop it. Here's Martha.'

It was almost like the plate episode in reverse, and her voice was not her usual one when addressing Tom.

I felt irritated to think that my presence had interrupted this inexplicable but apparently friendly exchange. Still, since the thing had been done, it might as well be done thoroughly, so I took the next three steps like a dart. My foothold on the landing was intercepted by my Aunt whose movement had been as swift as mine.

'What are you doing?' she asked, as if I had no right to go up to bed, and, while she asked that, I was able to see between her and the banister bend, to see, standing in Bob's bedroom doorway, Tom who had no clothes on at all.

Swiftly I was shepherded down the stairs where

preparations for my next ascent were performed with exceptional solicitude by Auntie. She made me Horlicks, she brushed out my hair, she asked if my throat felt all right. Then, accompanying me upstairs, she plumped up the pillow, tucked in the counterpane, told me not to forget my prayers and gave me a kiss on each cheek and my forehead. In this exaggerated concern I detected an effort to drive the incident right out of my mind, get me to sleep and begin a new day with the slate rubbed clean.

I tried to oblige, but my mind seethed with the strangeness of the things I had stumbled on; their soft, low voices, secretive manner and most disturbing of all, Tom's lack of clothing. The strange fact that he was undressing for bed at half past eight was hardly worth considering compared with the overriding fact that I had never before seen a man, or a boy, for that matter, naked. The image was too powerful to be banished by an act of will, either hers or mine. We had a horrible night. As I struggled to drift into sleep, this image grew, exploded into fragments and in its place was the dragon, ancient guardian of our three bedrooms, rearing itself, opening its huge toothed jaws and spewing out jets of flame and dirty smoke. Auntie didn't sleep, either. She turned from side to side, got out of bed, taking a long time about it in order to so do quietly, used the chamber pot in the dark, tip-toed round to my side, lifted and straightened the bed clothes pulled over my left ear. This willed immobility brought pain into my legs, pain that thrust upwards into my back. I broke into sweats that left me shivering. At last she snored, a night-time sound which I could tolerate, and only then did I move, turning on my back to see that the blind was bright with moonlight. My resolve to have done with the End weakened. It was the very witching hour of night. I shuffled out of bed, crossed to the window and lifted the blind. The full moon was pale as a primrose and unstreaked with blood. I crept back onto my side of the bed and slept.

But next day, in school, I came to the conclusion that something must be done, or I should never get to the High School. I had made mistakes in a couple of easy Unitary Method sums and had a total black-out as regards the trains speeding towards one another. They might as well have been flying apart, keeping company with the processes of disintegration in my brain. Why, I wondered, dealing automatically with sentences that had to be joined without using the conjunction 'and', why could I not question my Aunt about Tom's nakedness? I could and did ask her about a number of things, but the word 'naked' set up odd reactions in both my mind and body as well as recalling Miss Gibson's criticism of it in what I had considered my prize sentence – 'As far as the eye could see, the purple moor rose and fell, treeless and empty save for one naked house.' 'Good' Miss Gibson's red ink in the margin had read, 'but do not use the word "naked" use "bare" instead,' and had emphasized the point by putting three red strokes through the word in my composition. So much for *The New Gresham Dictionary!* I'd looked up 'bare' to find a better word. I can't ask her, I thought, dealing with a sentence about wheat being shipped over the Atlantic and stored in warehouses on the River Mersey. There's only one person I might ask, and that's Hannah.

It was Wednesday, Hannah's day for going to the library, so, after tea, I knocked at 112. 'Are you going to the library, Hannah?'

'She can't go,' called Mrs Kneeshaw's rasping voice, 'Mr Kneeshaw is in bed with a cold on his chest. He's away from work. Hannah Ellis must see to him.'

'I have done, Mother,' I heard Hannah say from the kitchen as I waited on the step. 'He's quite comfortable and I shall be back in half-an-hour.'

'Is he very poorly?' I asked as we left the house, Hannah clad sombrely as usual in her ankle-length costume which would not yield an inch to fashion.

'The cold's not on his chest at present, as Mother will have it. It's in his head. But the gas works are not healthy for people's chests. So we have to take care when he gets a cold.'

'How old is he?' At this time age was another heavy thing on my mind because of the sums dealing with this area of human experience. 'If Jane is twice as old as her brother, Tom, and two years younger than her sister, Anne who is fourteen, how old will Tom be in three years time?'

'Sixty-four,' said Hannah. 'He'll be retiring in November when he's sixty-five.'

'Grandfather would be eighty-one now, I think. It's three years since he died. That's a lot older than your father. Yet Grandfather was Mother's father.'

'Well, your mother was the last of a large family. Her parents were quite old when she was born.'

'Do children go on being born when people are old?'

'No, not after a certain age.'

'What age?'

'Well, it's different between men and women.'

'Why?'

'A woman has a lot more to do than a man in bringing up children. That's why she doesn't have them after a certain age.'

'What age?'

'Oh, about forty-five or so.'

We had reached the end of Aubrey Street and turned along Southfield Road. She was a rapid walker. I had to take lots of running steps to keep alongside her.

'Hannah, there's something I'm worried about.'

'Well?' Her pace did not slacken.

'Auntie and Tom Henderson have these rows. Did you know?'

'Most people quarrel occasionally. They get on each others' nerves. And, of course, Tom should stop drinking. It's very wrong. But the war was to blame. He didn't drink before then.'

'Did they have rows before the war?'

'I didn't know them well in those days, I was your mother's friend.'

'But do you think they had rows?'

'You shouldn't ask me really. It's all in the past. Everything goes into the past, and we have to forget.'

'Yes, I remember. I remember when Mother said that. But this is *now*. Auntie won't wash his night-shirts, so he has to sleep without anything on.'

We were now at the large double doors of the Library but Hannah stood stock-still clutching the two books to her chest. Her black, mint-bullet eyes were prominent; her lower lip sagged and the trickle of saliva escaped

110

unchecked. Her height made it difficult to keep my eyes fixed on hers, but I did so and held them steady without the flicker of an eyelid. At last she spoke – 'What *are* you saying, Martha?'

'That he has to sleep without a night-shirt.'

'How do you know this?'

'They had a row. Auntie said she wouldn't wash his night-shirts.'

'People say things unintentionally in the heat of the moment. I'm sure she didn't mean it.'

'She did, because I saw.'

'You saw what?'

'I saw him without any night-shirt. With nothing on at all.' Hannah turned. Using her shoulder, she thrust powerfully at the right-hand door and held it open for me to pass through. She went to the desk, presented her books, took her two tickets and went immediately towards a certain shelf. I glanced stealthily at her face. It was impassive. She did not ask if there were a book I might like.

I had made occasional visits with her to the Library and wandered as if in a trance between high walls of books. There was no separate area for children's reading; in fact no books specially for children. Moreover, the spell cast by this voiceless, book-built world, restrained me from even using my eyes to read titles on spines. I had been told not to remove a book, but if I were alone in an alley, I would run my finger tips caressingly down the rough or glossy backbones. Only when Hannah had chosen her two books and we had left the building, would I ask what she had got. She was allowed one of each, fiction and non-fiction, and the difference she had once explained to me.

On this occasion we were in and out in no time. We strode along in silence to the top of Egerton Street but, as we turned the corner, she said, 'You should have gone with your Mother, Martha. I really don't know why they let you have your own way. You see, your Grandmother didn't live long after they went and the whole thing has put Blanche into an impossible position.'

I considered this irrelevant, and said so. 'What has that to do with Tom?'

'Mr Henderson wouldn't have been there if your Aunt had still been able to work as a private nurse. It's so unfortunate that she had to give up her work. She's been very good to us. She went to a lot of trouble getting us a small pension for Dick who was killed after the armistice in some sort of accident before he was demobilised. They said we weren't entitled to a pension and I'm no use when it come to fighting with officials. But Blanche is very capable in such matters.'

'Yes,' I said, remembering the plates, 'she can fight.'

'But she really shouldn't have taken in lodgers, especially Mr Henderson. People did try to tell her.'

'She said she wouldn't take in washing. Lodgers are better than that. It's all because of money, you see.'

'Yes, I do see. But I honestly don't think *she* does. She's a very innocent person. There must have been an alternative to that.' Inwardly I grappled with her meaning. Then she helped me. 'Your Aunt does not realise that people can misinterpret things. She should have found another way out of her difficulties is what I meant. She'll have to get another lodger as quickly as possible.'

'But I thought you said, no lodgers.'

'I did. None at all. But, since she's taken one, she'll have to take another. And Martha, please don't ask me why.'

'Is that the alternative?'

'I think it's the only way.'

'Often she says it will all kill her. She'll be in her grave before the year's out. Then at other times, she says she's sure there'll be a way out.'

'I'm sure there will be.' Her voice had reached a brighter note as if we had turned a difficult corner. As far as I was concerned, we had not. I felt there were depths to that strange encounter on the landing which the arrival of three or four more lodgers would not sound. If anything, Hannah's suggestion had frozen the surface. I was more baffled than before.

When we reached the house, she handed me one of the books. 'Here's *Good Wives*, the sequel to *Little Women*.' (Hannah had given me the latter as a belated birthday present because she was tired of taking it back and forth to the Library.) 'Did I tell you it's about that part of America

112

where your mother lives now? The March family lived there at the time your grandmother was a girl. I don't know what I'd do without a book to read. You want to read *Good Wives*. It will take your mind off other things.'

For the following week too much was on everybody's mind. The cold in Mr Kneeshaw's head settled on his chest. His condition worsened. On Saturday he died. My Aunt said poor Hannah would never hear the end of it, and when I asked of what, she was sharp with me. 'Her trip to the Library on Wednesday night. You went with her, I understand. Mrs Kneeshaw told Hannah she shouldn't leave her father in that state. I must say she carries this library business a bit too far and it's caught up with her. She'll have it on her mind, poor woman, for the rest of her life.'

'But she wasn't away even for half an hour. He didn't die while she was out.'

'As far as Mrs Kneeshaw's concerned, he might as well have done just that. How I'm going to cope with laying him out and the funeral and lodgers coming at the weekend, I simply don't know.'

As if that weren't enough, two days later Mr Knaggs died. This was no surprise, Mr Knaggs of Granville Road being ninety-two and, for longer than I had lived, having never been outside his house. His daughter was almost as much a recluse. He had suffered a stroke at eighty, since when Miss Knaggs had waited on him hand and foot. He had been a friend of my grandfather's and I recalled having seen him twice. No sooner, then, had Auntie laid out Mr Kneeshaw but what this second call came on her services. With her nurse's training, she knew how to do that job properly and, as I would gradually discover, was often needed in that capacity. She would have taken Mr Knaggs in her stride had it not been for the lodgers. But, within one week, to see to a couple of dead and prepare for two extra living people was the reason, I am sure, for her anger when I unexpectedly put up a fight and tried to pit my will against hers.

'Wash your hands and face,' she said about seven on Tuesday night, 'and tidy your hair. We're going along to the Kneeshaws' to pay our last respects.'

I knew what she meant. I remembered Grandfather, Grandmother, and little Mary Johnson.

'I'm not going.' I kept my eyes on a page of *Good Wives*. 'I don't want to.'

'That's nothing to do with it. You'll do as you're told.'

It was our first real confrontation of wills. I had never flagrantly disobeyed her; she had never actually forced me against my will.

'I don't want to see any more dead faces or coffins. Besides, I never saw Mr Kneeshaw when he was alive. Why should I see him now?'

'You'll see him because of Hannah. What would she think, if you refused?' Which immediately sent my thoughts in that direction. What would Hannah think? She was different from the rest of Auntie's circle in that she had read a lot of books and from them had extracted what others termed a lot of queer ideas. These included what she called the rights of women and, stranger still, the rights of children. She would have abolished the use of the cane and have had the government pay mothers to help them bring up their children – a childhood pension as well as an old-age pension. She thought that women should have long educations and the chance of good jobs, even of being doctors. All the things which women, never mind men, in Middlesborough treated with ridicule if they bothered to think about them at all. I didn't know what she thought about the rights of the dead; did those include the right that children should be taken to view them?

While thinking this, I was also thinking – for it's a remarkable thing that you can think dozens of thoughts in the time it takes to speak one sentence – that Hannah could read and talk and have ideas, yet not be able to do much about them. She had not even been able to get the pension for her brother and had let her father die before he could get his. It took my Aunt to get things done, or people like her. I saw in a flash that learning was not enough. You had to fight. Fight against men, against your family, against principalities and powers (from somewhere in the Bible), you had to fight even with yourself. Fight, fight . . . I felt elated, carried away by the thought. And Hannah did not have that in her. Really, she was rather frail and helpless,

114

the opposite from what you would imagine when looking at her. All this shot through my mind like a revelation during the moments it took my Aunt and I to glare at one another.

Poor Hannah, I thought, and, tossing *Good Wives* onto a chair, I departed for the scullery, swilled my face under the tap, soaped my hands and dried them, took an old broken comb from the table drawer and drew it savagely through my hair, so savagely that I could feel a wetness which, being dabbed at with my finger, revealed that I had drawn blood. So I prepared myself to obey my Aunt, at the same time muttering, 'What does another corpse or two matter?' In this mood I went to kiss the marble forehead of a man I had never before seen and pay the same respects, two days later, to Mr Knaggs.

Chapter Twelve

On the morning of Mr Knagg's funeral – Friday – I stumbled coming downstairs and fell the rest of the way. I was asked why must I always run downstairs. Since I could not recall when I had managed to take the staircase on the run, and it seemed years since I had slid down the banister, I thought I would explain that my right leg had seemed to crumple under me. 'It's the growing pains,' I said.

Auntie looked at me and the expected tirade about all she had to do did not materialise. Instead, she told me to take off my stockings. She would give my legs a good rub with Sloane's Linament. In school Edith Turnbull, beside me, and Marjorie Burns, behind, managed to whisper that I stank, and this was immediately followed by Miss Gibson asking who had had Sloane's Linament applied. Shame reduced my temperature to nought degrees as I raised my hand. Miss Gibson said she wondered at my Aunt not leaving the application until tomorrow, Saturday. She opened another window and said that was enough. Let there be no more whispering on the subject. It wasn't the only unpleasant odour in the classroom. There was the worse odour of unwashed bodies. And that settled it.

At playtime I stood under the shed and wondered about the two lodgers. I did not think of them as being *new* lodgers because I could not class Tom as being an existing one. It was difficult to know into what category he fitted and this uncertainty seemed related to what I had seen on the stairs and also to what Hannah had withheld from me. That she had done so was obvious and I felt this was a weakness in her. From the enlarged world in which her reading habits had placed her, she should be prepared to pass on her knowledge if asked to do so. Then why had she shied away from my questions about Tom and my Aunt and a few other things as well? All I had learnt was that Tom should not be living with us but since he was, then we must have at least one more lodger. It made no sense, but I dimly perceived that it might have done had she told me all. Would more lodgers provide more information? They might, at least, lessen the number of rows.

They both arrived on Saturday having had no previous acquaintance with each other and they continued to remain unacquainted. Mr Dyson was given the bedroom which had been my parents', with the walnut suite. Cyril Binks, who looked younger than Bob, was placed in the box-room where, with a narrow bed bought for half-a-crown from Mrs Sidaway, he seemed happy enough to be hemmed in by a basketwork suitcase, two clothes horses, a cane chair and three rolled up rugs standing on end. I heard Auntie apologise, and him say that she needn't bother; he liked rooms of that sort; they gave you scope. There was no telling what you might make of them. My Aunt frowned.

Mr Dyson was thin, trim and grey looking. His oval, rimless glasses gripped his nose over the wide bones near the nostril so that he could look through them or over them. His clothes gave Auntie plenty to talk about for at least a week and Hannah a chance to say he was impeccably dressed. Pin-striped suits, grey or navy, were worn on alternate days, and a light overcoat draped his arm as he plied between the house and Linthorpe Road where he was temporary manager of a high class tailor's shop. He came from Huddersfield and all we ever learnt of his life there was his knowledge of materials for tailoring suits, both gents' and ladies'. He had hardly been shown his bedroom before he was shown Auntie's herring-bone tweed and asked for his opinion. Unlike Hannah, she was a little sensitive regarding fashion which had changed more radically since the war than in all her previous existence. Mr Dyson said the garment would need considerable reduction, not only the skirt but the coat also, which, by present standards, was long enough to be worn without the skirt at all. I heard her tell Mary Kitching afterwards that, had she not felt the need for politeness, she would have let her tongue run away with her at such a remark. Mary said lodger or no lodger, she herself would have given rein to

117

her tongue. This, I knew, was because Mary had an identical costume made at the same time and by the same tailor as my Aunt's.

On tweeds and allied subjects Mr Dyson had something to say if consulted. Otherwise he would not converse except on such topics as took us quite out of our depth. The first instance of this arose one evening when I was glued to the desk grappling with my Apollyon in the form of a sum which said, 'If four men working nine hours a day can dig a ditch in twelve days, how long will it take six men working eight hours a day to dig two similar ditches?' Sheer perversity impeded my progress with this type of problem which seemed so criss-crossed with ditches. Why were they digging them and how could every man be certain to dig out the same quantity of earth in a given time? Suddenly, as I struggled to set the thing down according to rule, I heard myself say, 'It's stupid, utterly stupid!' My Aunt would have taken no notice. Mr Dyson did. A dry, precise voice over my right shoulder said, 'You seem to be having trouble. Can I be of assistance?' and I felt he was speaking to a customer in his shop. I was as polite as possible in explaining my doubts. 'I mean, don't they leave off for a few minutes now and then? Or is there a man watching them all the time, like a slave driver in Ancient Egypt?' I knew about those from the story of Moses and wanted to impress Mr Dyson. I failed, because after a few moments of considering he said, 'Ah yes. The trouble is you are too young and the young can deal only in the concrete. What you have here is theoretical despite the ditches. Are you going on to higher education?' I did not understand, and told him so, politely.

'Are you intending to leave school at fourteen?'

'Oh no.' I was on firm ground there. 'I'm going to the High School. At least, I hope I am. You can stay there until you're eighteen.

'That is higher education. And that is where you learn to deal with the theoretical and the abstract. There you would be taught to use X for a sum like that; X standing for the unknown quantity.'

'How do you mean?' Only one thing seemed clear, that this was not for the understanding of babes and sucklings.

'Well, X is a symbol. It can equal nothing; it can equal infinity; or anything in between. To find X, you always work from the known to the unknown and the more you learn, the more you deal with unknowns,' and his laugh tinkled at the same high pitch as his voice, more like a woman's than a man's and which I found distracting. I dragged my mind back to X as he continued. 'It's disturbing to realise that what you know doesn't really matter. It's what you don't know that is significant. That sum, of course, doesn't need X. It can be worked in your head. The answer is eighteen days though, as you say, one lazy man might take a rest.' He laughed again, but I had a flash of insight. 'Is it like, now we know in part, but then we shall know – the unknown?'

'The unknowable. That's what we look for, and can't find. If we found it, we should have to invent another unknown.'

I stared at him and wished such a clever man could converse with Miss Gibson. Then another thought struck me. 'But the High School girls are not a bit like that. I mean, they are not so serious.'

'Young lady, never judge by appearances. We all wear masks, you see,' and, peculiar as this might sound, I felt it appropriate in his case, because his expressionless face with its thin hair and thin lips and the rimless glasses perched near the end of his nose did give the appearance of a mask.

With an effort I returned to the sum; the sort of thing that might well determine whether I left school at fourteen or at eighteen.

'I can't just put the answer. We have to show the working.'

From his breast pocket he took a pencil encased in what looked like gold but which I knew by now could be deceptive; and began to demonstrate the working. 'Yes,' I interrupted, 'I can do it from there. I know how to cancel down.'

I asked Auntie the age of Cyril Binks which she knew. He was eighteen. She did not know Mr Dyson's and told me it was bad manners to enquire or talk about people's ages. Cyril worked in a shop. I think it was the Co-operative Stores, but he had not said where he came from.

He was, in every way, the antithesis of Mr Dyson, being short, plump, red-faced, with a large mouthful of teeth and a thick lower lip. He, too, wore glasses, but they were round with dark tortoiseshell frames which gave him an owlish appearance. He was not quite our type, according to my Aunt, who was soon exasperated by his habits of plastering his brown hair with oil and playing a lot of foreign sounding songs on the organ. It was costing her a fortune in soap and boiling water to remove the brown stains from his white pillow-cases and he would *not* close the front room door when he used the organ. He didn't notice doors. He tossed aside my Beecham's Pill music books as being out of the Ark and produced his own sheets of music. Then, through the open doorways would surge his voice howling most peculiar songs – 'Who-o-o-o stole my heart away', 'Bye, bye, blackbird' and 'Mademoiselle from Armitiers, parlez vous.' Trouble stirred one night when Auntie, folding sheets in the scullery, heard Tom from the greenhouse join in the refrain of that particular song. 'Inky-pinky parlez vous' quavered his spidery voice in concert with Cyril's wail. I was in the greenhouse, having come from across the yard before going to bed.

'That'll do,' Auntie ordered. 'Have you gone mad? Isn't it enough to have to endure his caterwauling?'

'Inky-pinky parlez vous,' sang Tom on a higher and deliberately squeakier note. My eyes encountered his. A gleam of mischief, unmistakable, glanced back at me. I couldn't believe it! He was teasing her!

'I've said that'll do, and I mean it. Men! Like babies. I don't think that young man will be here long.'

But he was. He stayed longer than any of them, almost as though he had taken Bob's place. He stayed, I think, because of the food. Once he said to me, 'It'll do me good here, getting used to the nagging. I'll stand it better when I'm married. Being inoculated, you might say. Besides, Miss D. feeds us well.'

I asked him when he was going to be married which he seemed to think was a silly question because he said, 'How should I know? I suppose it'll have to come some time, but there's no rush. I've seen too much.'

My Aunt put up with him because, as she once said,

'He's harmless and he has nowhere to go,' which was all she knew about that.

Two things happened towards the end of October – the General Election which put Ellen Wilkinson into Parliament without the help of my cousin, and my acquisition of four mice, two white, two black. These events were connected, though deviously. Only one aspect of the election affected my Aunt, that being the widespread prediction that the reigning Liberal candidate, Penry Williams, would topple to the bottom of the poll. She was deeply angry.

This man with the, to me, ridiculous name of Penry instead of Henry had come to assume heroic proportions in Auntie's eyes, how or why I was never to know, although I knew a great deal about her hero in the medical world. What I did perceive was that personalities and not the House of Commons mattered with her. It took her a full week to recover when Penry fulfilled the prediction and lay, as I heard people tell her, with everything in ruins about him. It was a pity, but I could not feel sad myself.

During the preceeding week, Tom had taken me into Lily Allinson's zoo. At least that was how their back yard appeared to me, one entire wall being lined with a vast disarray of hutches, kennels and cages. I had been only once in contact with a pet, Bob's jackdaw whose sojourn in our shed was brief, so that naturally I was overcome when led into the proximity of dogs, rabbits, guinea pigs, ferrets, rats, mice and various birds. Lily said she didn't keep cats as though that were the only species of living creature not represented.

'You can master everything but cats,' she explained. 'Cats have wills of their own. You can never really make them do as you want. Besides, there are the mice,' which was true. There they were, twitching inquisitive pink noses behind the wire netting of two ramshackle cages. 'Mice can put up with dog smell, but they hate cat smell. Cat smell's a lot stronger, isn't it?'

Hastily I assured her that this was so, while struggling mentally to find a rough parallel amongst smells familiar to me. Sloane's Linament and lavender, for instance. I must not allow this tall, knowledgeable girl who had just left school to be aware of my total ignorance of cats and dogs. Besides, there was the intimidating business of her father's profession. He was a policeman. Tom had told me so and I was a bit worried at the thought of going there.

'How is it that you know a policeman?' I had asked, feeling that here was another tangle to be unravelled. Bobbies, as most children and many adults called them, walked the streets with a slow deliberate tread clad in their thick, many buttoned uniforms, gloves and high helmets. I had no reason to be afraid of them, but many children were. They would make a detour round the block if they saw one approaching. I gathered that pubs and fathers getting drunk were the main things mixed up with their fear, and the most petrifying sight was the Black Maria coming slowly along the street. Everyone stopped to stare. Inside that windowless van, we children thought, were people going to prison and probably going there because they were drunk.

I would have expected Tom to fight shy of policemen because I had learnt recently, in school, all about drinking. Miss Byers had brought into the classroom a man who, she said, had something important to tell us. It turned out to be this, that if you took one drink of any liquid with alcohol in it, you were likely first, to be drunk and end up in prison and secondly, to have your insides shrivelled up. To illustrate the second he had two glass jars, one with water in it and one with gin. They both looked alike. He then took two long worms out of a tin box and let us watch them wriggling healthily in the air with many loops and twists. We were all attention, especially since some girls wouldn't touch a worm. He then popped one in each jar and held them aloft for our inspection. Both sank to the bottom and lay there struggling feebly. The jars were left on Miss Gibson's desk while he told us a great deal about men getting drunk and striking their starving wives and children which was the main cause of being arrested by the police and charged at court. He then fished out the worms. Naturally, I had expected both to be drowned and was already in agony about this dreadful cruelty, but at nine I was too self-conscious to make a verbal protest as I had once done to Miss Bailey, and certainly too old to throw a tantrum as I had done when Bob's jackdaw swallowed a worm. But, as we watched, we saw one worm recover – the one that had been in water – but the other poor thing was shrivelled up and dead. So, we were told, the only way to keep our insides from becoming like this rotted worm was never, never to touch alcoholic drink. Because once you started, you couldn't stop, but rushed headlong either to prison or to death.

After that I had seen my Aunt's outbursts about Tom's drinking in a new light. She was doing her best to save him from death or worse, prison; and I thought I ought to join her in this campaign. So it was not surprising that I was perplexed at finding Tom to be on joking terms with a policeman.

Lily lifted from its cage a shining white mouse with pink eyes and placed it on the cuff of her father's black sleeve where, for a few moments, it showed up to great advantage; then, in the twinkling of an eye, it was on his shoulder, sitting bolt upright and sniffing at his ear. It then reared on its hind legs to investigate the peaks and hollows of that ear. Its own ears were flat and transparent and each of its tiny claws gripped an edge of his ear lobe. 'There's no food to be had in there,' Lily laughed, just as it raced to the top of his head and surveyed the great space around and the great distance below, for he was a tall man. Lily poised a morsel of cheese on the parting of her father's hair. It was sniffed at, then nibbled.

'Where did you get it from?' I breathed.

'I bought her and a black one from a pet shop in Newport Road for a penny apiece and I've sold dozens at twopence each.'

'Dozens? Where did they come from?'

'From her and the black one and their babies and their babies' babies.'

'Unto the third and fourth generation,' I said, and could have bitten off my tongue. Constable Allinson laughed so much that Sal, as Lily had called the mouse, sprinted all the way down to his boots. Lily picked her up by the tail and put her back in the cage.

'You'll have to manage it somehow,' the policeman chuckled to Tom.

I shall never know how the four of them did manage it; a rare feat of collusion, manipulation and timing. What I remember is Tom appearing just before tea-time, crossing the yard with a wooden hutch in his arms and planting it on a low shelf in the shed; then sending me to tell Auntie I had something to show her; finding her buttering bread and being told that whatever it was it could wait until after tea; Mr Dyson hovering in the doorway and uncharacteristically breaking into speech, suggesting that it might be wise to delay tea on Polling Day since some people would be at the Town Hall till after midnight awaiting results. If tea were early, they might want something more substantial than supper on their return. The three of us then making for the shed, Indian file with Auntie between us and finding there not only Tom but Lily and P.C. Allinson uniformed. Then, when she saw what was to be seen, the anticipated storm, tempered, however, by the presence of a policeman and not aimed exclusively at Tom. The gist of her outburst was what did we take her for, a woman who had laboured all her life to acquire precision in the setting of mouse traps? No dirty mouse ever escaped one of her traps. She could have earned her living setting mouse traps for people who were too clumsy-fingered to set them properly. What did we take her for, she wanted hysterically to know and told Tom to pick up that hutch thing and be off with it. Then Mr Dyson's voice, as precise as a well set trap, asking if she, as an enlightened woman, couldn't see the advantage to children of keeping live-stock? Mr Henderson was merely offering me another step forward towards higher education, his first having been the *Gresham Dictionary*. The study of Life, Biology as it was called, would be taught in High Schools before long, might even be there already in so progressive a High School as we had in Middlesbrough. And urban children would be disadvantaged, having, unlike rural children, so little chance to study animal behaviour at first hand. Take the pupils of Yarm Grammar School for instance, children of farmers some of whom were customers of his. They would excel in Biology. He felt that P.C. Allinson and Mr Henderson were rendering me a service by introducing mice for my daily observation. Then the policeman assuring her that these mice had been born and bred in a hutch, did not like life outside it, were unlikely ever to leave it and would starve if they escaped and failed to find their way back.

After saying this, he opened the door, closed his hand over a black mouse and transferred it to the top of his head where it sought out the thickest part of his wiry hair and hid itself except for its tail and its bright beady eyes fixed upon us. Lily said it was a male and she had christened it Penry hoping it would be a good omen for the Liberal Party.

I can still see my Aunt and that mouse in confrontation. It had the advantage of height but, I thought, it saw her as a potential enemy, for it remained motionless. Lily must have sensed that I was about to burst out with something like, 'Oh, isn't it lovely, Auntie? Please, please let me keep them,' because suddenly her hand took mine and held it in a grip like a vice and the words were not spoken. I dimly understood her thought, that such an approach would not work with my Aunt. Otherwise, they would have let me get a word in before then.

My Aunt's view about the opinions of policemen was uncertain, but it was clear cut regarding Mr Dyson's. He was a suitable addition to the household, raising its tone by his education, his occasional clever remarks and those qualities she attributed to a perfect gentleman. In fact I had never heard her challenge what he said, and she didn't this time, except to ask what we thought we would do about the smell. Lily said I would clean them out daily and she would provide clean straw and I could buy food from her too, and when my Aunt, seeing a loophole, demanded, 'Buy food with what? Where was the money coming from, pray, to buy food?' Lily gave the airy reply that I'd soon make a profit by selling them because of the growing fashion for keeping pet mice. I'd bought them for two-pence each and I'd soon be able to sell them at fourpence apiece. My Aunt said oh well, if I wasn't planning to keep them for more than a week or two, disregarding, as usual, the fact of multiplication, or, as Mr Dyson would have put it, but wisely refrained from doing so, the fact of repro-duction.

Then the other smell came, just at this moment of wavering, Auntie raised her chin, sniffed the air, then wailed, 'My bacon and egg pie! Now you'll have it to eat burnt and I must say that will serve you right.' We listened to the opening of the oven door in the greenhouse and no one moved as the smell floated out across the yard. No one except Penry who lifted his nose above his nest of human hair and sniffed.

The excursion into keeping mice was a not insignificant aspect or recollection of my childhood. Years later I believed it had been my first lesson on how living creatures can adapt, and will do, to almost anything, providing they are neither too undernourished nor too ill to have energy. Many times I would dwell on the plight of prisoners surviving for years chained in those dark dungeons which had a tourist appeal as the century wore on. My four mice, two black, two white, a male and a female of each colour, according to Lily, were neither chained nor in a black and fetid hole (though such, I suppose, was their natural habitat) but they were imprisoned in a space which, compared with that enjoyed by wild mice, was certainly confined. The hutch, as nearly as I can recall, would be some eighteen inches by twelve and about eighteen in height. Three sides were netted with fine wire mesh. Half way up was a horizontal partition dividing the whole into two storeys with a hole in each far top corner from which a ruler wide plank descended to the lower floor. Tom had made the upper storey their sleeping quarters, covering the floor with a layer of straw. Below, where he expected them to eat, he left the wood bare and on it placed three shallow potted meat dishes, one for quaker oats, one for milk and the other for scraps of cheese, bacon or meat, because Lily declared they must have something called protein which was present in those foods. I took a candle into the shed that night but saw none of them eating. They were up in the straw asleep, I supposed.

I was in the shed next morning as soon as it was light enough to see. The mice were still upstairs, sitting here and there on the wooden floor and nibbling. I saw a white one drop something from its mouth, retrieve it and nibble again. The combined movement of jaw, nose and whiskers was so comical that it was a few moments before the change struck me. This morning all the straw was downstairs, strewn about so that little of the three white pots was visible. Just why, I pondered, had Tom decided to move it. At that moment a black mouse appeared on the left hand side. Penry, I thought, and wondered who had won the election. He descended cautiously, twitching his whiskers, then rustled through the straw, found the edge of a pot, snuffled in it, then turned and was up his stairway in a flash. I saw his black head rise from the hole and followed his movements till he settled down and began to nibble.

Tom declared he had done nothing with the straw, Mr Dyson likewise and I knew Auntie would not place her hand in the hutch. So that left only Cyril and of him I was a little suspicious. I hadn't known him long, but he looked the type who might play practical jokes. But when tackled, he said *I* must be joking. He wouldn't touch mice with a barge pole. Not since the time when he worked in a warehouse and one of the buggers had run up his trouser leg. There is no need to comment on what my Aunt said to him. He left the breakfast table disgruntled.

'Well, it's a rum thing,' mused Tom, opening the hutch door so that we had a better view of the straw all laid out on the lower floor. I extracted a piece and fingered it, half expecting that it had turned into gold.

'It *is* rather like Rumpelstiltskin,' I commented. 'A sort of magic or a small miracle. Just how has it got there?'

'By only one means as far as I can see. Those mice have decided they want it down below and they've moved it stick by stick. It must have taken them all night. I suppose they want the food upstairs, a contrary sort of arrangement.'

He gave me a few bacon scraps from his plate to drop into one dish and I replenished the quaker oats and milk. Then we moved the three pots upstairs.

'Perhaps it's because they wanted something to do,' I suggested. 'I wonder if they'll move it back again?'

They didn't, although before long they were busily transferring it to corners of the lower floor, piling it away from the centre. They were helping me to forget my aches and pains as I watched them darting about with the feather-weight sticks protruding from either side of their chinless faces.

Chapter Thirteen

A letter came from Bob in early November.

'Well, he's got there,' said my Aunt, 'but after a terrible voyage and then two days on Ellis Island. He says the Statue of Liberty should be smashed, the way they treat immigrants. Thank goodness the cake arrived intact.'

'Is he all right now?'

'As right as can be. He's working, that's one thing. For some people called the Youngs. They're giving him a pumpkin for the Thanksgiving dinner.'

'A pumpkin?' I was familiar with Cinderella's, but never thought you could eat the thing. In the picture it looked too big to eat even before it was turned into a coach. 'What does he mean? You can't eat a pumpkin.'

'In America it seems you can. They're having pumpkin pie after the turkey. I can't imagine the taste of turkey, let alone the other. Here, read it for yourself. No one will persuade me to go there. I'd never get used to such strange habits.'

It was a long letter that must have tested his patience severely though only two things were clear cut – he was earning money at last but hadn't heard from Doris. Had she been to tea and would Auntie ask her to write? A cottage on the Young's estate was at present inhabited by the head gardener, but he was getting on in years. I gained the impression that Bob had high hopes in this direction.

'He didn't ask about the election,' I said.

'Oh no. He'll have put all that behind him.'

Then why not Doris, I thought. Surely in a huge place like America there must be some nice girls.

At school, while Sylvia was out of the room seeing Miss Byers, Miss Gibson told us that next Wednesday an Inspector would be spending the day in our classroom examining Miss Sykes' teaching ability.

'It is an important day for her, so you will all do your

best in everything she asks you to do. I shall not be in the classroom but I'm warning you, I shall know if anyone has let her down and you are aware of the consequences. Miss Sykes will not be working with Standard Six after tomorrow. She will be with other classes so that I can get on with scholarship preparation. She will leave the school at the end of next term and will expect, in due course, to pass on into College. She has had good training under me and she wants a good report from this Inspector. So see to it that she gets one, and no nonsense of any kind.'

That should be enough, I thought, for Edith Turnbull and her cronies. I felt bruised by the knowledge that Sylvia was leaving. November was a horrid month. Grandfather had died just before November when I was six, and in November when I was seven the War Memorial had been unveiled and we were reminded, in a spectacular way, of the three thousand dead. In the same month I had learnt of the non-existence of Father Christmas. In November, aged eight, I had broken Grannie's umbrella and soon afterwards she had died. Now I was nine Bob had just departed and after tomorrow Sylvia might as well be gone. Who was left? Auntie, her friends, two lodgers and Tom. By now I was aware that underneath Auntie's outbursts, her rows with Tom, her insistence that she had one foot in the grave, she was really like a rock, though with jagged edges. And as for Tom, who couldn't stop drinking, well, we had always been good pals. For a while now I had wondered on and off what it would be like if Auntie and he were married. Would things be better or worse? Would they grow used to one another, as Cyril had said married couples must?

Miss Gibson saw that we were well prepared for Wednesday. We knew "Lochinvar" by heart, that is to say Sylvia knew which girls could recite parts of it without stumbling. We knew the whereabouts of the Eske River, Netherby Hall and Cannobie Chase, also that Sir Walter Scott had lived at Abbotsford near the Border. We knew about the Cheviots, the Southern Uplands and the Solway Firth and we were well up in *Ivanhoe* and the peculiar things people had to get used to in those far-off days. We had done *Julius Caesar,* of course, but were told that this did not come into Miss Sykes' time-table for Wednesday. As far as that day was concerned, Shakespeare was out. In arithmetic we knew we were to do percentages as applied to simple interest on loans. Miss Sykes would demonstrate them on the blackboard just as if we were learning them for the first time. A bit peculiar, I thought, for it seemed years since Miss Gibson had first taught us this process. For English there would be no Analysis, Miss Gibson said. (So I should never be able to help her again with that.) We would have a group of sentences to join with suitable conjunctions, a group we would revise next Tuesday, and some simple words with the same sound but differently spelt.

On Tuesday morning Edith Turnbull and Marjorie Burns cleaned out the inkwells and we endured a verbal bombardment from our teacher because of their contents – mushed up blotting paper, old pen nibs and even a couple of small chalk marbles. The two girls, with blue hands, brought them back in inkwell trays and each desk hole received an inkwell in pristine condition.

But Miss Gibson herself took charge of the ink can with its long, tapering spout and refilled the wells exactly to the rim, not overflowing onto the brim which was one cause, she said, of our exercise books being decorated with blots. To our astonishment, we were then provided with new penholders as well as new nibs, a procedure that normally occurred only after the summer holiday. We were so awed as to be impervious to her harangue about the condition of the used penholders with their damp frayed ends. 'Look at them,' she demanded, 'Look at their size and then think of your stomachs trying to digest inches of ink-stained wood!' It was almost four o'clock, so she had to settle down in order to issue final instructions.

'Now see that you smarten yourselves up for tomorrow, both inside and out. I surely don't need to elaborate on that. Have a bath, if you can. If not, then a good wash, not forgetting your necks and feet. I want the classroom to smell fresh. Use a brush and comb for once and keep yourselves tidy in the school yard before the bell rings. Remember this examination is not only of Miss Sykes, but also of Standard Six and of Victoria Road school.'

On Wednesday morning some girls were in their Sunday best and Sylvia had certainly put on a new dress of forget-me-not blue. She looked beautiful and I feasted my eyes on her, at the same time trying to detect in the Inspector any sign that he too was duly impressed. He appeared indifferent. Too old, I thought, to be sensitive to beauty. I tried to estimate his age. Not for the first time, I thought how odd men were. Take my cousin, impervious to Sylvia's charms as reported by me, and now this aloof looking man without so much as a smile for her, interested only in how she could manage us. Then I remembered one man who came in periodically, a school attendance officer, who had not been indifferent to Sylvia.

My thoughts on this subject receded as the morning's teaching began and, as far as I could judge, passed without a hitch. Our first task of the afternoon was to write a short essay on one of three given subjects. Sylvia had written the titles on the blackboard and set about preparing us as she had seen Miss Gibson do. She was interrupted by the Inspector.

'One moment, Miss Sykes, if you'll excuse me. Why not let the girls choose their own subjects? Free choice, you know. Set subjects for composition are just a little old-fashioned. Give them free rein, and see what they do.'

A catastrophe! Never before had we been given free rein either in composition or in any other subject. I sensed bewilderment on all sides as the class looked helplessly from the man to Sylvia and back again. I glanced along my row and saw two or three girls demolishing the new penholders and with expressions which the man might have interpreted as thoughtful, but which I guessed to be blank. Just the way those pet mice would look and feel, as Constable Allinson had assured my Aunt, were they to be set free. And whatever would Miss Gibson think, she who disapproved of a one out of three choice on the grounds that children wasted time thereby? And she was right. That was exactly what we were doing. Wasting time. 'What on earth shall I write about?' circled through all our minds, plunged into this alien waste of limitless choice. 'What on earth shall I do?' I could hear a liberated mouse squeak fearfully. I dipped my pen into the inkwell and wrote my lengthy heading, 'A White Mouse Escapes into the Wide, Wide World'.

It was a start, for soon I was conscious of other pens scratching across pages while the man wandered up and down the aisles between our desks. He stopped beside me, looked over my shoulder, then said, 'Keeping mice! That's interesting. My grandson has just bought some.' And I felt a glow of pride at being placed in a category with this Inspector's grandson. After play we sang, avoiding those songs which caused Sylvia too much trouble on the piano. Our latest was "Orpheus with his lute made trees", and the Inspector asked if we knew where the words came from. An absurd question, I thought, for song words, like poems, were surely written by someone, they didn't come from anywhere. No hand was raised, and, when he said we ought to know, I felt terrible for Sylvia who looked uncomfortable. Here was something Miss Gibson had not foreseen, but I couldn't blame her since she had nothing to do with music lessons. Wherever had the words come from? The Inspector then told us, at least in part. From a play by William Shakespeare. At which Marjorie Burns shot up her hand and said, *Julius Caesar*. A good guess, the man said, but, as far as he knew, there were no song words recorded in *Julius Caesar*. (Marjorie Burns knew further than he. She was certain that play contained no song words. Like many of us, she knew it almost backway first. She just wanted to show off.) The man did not tell us immediately. Instead, he asked if any of us had plays by William Shakespeare at home and, though most reluctantly, I raised my hand, keeping an eye on Sylvia who now looked the picture of worry as though she were wondering where all this might lead. The man asked me which play I had and when I said I supposed all of them since the title said Complete, he then told me to look for the Orpheus song in the one called *King Henry VIII*. I said, yes Sir, I would. Then, to divert his mind from Sylvia's deficiency regarding the song's origin, I added that there was a lovely fairy song in *A Midsummer Night's Dream*. It did divert him, and my classmates too, who later told me I had a cheek to talk to an Inspector like that. He was higher than a teacher, and no one in their right minds started up

133

conversations with teachers, let alone inspectors. They were right, of course, but I didn't care because, when the man turned back to Sylvia, it was almost home time and he said, 'Well done, Miss Sykes.' Sylvia suddenly looked radiant and I felt a sort of vicarious triumph, if I'd known that word. Sylvia would pass on into College and become a teacher, as long as she didn't get married which I thought was much more probable.

The days were so short now that Tom had fixed an old oil lamp on the long shelf in the shed. He drew the line at allowing me to carry one, although I was used to carrying candles across the yard or upstairs to the bedroom. My Aunt maintained that candle light was cheaper than gas light and, in any case, the gas fitting was near the window, a long way from the bed. You could see to read in bed by the light of the candle stuck firmly in its enamel saucer-shaped holder and positioned on the commode. But the oil lamp in the shed was of little use when it came to observing mice behind wire netting. In order to clean out the hutch, my hand had first to find the mice amongst the straw and then lift them one by one into a shoe box and put on the lid whilst I swept out the hutch and replenished the straw all in semi-darkness punctuated by the rise and fall of the guttering flame. Only at weekends could I see what I was doing and what the mice were doing. The first Saturday in December being fairly bright, I opened the hutch door and saw Penry upstairs sitting on the rim of a dish with his tail in the milk. He swung it back and forth, curled it round him and darted downstairs where I saw him skirt the back wall to where a white one, possibly Ellen, though I couldn't tell from my standpoint, was sitting in the corner. He turned with his tail towards her and she appeared to nibble it.

'Tom, Tom,' I called, for I could hear him hammering in the greenhouse. 'Come quickly, please.'

'What's to do?' he asked appearing in the shed door.

'Look, she's nibbling his tail. She'll nibble it off.' Tom peered into the corner and Penry darted away and back upstairs.

'Be quiet,' said Tom. 'Just watch.'

And what we saw was this mouse giving his tail a good

swish in the milk, curling it up and returning to the white one as before.

'Well, I'll be jiggered,' said Tom. 'It's hard to believe. I'll swear he's been bringing oats down, too.'

'But why? Why isn't she upstairs to eat?' Without replying he reached gently into the back corner and extracted the white mouse. It sat, quite still, on his hand.

'Look,' he said, 'can't you see how big she is? Even Lily didn't think of that. But then her hutches are one storey not two. It was my stupid idea to have an up and a down. She's too big to get through the holes.'

'You mean, she's grown?'

'Only temporarily. She's going to have a litter. Any time, I'd think. And a lot, at that.'

I stared at the mouse and felt slightly sick. Was this what Mr Dyson had meant by Biology? The sick feeling made me light-headed. I thought I might faint.

'It's nature,' I heard Tom's voice say. 'Nature, that's all. And you might sell them at threepence each. Fourpence is profiteering. Lily shouldn't be doing that with Ellen Wilkinson in Parliament!' He let out his trickle of laughter. 'Now then, have a look at that stomach. You can even see them moving.'

I swallowed hard, trying to cope with the sickness which still persisted despite the promises of threepences. Then I said, 'How do they get out?'

'Oh, she opens up.'

'Where? her stomach?'

But Tom brushed that aside with a muttered, 'In a way, yes,' and quickly drew my attention to the mouse's problem.

'They've made a nest in that corner but she's too big to get through the hole to feed upstairs. A difficulty I had not foreseen. For the time being we'll put some food downstairs, then sometime I'll have to enlarge the holes. The black one's her mate and he's trying to feed her. But bringing her milk on his tail is something you'll never get people to believe unless they actually saw it for themselves.'

'Like Thomas,' I said.

'Like who?'

'Oh, it doesn't matter. The disciple who wouldn't believe unless he saw it for himself.'

She had eight young. Lily warned me against calling them baby mice.

'They're not babies,' she said. 'Babies are the human young.'

'Well, we've not had the name for the young of mice at school. What is it?'

Lily said she didn't know, either. She didn't think there was one.

'Just say, their young,' she told me. 'Eight of them. That's very good for a first litter. Put an advertisement in Ryan's window, and in Wilson's. Miss Swales might even let you put one there.'

'I can't sell them yet,' though my hands could almost feel the pennies.

'Of course not. Not until they're eating for themselves. A couple of weeks and just in time for Christmas. She couldn't have hit a better time. Get your ads. up. People will want to buy them as Christmas presents for children. Tom ought to knock up a hutch or two and sell those.'

Like most newly born, they were hideous to look at, pink skinned, large-headed, protruding eyes and legs that would not support them. They squeaked a lot. What colour will they be, I wanted to know and Lily said I'd have to wait and see. That, in fact, was the next incredible thing. Two became pure white, one all black, three were black and white in patches, but two turned out to be pale brown and white.

Mr Dyson was intrigued and questioned Lily closely about their ancestry. She said her blacks and whites were kept in separate hutches and no browns of any kind had mixed with them. 'It's a throwback,' she said, 'but it must be at quite a distance. It'll be interesting to see what happens next.'

'It can happen,' said Mr Dyson, 'with human beings. Recessive genes that turn up once in several generations. Biology is certainly a most fascinating study. Did I not tell Miss Drinkhall what a lot you would learn from these mice?'

I hadn't learnt all, and I knew it. In retrospect I am

puzzled by what it was that held me back. On the brink of an important discovery, I had been side-stepped by Tom, but there was nothing to stop me from persisting, or even from asking Lily who would not have been slow to tell all. Not long before that, I had mentally reproached Hannah for her deliberate reticence on certain subjects; now, having learned so much, I myself had deliberately held the rest at bay. Even then I perceived, though dimly through that dark glass, that the tangle inside you is the hardest one of all to unravel.

Chapter Fourteen

Apart from the birth of mice and the sale of five which gave me a total of 1s 5d towards buying something to fill my Aunt's stocking and left me with four pure white mice and three black because the buyers preferred the multi-coloured, the outstanding event of Christmas 1924 was my precipitation into the out-patients department of North Ormesby Hospital which, in itself, was the direct result of our Good Works scheme at Sunday School.

During 1924 there had occurred slowly though surely a shift of emphasis in our religious observance at Chapel. To sum up, it was a shift from personal salvation to philanthropy and, had it not been reflected in the minister's choice of hymns, it might have passed unnoticed. Those hymns that had been the backbone of our worship, 'Just as I am without one plea', 'Rock of Ages', 'I heard the voice of Jesus say', were numbered less often on the Hymn Board, while some near the back of the Hymn Book, where the pages looked new, were having to be learnt by a reluctant congregation.

> To comfort and to bless,
> To find a balm for woe,
> To tend the lone and fatherless
> Is angels' work below.

My Aunt did not care for these hymns. She said they had no spirit, the tunes had no swing and the words were all mixed up. Chapel was moving away from its great founder, Charles Wesley. What would he have thought, for instance, if confronted with the jumble at the end of number 923.

> Whate'er for Thine we do O Lord,
> We do it unto Thee.

It hardly made sense. And so she would grumble on throughout Sunday, anticipating the evening service and occasionally voicing her resistance by breaking into a rendering of her two favourite hymns, 'O Love that wilt not let me go', and 'Nearer my God to Thee'.

Hannah was not perturbed by the switch in direction. 'It's nothing but a fad,' she affirmed, 'not likely to last long. Fashion goes in cycles.'

The choir had to master a modern anthem requested by the young minister – 'O brother man, fold to thy heart thy brother,' which did not meet the approval of the older congregation although choir and organist gave it their all.

This fervour of communal benefaction filtered through to the Sunday School. We heard fewer stories of Jesus and more of Doctor Barnardo and the orphan boys he rescued from the roof tiles of London. We heard about the homes for waifs and strays which bore his name, and, one Sunday in early December, we were asked to bring, in two weeks time, some gifts of toys and sweets which we could then take, as a Sunday School, to one such Home in North Ormesby near the Cottage Hospital.

I was given threepence to buy a quarter of dolly mixtures at Ryan's shop and told that I might as well take the Noah's Ark that my father had made for us a long time ago. It was just a nuisance, Auntie said, taking up space in the under-stairs cupboard. I thought two white mice would be a suitable offering, urging Mr Dyson's arguments in favour of keeping live stock. Actually, they were breeding so prolifically that I greatly doubted their value in terms of money. The supply had outstripped the demand and they all had to be fed. My Aunt had a word with the Superintendent, but he firmly opposed the idea.

So, dolly mixtures in one hand and in the other the Noah's Ark airborne in a string bag, I joined the procession that Sunday afternoon before Christmas and we made what seemed an immensely long trek to North Ormesby. A bitter wind swept across the river. Our teachers had to keep urging us on both from the front and the rear because that is the only way to keep a dawdling string of children on the move. Packages not too well strung fell apart and ended up in baskets carried by teachers. We had been promised that we should present our gifts personally, so that each could feel the glow of giving, like one of the

139

Wise Men; therefore, as more and more children relinquished their parcels, I foresaw what a sorting out there would be on arrival. The Kings, I argued inwardly, had had camels to carry both their gifts and themselves; nor, as far as we knew, had they been unseated by a gale, nor caused by its icy nature to need the W.C. which was now being required by several of us. A teacher was informed. She looked distressed and annoyed and said she knew of no lavatory between Woodlands Road and North Ormesby. She muttered something that sounded like 'a fool's errand, not a labour of love,' and removed herself from our proximity. I concentrated on the Kings and their desert situation. No problem there, I thought. Each in turn would dismount and use the sand while the other two reined in their camels and looked at the opposite horizon. By the time we reached the Home, we were low in both body and spirit. These were quickly revived by the amazing disclosure of some *indoor* water closets, the first most of us had ever seen.

The outstanding recollection of the room where we were to present our gifts was the rocking horse, a creature so enormous, with such a mane, tail, flaring nostrils and staring eyes, that I'm sure many of us felt we had landed in a fair ground. We surrounded it in silent awe. I failed to believe that anything so huge, elaborate and splendid could belong to waifs and strays. I thought of my ark and animals, sturdy enough but needing coats of paint; I thought of a few more battered toys protruding from their wrappings. How were they going to look in a place already so well equipped with toys? Because, when I could tear my eyes from the horse, I saw other toys ranged neatly on shelves and cupboard tops.

When our lot had claimed their property, we were asked to sit on the floor at one end of the room while the Barnardo children sat on the floor at the other end. Like the Israelites and the Philistines, but we had a table, not a valley between us. The table was covered with small tumblers containing a clear liquid which I hoped was lemonade, not water. While our Superintendent talked to the man I supposed was theirs, we had our eyes on the liquid hoping to detect a bubble. Then a lady handed round glasses and, as soon as the first child had taken a sip, we knew that it was indeed lemonade. By now I could sense the general feeling amongst us, that we had come to a party rather than to do a good deed.

While we sipped, their Superintendent gave us a talk. He told us about Doctor Barnardo and then supplied numerous figures – how many Homes there were, how many children looked after, how many when the first Home was opened which could not hold them all, how many came in each year, how many left, how many there were in that particular Home, how many girls compared with boys and how many people were employed to look after them. He numbed my mind with figures, then said something which started it working again.

'So you see, children, it costs a great deal of money looking after all these boys and girls and it can only be done by the generosity of the public, that is, people like yourselves.'

I felt most uncomfortable. Why was there no mention of toys and sweets, only money? We hadn't brought any money, so what would he think? Surely our Superintendent should have known that it was always better to stick to money. We could have easily brought our collection instead of a lot of old toys and sweets that by now would be sticky and unpleasant to look at. With dismay I heard him tell the children to rise and form a single file, then pass in front of us. They did so, each taking one toy and some sweets from one of us. They said 'Thank you' under their breaths but did not raise their eyelids to look at us. Thus they changed hands, the sweets together with the scruffy teddies and dolls, stuffed dogs and rabbits, battered books, two whips and tops, some model horses, a railway engine and much besides.

When these had been displayed on an empty shelf, their man asked if we would like to play together for a few minutes, which meant, on our part, a mad rush for the rocking horse and, on theirs, a ruminative chewing of sweets.

'Hand them round,' called their man as he and our teachers sat drinking tea. The timing was unfortunate for me as I was about to mount the horse. My foot was in the stirrup as a girl shoved a crumpled bag at me. I put in my hand, withdrew a sweet and stuffed it into my mouth, then struggled to heave myself high enough to throw a leg over the horse's back. That was the moment when I choked, my last thought for some time being, I've always known that choking would be the death of me.

Emergence from unconsciousness has intrigued me ever since that first experience of it. Unconsciousness, that is, induced by either anaesthetic, accident or the breakdown of some physical function. After repetitions of this later in life, I have striven to put into language the 'coming round' and have failed to do so. The process is so different from waking after sleep, no matter how deep the sleep. When you wake, you know you have slept long and soundly or otherwise. You know whether you have dreamed or not. You know some time has passed since you fell asleep. But such awareness is missing when you recover from loss of consciousness. Between the then and the now there is nothing. The two are glued together with no space and no time between. I have recovered consciousness with a unique sense of having been freed; freed from the prison of time.

At the age of nine, I did not know what to think, feeling myself laid on my side with a white shape limiting my range of vision. A head? A head of a nun? Of a nurse?

'Feeling better, dear?'

I moved my lips, but whatever passed through them was soundless.

'They've gone for your Auntie. She'll soon be here.'

And she was. Before long I heard her voice approaching. And soon I could hear her words.

'No, Doctor, I had no idea she had tonsils.' I heard people coming through a door. It closed behind them.

'We've all got tonsils. Hers are enlarged. In fact I've seen hundreds of pairs of tonsils but never whoppers like those. No wonder she had a fit of choking. I'm surprised she can swallow anything but slops. They should be removed as soon as possible together with her adenoids. But Christmas week we only do emergencies and after that I'm afraid we're choc-a-block for seven weeks.'

'You mean you can't remove them until late February?'

'That's what I do mean. Scores of children having

142

tonsils out! If you don't book her in, it could be another seven weeks.'

'You see, Doctor, she's due to sit the scholarship examination about that time. '

'The scholarship? You mean for a place in the High School?'

'Yes, Doctor.'

'But she doesn't look old enough,' and I had the feeling he thought Auntie not quite right in the head. 'How old are you?' he barked at me.

'She's nine,' my Aunt answered for me. 'She'll have another chance next year, of course.'

'Then what's the fuss? She's not fit to take an exam in February. Has your own doctor not seen her throat?'

My Aunt said no, and I hoped the questioning would stop there. I didn't like her having to tell him that no one had seen my throat. In fact I had taken as great a dislike to this young man as I had taken, when I was eight, to Doctor Armstrong.

'Then I'll give you a gargle for her and Sister will book her in for the last Tuesday in February,' and, with a nod to Sister, he departed.

'Come along, dear,' she said, and helped me off what I now discovered to be an excessively high bed with no head or foot to it.

'Well, that's that,' said my Aunt, taking my hand as we went out into the dark, strange street and began the long walk home.

It was a singular Christmas, a mixture of sudden, cheerful surprises and an overall despondency. School was now closed, thus postponing the moment when Miss Byers and Miss Gibson would be told the news. I both dreaded that moment and wished it were here, feeling that then, at least, my Aunt would have someone to talk to who was as genuinely disappointed as she. The reactions of her relatives, friends and neighbours had been predictable. She had tried to keep the news from Aunts Gertrude and Lena but you might as well, she said later, have tried to keep a tiger shut up in the house. Christmas looked brighter for them. Each said a party would be arranged and I was invited. Both Hannah and Minnie insisted that health came first and it was not as if this had been my only chance. Mary Kitching said it was a very good thing. I was fortunate to be having them out. The removal of tonsils and adenoids had two beneficial effects; it helped you to breathe through your nose and improved the shape of your face. Unfortunately, it wasn't in fashion when she and John were children, and of course they wouldn't perform the operation on adults. There was too much loss of blood. But, if she and John had had it done as children, their marriage might have been easier.

'How do you make that out?' My Aunt sounded both curious and suspicious.

'Well, John would not have snored and my face would have been a more refined shape.'

'There's nothing wrong with your face,' Auntie snapped. 'You and I are supposed to look alike, aren't we?'

Mr Dyson said something inscrutable about warding off the prison walls for a bit longer. He was going to his sister's for Christmas Day which was Thursday and staying until Sunday night. Auntie was icing the Christmas cake on Monday night and when Mr Dyson saw the mouse and pig that she moulded for me out of two lumps of almond paste, he showed interest and wanted to know where she had learnt that custom.

'It's not a custom, Mr Dyson. My Mother used to make them for us and I've just carried on.'

'*That* is custom,' said Mr Dyson. 'Making these images in paste is a Yule-tide custom in parts of Europe and, it appears, in some parts of England too. Your niece must keep it going when she grows up and pass it on to her children.'

Neither of these states, being grown up or having children, was conceivable to me, but Auntie was so impressed that she mixed a bit more paste and told me to get busy practising and not to eat it all that night.

Cyril, who still seemed to have nowhere to go, said what did the scholarship matter, and thought we should have a Christmas tree, one big enough to occupy the corner of the kitchen. Tom had nowhere to go either. He said we could both do the special crossword that would appear in the Christmas morning newspaper and give the mice a special Christmas clean out and some bits of meat for their Christmas dinner. He had enlarged the holes and fixed a string taut from the top right hand corner diagonally across to the bottom left hand corner. The mice had already begun to use it, climbing down it either right way up or upside down. It strengthened my belief that they needed something to do. You can get used to anything, I thought, except perhaps having nothing to do.

The post from America had brought two Christmas cards each depicting low red houses that looked like barns built of strips of wood. They were half buried in glittering snow and the glitter was rough when you ran a finger over it. There were short letters. Mother was helping at the big house where lots of people were coming to stay. Mr and Mrs Adams were entertaining all over Christmas. My Father and Bob were busy on the pond cutting blocks of ice for use in things called ice chests to keep food cool. (Why should they need something to keep food cool in a climate like that, Auntie wanted to know.) The letter said the ice was already twelve inches thick and would get thicker. She was buying the children skates for Christmas so that they could learn to skate on the pond. Auntie expressed her fury at this lunacy and I thought we should not hear the end of the letter but when she read out the next bit which stated that any spare time they had was spent in trying to deal with the rats in the cellar, the trouble being that they *would* get up into the house, then I really saw my Aunt's face turn purple. At that moment she was at a loss for words, but found them all by night when she sat up until two in the morning writing a long letter telling my Mother how to deal with rats. She had had to deal with them only once, at her second place in York, that dreadful Miss Beecroft's when she was fifteen. No rat had survived in that house after her first few weeks there.

Out of the ten dollars that Mother sent and two from Bob, Auntie gave me one to spend as I liked. I had five shillings all together having given Lily eightpence for straw and oats and I went to Miss Swale's shop on a corner a few blocks up Acton Street.

The two Miss Swales had turned the front room of this little house into a shop with counters fitted round three sides. The counters were just the right height for me. They had been fitted to suit the height of the two tiny ladies, an inch or so higher than I. Ordinary sized grown-ups could not have squeezed into the space behind the counters which was suitable for the Misses Swales, and no more than two customers at once could get into the shop and close the door. Once there had been only two counters set out with very small things – everything you were likely to need in the execution of plain sewing, darning, knitting or simple embroidery. No material or wool. But that was when the elder Miss Swales was still giving piano lessons as well as lessons in elocution in their other little room. The time came, and I believe it was partly due to Felix Corbett, when there was an upsurge of piano teachers who entered children for the Colleges of Music Associated Board Examinations. Those children who passed received certificates which could be framed and hung on walls. Miss Swales was unable to compete, although these teachers charged twice as much for lessons as well as entry fees for examinations, and mothers even had to pay in advance. All this we had learnt from Mrs Burt. Still, the certificates were worth it and those parents who aspired to piano lessons for their children – mainly, though not exclusively, girls – had to economise in other ways and drop Miss Swales in favour of a teacher who could produce certificates. So the Misses Swales had been obliged to add another counter, people said, to make ends meet and expand in trade which was not at all to their liking. I knew this because, after the elder Miss Swales had heard my old-fashioned garden poem, she happened to say, 'Oh dear, we never thought we'd be brought down to keeping a shop.' 'Brought down?' I'd asked, out of my depth. 'Well, you see, dear, we were brought up to better things, Amelia and I. Our father left us shares, fully trusting we would be secure for life.' 'Stocks and shares?' I'd asked. 'No, just shares. They fell, you see. I was happy to take pupils for piano and elocution, but the shop . . . Our father would never have dreamt . . . It's just a little demeaning, you see.' I had kept the word in my head, looked it up in *Gresham* and found she was right. To debase, to lower, it said, though why keeping a shop should lower them, I could not imagine.

The extra counter accommodated ladies' underwear, stockings and handkerchiefs both ladies' and gents'. At Christmas half-a-dozen tea aprons were added, a few sensible ties for men and, this time, some rectangular pieces of silk stitched and embroidered in the same colour as the material. I could not guess at their purpose. When Miss Swales had commiserated with me on my double misfortune, not being able to take the scholarship and having had to miss the Anniversary, she ended on a more cheerful note. Everything was ordained for the best, she said, and these things probably meant that I should soon join my family in America. People who came into the shop said that that was where I should be. Her sister, standing beside her, was unable to nod in agreement for the simple reason that she nodded all the time, a peculiar affliction, my Aunt used to say, for which there seemed to be no name. So her head went on shaking and I nodded, anyway, whether I agreed or not and said I would like something to put in Auntie's stocking.

Miss Swales was all approval and immediately shook out a pair of long black woollen stockings.

'What better than stockings, dear? Something Miss Drinkhall will always need. Best quality wool. We only keep the best, and only one-and-elevenpence half-penny. But perhaps that's too much for you, dear?'

'No, I can afford that. But,' I hesitated, 'Wouldn't it look a bit odd, filling her stocking with a pair of stockings?'

Miss Swales creased her tiny forehead, bringing together the two thin loops of white hair.

'I can wrap them in a little packet for you and tie it round with ribbon.'

I felt that Miss Swales was pleading with me to relieve her of the stockings. Perhaps they had been in the shop for a long time, I thought, and suddenly realised that I was right. Some women, though certainly not Auntie, were beginning to wear grey or brown stockings. You could see them as skirts shortened to the middle of the calves. My eyes swept the counters. I knew Auntie had all she needed for sewing, darning and embroidery as well as piles of handkerchiefs that she had made out of fine lawn or linen. I knew too that she would have no use for tea aprons. She favoured cross-over overalls made also by herself. She was self-sufficient as regards most of the articles in Miss Swales' shop. Except for those rectangular pieces of silk of which, to the best of my knowledge, there were none in our house.

'Those,' I said, pointing them out, 'are they fancy handkerchiefs or babies' bibs?'

'Dear me, no. Neither, dear. Hankies have to be square and silk is no use for bibs. They are called fronts, because ladies put them in front of their dresses now that the neckline is being lowered. I understand they were once called stomachers, a strange name, but that was a long time ago when ladies wore necklines that did not meet until they reached the waist, or even the stomach. How very naughty people were then,' and Miss Swales tittered at the thought. 'Of course, it will never again come to that, but V necks are certainly coming in and these fit inside the V and over the camisole. I, personally, have never seen them worn, but our salesman assures us they will be in great demand.' She hesitated for a moment and peered at me anxiously. 'It's hardly likely, my dear, that your Aunt will possess a dress with a V shaped neckline?'

This sounded part statement, part question, and it was not easy to answer. I did not know exactly what Auntie possessed. Nor was I ceretain of what she ought or ought not to possess. But these were pretty things – a far cry from black stockings, and I decided to buy one that would go with brown.

'Beige, it's called,' said Miss Swales, and was obviously delighted when I said I would take the stockings also. She wrapped each parcel separately in coloured paper and tied them with contrasting lengths of ribbon which the younger Miss Swales managed to cut from a large reel. I paid three shillings and fivepence-halfpenny which left me with one shilling and sixpence-halfpenny to buy some tobacco for Tom, a few brazil nuts, Auntie's favourites, and a quarter of pomfret cakes. I doubted whether the money would stretch to it and, for the first time, fully understood what people meant when they said that money wasn't elastic. You heard this so often that you did not stop to enquire into its meaning, although a long time ago I used to wonder why people insisted on telling you a fact that was so obviously true.

I hoped that filling her stocking would cheer her up. It was a severe blow to her, my missing the examination. I would not get into College a year early, nor be able to help her in whatever way it was that she anticipated needing my help. I made use of Tom, as Father Christmas, asking him to put the stocking on the fender after she had come to bed.

The Tree, the umbrella and the dolls highlight my recollections of that Christmas, each in its own way. Cyril brought in the tree at dinner-time on Christmas Eve. He had to gobble down his meal, having spent half of his dinner hour going into the old town market at the other side of the Albert Bridge. With the tree were a few sprigs of holly, but no mistletoe. There wasn't much, he said, and it was too dear. Besides, what point was there in having mistletoe in this house? He would bring some wire from the shop, there was plenty of that on old crates, and make a mistletoe.

'How can you make a plant?' I wanted to know.

'It's not a plant.' He was talking with his mouth full which Auntie couldn't stand. 'It's two wire hoops crossed and covered with crepe paper. The only decoration I remember.'

'What part of the country was that?' asked Mr Dyson.

Cyril shook his head, chewed hard, swallowed and drank a glass of water.

'Must be off,' he said, rising from the table.

'He's blunt,' said my Aunt. 'But I think he must be an orphan. Can't get a word out of him about his home.'

'A waif and stray,' I suggested, dipping bread into a cup of beef tea. To swallow was still painful.

'Nothing waif-like about him. He's much too fleshy.'

'I was not being inquisitive about his origins,' explained Mr Dyson. 'I would like to trace the source of that tradition. Decorated wire hoops. It must be a substitute for mistletoe because, though there's no resemblance, those wire hoops go by the same name. An ancient custom, undoubtedly.' Then he gave my Aunt a look – quizzical, Hannah might have called it – and said, 'O past that wilt not let me go!' It was lost on Auntie. He rose, excused himself, wished us a happy Christmas and said he would be back on Sunday night.

'A clever man,' she said, after he'd gone.

'Has he paid you?' I asked anxiously.

'Of course he's paid. Last night, and for the whole week. He's always on time with his board money – not like some I could mention. What in the world Cyril will do with that enormous tree, I don't know.'

After tea, however, she humoured him, allowing him to re-arrange the furniture and even remove a chair into the front room. Why he didn't put the tree in there, I never understood. He and Tom planted it in a bucket of soil, placed it in the far corner beyond the window and balanced it with stones. Then I stood on a chair and hung up the glistening balls with coloured funnels leading into their hearts and the gold trumpet on which you could actually blow an elfin note and the bird with the long, loose tail that was always coming out and had to be pushed back in, and the little dwarf on a swing of glittering wire. My Aunt insisted on dealing with those decorations which, she said, were so old that she didn't remember where they had come from – misty pearl balls and baskets with delicate pictures painted on them, and a blue peacock, all sitting in holders of ancient tinselled wire. They were more reticent than the newer trinkets, veiling themselves in a sort of secrecy.

But Cyril's candles caused that tree to stay clear and vivid in my memory. I suppose he brought them from the shop. It was the first time I'd seen a Christmas tree lit and perhaps not again until electric fairy lights made their appearance. During the time between, people became more conscious of fire risk which, up to then, had received little attention in our house. Cyril clipped at least two dozen tiny candle holders on to that tree and stood in them candles no longer than my little finger and only half as thick. And when they were lit, the sombre green spruce was irridescent with light and movement.

The only request I made of Auntie regarding my own stocking was for an umbrella. A child's umbrella, that is, which causes me to wonder whether children's umbrellas had just been invented or had just become the rage. Or perhaps I had a purely practical urge to be sheltered from downpours. In that respect, I have no idea how we were protected. I don't recall owning, at that time, anything called a mackintosh or raincoat. I think our coats and caps were soaked, dried, and soaked again and I hardly think this roused me to seek the desperate remedy of making an umbrella my only request for Christmas.

Just over a year before I had broken an umbrella – my Grandmother's – and in so doing had reached a particular milestone in my life. I had deceived, lied, suffered and lost, and I think I had been inclined to blame my doll, Hazel. She had been placed at the helm in the upturned umbrella-boat, had fallen forward drunkenly and caused me to lean on the handle and snap it off. A few weeks later I had wrapped up her jointed porcelain beauty in some strips of rag, laid her in her original box and put her away on the high shelf in the front room cupboard. Another doll had arrived that Christmas just after my Grandmother's funeral. At least I understood so, later on, the event itself remaining a blank in my memory. I do remember, however, the day I christened her, this other china doll of the infant type with limbs set in permanent curves so that she could never stand to become even a toddler. (She was jointed at the thighs and shoulders but the acute curves of arms and legs seemed to nullify any purpose of the joints). As I looked critically at her short dark curls, her shell pink cheeks and black-lashed moveable eyes, I remember saying, 'I name this doll Dorothea,' then laid her in an extra large shoe box procured by Tom and, standing on the embroidered footstool, placed that box beside Hazel's. Even still-born babies had to be christened, I had gathered from scraps of conversation.

'Where's your doll?' my cousin Margaret had asked one day, coming into our house with her father.

'Buried,' I had said, 'in a pyramid.' It sounded more sensational to add that, and I was satisfied when Margaret said, 'Gosh!'

Information on the subject of pyramids and their contents had been given us spasmodically at school ever since the first news had filtered through two years before that an Egyptian king with a long peculiar name was no longer resting in peace. Egypt, Tutankhamen, sarcophagi, mummies, embalming, one or more of these had, at intervals, usurped fifteen minutes, which, in Miss Gibson's view, should have been given to syntax. It was obvious, even to us, that she had little patience with all the fuss. We lapped it up with all its inaccuracies and, outside of school, heard passionate bits of gossip about the consequences of meddling where you shouldn't, death in the form of mosquito bites and cities plunged into darkness to indicate the wrath of God. They would not entertain the plural of God. At Marton Road School Margaret had no doubt been similarly instructed, so, having said 'Gosh,' she requested urgently to be shown the sight. I asked her if she wanted to be bitten by a cobra. She said, 'Don't be daft,' and pestered me until I opened the cupboard door and she saw for herself.

'That's not a pyramid,' she said.

'As far as I'm concerned, it is. What is a pyramid but a cupboard with shelves to stock boxes of embalmed mummies?'

'Don't you ever play with them?'

I said no, playing with dolls did not appeal to me and they were not to be interfered with. I was on home ground and could say yes or no to her suggestions.

Therefore, the sight of what lay on my bed early on Christmas morning came as a shock. Auntie had snuffed out the candle with her fingers and tiptoed downstairs. I, having feigned sleep until that moment, gave her a minute or two, then opened my eyes. I felt for the matches and re-lit the smouldering wick. Soon my eyes made out two parcels lying near the foot of the bed. Neither had the shape of an umbrella. Then, beyond them, and rising above the brass rail was something long and thin. That's the umbrella, I thought, pushed into the stocking. Reassured that I had got my request, I drew towards me the first parcel which was enormous and shaped exactly like a mummy. Thick brown paper encased it and a criss-cross arrangement of narrow purple ribbon which ended, incongruously, in a neat bow just below the shape of the head. I set to work untying my Aunt's handiwork, unwinding the ribbon and unwrapping the carefully arranged sheet of paper. Then, a doll stared up at me, a doll as large as a human baby with a massive celluloid head moulded to show a short tawny wave of celluloid hair ending in a curl. The cheeks were red and fat, the eyes pale blue, the mouth small and the expression, when I drew it nearer to the candle, was mischievous and beguiling. The solidly stuffed body was covered in a vest made of fish net. I lifted it, stood it upright by the bed and its head came level with the counterpane. A massive doll! I wondered if Cyril's shop would have a box to fit it.

The contents of the other parcel, enclosed in a lady's shoe box, almost convinced me that this was some dream. For here was another doll with another solid stuffed body and excessively short stuffed legs. But the head was porcelain and was that of a newly born baby. (I could see it was a baby but was told later that it was the newest thing in dolls, newly-born.) As I lifted it, the eyes shot open, then closed again as the bald head fell back. I thought it was about to fall off, but no, it hung there, lolled at a deep angle from the body. I cupped the head in one hand and lifted it. The eyes opened again, looked at me, then closed. Aunt Annie's baby girl, I thought, as my palm held the back of the head which curved steeply out from the nape of the neck.

· I unwrapped the umbrella. It was black as were all adult umbrellas I had seen, but it was the right size, a child's. I released the catch and opened it, keeping it upside down because of the bad luck which would come if you held it over your head in the house. Worse luck, I thought, in a bedroom. I let it rest on the mat and sat between it and the dolls, not bothering for a while with the other contents of the stocking. They were predictable. An apple, orange and nuts with perhaps a box of sweets. I felt jaded. Not that I had been too excited or too hopeful. But the dolls worried me. If only they had been books. By now I would have been well into one. But dolls! I didn't like playing at being a mother. 'You don't want to take on that job yet. It will

153

come all too soon.' My Mother's voice, the Christmas when I was seven and had wanted to help her fill my sisters' stockings. Yet she had given me a doll for my birthday to make up for leaving me, that was evident. I'd had a doll last Christmas to make up for Grannie's death. And two dolls this year for two reasons, I supposed, going to have my tonsils out and not being able to sit for the scholarship.

'And when you came, early morning, in't room above this kitchen, it were like you made up for all t'misery.' Huck-a-Back, and Cousin Liz talking to my Mother when I was six.

Auntie was climbing the stairs, coming through the door with a tray.

'Happy Christmas,' and kissed me on the forehead. 'What a surprise to find Father Christmas had filled *my* stocking. I haven't had a Christmas stocking since I was your age at Sutton. I can't get over that little "front". Your Aunt Gertrude was on about them the other day.' Tea was tinkling into the cup from a small china tea-pot patterned with roses. A special tea-pot for a special day. 'That "front" means I'll have to borrow a pattern from Gertrude and sew myself a dress with a V neck. And while I'm using the machine, you're going to learn to use it and sew clothes for your dolls. I've no patience with those under-sized aprons and outsize knickers that you sew at school. Let's have your dolls rigged up with clothes. I've plenty of scraps so we can start today as soon as the dinner's cleared away. It's a nice piece of pork.'

She picked up the large doll.

'This chap will be easy to dress, he's so big.'

'Chap?'

'It's a boy doll. At least that's what it looks like to me. I've never seen one quite like it. I got them at Dickson and Benson's. Both new sorts of dolls, they told me. You can leave the new-born baby. I'll make her a christening robe and petticoat while you're in hospital so that you've something to come back to. You get those two skeletons out of the cupboard and let's have your family all together. You can sit them round the little table at tea time and have your doll's tea set. Give them a Christmas party with a

154

spoonful of raspberry jelly and some dolly mixtures. Not the baby of course. We'll have to rig her up with a bottle. There now, drink your tea and then get dressed.'

It looked as if I might meekly submit.

Chapter Fifteen

In late February I was duly taken to North Ormesby Cottage Hospital, my Aunt carrying in a bag nearly all the underwear I possessed. The ward would be cold, she said, and I would need extra clothing in bed. Also, it was as well to be prepared for contingencies. You never knew, with these things, what might happen. I did not ask her to enlarge on this eventuality.

A nurse, whom Auntie addressed as Sister, told her to take home all the clothing including everything I had on my back and return tomorrow with warm clothing for me to wear on going home.

'I've been a nurse,' said my Aunt, 'and I know what wards are like. They can be very cold at this time of the year. I thought a vest . . . And what about her night-gown?'

'There are hospital nightgowns and the ward is warm enough for children. Cold air is better for them. Sterile, you know. And no clothes to be left, please. That is regulation.'

I removed my clothes and Sister looked me over. 'I don't think she needs a bath. We have to economise on heating water. She looks clean enough.' 'She *is* clean,' Auntie snapped, 'and you don't need to look at her head, either.'

I had just felt Sister part the hair in two places, then lift it and push forward my head as if examining the backs of my ears. She seemed satisfied and dropped a coarse flannel nightgown over my head, then said, 'Come this way, please.'

'I'll see her into bed,' said my Aunt.

'No. No visitors allowed in the tonsils ward. In and out in no time. A matter of routine, as you will know, having been a nurse.'

There was nothing my Aunt could say to that, so she kissed my cheek, told me to be a good girl and she would see me tomorrow when it was all over.

In the long ward each bed we passed was occupied. By the time we reached the third pair facing each other across a narrow gangway, I realised that each bed was doubly occupied. A girl's head at the top and one at the bottom lifted to stare at us until we reached a bed with a single occupant, a very dark girl. Apart from this impression, the first noticeable feature were her broad feet exposed on a flat pillow when the nurse turned down the grey blanket.

'Move your feet over, Myra,' instructed the nurse, but the girl seemed disinclined to obey, so the ankles were grasped and the legs moved to the opposite edge of the mattress.

'You'll have me out of bed in a minute,' the girl grumbled.

'And you'll have very cold feet if you don't pull up your knees.'

I had always slept with someone, but never top to tail and never in so narrow a bed. These beds were not designed for plurality in whatever position. But when the nurse departed, we both sat up which improved matters.

I noticed at once that Myra bore a strong resemblance to Fanny Barnston except that she had jet black hair, not red. She was scratching her scalp.

'Have they done your hair?' she asked.

'No, I don't think so.'

'You'd know if they had, by the smell. They've doused mine with sassafras: I hate it. Why can't they leave it alone? I'm not coming in here again to have my tonsils out.'

'You won't have to, once they're out.'

Myra only said, 'I'm hungry. I hope they won't be long with our supper,' and started to scratch again.

My Aunt had fortified me against the experience of having my tonsils out by repeating her stories about Doctor Howell. 'You'll know nothing about it. You just go to sleep in a room called the theatre, then wake up in the ward to find it's all over. Not long ago people weren't put to sleep and tonsils were removed on the kitchen table, a horrible thing to go through. Doctor Howell was a pioneer of chloroform in Middlesbrough and he used it on

157

himself before he would give it to a patient. That was the sort of man he was. Now, it's as safe as houses,' so that I received the quite erroneous impression that he had been the sole pioneer in making surgery painless and harmless. This also inspired in me a sense of his presence attending me during the ordeal, when I should, of course, have been thinking of God's.

What my Aunt had not prepared me for were all those other minutes apart from that particular minute when the tonsils were being whipped out. She had not prepared me for having a girl at such close quarters. There was not much space between us as we sat top to tail and, as she scratched, I saw things dropping onto the blanket – and still moving! I started to scratch my own head.

'I don't want to get those in *my* hair.'

'Aw no, you won't.' She was unresentful. 'They've been poisoned with sassafras. I told you. If they weren't poisoned, they wouldn't drop out.' She eyed me with speculation. 'You won't get them, anyway. Your hair's too thin. The old man says they only like thick hair. It's the price you pay for having thick hair, that's what he says.'

I was glad she told me, because for a few years afterwards, when I was fed up with trying vainly to make something of my thin hair, I could recall this conversation and this sight and attempt to count my blessings.

A nurse was zigzagging along the ward from bed to bed giving each girl a brown enamel mug. 'Cocoa coming up,' she was repeating. 'Cocoa coming up any minute.'

'What about summat to eat?' asked Myra, reaching for her mug.

'No eats, dear. No eats the night before your op. You'd be sick in the theatre, then how could doctor cut out those nasty tonsils?'

Apparently Myra couldn't believe her ears. 'I won't be sick. I promise I won't be sick. I've never been sick in my life, so I'm not likely to be sick tomorrow. I want some supper. You can't keep us here all night without supper. It's not right. We might as well be in an orphanage.'

'That's not right, either,' I hastened to correct her. 'They do get supper in orphanages. I happen to know.'

158

'Aw, shut up, clever clogs.'

'Hold your mug straight or you'll get no cocoa either.'
This nurse was out to stand no nonsense. 'It would do you
no harm to go without cocoa and that's what will happen
if you don't quieten down.'

So, apart from the sound of cocoa being drunk, or
sucked in Myra's case, the ward was quiet. I reckoned that
there must be dozens of thoughts weighing down the air,
for you couldn't drink cocoa and not think about something. A phrase from the Bible crossed my mind. (When
would they stop doing so?) I rejected it, then thought it
was apt and changed it into the plural. 'As sheep before
their shearers are dumb, so they opened not their mouths.'
The other bit about slaughter would hardly do. Shearing
was more correct, for tonsils.

I hadn't finished my cocoa when the nurse came to
collect the mugs and give us bedpans in their place and I
shall not forget balancing on mine face to face with Myra's
sullen countenance as she squatted on hers. It was then I
dared to ask her age – a consuming interest with me – and
she muttered, 'Twelve.' Her thoughts dwelt darkly, I
could tell, on the injustice of no supper and her next
remark left *me* groping in the dark. 'I'd as soon have a baby
as have my tonsils out.' Nurse was now piling bed-pans
on top of one another and there seemed no chance to seek
an explanation because the lights went out and we were
told to sleep. I think Myra slept, but she was one of the
unquiet sleepers. Her feet were never still, causing me to
cling to the edge of the bed. I was afraid to sleep in case I
fell off that edge, and in such circumstances a night seems
endless.

Now I am lying on a table. The operating table, as
Auntie had said when preparing me. I am covered up to
the waist but a doctor all in white is planting a round thing
here and there on my chest. Making patterns all over it.
Some rubber tubes lead from it to each of his ears. I watch
his eyes. Brown tarns. You can't see the bottom as you
could in the dream pond. His eyes are brown and murky. I
don't know what his thoughts are. Why is he thinking,
anyway? I've only come to have my tonsils out. A
minute's job, they all say. Not a carry on like this. He

159

raises himself, takes the tubes out of his ears and hands the whole contraption over to the doctor on my left who sticks the tubes into his ears and repeats the marking on my chest.

Then the first doctor says, 'What do you make of that?'

The second one stares at me and I begin to think there is something wrong; that I am not the way I should be.

'You've had rheumatic fever?'

It isn't a question, but he makes it sound like one. I say, 'Pardon?'

'Have you had rheumatic fever?'

Really I don't know what he's talking about, but this is certainly a question so I say, 'No, I don't think so.'

The other doctor says, 'Probably doesn't know,' and I think frantically, I ought to know, I ought to know. 'It's not on her form,' this doctor continues. 'No mention of anything except the usual, measles, chickenpox, mumps.'

The one who questioned me is not satisfied. 'Have you been ill in bed for a long time? A rather long time without getting up? And had a doctor coming to see you?'

What does he take me for? I think. Someone who doesn't know what's happened? Who has no memory at all?

'No,' I say, 'I've only stayed in bed for a day or two when my throat's been sore.'

'You're sure no one mentioned rheumatic fever? Or took your temperature often?'

I can answer that one. 'Auntie's always taking my temperature. She's been a nurse.'

They laugh. But this doctor says, 'Better not do her,' which seems to irritate the other one who says, 'Oh, let's get on with it. Have them out in a minute. Just give her half.'

My face is covered and a strange sickening smell assails me as a voice says, 'Start to count now, please. One, two, and go on counting as long as you can.'

This is the chloroform. I will go on counting and I will not stop counting. I know I am stubborn but that's how I'm made. They will not do what they like with me. I will go on counting until I reach a thousand and they can't start until I stop counting. Forty, forty-one, I can hear my voice though a long, long way out over the sea, like the horizon at Redcar. Forty-two, forty-three . . . And another voice says, 'Good Lord, not out yet.' That's forty-four, but it's very slow. They-will-not-stop-me-from-counting. Then I see coffins, golden coffins descending one after the other. One-two-three. I am counting them as each one lands with a thud on my chest, vanishes and another drops down to take its place. They continue to come as I count – floating lightly down but landing with that ponderous thud. The space between each thud is longer – and between each count. Now I am being lifted, wheeled away, lifted again and laid down.

I opened my eyes to see the doctors still standing over me. I've had my tonsils out, is my first thought. One doctor is holding my wrist.

'Feeling better?' he asks.

I nod and, after a while, they go, leaving me with a nurse.

When my Aunt came for me, she was told, it seems, that they must keep me in for another day or two. I could hear her penetrating voice long before she reached the bed of which I was the only occupant.

'I insist on seeing her and I want to know why she has to stay in, Sister.'

Sister was saying something about a little complication. Nothing, really, Doctor just wanted to keep his eye on her for a day or two.

'That won't do for me,' said my Aunt as they reached my bed. 'I should like to see the doctor concerned, please.'

She kissed me and asked me how I was. I nodded. Sister took a large, blood-stained rag from me and gave me a clean one. It became apparent that my Aunt would not remove herself. 'I will not go,' she said, 'until I have seen that doctor. Or otherwise, Matron.'

That seemed to settle it. Sister went and in a short time was replaced by the doctor, the one who'd said, I recollected, 'Let's get on with it.'

Then a battle raged which it was hard to keep track of, but all my senses had returned. Only my throat felt worse than I could ever remember. He said I'd had rheumatic fever and she said I had not. He said, how could she know

161

having had me in her care for only two years, according to Sister. She said what was Sister talking about? I'd been in her care on and off since the hour I was born. And what had this rheumatic fever to do with a simple tonsil operation and he said it affected the heart muscles and I couldn't be given the full dose of chloroform. I was coming round before he could get the other tonsil removed. She asked if they really knew anything about administering chloroform. Removing tonsils was no more than a minute's job. She'd seen it done. Such a thing as taking one and leaving one was preposterous. It would never had been heard of in Doctor Howell's time. He said he had no knowledge of Doctor Howell but would she kindly give him credit for doing the job he'd been trained to do, to which she replied that obviously medical training was not what it used to be. I thought they had forgotten all about me and they had certainly not seen Sister come up behind. I made a stupendous effort to speak and got out, hoarsely, the words, 'Has Myra gone home?' My Aunt and the doctor stared at me in such a blank way that I knew they really had forgotten my presence. Only Sister understood and said, 'Yes, they've all gone home. They've all had their tonsils out without any trouble at all.'

This diversion cleared the air a little. Auntie said she would go to order a taxi cab. I wasn't in a fit state to walk home and the doctor said, 'Bring her back next week and we'll take out the other one.' But when my Aunt said, 'Certainly not, she's having nothing more done until I consult my own doctor,' there was a sudden change in the hospital doctor's manner which became less abrupt.

'Look, Miss Drinkhall,' he said, using her name for the very first time. 'If you like to wait in the waiting-room, Sister will get you a cup of tea, and I'll take the other tonsil out with a local anaesthetic while you wait. And you can take her home afterwards.'

'What do you mean a local anaesthetic?'

'Just something to numb the tonsil.'

'You mean no chloroform? The child will be awake while you take out her tonsil?'

'That's right.'

There was one terrible moment when I thought she

would strike him, as I had seen her strike Tom – on the cheek. But she controlled her arm and transferred her wrath to her vocal chords, then said, 'What do you take me for? I might be a defenceless woman, but I will not be a cover-up for your blunders, nor the child a hostage to your incompetence. She comes with me this minute.'

It was a wonderful battle cry, comparable with that of the defenceless David challenging the outsize Philistine across the valley of the Jordan. Thou comest to me with a sword and with a spear and with a shield, but I come to thee in the name of all – all that is right (a simple substitution for the Lord). And David prevailed over the Philistine as did my Aunt over the surgeon who surrendered with a shrug and strode off. And why should I feel sorry for him, being the one who wanted to get on with it, who said, 'Give her half.' Half, that could only take out one, and what was the use of losing one tonsil? It was as bad as losing one glove.

Auntie girded herself and took me to Doctor Armstrong's surgery.

'She'll open her mouth and say 'A-a-h' Doctor, if you'll go steady with the spoon handle. The trouble is, she's always been afraid of choking.'

'Afraid is she? Of choking? It all comes of being bottle fed. I told you she should have been on the breast.'

'I think it was that mint bullet when she was two. But never mind. What's to be done, I wonder, about her throat?'

He managed to see all he wanted to and said what a mess. Unaccountably, I even allowed him to paint it with a paint brush dipped into some purple liquid that looked exactly like potassium permanganate.

'I shouldn't let her go back there. Leave her throat alone for the present.'

'But what do you make of this rheumatic fever business?'

'What *can* I make of it? She may have had it. Lots of children go through phases of illness and grow out of them.' His moustache widened in what was intended, I think to be a smile but did not completely reassure my Aunt.

'I'd like you to sound her, Doctor. The surgeon talked about weakened heart muscles.'

163

'Certainly, if that is what you wish.'

Being upright this time, I was able to see my chest ringed here and there with his stethoscope. When he'd finished, he told my Aunt there was a little trouble which would right itself in time.

On the way home Auntie said she was sure she had done the right thing. She had stood her ground and had had Doctor Armstrong's support. There should be no more meddling with my throat. In the course of time, the tonsil which had been interfered with – badly mauled, was how Auntie put it – renewed itself and grew to almost match the other in size.

Nowhere could anyone have found a prettier robe than the one Auntie sewed for the baby doll during my one night in hospital. Made of fine cotton, it had a wide front panel of broderie anglaise running from the neck to the hem and exquisite little frills round the wrists. Within the week she had completed its christening outfit by making a bonnet, petticoat and a hemmed nappy. All had been contrived out of remnants from her blouse-making days. Minnie, who had no children, rhapsodized when she saw it. 'It has the face of an angel,' she crooned, and, although I had never seen one, that was the way an angel's face should be, I thought, so purely carved, so delicately tinted, so serene. My aversion to dolls was almost overcome; and, as for Myra's declaration that she'd as soon have a baby as have her tonsils out, I was further than ever from being able to see any analogy between these two things.

Although Miss Gibson coached me along with those who had passed the first stage of the examination and were now being inexorably forwarded to the second, I sensed the change in her attitude towards me. Until then I had been one of a few star pupils but now, one who had fallen by the way. The sense of fall was great. I resented Edith Turnbull and others now approaching the climax of their efforts to win bicycles. I avoided the vicinity of the High School, making detours this way or that, and would turn into a side street or shop doorway at the approach of a girl in that uniform. I began consciously to dislike people.

There occurred, too, a distinct change in my life style.

Auntie now ranged herself with those who had never seen the need for me to stick at homework or books. I could leave all that, she said, until after the summer holiday. Instead, she carried out her plan for teaching me to sew and unwittingly, provided a compensatory fantasy that did much to offset my frustration. I sent the dolls, Hazel and Tony, to High Schools in uniforms which were neither navy nor green nor wine – these being respectively the uniform colours of the High School, Kirby School and their Roman Catholic counterpart, the Convent. Hazel and Tony went to Greystones, segregated of couse, and were uniformed in grey. The predominance of grey in Auntie's scrap bag may have prompted this choice. Auntie helped me make a real gym tunic for Hazel with a yoke and three box pleats back and front, and master the difficult process of fashioning trousers for Tony. They both wore grey blazers edged with scarlet bias tape and a scarlet badge was stitched to the breast pockets. Each morning I dressed them, packed them off to school and accompanied them mentally.

The mice multiplied at an alarming rate, and I sold a small percentage, Frank Smith pestered his mother who said she wouldn't have them within a mile of her. Far too often I caught sight of Tom crossing quickly from the shed door to the W.C., his palm closed about something wrapped in newspaper. Gradually I realised what this was, a paper shroud enclosing the newly-born, and I would stuff my fingers into my ears against the sound of the lavatory chain being pulled. The thought of the guillotine would enter my head. Surely some people did not knit, unperturbed! Surely there were a few who plugged their ears, shut their eyes, wept inside themselves when the mechanism started up to release the blade. It depressed me, though Tom, I think, believed I should get used to this necessary control of population. The mice were always having young which was a nuisance, as well as the problem of their being bored which worried me. Keeping them as pets was not all pleasure and perhaps the end had to come before long, though I wish it had done so in a less violent way.

One young mouse had turned out to be of special

beauty, the sort that is thrown up at rare intervals in a human family where interbreeding is common. It was white with even, bright brown markings, not daubed as many were, with haphazard patches as if a small child had been dabbing away with a paint brush. Lily was quite taken with it.

'It's an aristocrat,' she said. 'No doubt about that. Look at its long, thin face, mass of whiskers, tiny ears and magnificent tail. You should enter it in the Show that's coming up on Clairville Common.' She had it perched on her left forefinger and was stroking it from nose to tail with the same finger of her right hand. The mouse looked mesmerised. Lily certainly had a way with animals, I thought. The stray dogs her Father brought in from the streets were quickly trained by her and my Aunt said they must spend a fortune on pet food. That day she had a tiny Yorkshire terrier sitting still and patient at her heels.

'Is it safe?' I asked, 'to have Marmaduke out while Scrap's here?'

'Couldn't be safer. I've said, "Stay," and Scrap won't move till I tell him to.'

Scrap didn't move, but Lily hadn't reckoned with a bee. It sailed across from the London pride now blossoming and hovered as bees do, just above the dog's nose. Scrap snapped, gave a little yelp, and the mouse had gone. A flash of white streaked over the shelf and vanished into the ironmongery at the end of the shed.

What shall we do, what shall we do, what shall we do?

Lily moved the bicycle, my tea-chest desk and stool out into the yard, then spread the rest of the paraphernalia over the shed floor so that the returning mouse could see its hutch and we could see it more easily. Since no mouse emerged, the shed was left in this state and my Aunt threatened to set traps. Lily's father restrained her.

'It's still terrified,' he said. 'It will come back when it's hungry.' But, though my Aunt covered everything in the pantry with bowls and basins, hunger did not drive this aristocrat to give itself up. On the third day Tom devised a trap using two pieces of glass propped against the side of the hutch which had been put on the floor. A large piece of cheese was pushed along to the closed end. Nothing

happened the following day and Constable Allinson assured my Aunt that the mouse would now be dead.

'Dead where? That's the point. Left somewhere until it
smells the house out.' Her nerves were in shreds. Anger
that she should be worried to death by mice at her time of
life was paramount. Then, on the following morning,
there it was, inside the glass, nibbling ferociously at the
cheese. Tom covered the open end, slowly lifted the piece
of glass opposite and the mouse ran into his hand.

Joy abounded. He gave it to me to be stroked and
caressed before letting it go home to its relations one of
whom stretched backwards to at least the fourth generation. I identified myself both with it and with those
waiting to receive a lost one whose sufferings must have
been unthinkable out in the wide, hostile world. I experienced afresh that upsurge of relief and security felt as I lay
in bed that night after Bessie's Redcar adventures, Bessie
and I on either side of Grannie, and everyone safe under
the same roof. At dinner time I raced home, through the
back door, over to the hutch, looked in, opened the door.
Something fell out. I closed the door and picked it up. It
was a leg. There was no mistaking the fact. A leg with tiny
claws spread out as if in protest. I *did* open the door again,
though unaware of doing so, and saw the rest. More legs,
a long white head with ears like tiny shells and a red
tongue escaping from the opened mouth, two jagged
pieces of brown patched body and the straw stained red.
The door swung open a fraction further and a tail fell
partly out. Being so long, it stayed hanging there, its top
end held by a wisp of straw.

Constable Allinson, trained as he was to deal with
offenders, found this one of the worst cases of violence it
had ever been his lot to handle. It taxed all his resources to
know what to say to me, what to say to Auntie, how to
cope with his daughter who raved about how such a thing
could have happened and all because of a bee; what to say
even to Tom who had dashed his shirt sleeve acress his face
after he had taken in what I had to show him and before he
could bring himself to gather up the remains. When we
had heard from Auntie countless times that afternoon, for
I didn't return to school, that she had been right from the

167

start, she should never have given way and allowed me to have such horrible inhuman creatures which were nothing but vermin, and I understood she was overwrought mainly because there was nothing she could do to console me; when Cyril had remained unmoved and I hated him for it; when he and Mr. Dyson had eaten a good tea while the rest of us toyed with the food; and I had just said for the twentieth time, how could they have been so cruel when they had been so kind, feeding the mother who couldn't get through the hole, how *could* they? – then Mr. Dyson spoke.

'It's hard,' he said, 'but it's nature. It wasn't the individual mouse they had to kill, it was the threat to the colony.' And, when no one said a word, he went on. 'The mouse had been in unknown territory. It returned with unknown smells on its claws, its fur, its whiskers. These constituted a threat to the rest and they reacted with violence. Men have done the same in similar circumstances as I'm sure you all know.' Judging from the silence, it seemed improbable that we did.

'If you had given it a thought,' he continued 'you might have put the creature in a separate container for the time being until it had cleaned the smell from its coat, as undoubtedly it would have done.' His superior wisdom was cold comfort to me, and when my Aunt's face glowed as she watched him consume a second portion of her lemon cornflour cake, I saw such a downcast expression on poor Tom's face that I was convinced he and I were in the same boat, the sinking one, while people like Edith Turnbull and Mr. Dyson sailed effortlessly towards some blue horizon.

Lily took away the hutch with its mice. She said she could give them away if she failed to sell them for me. Whether she sold any or not is uncertain, but on Saturday she came with half-a-crown and I felt like Judas taking it – thirty pennies, the price for the victim of violence. I hardened my heart. It wasn't my fault, I reasoned, and I might as well have it. Lily said would I like a little dog instead. There is no need to dwell on my Aunt's lengthy reply.

Chapter Sixteen

We were to hear from Mr Dyson only a few more words of wisdom before the dispiriting news of his imminent departure. It was the second Sunday after Whitsuntide and I had emerged from the Waterloo Road door of the Chapel after morning Sunday School and had paced the few yards to Woodlands Road when I was brought to a halt. Woodlands Road was full of people; a host of them moving with what I imagined to be the speed of a glacier towards Park Lane. From their midst rose some sort of dirge chanted in a foreign sounding tongue.

This Whitsuntide had not been the first time — nor would it be the last — when I should ponder the remarkable events of Pentecost. In our Chapel the celebration had reached its peak with the singing of "Gracious Spirit, Holy Ghost" which, being sung only once a year, needed a vigorous lead from the choir. This had been provided mainly by the women's section, the men trailing behind with less conviction. Six times, once at the end of each verse, came the invocation to the Spirit to give them love; and, heartfelt as this sounded from the ladies, it left me unmoved. I was unmoved because my thoughts dwelt on the Pentecostal Spirit's other gift to the disciples, the instant ability to speak with other tongues. This curious occurrence was, I'd feared, one of several stumbling blocks in my progress heavenward. Because, what else could be meant other than different languages; foreign ones which took ages to learn, or so I'd been told? Therefore, though I did not doubt that God could bestow the power to learn them instantly, I could never see the point. What were those listening to think when Peter addressed them in French, for instance, or in the language of the horrible Germans whom we had not yet forgiven; or the still more horrible Turks? I was not surprised that the crowd pronounced them to be drunk.

And here, in our own town, close on the heels of

Whitsuntide, was another lot of people chanting in some foreign tongue. As they inched their way along, I realised that this was some kind of procession, though quite different from the straggling groups which had shuffled along the streets to the strains of that Wilkie song. Not that these people were better dressed; you could hardly say they were in their Sunday best. But, for one thing, they occupied both pavements as well as packing the road; and, for another, they exuded an aura and an odour that had been lacking in those Labour processions and were strange to all my senses, causing a tightening of my muscles, a quickened heart beat, a fear, or an opposition to something alien, I wondered, as with the mice. I looked up Woodlands Road and could see no end to it. Did it have an end, or did it wind all through the town to goodness knows where?

At that thought the business of Sunday dinner arose. How was I to reach home? If I turned and went by Laura Street, I might be no better off if the procession were heading down the Lane in the direction of the main Park gates. Yet to battle a way through it to reach the other side of Woodlands Road seemed like throwing yourself under a steam roller. Not that I really believed these people would flatten me, but there were glimpses between their bodies of what moved in the centre; flashes of white, gold, scarlet; figures dressed up; and it would never do to get mixed up with them. So, while I was standing there, glued to the Chapel railings in Waterloo Road, the Yorkshire puddings would burn or drop flat because of the waiting, and we should have a disagreeable afternoon.

Then, from my position apart from the crowd, I saw, approaching, an object borne aloft above the heads of the throng – a purple platform under a purple canopy fringed with gold. Two women, also watching a few paces abreast of me, each made some movements which Auntie would assuredly have termed peculiar – an awkward sort of curtsey followed by an arm movement down and across each chest. It was at that moment when the platform had drawn level with us and seemed to pause, so that I saw, poised centrally upon it, a small, square, pointed tent, its sides festooned with sea foam, frothy white.

I was now too old to confuse one thing directly with another. I knew that this was not the Ark of the Covenant, because that belonged to the very distant past. But, whatever it might be, it brought that Ark to mind, borne aloft as it had been across deserts, rivers and plains, overlaid with gold and carrying the pot of manna and the tablets of the covenant. This veiled thing was too small, of course, to hold slabs of rock. Nor was there room for the wings of the two cherubim to meet across its top. No, it was like the Ark, yet unlike, as it resumed its slow deliberate course. It did not need the cherubim. It stood alone, whatever it was, on its stage draped with a purple cloth that hung in folds. Like the gown of the purple lady in Nazareth House grounds! And in a flash the mist of unknowing was gone. I knew I was watching a Catholic thing and shouldn't be, so I'd better find a way home somehow or be drawn in, never to get out. Without further reflection I stepped forward, turned right and became one of the children who along with women seemed to be on the fringe. We moved very slowly, in a mass, nudging each other along, and I breathed in that smell again being sifted out from the smell of bodies. The pocket of air in which I walked seemed blue like the haze round a peat fire, I remembered. But not like the smell. This smell was sweet like honey and the honeysuckle that had made those bees at Nunthorpe drunk. Was I drunk? Something strange was happening to me. I was rising, being drawn upwards like a bee, floating above the crowd and keeping pace with the platformed tent.

'You all right, love?' A fat woman was clasping me to her, her large body like a bolster. 'Here, sit on this ledge by the railings. She's come over queer and no wonder, Sure it ben't fit for kids! If I'd known it'd be like this, the Bishop himself wouldn't 'ave dragged me out. Best go back love, where you've come from, if she can, that is.'

I felt myself rising again. A very strange business because, ever since, something tells me I had found the key to levitation and should be able to find it again. I grasped at the woman's shoulder to anchor myself and heard my voice say, 'Park Lane. Not far, if I can get to the other side.'

'There, there.' She attempted to pat my back. 'It's a bit

tight and no mistake. The corner's the trouble, turning in at the Lane. It's narrower than this 'ere road so we're stuck till they get going.' Then suddenly, 'Everyone stand still,' she yelled to the oncomers. 'All of us'll be fainting next. Stand still, I say, or yer'll be on top of us like a bloody steam roller. Have you no sense? We can't move now till they're past Nazareth House. There now, just sit a bit love, and get your breath back. Here, I'll pop you through this gate. People won't mind and you'll be out o't' way.'

I recovered enough breath to say, 'Can I get through to the other side, please? You see, I'm not really with you. But thank you. I'm just trying to get home.'

'Well, I'll be damned! The poor kid's just trying to get home. No more than across the road! Sure and we'll get you across some way. Make way, make way, let her through, you buggers. Move yer body back, Pat O'Riley or you'll feel my fist on yer nob. Fancy a kid not being able to cross the road to her own place.'

She battled her way through until I was landed by the railings on the other side. Behind these stood a woman who called out, 'Here, I know who she is. I'll take her in and give her a glass of water,' and I managed to thank the fat woman again before going with the other one along her garden path. 'I must get home,' I told her, 'because the Yorkshire puddings will burn.'

'Good gracious me! However did you get mixed up with that lot? Come through the house and out of the back door. Then we're only a few steps from Acton Street. I'll take you. They'll not hold me back, jamming the streets like this. It was good of that woman though. It just goes to show.' I agreed about the goodness of the woman and did not bother trying to interpret what it went to show. When we had managed to reach Acton street and crossed to our back arch entrance, this woman wanted to complete *her* good deed by taking me to our back door and delivering me up to my Aunt. I don't know how I stopped her, but I knew what would happen if my Aunt should be further distracted from her supervision of the Sunday dinner. I knew the trouble already brewing in that region. The woman kept her eye on me until I pressed down the sneck of the back yard door, then waved as I opened it, and at that very moment my Aunt must have opened the gas oven door — she used the gas oven in summer — because, as I entered the greenhouse she was placing on the oven top the first tray of nine individual Yorkshire puddings.

'Just where have you been?' she asked without looking round.

'Nowhere. I came straight home, honestly.'

'Then what's happening at Sunday School to be finishing late?'

'It didn't. I couldn't get along because of the procession.'

A second tray of puddings was on the oven top alongside the dinner plates and she was transferring puddings to plates with a carving fork. Tom hovered near waiting to carry in the plates. Auntie glanced round. 'What procession? Surely the Labour lot haven't sunk so low as to have demonstrations on Sundays?'

Tom intervened. 'No need to get upset. It's not Labour. It's the Catholics. I did say when we heard the band, but you insisted it was the Salvation Army.'

'The Catholics!' This expressed much, but she looked at her puddings. They were sinking by the second. 'Get to the table,' she ordered. 'I've had to fiddle no end with the oven just waiting for you. I won't have them ruined.'

Of the eighteen puddings, Cyril usually ate five, Tom and Mr Dyson four each, and my Aunt and I made do with two and a half apiece. They were always delicious. As she strode into the kitchen carrying three plates on a tray, Tom following with two, the three of us waiting at the table were already aware of sounds outside. Cyril and I were watching torsos edging past the two gaps between the pairs of lace curtains. I thought, it's still very close, nothing but a wall and two narrow windows between us and it. My Aunt spoke as the gravy boat was being passed round,

'Whatever is this rabble passing our house right on Sunday dinner time?'

There was a long pause before Mr Dyson, pouring carefully a little gravy into each of the four wells in his puddings, said. 'I believe it's the first Corpus Christi procession to be held in Middlesbrough. Our customers were discussing it. The Bishop expected a turn out of ten thousand.'

We digested this along with our puddings in a silence broken only from outside. It continued until Auntie had brought in the meat, already carved, and the vegetables. She served out the meat. We helped ourselves to the rest. Some of the ten thousand were still darkening our windows. The chanting would rise, then fall and vanish before being taken up again.

There was much I wanted to know when I felt recovered enough to ask. The silence would provide a chance, for too much food was consumed during the Sunday meal to allow time for trivial conversation. I swallowed my first piece of meat, then said,

'Is it French?'

Auntie, of course, wanted to know what on earth I was talking about.

'The language they're singing. It's foreign.'

Mr Dyson gave his genteel laugh and said no, not French but Latin, the language used in much of the Catholic services. I was astounded and wanted to know how long it took the people to learn it.

'They don't learn it. They understand the meaning without the words. They memorise some of it from childhood. It's hardly likely they're all chanting the same bits. It doesn't matter. There are songs without words, you know.'

We didn't. Nor did we understand why he laughed again. But I knew what he meant when he added, 'Do you always listen to the words when your ministers offer up their lengthy prayers?'

Before Auntie could reply to this, I asked him what the word meant, the one he'd used for the name of the procession.

'You mean Corpus Christi?'

'Yes.'

'It means the body of Christ.'

We chewed beef. Cyril, who was about ready for more, scraped his knife along his plate gathering up the remains of the gravy. Auntie glared at him. The low chanting continued, monotonous. She rose, took Cyril's plate and returned with an extra piece of beef on it. She settled down to finish her portion and said,

174

'I don't know what the town is coming to! When I remember the days . . .' We had to wait a minute while she chewed. 'The days when the town always elected a Liberal. Havelock Wilson, then Penry Williams. I can remember when Lloyd George visited Middlesbrough. What a day that was! He wiped the floor with the Tory man, Sadler. He made fun of his fancy waistcoats, and rightly so. There was work in those days for honest men who wanted it and were ready to give as much and more than what they got. Honesty was the best policy and people always held to that. Now we have men not content with their wages to help get the town on its feet again after the war. So hordes of Irish Catholics come who will work for next to nothing. Just look at them!'

In fact there were now only intermittent stragglers left to look at, the tail end of the procession. Still, a multitude had passed by.

While the apple pie and custard were being served, I got in my question.

'What do they mean by the body of Christ? Jesus hasn't a body like ours now. It's a spirit body, not one of flesh and bone.'

Naturally, the answer came from Mr Dyson.

'The Catholics, Roman or Anglo, would agree with that. But they believe the spirit body can still inhabit matter like bread and reside in the tabernacle in their churches. When they go to the service which you call the Lord's Supper, they partake of this body.'

'How do you mean?'

'They eat it.'

'Cannibals,' said Cyril.

'What is the tabernacle?'

'Didn't you see it? I heard you say you were caught up. This is the first time in Middlesbrough that they have carried it through the streets.'

'You mean that white tent?'

'Where people get such heathen ideas from I don't know,' said my Aunt.

'But it's in the Bible,' I argued. 'In the Old Testament, anyway. Haven't you read about the tabernacle and the Ark inside it, and inside that the holy shew bread that

David forced the priest to give him and his men to eat, although it should be eaten only by the High Priest.'

'Were they hungry?' asked Cyril.

'Yes.'

'Then I'd have done the same. I'd have stolen it, never mind having a chat with a priest on the matter.'

'Cyril, watch your tongue, you know nothing about it.'

'He is still entitled to his point of view,' said Mr Dyson. 'The shew bread came from a pagan custom of putting out food to propitiate a god.'

'There you are. A heathen custom, as I said.'

'But one can still trace analogies, Miss Drinkhall, between that and the crucified body of Christ which the Catholics wish to become part of, or the other way round, at their Eucharist. Of course it might be seen as an interpretation of the cycle of life in all of nature, if that suits you better?' Auntie showed no sign that it did. She was obviously enjoying her apple pie. She was fond of apples in any form. Mr Dyson had not quite finished.

'And then, again, it is an embodiment of their search after the mystery. Their quest for the Holy Grail, if you like. Their desire to know the unknowable.'

'How far will they get?'

'What, in their search, you mean?'

'No. I mean the procession. How far will it get?'

'Back to the Cathedral, I suppose. A round tour. There isn't anywhere to end except at the beginning.' And this profundity was what he left us with because the following Saturday he gave Auntie a week's notice.

His firm had called him elsewhere and during that week she told and re-told everyone what a model lodger he had been. Why a man of his worth should be forced to take up his bed and walk to the ends of the earth (Newcastle, to be exact) she failed to understand. She said as much to Mr Dyson who told her that only by going from branch to branch could he ever hope to reach the top of the tree.

His leaving so depressed her that, before seeking a successor, she took me to have tea with the undertaker, Mr Whittingham, and his wife.

'He invited me to go sometime to see their new house between Ormesby and Nunthorpe. Mary says it's almost as grand as Miss Jonson's. Undertakers do well because the dying are always with us and the money's pretty sure these days with the penny a week death policies. If your mother had left your father alone, he'd have overcome his dislike of the job and be still working for Mr Whittingham or even setting up on his own.'

She was right about the house. The lawn was as large as a field but with the grass all shaven, and to one side a swing, a see-saw and a tree. I played with his three children on the first two and desperately wanted to climb the other. I doubt whether I could have pulled myself onto even the lowest branch, yet of late I had been plagued by this compulsion to climb a tree. But the Whittingham children did not climb theirs. They said their father liked a tree on the lawn, but he didn't want them to break either the branches or their necks. The boy said, 'He doesn't like the idea of making coffins for us,' and I suppose I should have laughed.

Two weeks later Mr Rouney arrived. The fact of his elevated status had preceded him as Auntie put all her friends and neighbours in the picture. He was a school attendance officer recommended by the borough Education Authority. Reactions to this news varied. Mary Kitching, living with her husband a childless life in Linthorpe, had never heard of such. Minnie, also childless, but living not far from us, had certainly heard of them.

'It's a good thing you don't live in Jervaulx Street,' I heard her say. 'And what about the Lower Lane? People down there will take a poor view of one of those men living almost on their doorsteps.'

I knew what she meant. Our school was visited once a week by the attendance officer, not always the same one. He would arrive about nine-thirty, examine the register, count the children present as a check, make a note of any absentee whose absence had not been satisfactorily accounted for, and then say, 'Right. I'll be round there this morning and chase them up.' Auntie, accustomed to me going to school when she thought I should be in bed, had no patience with this remark.

'Where would you find a more respectable lodger than one employed by the Education Authority? Of course he'll be unpopular with women who keep their girls at home to mind babies, or their boys to earn a copper or two doing paltry jobs. Or mothers too lazy to get out of bed to see their infants off to school. They're breaking the law as well as being lazy and dishonest. You surely don't encourage that, Minnie?'

'No. But there's such a thing as a woman being too ill to crawl out of bed. As well as the business of childbirth.'

'Which we needn't go into, Minnie.'

The moment I saw Mr Rouney I recognised him. It was he whose appearance through the classroom door caused Miss Gibson to come amongst us and immerse herself in our work. From this position she answered his questions. No other visitor affected her thus, and when she had had to introduce him to Miss Sykes, I'd thought I detected a reason. He had taken Sylvia's hand in his and held it while he chattered at her; and, since he had so much to say, he might have held it for the entire lesson had not Miss Gibson intervened. As for his appearance, Auntie had described it to Minnie with reasonable accuracy. A fine, strongly built man, black-haired, dark-complexioned, a bit of Irish or Italian in him, she wasn't sure which. This was puzzling since she habitually connected red hair with Irish extraction, black hair with Italian. The matter was clarified when she added that, like the Irish, he seemed fond of a joke, a little too fond, perhaps, for a man in his position.

When he first saw me, Mr Rouney cupped my chin in his left hand, looked hard at me and said. 'You creature with the eyes.' He then glanced at my Aunt, back at me, and one of his dark eyes closed in a slow motion wink. 'All eyes, isn't she? Where's her face?' he asked Auntie who was clearly unprepared. 'I'll take one of your cases upstairs, Mr Rouney, if you'd like to follow with the other.' But Mr Rouney picked up a case in each hand and said, 'Certainly not, my dear young lady. Certainly not. You lead the way and show me the chamber where I am to sleep the sleep of the chaste.' I crept half way upstairs to listen; it was so silly calling my Aunt young. I had calculated her age to be forty-two. He seemed to be grumbling about the bed. 'What a bed, Miss D. What a sight for sore eyes!' Whatever, I thought, could be wrong with the bed? Auntie prided herself on her beds and the way she kept them.

'How thankful I am, Miss D. that you're an old-fashioned landlady, a young one of course, who doesn't deny her lodgers the comfort of a real double bed. What matters in the bedroom, I always say, is the bed. If the room's too small, then throw out the rest of the furniture but keep the double bed. I've no patience with this new fad for beds they call single. What a man needs is a bed to stretch in, roll over in, throw himself about in, bounce up and down on, not an object as confining as a coffin. I think you and I have the same tastes, Miss D. It will be a real pleasure to use this bed.'

I was not surprised that my Aunt said nothing for a minute or two. Then she found her voice.

'I'm glad you like the bed, Mr Rouney. I can assure you it will be kept clean. I hope you don't mind if I ask you to use my full name?'

'Certainly not, though I'll have to know it. What is your Christian name?'

'Oh no, no. I didn't mean that. I should prefer you to call me Miss Drinkhall. I shouldn't like other lodgers to take advantage, you see. Especially young Cyril.'

'Of course, I see. We must not have young Cyril taking any advantage. One never knows, with the very young. I only wanted to assure you that I am on your side, Miss Drinkhall, and I hoped we should see eye to eye in most things. And I don't want you to think me selfish in what I said about the bed. Wanting a bed like this all to oneself! It does sound ungenerous.'

'Well, it is customary, so I'm told, for gentlemen lodgers to share a room of this kind. Now, if you'll excuse me, I must get on with the dinner. There is some hot water in the jug. At least, it *was* hot. I'm afraid it will have cooled off by now. And a jug full will be brought to you each morning. My previous lodger, Mr Dyson, appreci-ated that.'

'Don't worry, my dear Miss Drinkhall, so will I. So will I,' and this was the last I heard as I made myself scarce before she reached the lower landing. I had found in

Mr Rouney a focal point for my general dislike of people.

Auntie's routine allowed for no flexibility regarding mealtimes. She arranged that we should eat our meals together, and breakfast was almost a ceremony with bacon and eggs for the men and shredded wheat for us. Mr Rouney had one idiosyncrasy about food — he would eat no fat which annoyed my Aunt because of the waste and because she deplored pickiness over good food. It annoyed her even more when Mr Rouney found it a subject for obscure jokes.

'My dear Miss Drinkhall,' he would begin, 'I'm greased enough inside. All my parts in perfect working order. I can prove it to you if you'd like me to.' He would then wink at Cyril who was too busy chewing to say anything but, 'Haw, haw, very funny that. Very funny indeed, I must say.'

Tom's eyes were always on his plate whenever this joke was repeated, and Auntie would remark, 'That may be so, but all the flavour and the goodness of the meat is in the fat. You miss a lot.' Then came the time when Mr Rouney had a reply for this. 'So I miss a lot, do I? But I'm not the only one who misses out. If I may say so, you miss a lot, Miss Drinkhall, by remaining a Miss.'

The silence was like a shock before she replied. Then, 'I've seen enough, thank you, quite enough to know what I miss, and I prefer to miss it.'

I knew she was angry, but not as angry as when he had a few words to say about school.

'So you're at Victoria Road School. In Miss Burns' class?'

'Oh no,' Auntie interposed. 'Miss Gibson's. She's been there almost two years.'

'Merciful heavens!' he feigned shock, then continued in almost a whisper. 'However have you survived two years under that rule of thumb?'

'Martha's come on very well. Very well indeed under Miss Gibson. She doesn't mind her strictness. After all, it must be very difficult for teachers having such new-fangled stuff to teach — things *we* never heard of. Martha's to take the scholarship next year.'

'Ah, the scholarship! That pinnacle of achievement. And

with what in view, may one ask?'

'In view?'

'Yes. What have you in mind for her if she should pass?'

'Well, the High School, I suppose. Her mind's set on that.'

'Set on going to the High School? Where you'll have a headmistress who might as well be called a headmaster? Believe me, Miss Gibson may be more man than woman, being a regular martinet, but even she has feminine charm compared with that dragon in charge of the Girls' High School. They'd need call her Biddy. Bismark would be more fitting. I'd be surprised if she allowed that her girls had fathers, let alone brothers in the school next door. What *are* they going to make of you there?' and his eyes scoured me in a search, it appeared, for my future fate.

My Aunt was ironing a handkerchief. She folded it and plonked the iron down heavily to press in the fold. I noticed her lips, clamped together like the iron on the handkie, holding back words.

Ages afterwards, it felt like, she opened them.

'Mr Rouney, it's not right to speak like that of Miss Bedford. She was headmistress of the Girls High School before we came to Middlesbrough and is highly respected. Everyone speaks well of her.'

'That depends on what they want their daughters to be.'

The subject was raised once more when we were sitting at breakfast with Mr Rouney meticulously cutting an edge from a rasher of his bacon.

The fat had been removed, melted down into dip, and my teeth were breaking through a piece of crisp, salty bread which had been fried in that dip.

'There's no fat left on that!' Auntie's voice lashed out like a whip! And she hadn't used his name, I noted.

'Just the tiniest thread. Invisible to your eyes, perhaps, but mine are sharp.'

Hatred flared in me. I came blundering to my Aunt's support. 'Women are not picky like that. You weren't right, Auntie, when you said men were easier to satisfy than women.'

Her nerves were already on edge and I expected to be told to mind my own business, not to speak unless spoken to, and so on. What I was quite unprepared for was the effect of my remark on Mr Rouney. He fell into a fit of laughter. His knife and fork clattered to his plate while he fished from his pocket one of the ironed handkerchiefs in order to wipe his eyes. He might choke, I thought, and a good thing if he does. His will be one forehead I shall never kiss. Eventually he controlled himself and wiped the mess from his lips.

'Did you really say that, Miss Drinkhall? And she's remembered? Now I know what goes on behind those eyes, don't I, young lady? You can take my word for it, she doesn't need to go to the High School to learn how many beans make five. She'd stir up a hornet's nest there, and no mistake.'

What do I know, what don't I know, what ought I to know? The whole business and his laughter made my head whirl.

'I really don't see what there is to laugh at, Mr Rouney.' My Aunt rose to clear away the bacon plates. 'I suppose you will have your joke no matter what's said. Martha was only referring to your pickiness over fat. Anyone with sense knows the value of fat as well as its being the tastiest part of the bacon.'

'But I'm not referring to fat, Miss Drinkhall. I'm referring to this niece of yours who has more in her head than you give her credit for. I still think she shouldn't be aiming at that nursery for blue stockings. She wants to enjoy herself.'

'That's one reason why I want to go. They do enjoy themselves.'

He sat round the corner of the table from me. For the second time he took my chin in his hand and brought his face close to mine. The red mouth, yellow teeth and smell of masticated bacon revolted me. Rage urged me to wrench away my chin, open my teeth and plant them over his hand, or finger at least. I don't think I had been one for biting people as some infants are, but at that moment I longed for the teeth and jaws of the crocodile in Peter Pan to have taken off this man's hand by the wrist. I did nothing, remembering that Auntie had to have lodgers and ones who paid on time, which Mr Rowney did. He gripped my chin, shook my head back and forth, laughed, then let me go.

'You'll find out. You're not really one of them, though you might like to think so. Anyway, they're a bunch of snobs, and that you'll certainly learn to your sorrow, if you get there. You live, my dear girl, and learn.'

From then on I avoided him. I removed myself from room to room in order never to be alone with him. I don't think my Aunt noticed. I heard her tell Hannah that, unfortunately, he was not a second Mr Dyson and how the Education Authority could employ someone who talked as he did about teachers was beyond her. He was never happy unless he was making a joke out of something or someone, and Hannah said she'd read of such men. They were like babies, really, always drawing attention to themselves and the best thing to do was to ignore them. The only cure would be having children of their own.

I did not tell Hannah how utterly I disagreed with her or with what she had read on the subject. To have him for a father! I could not speak about my feelings which were, I realised, beyond expressing. The indefinable thing which prompted me never to allow him and me to be alone together, this I found impossible to put into words. 'Now I know what goes on behind those eyes.' What had he seen, so deeply implanted that it could not be forced even into my own consciousness? The thought that he knew me better than I knew myself was unutterably disturbing. Nor could I ignore him, as Hannah had suggested, because my mind was on how to keep out of his way. I believed he was aware of my manoeuvres and that he saw this as another joke or some sort of game, like cat and mouse; that he would allow it to go on for just as long as he chose and no longer. Therefore, the whole affair came to have the quality of a nightmare and from there, an identification with the Thing. He came to stand for whatever it was from which there was no escape precisely because it came, as he had seen, from inside me. And from somewhere inside me, I had begun to think, sprang the Thing. I could no longer believe that witches swooped out of the void to gather me to them. Had I not memorised those words of

Cassius, 'The fault, dear Brutus, is not in our stars, but in ourselves'? These thoughts churned themselves in my mind but could never be told to anyone.

He caught me at last. In recollection I can only say that there was no one about, that I thought I had the house to myself. Even so, I was in the tool shed underlining prepositions and copying out a passage which had to be changed into the future tense. The ink in the bottle was at so low a level that a lot of time was being wasted tipping it up, and I remembered another bottle in the kitchen desk. I ran through, lifted the lid, fished it out and had turned to fly back when he stepped out from behind the half-opened door. Nothing was said. I was lifted until my toes left the ground. I was aware of red in his eyes and the red cavern of his mouth just before it was clamped onto my face. I was drawn into it, for it was large enough to devour me, cheeks, nose, the lot. And for a second, or was it longer, something from the depths of me uncoiled like a loosened spring to meet whatever it was he intended. Then, his great lips, sucking in mine, stopped me from breathing, for my nasal passages, choked with catarrh, were useless. He hadn't reckoned with my reaction to the fear of choking. The only muscular strength I had ever possesed lay in legs developed by the organ pedals. They had let me down of late, especially the right one, but I levered the left one backwards using his great body as a support, and fury lent it strength as I threw the bent knee forward. It landed between his legs where something hard slackened and gave way. A bone, I thought, and I'll break it, and kicked again. As he let me drop, I seized his hand in both of mine and bit it viciously with my large front teeth and saw blood well up above the thumb joint.

'You devil! You little devil! They'll make a teacher out of you yet.' These words, hoarse, thick, snarled under his breath followed me through the doorway and continued to repeat themselves as I fled into the W.C. and shot the bolt.

That was Thursday. On Friday morning my Aunt was moody. No words were spoken as she poured hot water over my shredded wheat and drained it with the aid of a saucer. Cyril and Tom were eating poached eggs on toast. I was aware of Mr Rouney's absence, but would not utter his name to ask why. We ate in silence, Auntie buttering slice after slice of bread for Cyril to spread with marmalade as compensation for the lack of bacon. At last her grievance could be contained no longer.

'I just don't know what to make of Mr Rouney going off like that.' Relief flooded me.

'Do you mean he's gone?'

'By half-past seven. Asked if he could possibly have his breakfast by a quarter past, putting the whole of my black-leading morning out of joint. Inconsiderate, to say the least.'

'Didn't he have to give a week's notice, like Mr Dyson?' I might have been a wasp, the way Auntie regarded me.

'Whatever are you talking about? He hasn't gone for good. Only for the weekend. He's never mentioned having weekends away. It can't be the food. He's always praised it on Saturdays and Sundays. However, it's one less to be cooked for and washed up after. If only he'd said where he was going, and why.'

'Didn't you ask him?'

'It was hardly my place to do that, although I should have thought it a matter of common courtesy for him to tell me.'

'Some woman, I suppose,' Cyril suggested, and, since this produced no tirade, I wondered if Auntie thought there might be a woman in it, though why there might be, and why Cyril should suppose that, I couldn't imagine. Except to be married, in which case why was he coming back here to live? Swallowing the shredded wheat was painful. My throat was swelling again and I should have to gargle. It looked as if Hazel and Tony must stay home from school. Thank goodness Greystones had no attendance officer!

'Did he say anything to you, Martha? You were in last night while I was over at Mrs Burt's.'

I coughed up a chunk of cereal.

'No,' I lied, 'I was in the shed.'

'You spend too much time in there.'

'I don't. It's nice there in the summer. I'm making it into a den, I'd like to live and sleep out there. Camping. Like Laura's going to do with the Guides. May I, Auntie?'

185

Naturally, I knew this would be ignored.

'Well, I just don't know what to think.'

'It might,' said Tom, 'have something to do with his work, and that would have to be confidential. He won't be able, you know, to tell you about it.' And that hit the nail on the head with regard to my Aunt and me. I couldn't tell her about it either. I could easily imagine the brief conversation.

'Last night Mr Rouney kissed me.'

'Oh, did he?' Preoccupied.

'I didn't like it.'

'That's nothing fresh. You always were peculiar that way. I don't believe you even like me to kiss you.'

'It was horrible. And why should he want to kiss me?'

The first bit she would disregard. 'Either he was trying to be fatherly, or he was teasing you. And you know perfectly well what you're like about that.'

'He called me a little devil.' She would register shock.

'For goodness' sake, Martha, whatever were you doing?'

I knew the conversation would never reach that point, for how could I tell her that I bit him? The bite worried me. I thought it might have something to do with his disappearance. That the kick might have been worse than the bite did not occur to me. In twenty years time, but not until then, I would look back and consider the kick. His last remark, 'They'll make a teacher out of you yet,' struck me as nonsense in the context. Whatever had kicking and biting to do with being a teacher? Mr Rouney gave you the impression that he disliked teachers, but surely not because they kicked and bit. He disliked Miss Gibson, he disliked Miss Bedford because . . . I could not find the adverbial clause of reason. I did not know it. 'But you ought to know,' someone had said. A reason did exist which I must find, and also why he'd said. 'You're not one of them.' I would not think of it. And yet I must. If I got to the High School — it was always 'if' now — would I not be one of them, the thing I desired above all else to be? A somebody. Somebody who could take life easy. What had he seen in me that would one day grow and surface? Like those bulbs?

In Assembly Miss Byers said she had very good news for

186

the school. Four girls had gained scholarships to one of the two High Schools and six who had passed stage one were going to Hugh Bell Central School. That was one third of Miss Gibson's class, a fine record and a tribute to her training. Those who were staying on here would certainly benefit, too, from that training. More girls were finding good work as shop assistants in the large, expanding shops like Hinton's, Wright's, Newhouse's and Dickson and Benson's. Even cashiers' posts were now being given to girls. I could always do that, went through my head. Sit in that little glass tower in Newhouse's to receive the wooden containers that whizzed along the wires like flying coaches, carrying coins, notes and bills. I would work out the exact change, scribble my name on the bill, push both into the container, screw on the lid, pull a lever and send it flying back to the right counter, to the assistant whose job was not on the same level as mine, to tease out, straighten and give to the customer. All day long the containers whirred back and forth from all the different counters, like a spider's web full of life. I could do that if I didn't get to the High School. My Aunt seemed to be on familiar terms with John Newhouse. At least she often said so, though I had no idea why she should be.

Thinking about this, I missed the names of the girls being read out, but back in the classroom I learned quickly enough. Edith Turnball would get her bicycle, Marjorie Burns, Gladys Morton and a girl who had only been at our school since Christmas. Never for one moment, we had often heard, had Miss Gibson expected her to pass. She had not taught her long enough. Nor had I expected to make friends with her, temporarily, as it now turned out. Her christian name was Olga, but we were unable to get our tongues round her strange surname because her father was foreign. I had actually been home with her twice to a room above a shop in Linthorpe Road not far from the Cenotaph. I remember the narrow staircase and three turns with small square landings. They lived in one room with a tiny bedroom fireplace and a gas stove on one wall and shelves of books on the other. To wash up they carried water up the stairs and got washed, Olga told me, in some outside place in the yard beside the W.C.

Only in retrospect did I consider the limited space and lack of reasonable amenities. At the time I noticed only the yards of books and wished I could exchange all our rooms for their one.

At playtime I asked Olga if she would tell me about the High School when she went there. It was only then that I learned she was a Catholic and would be going to the Convent.

'Shouldn't you be at a Catholic school?' I asked as we propped ourselves up on a ledge that ran round the bicycle shed, like two monks on their misericords.

'I was at St Philomena's, but my parents wanted me to pass the scholarship and Mother knew Miss Byers. Mother's English and only turned Roman Catholic when she married Father. He's Polish. The children of Catholics aways have to be Catholics, but when I grow up, I'm going to change all that.'

My interest in Olga rose. Here was a girl who aspired to higher things than teaching or being a cashier. I wanted to know how she would effect such a change.

'Well, you can't really say, not at my age. I'll have to go to America to learn how. Dad wanted to emigrate to America but Mother wouldn't go. Over there Catholics and Protestants go to the same schools and no one fusses about your religion. It doesn't matter much, as it does here.' This was a new aspect of America and one I had not considered. What were my own parents doing about their religion? No letter had mentioned the subject, nor had my Aunt. Had my mother and Bob given up Chapel? My father, to the best of my knowledge, had never gone there. But I could not imagine life without Chapel.

'But you have to have a religion, don't you?' It was an argument I felt obliged to make.

'I suppose so. But people shouldn't fuss about it and insist on theirs being the only true one. Everyone should be able to choose. And I'm going to do something about it when I grow up.'

The head monitor was ringing the hand bell and everyone was scattering towards the long flight of stairs at one end of the building or the senior girls door at the other. Lines were being formed ready for the march in. My thoughts had left Mr Rouney and dwelt on Olga who did not fall within the category of those I now disliked. She neither skipped nor threw balls about; nor wished to cross her outstretched arms, join hands with a girl and whizz round in giddying circles; nor try cartwheels nor think about owning bicycles. Nor, when I'd been to her room, had she wanted to play fathers and mothers. We'd played a word game called Scrabble at which her mother was extremely clever and her father, for my benefit, had said a few sentences in Polish. When we grew up I might go with Olga to America and change the world. In the meantime I would write to my mother and Bob about the need to go to Chapel and sometime I would go and look inside a Catholic Church which Olga said were never locked, as Chapel was.

After tea that day I told Cyril he could not have the organ for an hour. I looked for Polish songs but could find none, so I tried to play all the Irish ones, 'Killarney', 'Mavoureen's the flower', 'The Mountains of Mourne' and, several times over, 'The Londonderry Air'. The Irish were Catholics as well as the Poles.

Chapter Seventeen

Mr Rouney returned on Sunday night, apologetic enough to tell Auntie not to bother with supper for him but quite prepared, however, to sit down to what was on the table. Throughout the meal I did not meet his eye though I saw a piece of sticking plaster over the base of his thumb. I could sense an initial diffidence, but this faded as the meal progressed. My Aunt offered him the last egg and tomato sandwich which he politely refused but her gesture seemed to open up the way for conversation.

'I hope my going off so suddenly did not inconvenience you too much, Miss Drinkhall.'

My Aunt intimated that she liked to have a little notice regarding a change in routine. Of course, if it were something quite out of the blue . . .'

'You might say that, my dear Miss Drinkhall. I went to see my mother in Blackpool.'

'Oh!' She was plainly taken aback. I sensed that she had never connected Mr Rouney with a mother, though I saw no reason why not. She had had a mother until a year and a half ago and he really looked no older than she did. Perhaps forty-four, I estimated.

'I hope she's not ill.'

'No. Not ill. My Mother's never ill. I had to see her about her will.' Instantly my Aunt was won over.

'You have my sympathy there, Mr Rouney. I've been through it myself. My own Mother died intestate and, as I've said so often, you really can't talk to your mother about making a will. It sounds as if you're waiting for her to die.'

'I have no misgivings on that score regarding *my* Mother. She thinks about nothing else but her will. She has a fresh one drawn up or a codicil added at least once a month, being determined to buy her way into heaven. The trouble is she can't make up her mind which good cause is most likely to do this for her, the Salvation Army, the

190

S.P.C.K., Doctor Barnardo's or the Girl Guides.'

Nothing could have more effectively erased Mr Rouney's shortcomings from my Aunt's mind than this unusual family problem. It was meat and drink to someone who loved to pass things on, elaborate a little here, detract a little there.

'Oh dear, I'm truly sorry, Mr Rouney. Personally, I think people should make provision for their own first and foremost. I have always believed that charity begins at home.' And Mr Rouney naturally said he couldn't agree more.

In this manner the breach between them was healed, and, during the last week of school before the four weeks summer holiday, the whole business of how people should leave their earthly goods was investigated thoroughly in the kitchen of 85 Park Lane; and all the while I did not know whether to believe Mr Rouney or not. A visit to a sick mother was one thing, a plausible excuse; but a visit to a mother who changed her will all the time was another matter altogether, being hardly an excuse that would readily spring to mind. Perhaps he really had been to Blackpool and the kiss and the bite were coincidental. As it turned out, I did not have to consider for long. His days with us were numbered and all because of Mrs Burt's determination to do something about me. To give me a nice change, she explained, and to give Auntie a bit of peace.

On the Saturday which ended the first week's holiday, she invited me to have tea with them and to stay there overnight; then to share Laura's Sunday morning treat and return home in time for Sunday dinner. She saw no reason why I should not miss Chapel and Sunday School for once. Chapel at night was quite enough for any little girl. And, if I liked staying with Laura, I could go again, perhaps often, she went on with rising enthusiasm. Auntie acquiesced, although I said it seemed silly sleeping at Laura's when her house was just across the back arch. I said this again and more emphatically, on learning that I was to share her bed. Why couldn't I simply change places with Laura; go to sleep in her bed and let her come to sleep with Auntie? Because she was one of the very few children

I knew who had a bed to herself. Most of them slept either with adults or with other children, and when neighbours tended to pity Laura for being an only child, I thought that having a bed to herself must be ample compensation.

As Laura and I drank our cocoa in bed, I said, 'You're lucky. Luckier than the rest of us and luckier even than the Fairy Queen. She had to share a bed.'

'Who with?'

Laura was now in Standard Six, but she did not take seriously Miss Gibson's rules of grammar. Why worry your head about where unimportant words like prepositions went? As long as people understood you, what did it matter? Her little difficulty with enunciation, short-tongued, people called it, together with her pigtails and artless expression seemed to cut a year or two off her age and reflect what was indeed a placid nature.

'Oberon,' I told her.

'Who's that?'

'The Fairy King.'

'Were they married?'

I found myself unable to answer this with certainty, so I said I supposed so.

'Well then, they *would* sleep in the same bed, wouldn't they? All married people do.'

'But,' I persisted, 'Titania didn't like it. She foreswore his bed and company.'

'Meaning what?'

'She wouldn't sleep in his bed or have anything to do with him.'

'How silly.'

'I don't know. It would be nice to sleep alone. Your dreams might be different.'

'I never dream.'

'Never?'

'No. I just sleep.'

'Lucky thing.' My mind slanted away at a tangent.

'Minnie Gatenby and her husband have two bedrooms and no one else in the house. And I don't think they sleep in the same room.'

'Well, that's not right of them, is it?'

Again I supposed not, but wondered why such an issue

as sleeping in the same bed or not should be either right or wrong.

'There's nothing about it in the Commandmants,' I argued, 'though perhaps that's because they slept in tents.'

'We're going camping sometime,' said Laura, 'Dad's going to fix a folding tent on his bicycle. When you get a bicycle, you can come camping with us.'

'And all sleep in the same tent?'

'Yes. It's what they do in Girl Guides. Mother says you should have joined the Brownies and then become a Guide. She says that's the sort of thing you need. I'll be a Girl Guide next year. I'm going to sleep now,' and she turned on her side away from me.

'They might suffocate,' I said, turning the other way, my face an inch or two from the wall.

'Who?' Her voice was muffled under the blankets.

'All those Girl Guides in one small tent. There wouldn't be enough air. I'm sure I should suffocate, anyway.'

But Laura was asleep.

For some time I turned from side to side, straightening the pillow, pulling it under my shoulders, unravelling strange pieces of bedclothing that got entangled with my nightdress, until finally I fell into dreams from which I woke at intervals, repeated the performance with the sheets and blankets, then drifted into another dream. My Aunt was in the background of them all, not separated from me until the last, and in that she was seated at the back of one of the new buses and I was about to leave her. Her facial features were like cast iron, set in a mould of grim disappointment, and I dwelt on them with more concentration than I had ever done in my waking hours — the greying hair that frizzed of its own accord when she washed it, the bushy eyebrows above the spectacle rims, the wide rounded chin and tightly closed lips with that little mole to the right of them and the single, wiry hair growing from it. I took in all the features of her face and her expression, hard with grief and disapproval. Remorse welled up in me.

'Goodbye, Auntie,' I said, 'I'll see you in the morning,' and waited for a reply.

No sound came from her lips, nor flicker of response

from her countenance, and I walked unsteadily to the front of the bus and down the steps to where another bus was waiting facing the other way. I paced the narrow gap between these two exceptionally high buses searching for the steps by which to mount the second one. There were no steps, nor door, not even a crack. Just green sides with windows above. Panic gripped me and I scurried back through the tunnel, and there saw a step and a door at the other end. But before I could alight, a roar from the engines shook both buses sideways. They rocked unsteadily, then moved away in opposite directions. Auntie's mask-like face behind the glass passed me by and I was left in the middle of the road with no one and nothing in sight.

I was used to that dreadful business of telling yourself that this is only a dream yet being unable to break away from it and waken. After several agonising attempts I managed it and immediately was conscious of the lateness of the morning and the unaccustomed silence. The Woodenheads in their file crossed my mind. Something was wrong with the morning. Something was about to happen. The light through the thin, drawn curtains was strong and bright, yet Laura lay inert in her half of the bed and no sounds rose from below. Why was no one moving, clattering fire irons, doors, dishes, running the tap or talking? Where were the everday sounds that absorb the night and the dreams and prove them airy nothings?

The unprecedented experience of emerging from a dream into someone else's house was distressing. I felt shackled; trapped in silence, not daring to turn, nor sit up, nor call out. I tried to deal with my quickening heart beat by taking my bearings. We were in the back bedroom facing the yard and the back arch which explained the absence of street noises. But where were Mr and Mrs Burt? For how long must I lie, doing nothing, sandwiched between Laura and the wall? Why was I the only one awake in this lifeless house?

At home, if my Aunt were indeed there and not being driven out of reach in the back of a bus, breakfast would be over and I would be on my way to Chapel where I ought to be, rounding the corner of Woodlands Road and seeing the familiar red brick building appear. Even though we had to sit, unmoved, through the preacher's funny story for the children, then be wearied by his endless praying, there were always the hymns. My enjoyment of those had never dimmed. In any case, anything was better than this irksome need to lie doing nothing because everyone else was asleep. I repeated, mentally, our latest poem learnt about three weeks ago, the summer holiday having by now run two weeks of its course.

> 'Abou-ben-Adam, may his tribe increase,
> Awoke one night from a deep dream of peace,
> And saw, within the moonlight of his room,
> Making it white like a lily in bloom,
> An angel writing in a book of gold. . . .'

I had just reached the line, 'Made of all sweet accord' when a faint sound registered in my left ear. I raised my shoulders a few inches and slewed round my head to see over Laura. And what I saw was the door knob turning ever so slowly. Nothing is more confounding than to see an object which shouldn't move of its own accord, do so; and for a moment the turning knob quite petrified me. Then I remembered that other bedroom where Aunt Gertrude's expressionless eyes must have watched that other knob. Why were bedrooms so secretive that doors must be opened furtively; and who, when this knob had completed its revolution, would stand there spying on us, as if we were doing some forbidden thing? Ought I to be asleep like Laura? I shut my eyes and waited in my own darkness.

'Both still asleep?' a voice whispered.

'I opened my eyes and there was Mr Burt with his round face and bald head — well, there was no hair to be seen from the front.

'Laura is,' I whispered. But at that moment she stirred, as if given the cue, turned on her back, pulled out her arms and looked at the ceiling,

'Wakey, wakey, young lady,' said her father and kissed her forehead. He bent towards me, similarly intentioned, but I switched my head and my ear received the kiss.

'Come along, girls. It's after ten. Sit up for your Sunday

treat,' and he extended, in each hand, a bar of Fry's chocolate in a dark blue and white wrapper.

So we each sat propped by a pillow against the wrought iron bed head, painted white, and nibbled our way through the bitter chocolate with its firm white filling, and the only sound which broke our mutual silence was a sneck lifting, an outside door slamming and then a peremptory knocking on another door.

'I want to go to the W.C. Laura.'

'All right. Go.'

I clambered over her and pushed my feet into Laura's slippers − her mother had said I need not take any, guessing that I had none to take − and was tiptoeing down the stairs when the sound of my Aunt's voice arrested me. It certainly was her voice, there was no mistaking that, but its tone was unfamiliar − not complaining, not sharp, not even chatty. I struggled to define it from a limited vocabulary, but failed to come up with the word I needed, outraged. On the fourth step up, I clung to the banister and listened.

'If anyone had told me he would turn out like that, I wouldn't have believed them. I'd have said they were deliberately blackening his character.'

After a pause Mr Burt's voice said, 'It's a job, and no mistake.'

Then Mrs Burt's voice, 'He actually *came* into your bedroom?'

'He came into my bedroom.'

'Were you asleep?'

'No, I hardly ever get a night's sleep. You know that,' and Mr Burt's voice rounded that off with, 'It's a good thing, last night, I'd say,'

My thoughts were in a whirl with Tom at the centre. Whatever would he be wanting in Auntie's bedroom? I recalled seeing him naked in the doorway of his own. I strove to keep up with Mrs Burt's words. 'It's hard to know what to say, Auntie. But something must be done.'

'In one way then' said Mr Burt, 'it's a pity we asked Martha for the night. She was always a sort of safeguard, if you see what I mean.'

'Well,' the pitch of Auntie's voice dropped, 'Martha's been acting very strangely with him lately. I've had to pull her up at times for her curt manner. And now, with this happening, you begin to wonder . . .'

'Oh no!' It was almost a scream from Mrs Burt.

'I'd like to tell him to get out today, but I suppose I must give him time to find another lodging. But, depend upon it, the Education Authority will be told. How he comes to be in their employ I can't imagine.'

'But he didn't actually *do* anything? You know what I mean.'

'Of course he didn't. I'd like to have seen him try. It was what he implied, the dirty-minded brute. If you must know,' and it seemed she thought they must, 'he told me, bluntly, that there were easier ways for me to earn a living.'

'Good God!' and with this exclamation, obviously from Mr Burt and I was surprised to hear no reply from my Aunt, they seemed to be moving. At least chairs were shuffled about and someone turned on a tap and I beat a retreat back to the bedroom where Laura asked me if I'd been.

'Yes, but I think I'll get dressed.'

Laura looked up from her comic. 'What about the cup of tea in bed. They're late with it, but Mother always brings one. It's part of the Sunday treat.'

'Oh! Well the chocolate was nice, thank you. But I'd better be going. I shouldn't really miss Sunday School. I have to help with the little ones.'

While voicing these excuses, my mind was turning over the extraordinary affair of Mr Rouney's dismissal. Although I should be profoundly thankful to see him go, I could not understand my Aunt's wrath at being told there were easier ways for her to earn a living. Were these ways only possible if she didn't have me? Like going to Ayton, like giving up our house, like sending me away? Other people suggesting these things had not roused her wrath. And why should he have to go into her bedroom to tell her? Bedrooms were places where strange things happened and I wanted to get out of this one. If only I could sleep in Uncle Watson's allotment under the stars. Or even in our shed amongst the friendly clutter. Where, if Auntie had been last night, she might not have had to suffer an intruder. Still, if that was why he was going, I thought, tying my shoelaces, I'm glad it happened.

There had not been time for matters to simmer down when Cyril told Auntie, while she was sprinkling clothes, that he was taking his holiday the following weekend. He was going to Blackpool on Thursday and wouldn't be back until Tuesday. He was going to see his Ma. Auntie's sprinkler was a vinegar bottle with holes in the screwed-on top. I really thought she was going to throw it at him. In fact, I grabbed her raised arm and said, 'Don't throw. Please don't throw.'

'Take your hand away,' she snapped. 'So this is your idea of a joke, Cyril Binks, is it? This is the thanks I get for all I've done for you. Scrubbing my knuckles bare to clean your pillow cases dyed with that filthy hair oil. This is your gratitude for my putting up with the bedroom walls being plastered with grinning girls, a thing I never allowed even my nephew to do. He had more sense, anyway. This is my reward for treating you as my own son.'

She was certainly on the verge of tears. She had been through a lot lately.

'Well,' she finished, 'all I can say is, you, too, had better go in a week's time,' and her voice broke.

'Don't, Auntie. Please don't,' I said.

'Now look here, Auntie,' it was the first time I had heard him address her so, and she flopped onto a chair and seemed to crumple up, 'cut it out, please. I don't know what I've done.'

'What you're doing is plain enough for any fool to see. You're making fun of me, having one great, big, stupid joke at my expense. Telling me you're going to Blackpool to see your mother and only a month since that wretch, Rouney, spun the same tale. What do you take me for?'

'Let's get this clear,' argued Cyril. 'No one was better pleased than me to see that rotter depart. I don't know whether he had a mother in Blackpool or not. But I have, and now and again I feel I've got to see her, worse luck. There, read that. It's in black and white. A letter from her. On the beg as usual. You know what she spends it on?

198

Well, you can guess. Here, read it, and look at the address and all.'

Before that night, I had come to the conclusion that Cyril was impervious to my Aunt's tirades. A good example of one of those similes we'd had just before the holiday — flowed off him like water off a duck's back. Not like Bob who took everything she said to heart, probably, I had thought, because she stood in the place of his mother. This time she had upset Cyril. He kept urging her to take the letter and she kept shaking her head. She took off her glasses and wiped one eye with the corner of her overall. I could count on one hand, as they say, the number of times I saw her do this through the forty and more years that were still to come, and I knew they were times when she saw life as not worth living. At that time I thought, she'll have to find another lodger. She can't make do without, and what will *he* be like?

She replaced her glasses.

'No, I don't want to read your mother's letter, Cyril. That's none of my business. I'm sorry I'm so upset, but you must admit it's peculiar, these mothers in Blackpool. And what do you mean by worse luck? Whatever your mother's like, she's still your mother and you should want to see her.'

'Well, you see, you don't know her. Anyway I'll go. Have a look at her and get a breath of sea air and have a go on the Maxim Flying Machine and maybe get to the Tower Pavilion and hear the latest hits. I'll play them for you when I get back.'

It sounded like the most stupendous favour and I saw her lips quiver in a weak smile.

At bedtime, when she handed me a mug of Horlicks, she said, as if to herself,

'It might be a good idea to go to Guisborough on Monday. I'll drop Ruby a postcard.

Naturally I wanted to know where Guisborough was and who Ruby was, but had to be content with two facts, that Ruby was a cousin on Grandfather's side who lived in Guisborough and that Auntie had plenty to tell her. Yes, that is so, I thought as I watched her open the top drawer

199

of the kitchen desk and draw out a postcard of Middles-brough Town Hall.

When writing to America, my Aunt naturally used the letter, having so much to report about our health and her difficulties. Otherwise she used the picture postcard for correspondence. So did most people I knew. Postcards were cheap, went through the post for a halfpenny and were the perfect excuse for penning no more than was strictly necessary. During the first quarter of the century they flew to and fro between our house and Nunthorpe, Marton, Guisborough, Great Ayton, Castleton, the U.S.A. and Canada. They came, in the latter two cases, from the erring Joe Davison who wrote nothing but an enigmatic caption beneath the picture itself. What Auntie wrote to Ruby on the back of Middlesbrough Town Hall, I didn't know. But on Saturday morning a postcard of Guisborough High Street shot through the letter box. After reading it she said, 'That's all right then,' and left it on the table while she went to bring in the breakfast. I examined the picture, turned it over and read, 'Dear Blanche, Sorry, working at the Hall until two. Will pick you up at the gardener's lodge in Bow Street on my way back. Mrs Lazenby will see to you till then. Look round the Priory. Love Ruby.'

Chapter Eighteen

I was on top of the world that Monday morning. Fast asleep one moment, wide awake the next, elation flowing through my veins. The blue between the curtains looked promising though I remembered that the weather was no respecter of promises. Fine before eleven, rain before seven was as likely as the other way round, though people usually quoted the latter, setting out in a downpour.

Auntie was clattering about below, but I had been told to wait until she brought some tea. She got on better with the place to herself, she said. So I lay and considered this novel sense of well being. We were going to Guisborough, a place where Ruby lived, a place I didn't know. But who knew what might happen there, and I felt strong and ready, as I shall do on the morning of the scholarship next February, I thought. Suddenly things took a hand in your affairs, pointed the way. I flung off the bedclothes and was standing in my nightgown when the door opened and in she came with the tea.

Making for the station, Victoria Square seemed a painted garden. The flower beds, red or yellow centres, blue and white borders, jumped from their surround of grass, blazed and shouted at me, grew like bushes. I was Alice with the key in my palm, Tom's threepenny bit pressing a tiny imprint into the flesh. Hinton's long window passed us by with Auntie's voice saying, 'Walk properly. There's nothing wrong with you today,' as though aggrieved. We stood for a tram to rumble past. Sparks of burning blue shot from the wires overhead, shot like rockets up to the sky. We caught up with the people alighting from it at the bottom of the long, straight flight of station steps that rose as high as the bridge. As my legs reached the top, my spirits plummeted. I made for a seat and sat, with Auntie's eye fixed upon me. 'It's the steps,' I heard her say, 'and you get over-excited — up one minute, down the next. It's bad for you.'

In the train I felt better. 'No,' she said as we left the docks behind, 'we do not go through Redcar or Castleton. We go to Nunthorpe and a branch line runs from there to Guisborough. No, it doesn't go anywhere else. The line ends at Guisborough. It's a terminus. The train comes back from there.' Like the end of the world, then, or the wood that's there. Either you stay there or you come out the way you went in. This disturbing speculation ended when the train drew into Nunthorpe station. Two ladies got in and Auntie had a talk with the station master through the open window. A friend of mine, she told them as the train pulled out. The next station had bright flower beds and trellises sprayed with small pink roses — Dorothy Perkins, I felt sure.

'Pinchinthorpe,' Auntie said. 'It often wins the prize for the best kept station though Nunthorpe is quite as clean and pretty. This station master will be in with the judges, no doubt.'

'Perhaps they like the name,' I suggested. 'It is a queer one, Pinchinthorpe.' Then, as the train moved off, gathering momentum, so the rhythm of the wheels gathered up the name — PINCHinthorpe, PINCHinthorpe, PINCHinthorpe, and seemed to embrace my senses also. My eyes, fixed on the woman in the opposite corner, saw her shape blur, dissolve, and in her place sat Mike, the boy who had wanted to be a detective, who had tracked down my lost sister at the end of that dreadful day at Redcar.

'Pinchinthorpe,' I said aloud.

'Shut up, you ninny. Never say that word. It's a code word and mustn't be spoken. You pinch instead, though no one must see you do it. I'll pinch you awake.'

'I'm not asleep.'

'That's a lie. You do tell lies. I'll pinch you every time you tell a lie.'

'No. No. I don't. Not any more.'

'You're in a bad dream. Knock out of it, or *you'll* be lost this time. You'll be lost in Guisborough and *I* won't find you. It's the end of the line.'

Horror swirled about me, then lifted me in a rising spiral each turn being punctuated by the voice of Mike — You can only come back — where to — back to Redcar, of course, — no, no, not there — back to nowhere then, or stay in Guisborough at the end of the line — you've been before and you ought to know — I haven't, haven't, haven't — stop pinching me, it's not a lie — stop or I'll fall . . .

I fell, and knew a train had stopped, stopped with a jolt that pitched me forward.

'For goodness' sake, Martha, had you gone to sleep? Pull yourself together. We're there.'

We alighted onto a platform bounded by a trifling wooden structure like a doll's house and, looking beyond it, I saw a long straight hill that resembled the body of a headless lion holding up the sky.

I remember going through a green door to the right and seeing a trestle table to our left stacked with tight frilled lettuces and scalloped cabbages, long dark green pods of beans and plump light green pods of peas, three curved cucumbers and a basket of orange tomatoes. They clamoured for attention, looking exuberantly alive. It's the garden next, I thought. But instead it was a small room with cups, saucers and scones set on a round table. Then our tin with Queen Alexandra's picture on it was planted in the middle while Auntie and a small chubby woman were arguing about the sandwiches. The woman wanted us to keep them for our picnic, Auntie wanted to share them with her now. And when the fuss had subsided and we'd sipped some tea, I heard the woman say, 'This is not the first time you've been to Guisborough, dear.' Auntie answered for me that it was. 'But Harry would bring her to see her great-grandmother. He was at her funeral five years ago. Of course he wouldn't bring her then, but before that. He would surely want his wife and children to see her, a wonderful old lady.'

'I doubt it. He never talked of Guisborough or of his past.'

'Poor thing, you can understand it. His father dying when he was only four and his baby brother at the same time. An epidemic, I suppose from Middlesbrough. Then his mother re-marrying and a step-father. I can see your father in you dear, about the nose and mouth.'

What did she mean? I could not see my father in me. I

could not see him at ten. She was going on about him being a boy, a clever boy, and someone called a vicar took him under his wing. Like a hen, which sounded odd.

'Then his mother died with the birth of her next baby. So sad. The saddest of all deaths, I think.'

'Why do they die?'

That was my question and I often wondered how Mrs Lazenby might have answered it, had she been given the chance. She wasn't, because Auntie rose, thanked her and said we had better go. It would soon wear on to two o'clock and we must be able to tell Ruby that we had seen the Priory. And she would like to buy some of those lovely fresh vegetables, please.

'I'll fill your basket,' said Mrs Lazenby. 'Leave it here and take your tin of sandwiches. Go through this gate and you'll come first to the horse-chestnut. Jim, that's my husband, calls it the eighth wonder of the world. But his present Lordship doesn't see to the trees the way his father did. Spends too much time abroad, I'm sorry to say. Though how much longer his legs will carry him there, or anywhere, is anybody's guess.'

Beyond a stretch of grass rose what I thought was a forest. 'Which one in all that is the horse-chestnut,' my Aunt sensibly asked.

'All of it except of course those limes to the left. The ones that tower above everything. Those are what they call the Monks' Walk. Supposed to take the shape of one of the old stone coffins and surround the burial ground. But that's only a tale. All the same, they are something worth seeing, all eighty-four of them in a double row. You can walk right round between the rows. Then all the rest to the right is the horse-chestnut. Over three hundred and fifty years since the first Sir Thomas Chaloner brought it from Constantinople and planted it there. We have to remember these things when people come sight-seeing, though Jim says there's a good bob's worth of stuff to look at without any information thrown in. When you've seen the horse-chestnut, do the Monks' Walk, then the Priory itself and return into the gardens through the clipped lime hedges and you'll reach the lily pond. You can sit on a seat there for your picnic.'

'What lily pond?' It was the second time I'd spoken; my second question. And even to me it sounded abrupt and rude, as though a lily pond had no right to be there. But Mrs Lazenby seemed unaffected.

'An ornamental pool with water lilies and gold fish. It was the fashion for gentry to have one in their grounds. I'm sure it needs cleaning out. Jim says they're filthy things and he ought to have an under-gardener for such jobs. But there you are. It's a sign of the times, I'm afraid. His Lordship lays all the blame on taxes, but there's some that think otherwise. Still, nothing's been the same since the War.' My Aunt agreed heartily, and on that note of accord we made off over the grass towards the trees. For the fifth time that morning Auntie remarked that the weather was too good to be true, and this time I added that it was not just the weather, but everything. None of it was true. They were thoughts, really, which came out as words and caused Auntie to stop short in her tracks and say, 'Martha, if you're heading for one of your peculiar moods, then pull yourself together because I don't think I can stand it,' We then resumed our progress in silence and approached a wood that turned out, as Mrs Lazenby had said, to be a single tree.

It was not possible for me then to comprehend the unique nature of that tree. Even my Aunt, I think, was mystified. Twelve years later when I came to record details of its dimensions, form and manner of growth, I realised that it had been too massive and too remarkable. The bole, where you could count seven tree arms fused into one, was some thirty feet in circumference. At a height of six feet these arms separated and sprang out to form six huge arches (the seventh had been severed and the wound covered with protective lead.) Twenty feet from the bole these arches turned earthward, met the soft loam, grew sideways for a few feet forming six convenient seats, then, sending down new roots, proceeded skywards again as six towering trees in their own right though still connected to the parent tree at ground level. The circumference of this fringe of offspring measured one thousand and twenty-one feet, and the six arches, each with its network of branches, bore some resemblance to a monastic cellarium.

The tree deserves this mention from a later time. Though long since gone, it had been tended carefully through centuries, and, though not the eighth wonder of the world, it was a magnificent wonder of the locality. That day I could not, and did not need to, assess its stature. The mood my Aunt had tried to avert was now settled on me. This tree was unreal, though I sat on one of the fissured boles and fingered the strange pale green husks — soft unripe spheres whiskered with silky spikes; although I pulled a leaf and counted its nine outstretched fingers, thus repeatedly touching the actual; yet, intangibly, the tree was removed from me and dwelt in a lost and secret world. The same was true of the Monk's Walk, too narrow for us to proceed abreast. The double row of trunks formed a tunnel towering skyward; it was hard to see the top. But as we passed along, I caught glimpses to the right of a wild untidy place where the monks were said to lie. It goes on forever, I thought, then suddenly we were out. Out of the tunnel and confronted by the stones — a hill of them, all shapes and sizes, thrown randomly together, and beyond them, sentinel like, two strange trees.

'Well,' said my Aunt breathlessly, 'what a most peculiar place! And look at *those* two trees. Yews, decidedly. I would know a yew anywhere, Marton churchyard's full of them. But I've never seen one that didn't have branches from the ground upward. Somebody's made a real mess of those. Just look at them!'

I did so and saw two pale naked boles rising to a man's height and each supporting a spherical head of tightly packed dark green foliage. Guardians of the dead, I thought, as Auntie continued with her grievances. 'It's wrong to interfere with the shape of trees. All those lopped limes keeping out the sun. And why can't something be done with all those stones? What a shambles!'

The stones were piled in rank disorder, but someone had been busy with them, carving on them patterns like rows of teeth or parts of leaves or protruberances like grapes, and a wild rose on one. I inched over the pile spider-like, searching, hearing her voice on the edge of consciousness, 'It's people's duty to clear up their mess when they demolish things,' and then I saw the knight.

206

'Here's a knight,' I heard myself call. 'Well, there's some armour and a sword but no head or feet.'

'Well, the head will be somewhere, I suppose. Breaking things up like that.'

'Here.' I was glued hands and feet to my uneven perch. Here was a head, but not the knight's. A woman's.

I stayed on all fours, staring at the wide brow above the sightless eyes; at the sweep of the jaw and the uplifted chin; at the cheek bones firmly marked and the lips set in that kind of smile, the one I knew about, Grannie's, Willie's, pain and release from pain. With a forefinger I touched one of the jaundiced patches — lichen, had I known it — disfiguring her skin. Beautiful, her face was, like the face of a queen, or the queen of heaven, but with leprosy. I straightened my back, placed my hands under the head and tried to prise her up from her bed of stones.

'What on earth are you doing?'

'I can't move it. Come and help me. I'm going to take it home.'

'Of course you can't take it home. They belong to Lord Guisborough.'

'Then why does he leave her here? Why doesn't he put her on a stand in his house?' It was a question she thought too senseless to answer except by a command to come down at once, we must be getting along.

Along suggested the horizontal but, within a minute, we were confronted by the vertical, almost a thousand feet of it. There are some things which, seen or heard for the first time, leave you speechless and that was how the east end of the Priory Church left us. Probably for different reasons. I can imagine my Aunt wondering who was daft enough to build an arch of that height with nothing on either side of it. For that is what they left, and neither of us understood at the time that once there had been more to it! We had to move away over the grass before we could actually view it, the three blue sky shapes framed by the huge dark structure, like a mother holding a twin child on either side of her. And further back still to see patterns above the arch and four towers like pine cones erect against the blue.

Then I saw the boy. I had just counted the five patterns

surmounting the arch — lights had I known the word —that outlined blue shapes of robed and hooded monks, when I saw this boy move across, in front of them, from left to right. He turned, came back to the middle one and stretched out his arms as if to say, 'Look at me. I can see all the world from here!' Then he went back and melted into the stone.

There was a great to-do about this because my Aunt had not seen him. Her eyes weren't half as good as mine, yet, when I told her in excitement and terror because I'd been sure he would fall, she declared that I was seeing things again, which I was, though not in the sense she meant. No one could walk up there, she said. There was nothing to walk on, and the more I insisted, the more vexed she became. Then, causing us to jump out of our shoes, a voice spoke from behind us. If he might be permitted to arbitrate, it said, he could assure us that we were both wrong. My mother was wrong because there certainly *was* something to walk on up there, a passage which had once had a wall on this side of it. He'd walked along it himself a very long time ago; and once, also long ago, he'd seen a boy do it. But *I* was wrong, too, because no one could get up there now, not without a ladder. When the place was opened to the public, the lower steps in each tower had been removed to prevent people from climbing them. Too dangerous, he said, to leave spiral staircases accessible to the public. He took us over to what he called the north tower and the going was slow on account of his walking stick and his trailing leg. Inside, we looked up to the slab of stone which he said was the lowest step, now, of a stairway that spiralled to the top. Then Auntie found his arthritis or rheumatism more interesting than this climbing of heights and said he had her sympathy because there were days when she could hardly move with it, and this led to her telling him to take mustard baths and eat plenty of rhubarb and celery, and, while she was on about it, I slipped away to the other tower hoping to find the boy who must have come down that way. I found no one, but outside, to the rear, was a slab of stone propped upright against the wall. Had it not been of stone, I should have thought it a coffin lid, though for an exceedingly out-sized person. In a stupid attempt to move it, I caught sight of the end of a piece of rope. I drew the whole length from behind the slab, then heard Auntie's voice calling. I replaced it, this time entirely out of sight. (Twelve years were to elapse before I went there again, by which time the Priory was called an Ancient Monument, owned by the Ministry of Works and was undergoing extensive excavation. So I never found what might have been a decisive clue, some projection over which a rope could be slung and secured. In any case, I no longer ask for certainties. Once a boy had been up there — the lame man said so — and which boy I saw that day willing someone to look at him, I am content to leave in the air.)

My Aunt was being told to follow the path between the lime hedges which would take us to the lily pond where we could sit for a while on seats provided. She had thanked him more than once and said good-afternoon, when I opened my mouth to speak.

'Excuse me,' I began in my best speaking voice which I hoped would keep her quiet listening to me, 'There's a woman's head on the stones over there. To whom does she belong?'

'A woman's head? I hope it's made of stone, not bone.'

My leg was never easy to pull. I didn't laugh.

'Stone, of course, sir. Everything's stone over there.'

But he chose to laugh. 'On the surface, yes. Underneath, no. And you want to know who owns this head?'

'Yes please. Auntie said it would be Lord Guisborough.'

'Well again, she's not exactly right. I suppose you might say the head belongs to the Priory. It was dedicated to Our Lady.'

'Who is that, please?'

'Our Lady? I suppose the Virgin Mary. You've heard of her?'

'Yes, I've seen her. A statue of her, I mean,' adding this since he looked taken aback. 'It's a pity to leave her on that heap of stones. Lord Guisborough should put her on a stand in his house.'

The man looked at Auntie and said, 'Perhaps he'd prefer her with a body. But, I tell you what, I'll ask him to send her to a museum where they put heads on stands. She'd be at home there. Good day to you both,' and turning, he stumped off followed by his lame leg.

Once within the privacy of the clipped lime hedges, my Aunt said, 'I can't make that man out. He talks like one of the gentry and Mrs Lazenby said Lord Guisborough was lame. But he really can't have been Lord Guisborough, not in those shabby clothes.'

The pond came into view as we emerged from between the lime hedges.

'What a relief,' Auntie remarked, 'to be free of the need to crane our necks.'

'Will it be very deep?'

'How should I know? I've never seen a lily pond.'

'I hope it's not too deep. I don't want to look down from a great height.'

Then, as the thought of the boy and the dream shot through my mind, we were there, standing on the flags which bordered it.

And I'd seen it before; discounting the dream to which it bore little resemblance. The sense of having seen it overpowered me, but did not, as used to happen, remove me entirely from the present. I was adrift, struggling desperately to seize, recover, hang on to those elusive fragments that beckoned from that other time. The time when I had stood on this very flag and watched the slow, deliberate swish of a pinkish tail as a fat goldfish vanished under a dark lily pad, and seen the waxen flowers, cream, pink, wine-red, stabbing their petals at the sunlight; and the buds like swollen candle flames; and the stagnant water that lost its depth in murk and drew across its surface strands of emerald slime; but, for all that, real water giving back a blurred distorted image of my Aunt and me. And a smell was all about me, a musty ancient smell of old clothes stored for years in camphor and lavender. Each breath of it brought me to the point of grasping — whatever it was that lay out there beyond my reach; that other time. And each falling short was a bitter, wounding blow. So that, when I followed her to the wooden seat and sat upon it, I was chilled to the marrow, as they say, and could feel energy draining out of me.

'We couldn't have had a better day,' she said once more, unpacking the sandwich tin. 'But I do wish the seat had been further from that pond. It smells. Get on with your sandwich. Ruby will be here in twenty minutes.'

I remember nibbling at it, managing to empty my mouth into a handkerchief, and shaking out the half chewed food between the slats behind. I don't think she noticed because nothing was said, and I was aware of the strangeness of that, a silence which was so unlike her. We faced the arch in the distance and the pond opened at our feet. I could hear fish flick the water and a gentle cooing from a round building to our right. Then a flock of birds clattered from the lime trees and settled noisily on the church roof to our left. After a while, they too were still, as though asleep, and a peace that had substance dropped upon us. And that was how we stayed, it seemed for many years, until the church clock struck two.

'Goodness,' cried my Aunt, gathering up our bits and pieces, 'I'd lost all track of time. And if that isn't Ruby coming round the dove-cote.'

Concerning Ruby I had only the flimsy impression that her face matched her name. What I remember, and it is the hardest thing of all to record, is grabbing Auntie's arm as we crossed the road and then feeling the rush of tears down my face. Neither Ruby's astonishment, Auntie's alarm nor my own sense of shame could stem the flood; and when we reached a door that was Ruby's, I heard Auntie say, 'Right. I'm at the end of my tether and to a doctor she goes the minute we get home.'

The moment we got home she found Cyril there, returned a day early and not alone. With him was a young man much taller and much thinner than he whom Cyril presented as an old pal of his and a prospective lodger to take the place of that bloke Rouney. Ralph Gendall had been a chef in a Blackpool hotel but had answered an ad. and got a job with Sparks Caterers who were on the up and coming, catering for every big do in town. 'I told him this place would suit him down to the ground,' Cyril finished and thought that was the end of that. Auntie was suspicious, had never heard of men cooking, was angered by Cyril's presumption at not consulting her first, and also at being taken unawares. She had a lot to think about and a lot to say. The subject of doctors drifted from her mind until, in two weeks time, William Shakespeare forced it back.

When I gave my Aunt Miss Byers' note to say that the schools had been instructed to take parties of children to the Opera House to see a performance of William Shakespeare's *Macbeth* by a famous drama company, to take place early evening next Wednesday, her answer was predicatable. She said no, on no account was I to go. She still blamed this man for my insomnia despite having had to give way to Miss Byers on the grounds that he would personally be helping me through the scholarship examination and, although I did not agree that *Julius Caesar* and my sleeplessness were connected, I had to concede that there was a fair amount of that malady in the play itself. Brutus couldn't sleep, nor could Cassius because he was thin and thought too much, and even Caesar walked about in his nightgown.

'*Macbeth* is not about ancient Rome,' I started my argument. 'It's about kings of Scotland, castles and three witches. It's more like a fairy story.' I had read it and knew all that I was withholding. If anything, it was more bloodthirsty than *Julius Caesar* and had as much in it about sleeplessness. After coming into possession of *The Complete Works*, I had often wondered why we had not been given something a bit lighter than *J.C.* to study in school since William Shakespeare had actually written lighter things. Several years later, I could see the difficulties facing a selection committee. They were caused by the prevalence of sexual innuendos, especially in the lighter works. Even *A Midsummer Night's Dream* was about lovers, and how could Miss Gibson have explained, 'Ere I will yield my virgin patent up into his Lordship'? It was true that pupils were discouraged from asking questions, but since there was no written rule against it, these men might be ignorant on that matter. And they had to consider their necessarily unmarried and hopefully virgin women teachers and the possibility that some bold girl might ask of so obscure a phrase, 'What does it mean?' Murder, fighting and suicide were suitable enough if written by such a man as Shakespeare, but both pupils and women teachers must be safeguarded against any suggestion of sex.

That afternoon Miss Byers had given us a sketchy outline of *Macbeth* but with no hint of the important twist near the end. Had she but known it, Macduff being ripped from his mother's womb would have made sense to me and to Peggy, Irene and a few more, though I wasn't sure about Laura. We had reached the inevitable conclusion that, since the baby was inside the mother, then it must be got out in the region of the naval, that being the only thing in our bodies, except our mouths that remotely resembled a hole. It either opened by itself, or the doctor opened it. I had found the word 'womb' when searching laboriously through *Gresham* for a word to rhyme with 'tomb' in order to complete a poem. It said womb was a cavity containing anything and I remember thinking there was not much to choose between the two, in meaning.

'Fairy story or not,' my Aunt was saying, 'it will end the same as that concert ended, with a temperature and sore throat and a few days in bed. I'm not having it.'

'That was with having two tonsils. The biggest he'd ever seen, you know that doctor said. At least they got one, so I shouldn't have a sore throat. And that night I had to go with Miss Sykes. It was upsetting to go to something new with a grown-up. This is with children I know. I'm sure Aunt Gertrude will let Margaret go. Marton Road's going too. '

This was a clever point. Auntie enquired, found I was right and gave way though still maintaining that she wouldn't answer for the consequences, (If she wouldn't, then who would, I wondered.)

After tea on Wednesday I got into my best coat, jammed on a hat and closed the door on the safety of home to set out through a sulphurous atmosphere that was obscuring the westering sun. We assembled outside school, marched in crocodile formation to the top of Victoria Road, turned right and proceeded along Linthorpe Road to the corner of Southfield Road and the Opera House with its green dome. Other schools appeared from other directions and soon a mob of hatted children impeded all pedestrian traffic round two sides of the building. A clap of thunder seemed to surprise the teachers who said amongst themselves that surely someone would hurry to get us inside or we should be soaked. The thunder had not surprised me; I had smelt it all the way there and had conjectured about the power of William Shakespeare. Could he summon up real thunder storms for his plays? An unnerving thought! As a dull rumble continued to disturb the lowering sky, I hoped fervently that Miss Byers would allow me to squash into a dark corner. In fact, had I not been totally hemmed in, I would there and then have sidled a way out, headed for home and perhaps postponed yet again the threatened confrontation with the medical world.

Inside at last and ushered into a row of seats, it was comforting to discover that daylight was excluded, the only source of light being the gas mantles in brackets round the windowless walls. At least I should not see the lightning nor be aware of the darkening sky. We were like a horde of babies tucked into a huge, round womb with the proof of our security blazoned across a membrane in giant letters — SAFETY CURTAIN. With this staring at me and the comfortable hum of bodies encircling me, I was lulled into a sense of security soon removed, however, when I realised that SAFETY CURTAIN had shifted its position. 'Where's it going?' I felt compelled to mutter to the girl beside me. She didn't answer and, with awe, we both watched it sail upwards and disappear. With it went the hum of human proximity and in a sepulchral hush we stared at a velvet curtain hanging in dark crimson folds. Then this parted midway and both halves were also lifted heavenward exposing us to thunder, lightning, billowing smoke and fire and three black witches. Shakespeare had the right words for everything you could ever feel and, within seconds, the right words for my feeling at that moment were spoken. 'So from that spring whence comfort seemed to come, discomfort swells.'

It began to swell then in cold waves of terror but another fear, of being obtrusive, caused me to hold it in check. I sat with every muscle taut and rigid. In those days there was a wide gap between the reading or hearing of a thing and its visual image. We understood with our ears rather than with our eyes. For me, as for most of us, I believe, the verbal blood and thunder of *Julius Caesar* was not even imagined visually. We were never asked to picture it. We were not accustomed to pictures. But here a spectacle was spread before us with nothing spared in blood, lightning, ghostly and ghastly appearances. By the time that Macbeth, hands dripping crimson blood all over the stage, yelled 'Sleep no more,' I knew he needn't tell that to me. And when Banquo's ghost rose, chalk-white, out of the floor, all its dark ribs and red gashed head revealed, my heart had shifted its position and threatened to choke me. For once Miss Byers misunderstood. She manoeuvred our places so that she was beside me, passed me a handkerchief soaked in eucalyptus and whispered, 'It's better not to suck sweets.' Her face was untroubled, serene. 'It's not sweets,' I whispered back. 'May I go home?' and she replied, 'Not yet. Close your eyes if you want to. Have a little sleep.'

Naturally, I could not understand her, but that was nothing new as regards grown-ups. I dragged my gaze back to the horrors on that stage. The ghost had gone. Had I imagined it? All I saw were the actors thrusting out-sized goblets at arm's length before them, then raising these to their lips. But one goblet missed. It thudded to the floor and poured out blood in a spreading pool. A man screamed something which sounded like 'Out of my sight' and I saw the thing at which he stared. The ghost, present once more, its head level with the table and still rising! And at that precise moment the air above it exploded while the walls and the great domed roof were bombarded as if by a hundred monstrous cannon. I saw the ghost's head jerk backwards like a puppet's. The next instant it righted itself, but, apart from that, no one on stage moved until the first furious onslaught of sound had dropped to a lower pitch.

'It's in the play. It's all in the play,' drummed through my consciousness, but Miss Byers' voice, low though penetrating, said, 'Sit still girls. It's only a storm. It will pass in a few minutes.'

My worst fears were thus confirmed by the person I would never have disobeyed unless the circumstances were exceptional, were out of this world. Which was what they were now. I rose, and no one could have held me down, not even Lady Macbeth who now shrieked above

215

the continuing uproar from outside, 'Think of this, good peers, but as a thing of custom.'

It was not custom. I knew what it was, the thing I had just begun to think was beyond the bounds of possibility after having believed all my life that it was a mere step away. I battered my way between knees and seat backs, wrenched myself free in the aisle, flew up the long flight of shallow steps and out into the night which would be the last night of all. No hound could have got its nose to my legs along Southfield Road. Only supernatural forces, as Shakespeare said, could cause the elements to act so; white flares of lightning to split the ground at my feet and leave a blackness to be blundered into; or the sky above me to crack open monstrously and then explode in all directions. People are changed when the world ends, and this had happened to me. I was a demented being in a void without reason, a wraith in the lightning's flick, a lost soul astride the thunder claps. Rounding a corner, it would be Woodlands Road, I was hit, but not by lightning. I had collided with another body. I staggered, fell and was gathered up, awkwardly it's true, but placed back on my own two feet and my hand enclosed in a large one.

'Its all right now. It's all right. Your Aunt was worried. . . . She knew you'd be upset. Step it out. We'll be home in no time.'

And suddenly, as I strove to keep on my feet, the rain fell, bombarding us with massive drops which struck my felt hat like lead pellets and bounced off it.

Chapter Nineteen

I have a single sharp recollection of that night after Tom got me home — the moment I gave up the struggle to breathe and my last thought, how easy, how comfortable. Why, at other moments, had I striven to breathe?

This was nothing compared with my Aunt's version of the affair which I was to hear many times afterwards when someone sat by the bed while she made up the fire, tidied the wash stand, tucked in blankets more closely round me. I was flat, with no sheets or pillow and knew what was going on mainly through my ears. They heard two crucial facts, first that she had nearly lost me, and second that a doctor had run through the storm wearing a raincoat with nothing under it but pyjamas. In time these occurrences changed places, the pyjama clad doctor taking precedence over the near loss of me.

'Would you believe it,' I can still hear her voice telling someone, 'when Hannah ran to the bottom of Southfield Road for this new doctor she'd had to her mother, he answered his own door in pyjamas. Then he pulled on a raincoat, snatched his bag and came with her at a run. It was past midnight, and I knew someone must come. He was here while she was still turning the corner of Abingdon Road, and you know how Hannah can go. It was her skirts, she said, that held her back. They would, of course. He didn't even knock. Just tapped, let himself in and was climbing the stairs before I could get out of the bedroom. He saved her life. She was almost gone.'

Well, I'd known little about it, except sensations and that curious moment which I'd experienced only once before, the time when again I *knew* that I was *thinking*. The strangeness is striking, for mostly you think without being aware of doing so. That time I thought the face above me might be the face of God. Then the thinking left me and there was nothing but feeling. Steam rollers crushing my chest, sinking deeply, hurting, opening me up, causing explosions far off and near. They do so again and again, and the explosions multiply in many places and a hole opens and takes in with a gasp all that's thrown out. Bessie floats about on sand with a roller going over her. But my grandmother, where is she? In agitation I search, then find her. Under a tree in the garden of Eden, holding out her skirt while bright oranges drop one by one and land noiselessly on the thick black serge.

After a long time I knew the ceiling was above me and I stared up at it while pins and needles exploded under my skin and my limbs twitched violently. I realised that breathing had taken over again. I would stop that, and held my breath until the ceiling moved and spun round and I gasped. After several attempts I gave up. It was as hard now to stop breathing as it had sometimes been to breathe. This contrariness confused me. I slept.

Another long time, and I wondered about speech. I tried to say a-ah. My throat and lips were stiff; no sound came. Speaking was something I could control. I would not speak. That step would be in the right direction, backwards. Forwards, no. I did not want to go forwards, to that examination, to that High School and whatever might come afterwards. I would have none of it. Backwards, in the past, lay the only existence I would tolerate — a growing without effort, a condition without thought, a heather root holding the moor about it, a lily bulb unfolding a shoot. It was all there and you could go back by the long threads that grew out and linked you with it. And the first step was not to speak.

'Can't you tell us what you fancy to eat, Martha? Doctor Macphail says you must get on to a little solid food but I've to give you what you fancy.' My Aunt said this while lifting my head slightly and forcing my stiff lips apart with the narrow spout of a feeding cup that had been Grannie's. No effort whatever was required to stop myself from answering. I sucked the warm liquid and thought about words. All was silence in that wood where oranges dropped on her uplifted skirt. No one spoke a word. Like Bessie who had hated words. If she spoke, it was to herself. She had known. Sometimes I had suspected as much; now I was sure. She had refused to go forwards and

Father had never been able to force her. Nor would they force me, now that I knew. I wouldn't speak. And I wouldn't think either. Not about transitive and intransitive verbs and such like nonsense. In fact, I would think as little as possible. The spout was removed from my mouth, my head laid back and my mouth wiped. I slept, and dreamed the same dream about the oranges.

'It's a ridiculous thing, I must say,' the voice was Aunt Gertrude's flowing languidly along, 'that this new man can't say what's wrong with her and her voice.'

'He says she'll speak when she's ready to.'

'You don't mean he thinks she's pretending to be dumb?'

'I mean no such thing. There's something affecting the muscles. But, as yet, he will make no diagnosis.'

'It sounds very like Willie to me. They were never certain what was the matter with him. But he didn't lose his voice.'

'If you think back, Gertrude, Willie had very little to say. But I think Martha's trouble is all due to shock. Shock following that play. I've heard all about it from other mothers and I've written to Miss Byers. Children should never be exposed to such things.'

'It didn't affect Margaret. Nor anyone else that I've heard of.'

'You don't hear as much as I do. A lot of children had nightmares.'

'Children have nightmares with nothing. You can think what you like, but Watson and I believe it's all due to that excessive school work. We kept telling you. At least Watson did. Naturally, I wouldn't have dared. This will put paid to the scholarship.'

I looked at her as she rose from the commode, used of course as a seat. There was no mistaking the triumph in her voice and even in her handsome face. I did not care. Leaving my voice out of it, there was something wrong with me. I could tell by the fire in the grate, the blind pulled down though not entirely. Gradually I realised that the window was open at the bottom. Those who came to see me kept their coats on. I was wrapped in blankets and had two hot water bottles in flannel covers, one at my side, one at my feet. I was laid flat with no pillow or bolster, my temperature taken morning and night with Auntie writing what she read on a card that hung on the brass rail of the bed foot. The card interested Minnie who always examined it. And one day, long after I'd taken to my bed, I heard her voice say, 'It's steadier. Steadier than it was, even though it's still up. But steadiness is a good sign, Blanche.' Then she had bent over me and I had inhaled her special smell.

'You're getting better, girl. Do you feel better?' and I had gazed at her dumbly, inclining my head, shoving my chin still deeper into the blanket. It was too much trouble to speak, anyway, and the longer I refrained from speech, the easier that became. Words were nothing but a waste of breath, I thought.

No children visited me. I learned later that they were barred from doing so. But I was rich in visits from grown-ups who were intensely curious about my dumbness. 'What does the doctor say about it, and why isn't she in hospital?' Naturally Auntie told them I was better off at home; she was more capable than any hospital nurse. But what the doctor had to say was more difficult to answer. He said so little. She did confide in Mary Kitching that she had persisted with Doctor Macphail about my speech and he'd replied, 'That's the least of our worries. You know the saying, "Silence is golden". This produced a silence on Mary's part which was anything but golden, being short, meaningful and capped with, 'If he'd said that to me, I'd have sent him packing.' On hearing this interchange, I felt a stirring of conscience and had to stiffen my resolve to cut myself off from the world. It was hard on my Aunt, but she would just have to bear it. She bore it well, being more addicted to talking than to listening. In fact, whenever possible she had done my talking and answering for me, not allowing me to get a word in; so that, during the morning routine of seeing to the cleanliness of me and my bed, she was content to carry on a monologue and have no interruption from me. Mrs Burt thought she was being soft with me and soon began to try something firmer.

'It's time you were saying something, Martha. You *are* a lot better, you know.' (The voice of Doctor Armstrong! I heard it clearly, and saw him kneeling with his mouth to my Grandmother's ear, 'Mrs Drinkhall, come along now, waken up. You really *are* a lot better.' And she did not waken.)

'Come along now,' the voice of Mrs Burt persisted. 'What you need is to sit up and take an interest in things,' and, but for my Aunt's intervention, she would have lifted me bodily there and then. 'No, Mrs Burt, instructions must be obeyed. Doctor says she must lie flat for some time yet.'

'And that will pile up a bill for you before she's back on her feet. I must say they know what they're doing. No wonder they can live like lords.' Auntie told her she ought to see the curve in my spine, and I thought how strange it was that this phenomenon was something I should never be able to see. She had seen it when he'd examined me lying on my stomach. 'Straighten her,' he'd said, exactly like one of those military men, and I had felt his finger press slowly down my spine until, at one spot, its straight course was interrupted. 'Crooked,' I'd thought, and my body had twitched worse than ever and was some time before it returned to any sort of order.

One afternoon, Doris Mould arrived. After saying she was sorry I couldn't talk, she proceeded to do so herself.

'I've heard from Bob. He says he's saving a bit of money and might have enough to come for me in a year or so. I'll never be able to go, you know. That terrible voyage, with all those Irish people being sick! And water covering the portholes. Just fancy, living below water. If a porthole broke, just think what would happen. What *would* happen, do you think?' I could only shake my head. If I'd spoken, I could have said nothing, anyway. Nothing but speculation. Doris went on to answer her own question. 'Water would rush in and the boat would sink. Imagine it!' There was a break for us to dwell on this. Then a decision. 'No, I daren't risk it, although Bob says I wouldn't have to stay on Ellis Island if he gets his citizenship papers and marries me here. I couldn't have endured that place. Imagine having your body examined! As if you were a leper or something. As if anyone with a horrible disease would cross that ocean! Bob says the trouble is the Irish. A lot of them have TB. You die of it, don't you? So what are they doing going to America with it? I don't really think I'd like to be an American though I'd love to live in one of those marvellous houses you see on the pictures. If only there was a bridge across.' She sighed, then, from her perch on the commode, turned her head towards me. 'I hear you've got a new lodger?' I nodded. 'He's tall and handsome, isn't he? But don't tell anyone I said so, will you?' I gave my head a pensive shake.

'Oh, I forgot. You can't. So I can say anything to you, can't I?' and this thought sparked off a fit of giggles.

Mary Kitching came, saying that it was her duty to sit with me for a while. She had been asked, she said, to peel an apple for me. (Auntie still held that the apple was packed with nutriment.) Mary held out a wafer thin slice which I took and chewed ruminantly.

'I wouldn't get married,' she advised me. 'Certainly not if you don't get your voice back. They talk about the pen being mightier than the sword. Well, the voice is mightier than anything when you have a husband to contend with. You must know when to use it, of course, and when not to. When to act dumb. Nothing irritates John more than when I won't argue with him, won't open my mouth in reply to his harangues. But it wouldn't annoy him if I were really dumb and couldn't answer. So not answering would be no weapon to really dumb women, would it?' I shook my head, accepted another sliver of apple, then nodded in agreement when she told me I must be thankful I wasn't deaf too. There were things you could do if you were only dumb. Like dressmaking. You can listen to people's requirements, measure them and fit them without really saying anything. She rarely said anything. She let them do the talking.

'In a way,' she concluded, 'I would have been better off just dress-making and not bothering with a man in the house. Of course I don't tell everyone that, not even Blanche who is my best friend.'

But she knows, was what I thought as I swallowed the chewed apple.

Mrs Grayson paid me a visit. She said Auntie had asked

her to run up for a few moments. She said this while standing in the doorway and gaping at me as if I were a freak. I tried to smile and this brought her to the commode where she sat allowing tears to course unchecked down both cheeks. She told me I was in the best place and advised me to stay here away from the world's wickedness. The Bible was right to say that after the abominations would come the end, and the end was near. When men were brought down to the level of animals and behaved like animals, then the end was at hand and you were better off dead. She knew I wouldn't repeat this to anyone. It was a relief to get it off her chest. No one had known before what she had to endure.

I could not tell her that I was no wiser than before concerning the extent of her endurance, but that if she'd gained any comfort, then I was glad to be dumb. At that moment Auntie arrived with a pot of tea.

'Poor, poor girl,' moaned Mrs Grayson. My Aunt was brisk with her, 'She's in the best place, the way the weather is,' and poured her a cup of tea. She also stirred the fire into a hint of a blaze causing Mrs Grayson to say what a dreadful struggle she must have to keep two fires going and offering to bring across a pail or so of coal. 'If we can't help each other in our troubles, what point is there in living? This poor girl has done me so much good.' I noticed Auntie bestow upon me what, in a few years time, I might have termed a quizzical glance.

Hannah would have been on the commode more often had it not been for her mother. She squeezed in the occasional half hour and read aloud to me from a new author she had found, Jeffrey Farnol. There was too much boxing in his books for her liking, but she preferred that to the immoderate emphasis on horse riding in Zane Grey's novels. She said Farnol wrote tales of high adventure that might take me out of myself or even out of the bedroom. They had that effect on her. This was one called *Peregrine's Progress*, a far cry, she said, from *Pilgrim's Progress*. She read a page, turned over, read a bit more, broke off and remarked, 'Doctor Macphail is an adventurous sort of man, wouldn't you say?'

I couldn't, so I stared at the ceiling.

'I mean he's unconventional.'

Ah, I thought, you won't catch me out. You think I'll ask what that word means, don't you? Well, I won't, because I'm done with words.

'Very enlightened.' She seemed determined I should know about this man. I lowered my lids and looked sideways at her. Her long cheek appeared less sallow; it was almost pink, the effect, perhaps, of the firelight.

'That means he's in advance of his time. He's told your Aunt that the pains in your legs should have been noticed because there's no such thing as growing pains. Growing never causes children to have pains. Pain is an indication of something going wrong, especially in children — a sort of warning.'

I wondered when and where Doctor Macphail had spoken as many words as these.

'I've had him to Mother. He wouldn't give her any medicine. According to him, most medicine is only coloured water which he hates charging for. He's very honest. Mind you, he says most people would rather pay for coloured water than have nothing prescribed at all, and I'm afraid that's so with Mother. He says there's nothing wrong that couldn't be put right by a daily walk. But wild horses wouldn't drag her out of the house, so it's difficult.'

She paused. I supposed it might be difficult, too, carrying on all this conversation with a dumb person, and wondered if that were the end. It wasn't.

'He says there are people who make themselves ill in order to tie others to them, though they might not be aware of it. Mind you, I'm not saying that's so with Mother. Still, he says I should try to have a bit of life of my own, independent of her. It's very kind of him to think of me. He's a caring doctor.'

She was not trying to make me speak, of that I was now sure. She was talking to herself and letting out secrets knowing that they were safe with me. I felt a pricking behind my eyes and wondered if Doctor Macphail had a wife.

Would Hannah make a good wife? I'm sure I didn't know what was needed for that. But you heard a lot more about women making good wives than men making good husbands. I couldn't imagine Louisa May Alcott following

224

Good Wives with *Good Husbands* although she had followed *Little Women* with *Little Men*. The point seemed to be this, that a woman was expected to make a good wife. When a woman died, people said, 'She made him a good wife,' but when a man died, I'd not heard anyone say, 'He made her a good husband.' No one, to my knowledge, had said that about Grandfather — though the preacher had proclaimed him good in all sorts of other ways — nor about Mr Kneeshaw, and they wouldn't be able to say it about Mr Grayson nor, according to Mary Kitching, would they say it about John. Would it be said of my father if he were to die? I pondered this as Hannah's voice returned to the progress of Peregrine, and I reminded myself once more that life was horrible and I was leaving it, going to a place where there was no marriage or being given in marriage, no change, so no looking forward to any future event, no speculation, for instance, about Hannah's marriage with Doctor Macphail although she was a bit old to be marrying and what on earth would she do with her mother. What would it be like in a place where you could no longer wonder?

'There, that'll do for today,' said Hannah, 'but I'm dying to know what happens, aren't you?'

I bit my lower lip with teeth that were still growing if nothing else of me was. I had just stopped myself from saying a word.

Hannah rose, pinned on her hat and I thought was about to say, 'So long for now, Martha,' when instead she said, 'Martha, don't worry about your voice. I think it's psychological, caused by a shock to the nervous system and you've had your share of shocks. Do you remember how hard it was to get a word out of Bessie? Well, I think that was due to shock when she was born. I used to try to explain this to your mother and wanted her to see one of those doctors, a psychiatrist. They have them in America, I've read. But it's not been mentioned in her letters. I do think it's a pity.'

There was a silence. An agonising one for me, because at that moment the last thing I wanted to do was refrain from speech. Beyond everything else, I wanted to ask what had shocked my sister at birth. Had Doctor Armstrong been too rough when he pulled her out of that opening in my mother's stomach? My throat muscles tensed with the urge to speak; to demand that Hannah tell me the truth about this mystery. I strangled the words as they rose, wondering whatever people would say. What I had done was like telling lies over and over again, every day, although it was true that I had only been trying to die. Saliva came into my mouth. I swallowed hard. Hannah was talking again.

'I've written to your mother. She's worried to death by Blanche's letters. They haven't the money to come back yet and they've just got used to their new work, though it's very arduous. I've told her not to worry because you're in such excellent hands. I was worried myself about you until we got Doctor Macphail, but you couldn't have a more expert and understanding doctor. I wish I were in his hands. But I'm never ill. I should say, thank goodness. And I can't have him visiting Mother when he says there's nothing wrong with her. Now can I?'

I gave a slow shake of my head. I had not recovered from my desperation but it was blunted by a sadness on account of Hannah. Couldn't she marry Tom? He was kind to me, but would he be kind to a wife? Surely he would be happier with Hannah looking after him than Auntie who, most of the time, was horrid to him. Of course he could still rent our greenhouse for his cobbling. I wished I dare open my mouth and suggest it. Because there did seem to be indefinable obstacles to the possibility of her marrying Doctor Macphail although they were the same height and had the same sort of black hair.

The day had been exceptionally quiet. No visits, not even from the doctor, and Auntie getting on with her routine jobs in comparative silence. I wondered what was wrong with her. Was she heading for one of those nervous outbreaks that had not once occurred in my cloistered bedroom. Today, the pins and needles and twitches were not so bad. My body felt quieter. So did my head, with fewer thoughts bombarding each other like wild imprisoned birds. They had settled, like those birds on Guisborough church roof, had folded their wings and seemed asleep. I wished I could ask what month it was. The sun, which appeared in fits and starts, had a long slant to it. In the morning it had lain on the blanket beside my right cheek; then it had shone in my eyes; now it came and went like a light turned on and off over the blanket to the left of me. Turned off, the room grew dark and the window looked thick with soot. It couldn't be, because yesterday she'd cleaned it with a volley of grumbles about the filthy fumes from the steel works. I wished I knew the date, how time was passing. You were handicapped without a voice, though now I doubted whether I *could* speak, even if I tried and I'd quite forgotten the sound of my own voice. I turned on my side, knowing I shouldn't, but for the first time my body was free of twitches and sick of lying still in one position. It wanted to curl up, knees chin-wards, but I resisted that urge. The firelight was brighter because darkness was closing in though Auntie had not brought up the tea. I was thirsty. Above the wash stand the oblong shape of the wedding photograph could just be seen, but no faces. Still, I knew Grannie was smiling down at me; from a photograph, though actually from where? Where did she really exist, holding out her skirt for those oranges. . . ? I suppose I dozed, for suddenly I knew I'd wakened to the sound of voices drifting up the stairs.

'He's got to be asked outright, Blan. If you won't, then I shall. I'm her uncle with as much right in her welfare as you, and I'm going to know. He's going to tell us if he suspects paralysis. We can't let our bairns die while doctors just mess around. They need a man to deal with them. '

'Well, I'm sure I did my best for Willie.'

'No one could have done more, Blan. But you put all your trust in doctors. It broke me, the way Willie was experimented on. All that electrical treatment that the poor little chap dreaded and had to suffer.' The half-opened door came towards me. I was already in the correct position, on my back, straight as a poker.

'Here's Uncle Watson.'

He came and stood at the bedside, a bunch of flowers held in front of him. Auntie had struck a match and was lighting the gas jet. She turned it up and drew the blind to the bottom. With the light behind him, his face was indistinct, but he held the flowers towards me and I took them in both hands. They were Michaelmas daisies, the light purple ones with sprigs of dark orange and green threaded through them, and first I thrust my face amongst them and drew in with deep breaths the smell of earth, leaves, nectar, pollen, while the flower fringes lay soft and tickly on my cheeks. My eyes just cleared the daisies and stared at Uncle who said not a word. Yet, in that instant, I knew I had taken a stride forward, a stride in learning. I'd known that living was not easy; now I knew that neither was dying. It had been a hard thing for Willie to die. Even flowers might find it painful to grow, if we only knew. In fact my uncle did know, for most of them needed help except the ones called weeds which were uprooted or had stuff sprinkled on to kill them. No easy way, really, for anything. I held the flowers away from me, stretched the fingers of my left hand round the stems and with my right hand extracted a spray that had long, flat leaves like sword blades and small trumpet shaped flowers the colour of our copper kettle springing at intervals from a long, stiff stalk. I looked up at Uncle Watson . . .

During the next few days I grew tired of hearing Auntie relate this incident, and told her so. 'Everyone knows I've found my voice, so why are you telling them? It's silly.' It didn't matter when she told the doctor. I heard the tale as they climbed the stairs. 'She's got her voice back, Doctor. I said all along that you would be right, that it would return in its own good time.' A triumphant vindication of the medical profession, though I am sure she was glad too for other reasons. The doctor took my wrist between two fingers.

'And what were those words? The first ones you spoke?'
We answered together, not saying the same thing.
'Let her speak for herself. The first words you spoke were . . . ?'
'What's it called?'
He silenced Auntie again and looked keenly at me.
'And what was it called?'
'Montbresia.' I saw his eyebrows lift. 'It's a flower.'
I did not elaborate. Auntie would take over as soon as

possible. Also, I did find it hard to talk. My throat hurt. He had a look at it and said, 'Well, it tells us a few things, though not entirely why you lost your voice.' I stared him in the eye, though it wasn't easy.

'And are you able to tell us now what you fancy to eat?'

'Oranges, please.'

'Please Doctor.' The correction was automatic before my request had registered. Then, 'Oranges! Well, I never did! I've been giving her apples, Doctor, thinly sliced. They're so rich in iron.'

'Quite right. But she may need the very thing that oranges are rich in. Children often know what's good for them, if they're allowed to choose. Give her as many as she can eat.'

He examined the temperature chart, then gave it a flick with the back of his hand and said, 'Good. You can have one pillow under your head for a few minutes, no longer, morning and afternoon. You'd like to read a bit, that way? Or play with something?'

I nodded, and he gave me a sly look. 'And don't talk too much at first. You don't want to lose it again. Or do you?'

Chapter Twenty

Illness is not a subject on which to dwell. I was X-rayed at Middlesbrough Infirmary by a doctor who had literally given his life to the early development of the technique and was, at that time, dying from its effects. I must get to the hospital, Doctor Macphail told us, in the same prone position which had been my lot for three months, therefore a motor cab was unsuitable. My suggestion of Mr Whittingham's motor hearse raised the only laugh I ever heard from our doctor. Ambulances, if used at all, must have been in short supply. I went in a spinal chair manoeuvred by Sister Purvis, the lady in purple who had met me only once before when I was three. Auntie stalked alongside, a little disgruntled that her efforts to help steer the thing had proved mere hindrances; they were tricky things to steer and embarrassing to occupy. I was in no way dismayed by its resemblance to a lidless coffin, but greatly worried that I might be taken for a grossly overgrown baby in a pram. I kept my eyelids lowered and would not look at passers by. I was X-rayed in a window-less room with one small yellow light in a corner and this was extinguished while the machine was in motion. It gave out a curious grating noise as though in need of oil. The room was black as pitch.

After Doctor Macphail's next visit, Auntie had a great deal to write to my mother. All her worries had been justified. I had had not one but three things wrong with me — rheumatic fever for two or three years, some spinal tuberculosis and a dose of infantile paralysis. My spine had been curved and my right leg was short. After Christmas she must take me twice a week to the Infirmary to have massage and violet ray treatment to straighten the spine and draw out my leg.

I have no doubt she informed mother again that it was a wonder I was here and that my enlarged tonsils should never have been tampered with by a butcher of a doctor who did not know the harm he was doing. For all the neighbourhood now knew that tonsils were there to fight infection; that the larger they were, the more deadly the germs they were devouring. And it is true that Auntie was merely passing on the views of Doctor Macphail who had told her he was dead against this mass removal of tonsils and that mine had done well for me despite the one having been mashed. He was happy to say that, along with my body, it was recovering and beginning to grow again.

I was far away from a return to school. The doctor said he would issue a certificate of exemption from stage one of the scholarship examination and, hopefully, I should be fit to take stage two. I argued with him about this, saying what was the use, I would be unprepared. His reply was that I had been prepared enough; nothing that had been so fiercely hammered in could be forgotten, at least not until I reached a hundred or so.

This juncture in my affairs marked the end of a long chapter and the beginning of a distinct change in the quality of my existence. The Thing left me and never returned, thus allowing nights of comfortable sleep. The days changed too, because that part of me which had often dithered between two domains settled on a more equable plane of actuality. I had lost those 'blank misgivings', and, although Wordsworth would have deplored this loss, I soon knew that life was easier without them. No longer was I prey to peaks and chasms of condition, and no longer did a scene or situation hit me with such clarity as to stamp itself for all time on my memory. In other words, I was moving towards the norm and the change might be summed up and explained perhaps by the doctor having said, according to my Aunt, that she could put away her thermometer for the time being, put it safely away in her bottom drawer.

'Goodness only knows,' she exclaimed for at least the sixth time in my hearing, 'what he meant by that, unless they don't have bottom drawers in Scotland. He must surely know that I'm past thinking of marriage though he did say that I should have had children of my own because I'd have made a capital mother.'

What an odd expression, I thought. It doesn't sound like

Doctor Macphail. He said she was an excellent nurse, but if he said capital mother as well, then it was not in my presence. Not that it matters, I suppose. Then, when I heard her very next words, I began to wonder if it did.

'Anyway, I've got Martha and she's as near a child of my own as need be.'

These words came back to me two days later when I read a letter from my Mother. Being Christmas letters, we had one each addressed in separate envelopes. In mine Mother said she was returning no later than the coming summer and would take me back with her. They were changing their work after Christmas. Their present job had been so time-consuming and badly paid. My Father had found work joinering for a large building firm in Melrose. The money was better and there seemed plenty of part-time work for her to do. (She did not say what work.) I would not be ill out there with all the sunshine and the clean, dry air. It had suited her chest and it would suit me. As for this scholarship business, she was sure it had done me harm and I must forget it. It was typical of England that only money or studying to the point of nervous breakdowns could buy a good education. In America all children went into High School where they were taught the subjects provided in English High Schools. All children had the same education and the same opportunities. 'Worry is at the root of all your troubles,' I read, 'and really I can't stand any longer the worry of hearing from your Auntie that you are dying. I feel helpless being so far away. So have a nice Christmas and get on your feet again ready to come back with us in the summer.'

The letter lay on the quilt — there was no point in trying to conceal it — as Auntie came through the door with a face twice its usual length.

'What has your mother been saying to you?' She picked it up, read it and tossed it back. I heard with indifference her tirade about Mother doubting her word and about ingratitude. The difficult relationship between them seemed at that moment to lie on the periphery of things. Only one of her protests registered — thinking she can interfere with your two years of treatment at the Infirmary

232

— and I remarked, 'But I haven't said I will go.'

'Nor will you, I'll see to that,' and she furiously riddled ashes from the grate.

We had reached the stage where the fire was re-lit each morning, not kept going through the night. It was banked up about nine as I lay waiting for sleep, and threw dark rose tints over the middle of the room while leaving the corners in shadow. Whatever sort of cavity the womb was — and I was still technically ignorant about any part of the body beyond flesh and bone — this room, in the glow from cinders slowly reddening the top layer of slack, was how I imagined a womb to be. The window was now closed at night and opened an inch during the day. Also, I lay between the best drill sheets, neither too hot, as the blankets had been, nor cold like cotton; and I felt pleasantly lazy, and safe, knowing that sleep would soon lap over me in warm little waves. And yesterday, from my propped up position, I had actually caught sight of the slow effortless passage of some very large snowflakes. 'Will it really be a white Christmas?' Minnie had asked, popping in. How did she expect me to know?

Not that my new-found 'laziness' excluded all ambition. Now that I could read a little on and off, I had made a decision. I would read all through the *Complete Works* starting at the beginning and not skip about anywhere in Bob's gift to me. When Hannah heard this, she said, 'Well, there's one resolution that will be broken though I don't blame you for hitching your wagon to a star. What about starting with *Hamlet*, the famous one. I tried it once myself, but couldn't get round his way of putting things, almost as if it were a different language,' Then, while I tried to tell her it was a bit like the Bible in that sense, she picked up the volume, ran her finger down the Index and found *Hamlet* on page eight hundred and twenty-four. She studied the first page, then said, 'I see there's a ghost in it. It might be interesting. I should give it a try.'

I had done so and was soon stuck at the bit about Christmas which I read many times until I had to lie flat again. Even then, it still rang in my head because that was how I wanted Christmas to be this year. Come to think of it, that was how I had always wanted Christmas to be and had only just found it put into words, with the bird of dawning singing all night long . . . so hallowed and so gracious is the time. So hallowed and so gracious. That was just how things should be at Christmas. And here was Auntie all set to spoil it because of this letter from Mother who was also to blame, of course. Perhaps it would be wise not to grow up, after all.

Auntie had risen from her knees and lifted the pail holding the raked out ashes when I heard the front door open and close and a voice call, 'Blan? Blan, where are you? Upstairs?'

'It's Watson. Whatever can he be wanting at this time of day? I'm upstairs. What's the matter now?'

No one else called her Blan, but I'd have known his voice anyway, and his tread as he mounted the stairs. Everyone, I'd learnt, took the stairs differently. Uncle Watson started off well, slowed before reaching the top of the long flight, then rested briefly on the lower landing before taking the last four steps. I used to wonder if he was taking a look through the landing window. He came through the door and laid a slim bunch of button chrysanthemums on the quilt.

'There you are, lass. Alf Jackson's compliments and a happy Christmas. Blan, I wonder if you can help out? Could you possibly put up a man and his wife just over the Christmas week end? No, wait while I've finished. It's a young couple from Northern Ireland. No, they're not Catholics. Northern Ireland is Protestant. He's starting with the Prudential on Monday, the boss told me today. They want furnished rooms which won't be difficult, but the problem is Christmas. There's all that travelling and she's none too good.'

'What's that mean?'

'Well, she's pregnant. Baby due in two months, so you can see they really are in a tight corner. He's taking over that new estate between Grove Hill and Ayresome. The boss says he's a good man — can talk the hind leg off a donkey.'

'I want no more blarney. I've had enough of that. Anyway, what makes you think I can put them up. There's no room.'

'I thought Ralph and Cyril had decided to go to Black-pool since the shops aren't opening until Tuesday, although we start Monday. Didn't you say so?'

'Yes, but I wanted a bit of peace and quiet over Christmas and I think I'm entitled to it.'

'He'll pay you well, Blan. He can afford to fork out for the week end. And I thought that might be a help. There'll be no more work than if you were catering for the two lads. And I'm sure they'll move on after Monday. The boss is looking into it. It's just that everything comes to a standstill over Christmas.'

'Everything except the endless baking, cooking, serving and clearing up.'

'Well, believe me, I wouldn't have pushed this at you but for the poor lass being pregnant.'

'What's pregnant?'

The two words from me applied an instant brake on the dialogue's momentum.

'Keep out of this, Martha,' ordered my Aunt, and, 'Doesn't she know, Blan?' asked my Uncle. Both spoke together, and I replied, 'No, I don't. What's the matter with her?' while Auntie glared first at me then at him.

'She'll have to know, Blan. Sometime. I'm sure our Margaret knows.' It was hardly the moment for my poor Aunt to decide what I should or should not know. Her attention was torn between the Irish couple and, as she told people dozens of times afterwards, all she owed to Watson who therefore took it upon himself to deal out information. 'It just means that she's going to have a baby in two months time, that's all.'

'Oh, that.' Airily I waved away so paltry a meaning, letting him know that I did not lag behind Margaret in this area of knowledge. 'I know all about babies being inside their mothers. I thought being pregnant must be an illness.'

'No, it's not an illness. But babies are pretty heavy, aren't they? Heavy to carry about inside her, so a woman gets tired, you see.'

I saw, and remembered the journey to Bethlehem, and understood for the first time why Mary was always said to be tired, weak and ill; and remembered something else that

235

I must have read somewhere, that long ago people used to think it happened again every Christmas Eve and waited in the hope that the Holy Family would knock on their door.

'I said, 'It's funny that they are looking for somewhere to stay on Christmas Eve. You can't really say you have no room, Auntie. There'll be Mr Gendall's room, and you don't know who you're turning away.'

We both thought we were doing right, Uncle Watson and I. Auntie submitted. She let them in and they did not move out until June. Mrs O'Hurley took to Mr Gendall's bed on arrival, declining my Aunt's invitation to join them for the traditional Christmas Eve supper. Her husband carried up their supper on a tray. On Christmas Day an Irish doctor, unknown to Auntie, arrived and declared Mrs O'Hurley unfit to rise from her bed on account of her heart. I saw her only once, on the bright summer day when they departed, and, as for him, I came to know him well by ear due to the countless times he passed my door running up and down stairs after his wife either with scuttles of coal, trays of food, ewers of water or pails of slops. He ate his meals with her.

When Christmas had passed and they were still with us, our household was of necessity disrupted. Minnie offered to take in Tom for the time being. On returning from Blackpool, Ralph Gendall was asked if he would mind sleeping in the back bedroom for a mere night or two. His belongings had preceded him and were already neatly packed in Tom's drawers or hung on a hook in the door since there was no wardrobe, and covered, Auntie told me, by her own flowered print costume covers. These Mr Gendall had promptly returned to her insisting that she need only say the word and he would remove these people, lock, stock and barrel. 'And I think he would,' Auntie told me, 'with his height and those muscles and Mr O'Hurley being such a slip of a man. Cyril offered to help though he doesn't stand to lose so much. He's still got his view. Mr Gendall has lost his.'

'What view?'

'Oh, you know how ridiculous Cyril can be.'

'Yes. But what view?'

'The one over the grounds opposite. Of the nurses

236

coming and going. I'm sure I don't know what young men are coming to, these days. They never had such ideas when I was twenty.'

Looking back on the incredible business of the O'Hurleys coming for the Christmas weekend and staying for six months despite every kind of pressure being used to evict them, I think the man at the Prudential had put it in a nutshell when he'd said that Mr O'Hurely could talk the hind leg off a donkey. Mr O'Hurely *believed* in his flow of words when he told Auntie weekly, some times daily, that furnished rooms were waiting to receive them, were crying out for tenancy, although the local habitation, usually named, was already an airy nothing. He believed his wife to be at death's door and that Cyril and Ralph used the organ in the room below specifically to push her through that door. No sooner did I hear floating up the stairs the latest song hit, 'Me and Jane in a plane, soaring up to the skies,' but what Mr O'Hurley's footsteps could be heard racing down and his expostulating voice, 'You two young men wouldn't want to have the death of a woman and her unborn child lying on your consciences for the rest of your lives, now would you?' My Aunt's arbitration resulted in a ban on the use of the organ after eight-thirty.

When the baby was born, their doctor pronounced Mrs O'Hurley unfit to cope with it. Her husband drew out the bottom drawer of the walnut dressing table and asked Auntie for a pillow and a few scraps of bed linen. The baby wailed night and day and my Aunt told everyone that it was not long for this world, being the most undersized mite she had ever seen. Mr O'Hurely went to the chemist for two feeding bottles and set to work himself on the task of feeding it.

'And what's the use of that?' Auntie asked, 'unless he stays away from work. They are like a couple of children. When I told him that a baby has to be fed every four hours, he seemed to think I was joking. I'm at my wits end. Their doctor says she's too weak to feed it and I can't let it die, can I?'

I said I supposed she could. It wasn't her baby. My attitude towards the O'Hurleys had undergone a radical change since Christmas when I had pleaded their cause. If Auntie must feed and attend to this baby, then what about me? Would someone else have to push the bath chair which had recently replaced the spinal one and which Auntie had taken over? And would that mean an end to our visits, just begun, to the new little cafe in Linthorpe Road which was serving ice cream as well as cream cakes? We had called there last Thursday because with a bath chair, Auntie had said, it was handier than Merediths. A pleasant young waitress had helped to manoeuvre the chair through the door and pushed it well under a diminutive round table. She had then held a white chair, also diminutive, for Auntie to sit upon so that we faced each other with very little space between us, I with a black and white shawl tucked round me, she in her winter coat with its large astrakhan collar. How long was it, I wondered, since we had been in a cafe? Not since the time, I thought, when I'd questioned her about the workhouse when I was seven. She studied a small hand-written card, then asked the waitress if we might have a pot of tea and a cream cake. When the waitress said, 'I wonder, madam, if you'd like to try our ice-cream?' my Aunt's face was a study.

'Ice-cream? In a cafe? In February?'

The waitress seemed unperturbed by these blunt questions.

'I know just what you mean. We all connect ice-cream with summer and the Italians pushing carts round the streets.'

'That's so. And it's not fit to eat. I wouldn't dream of buying it.'

'Nor would I. But this is not Italian. This is pure. It's made with Brunton's milk which, you may have heard, is quite free from TB now.'

'Yes, I have heard. The Bruntons are friends of mine and I know all about their milk. Their little son was fed for years on milk from their prize cow. The boy died of tuberculosis and the cow was found to be riddled with it. Mr Brunton said no other child should die because of their milk and is paying the earth for some new process of killing off the germ. *And* he's bottling it for delivery. But what has that to do with ice-cream? I'm sure Mr Brunton

238

would never go in for making that.'

'No. But we buy his milk and make it and we serve it with cream fresh from his farm.'

I could sense that Auntie was having second thoughts. After a few seconds she said, 'Well, I suppose that puts a different light on the matter. But I still think it's the wrong time of the year.'

'Not at all. People are ordering it now for Christmas parties. It keeps its shape better in cold weather. There's nothing worse than half melted ice-cream.'

I looked at the bright fire burning in the small grate and felt warm enough to push away the shawl. Still, I raised my voice in support of this waitress who was trying to sell something. I knew no more about ice-cream than I did about insurance, but I did know how difficult it was to sell things — mice, for instance. People were not easily persuaded into thinking they wanted what you had to sell. Uncle Watson often worried about that, when he knew people hadn't the money to spend on buying insurance. Did we have the money now, to buy ice-cream?

'How much is it?' I asked. 'Is it more than a cream cake?'

The waitress gave me a ravishing smile. 'A large cream cake is fourpence and an ice-cream with fresh cream is only twopence more.'

'Can we afford it?' I asked Auntie.

'Yes, of course. Why must you ask silly questions?'

She knew it was not silly, but she would never admit our shortage of money.

'Very well,' she said, 'we'll try it. We can always get warmed up at home over a cup of tea.'

That was my first ice-cream. A pale dome set in a moat of primrose coloured cream and a triangular wafer like a flag stuck in the top. It was served in a round glass dish. Before tasting hers, Auntie spooned up some cream and let it fall in a viscous column on top of the dome where it spread in scallops round and down the sides.

'Yes, it's real cream,' she affirmed as if having harboured doubts. I dug in the spoon and managed to scoop out and get into my mouth a portion of the dome.

'Is it nice?' asked the waitress, hovering near, and I

nodded as it froze my tongue and gums, then gently melted round them.

It had been very nice indeed and worth anticipating during the process of undergoing the treatment when my body was battered by the slapping, kneading and stretching exercises devised by a Sister who persistently told me that she would soon have me ship-shape and then left me to cook under an arc of whitish light. Violet rays, Auntie informed me, and I found no chance to argue regarding the colour because, as she steered me along Newport Road, she was in full voice about the tragedy of Willie who might, she said, have been saved by these rays; and she wondered if there was any hope for the little boy whose turn was after mine and who would now be sitting with the same rays directed on the piece of nose that was left. Something called lupus had eaten away the rest.

All this had flashed through my mind when I heard her say that she couldn't let the O'Hurley baby die. All this and a little more. As long as her attention was on this baby's survival, it could not be on me and my mother's written intention to take me back with her. So I asked, 'Shouldn't it be fed now?'

'Not till ten. And what a carry on with those bottles, sterilizing them and preparing the milk. We shall just have to get used to its wailing,' and to some extent we did, during the daytime, that is, when it lay in its drawer placed across two chairs in the kitchen. But a night soon came when its father, asked by my Aunt to please take his son into their bedroom for the night, declined to do so. His wife was too ill with the three bad nights they'd had and if she couldn't recover a bit of strength, she would never be able to move into the furnished accommodation in Grove Hill that had been positively promised by the week end. If the baby wailed, then let it wail. Its heart and lungs were stronger than those of his poor wife. He would set the alarm for two o'clock and feed it downstairs.

That night Auntie heaved herself into bed and we lay still, hearing through the floorboards and the lino a storm of angry remonstrance from the kitchen. It was possible, I supposed, to cover your ears with blankets and, in fact, I was just drifting into a comfortable drowsiness when my

240

Aunt sat up, flung off the bedclothes and exclaimed, 'I can stand it no longer. The child's no bigger than that baby doll of yours. At this rate it will choke or burst a blood vessel. I could never have believed,' she went on, striking a match to light the candle, 'that such parents existed. It's inhuman!'

The next thing I knew was being told to move over and keep on my back. I could recover a bit of bed when she got settled. The bundle in her arms continued to yell as she laid it beside me.

'Oh, for goodness' sake stop it,' she ordered, easing herself back into bed. Then, unfastening the buttons on her nightgown, she drew the child to her bare chest.

'There, there, there,' she crooned. 'You poor little thing. They might as well have left you on a doorstep. Have you enough room, Martha? We mustn't smother it.' The baby had no worries on that score. In less time than it took me to make myself a ledge of sorts, its yells had subsided into fitful intakes of breath, and by the time I'd straightened out my legs, it was silent.

'Would you believe it,' whispered my Aunt, 'that's all the little scrap wanted,' and, without relinquishing her hold on it, she managed to twist over and snuff out the candle with her fingers.

Of the three, I was last to fall asleep. A doubt gnawed at me. Had Doctor Macphail really said she would make a capital mother? Why then, I reasoned, can't she breast-feed this baby. Why can't any woman, not just the mother, breast-feed a baby? (Though mentally I used the word 'breast-feed', I still could not bring myself to think of the word 'breast'.) That Encyclopedia I had acquired at Christmas — a wonderful gift — contained paragraphs about everything under the sun, yet I'd seen nothing on the subject of babies. It was time I found something out. I would soon be eleven.

Chapter Twenty-One

Meanwhile I was following the routine set by the hospital Sister. I was up and about in the house but must lie flat between two and four each afternoon. Outside, walking was a gradual progression, up to Aubrey Street and back, down to Acton Street and back, still up and down though the Lane was as flat as a pancake and the routine reminiscent of my three-year-old exploration. Gradually the distance was extended though I was not yet able to walk as far as Marton Road school where candidates for stage two of the scholarship examination had to assemble one morning in May. Doctor Macphail had kept his word and there I was scheduled to appear with those who had passed stage one, my cousin Margaret amongst them. I had not been allowed to return to school for coaching, but Miss Byers had brought round specimen papers and other work set by Miss Gibson. I had re-introduced myself to pen and ink and started. I knew it was generally thought that the whole business was a sheer waste of time, and I gathered from Auntie's attitude that Miss Byers thought so too.

'What did she say to you?' I asked.

'That it's been enough to pull you through those illnesses. Your health comes first,' and this reply strengthened my conviction that hopes of a teaching career for me were now abandoned.

Yet the doctor had been right I reflected, after completing the arithmetic revision. I had worked through the four rules in number, money, weights and measures, vulgar and decimal fractions, percentages, stocks and shares just as though I'd never been away from them. As for those problems about men working to time, my brain was not blocked, as it had once been, by their apparent unreality. What if a man did take some time off? Hadn't I done so? Not the odd hour, but months at a stretch. And, I reasoned, what difference had that made to the sum total of events? 'It boils down to the same in the end,' I had heard people say. As for the grammar, I had lost nothing since the time when I was helping Sylvia. He had been right. Nothing hammered home was ever forgotten. I slept well the night before the examination.

The test papers had no innovations. The material was much the same as on those I had completed and the one thing I recall vividly is writing an essay on 'Coal'. Although there was a choice, Miss Gibson need have had no worry on my account for I wasted not a second in deciding. I saw the title, 'Coal', and knew that I had more to write on that subject than time would allow. I felt, in fact, that I could write all day about coal. Not that I was the only child likely to make that choice. Most of us knew plenty about it — how expensive it was because of its use in the iron and steel works; how it was mined at risk to men's lives, blinding of ponies and deaths of canaries; how miners' wives had to slave to keep their husbands clean, always heating water for tin baths and spending so much on soap that went nowhere in hard water. How, when an accident occurred, old women and young stood side by side, dry-eyed, waiting at the pit head, fear, courage, agony all mixed together on account of coal. Then how the pit owners took all the profits and lived in mansions while the miners made do with tiny terraced houses and died young of lung disease. In one way or another most children were aware of these things, so that what examiners expected when they set 'Coal' as an essay subject for the scholarship examination in Middlesbrough just after the General Strike of 1926 is hard to imagine for me, now.

But not for me then. Because of the Encyclopedia and what I'd learnt about coal from that. My head had spun with an extraordinary excitement. It seemed that millions of years ago when the world was very young and unpolluted by people, coal had actually been beautiful. Not lumpy, black and dirty, but airy and green in the form of ferns like moor bracken enlarged hundreds of times. Tall, thick, juicy fronds like hands reaching high towards the sun and greedily absorbing its rays as they fell with force and heat through the still dazed air. The wood at the beginning of the world, I'd thought, which grew so fast and furiously that it then sank under its own weight deep into the earth, and, after a few millenia — a word I liked — had been transformed into coal. Avidly I had re-read these pages and saw in them a fact of enormous wonder and significance. Coal *was* sunlight and what did all the years matter? This change was fact, not legend or prophecy, and I had felt like that merchant who had found the pearl of great price. My Aunt did not want me to examine pieces of coal to find the imprint of a fern. She said my dirty fingers would leave black marks on everything. 'Just till I find one,' I pleaded, 'one piece, to keep.' So she humoured me and asked, 'Whatever next?'

I wrote that day until we were told there were five more minutes to go, and I managed to bring the essay to an end.

One day in June Mrs O'Hurley rose from her bed and, with the minimum of help from her husband, walked down the stairs and stood waiting in the hall until he removed their luggage to the pavement. A motor cab was due and would transport them to a house in the new council estate between Grove Hill and North Ormesby. My Aunt kissed Terence several times before giving him to his father and said she hoped they would be able to manage. She would have been fully justified in thinking the opposite but, in two years time we went to see them and there Mr O'Hurley proudly exhibited his son, red-haired like himself, tumbling about on a lawn the size of a man's pocket handkerchief. Mrs O'Hurley, the image of a pale pre-Raphaelite woman but with black hair, showed no sign of frailty except in a reluctance to use her voice. When Auntie asked, 'And how is the heart?' she seemed slow to understand, then said in a refined accent, 'I don't believe there's anything wrong with his heart.' Mr O'Hurley, who had just straightened up after somersaulting Terence, cut in on the last word. 'Miss Drinkhall refers to your own heart, my dear,' and went on to supply the information that Doctor O'Flannagan had high hopes.

We had a cup of tea and a cherry bun and, on the way back, Auntie was silent until, as we turned in at the top of the Lane, she said, 'And when I consider, if it hadn't been for me, that fine child would not be here! As for his mother's heart, that was a load of blarney.' Years later, when I leaned over to kiss the Blarney Stone, I thought of Mr O'Hurley.

Their removal from the house and Tom still staying with Minnie, gave Auntie a chance to spring-clean, out of season, as she said, in preparation for the influx from across the Atlantic. No sooner was this underway than it was brought to an abrupt halt by a visit from Miss Byers to say that I had passed the scholarship with my name near the top of the list for all the town. My Aunt, she said, would receive official confirmation. We had hardly managed to digest this, when confirmation indeed arrived along with a form to be completed by the parent or legal guardian of the child. My Aunt filled it in, signed her name and, not trusting the post with an important document, took it herself to the Education Offices at the top of Woodlands Road. In two days time a letter came asking for verification of my parents' deaths and documental proof that she was my legal guardian and this communication began the fiercest battle my Aunt was ever called upon to wage with officialdom because, when the Director of Education learned that my parents were alive and living in the U.S.A., he promptly closed my file and dictated a brief letter stating that I was not eligible to benefit from this scholarship due to the fact that my parents were not rate payers and she herself was not my guardian according to the law.

It was unfortunate for the Director that his office was so near. I am convinced that staff routine was interrupted in direct proportion to the wear and tear on my Aunt's shoe leather and bunions. She would make them pay, she said, for another pair of hand made shoes. Personal confrontation was at first the overriding ploy in her campaign, but when it failed to produce immediate results, she resorted to other methods. She thought nothing of Hannah's suggestion.

'You should get up a petition, Blanche. You'd get columns of names.'

'Whose names?' The reply sounded as if she were sucking an acid drop. 'And where do you think petitions land? In waste paper baskets without so much as a second glance at them. But I know people whose letters would not be ignored, and that's my next move.'

So work in the house came to a standstill while she wrote in her round, rather sprawling script. In a town no larger than Middlesbrough most influential men knew each other, but how they came to know my Aunt was a mystery. Often enough I had heard their names drop from her lips — Preston Kitchen, William Crossthwaite, Joseph Calvert, Sir Hugh Bell and Penry Williams, not to mention those from the top hierarchy of trade, Mr Dickson of Dickson and Bensons, Mr Wright of Sussex Street, Mr Lithgow and Mr Newhouse, and, more understandable, Mr Meredith. Her occasional references to them left an impression that these men, total strangers to me, were on visiting terms with our household.

'How do you know these men?' I had asked more than once.

'How do I know them? Wasn't your Grandfather a tradesman and a house owner in the days when Middlesbrough was a place to be proud of? Didn't he help to get Woodlands Road Chapel built?'

'How?'

'What do you mean, how? He agitated. This part of the town was growing like a weed. It needed a chapel. He made his voice heard.' And this was what my Aunt intended to do now on my behalf by writing to these personages as well as to Mr Outhwaite, representing the law, Doctor Macphail, the medical profession, Sister Storey, the hospital, Constable Allinson, the police force and, in respect of religion, the current Methodist minister whose name is mixed up with several in my memory, we had so many different ones. We lived on cold meat and a large emergency fruit cake through which Cyril and Mr Gendall hacked their way until a point was reached when Mr Gendall took over in the kitchen without a hint of protest from Auntie who was far too busy appealing to these men's sense of justice and telling everyone that they too were busy writing to the Director of Education on my account. She took time off only to wheel me to the Infirmary or knock once again on the doors of the Education Office.

Singularly, those who had condemned my taking the

examination as a waste of time for all concerned, now stood four square behind my Aunt. Even Aunt Gertrude which says much, since Margaret had not passed and was destined for Hugh Bell Central School.

'What is the Education Authority,' I heard Aunt Gertrude say, 'but a lot of upstarts who can't recognize a comma from a full stop? What do the likes of them know about marking papers? '

That was about all she did say, but she hoped my Aunt would put them in their place. The question, 'And what if her Mother comes for her?' was asked more than once and by more than one person, but I realised that it was asked merely to put my Aunt on her toes should the Director decide to ask the same question. Her supporters did not see the issue as being me, but as an opportunity to wrestle with the powers that be and bring them to heel. Auntie had become a champion for the underdog.

The postman was never off the doorstep. I gathered that all my Aunt's letters were answered, the replies read, digested, and a further letter posted to the sender. My Mother had been informed, but the letter would take eight days to reach her and she was never prompt to reply. Although I felt shelved, I must have had some grip on the situation because I recall asking Auntie, 'What can Mother do about it except get you to legally adopt me? Or come back here to stay?' My Aunt was too engrossed to think this over, let alone supply an answer.

When a director of anything closes a file, the odds are heavy, I understand, against his re-opening it, no matter what forces are pressing him to do so. In this case pressure must have been considerable because, towards the end of June, a single letter shot through the slot and fell on the door mat. When it was opened and read, Auntie was left stunned and silent.

'What is it? Please what is it?' I begged, because what would she do, I thought in anguish, if she had lost?

'It's you. They've asked you to attend for an interview this Saturday morning. Unaccompanied. Without me, that is. I don't know what that means.' Nor did I know. I knew even less than she because she, presumably, knew what an interview was. She had no time to explain, since today was Wednesday, half day closing, and she must get to Newhouses to buy something to make me a dress. It would take too long to search through her scraps and, if she could find any, too long to work out the intricate business of how to fit scraps together to make a decent dress.

I am guessing at the name of that material, a kind of silk rep, but its appearance and texture are sharp in my memory. I refused to be taken to the Education Office. The letter, I insisted, stated that I must go alone, and if she would persist in her intention of taking me to the gates and waiting for me, then I wouldn't go. What prompted my resistance to her reasonable proposal I didn't know, but can only surmise that I felt the ball had been pitched into my court and it was now for me to play.

So, for the second time in my life I walked up Woodlands Road in a state of intense self-awareness and in particular of my attire. The first time had been seven years earlier when I had headed for Victoria Road School to seek and demand admission and had been irritated by the wide scarf crossed over my chest, under my armpits and fastened at the back with safety-pins. This time I was in an unpatterned dress of prussian blue with a shiny surface that shimmered as if shadows passed over it as I walked. The skirt, which hung well below my knees, was just a piece of gathered material neatly attached to a simple magyar waist with a round and collarless neckline. It was a style which small girls use at the second stage of sewing dolls' clothes, the first being a plain magyar shape without a separate skirt. I reflected on the excessive simplicity of this dress, knowing there had not been time for even a fragment of decoration. Still, a lace collar would have improved matters, I thought; and, just as seven years ago I had blamed the scarf for locking me out of the school playground, now I felt I would blame the unadorned dress if this Board were to deny me entrance to the High School. A straw hat was jammed well down on my head and my hands encased in a pair of cotton hand-knitted gloves. What to expect at the Education Office was as much a mystery as my destination had been at the age of four.

What I saw on being ushered into a sombre room was a

sort of arc − not quite a semi-circle − of narrow table-top along the far side of which sat a number of gloomy men. I felt all eyes on me as I was positioned by the man who brought me in to a central spot with the seated figures ranged equally to right and left and curving round at the ends. Exactly, I thought, like a target for a firing squad. The fate of deserters during the war had exercised a morbid hold on my imagination. A fleeting wish to be blindfolded passed through me. It vanished and I looked at these men.

I had not been pre-disposed to greeting them with a friendly smile. Neither was I at that time predisposed to liking people in general. But let there be no question about it, this interview was the moment when I ranged myself as a female on the side of all females fighting for recognition in a man's world. Whatever the cause for which my Aunt and her friends had fought, my own thoughts, as I stood there in a home made dress of prussian blue confronted by this band of men, flew to the cause of women.

'Your name is Martha Bryce?'

'Yes, sir.'

'And you live at 85 Park Lane?'

The questionnaire continued for a while with such particulars. Then, without preamble, a man to my left asked, 'If a herring and a half cost sixpence, how much would four herrings cost?'

Really, for a moment I was convinced that this was a joke; the sort of facetious remark of a Mr Rouney or the thoughtless jesting of someone like Cyril. Then I saw it as neither. It was a joke, but with intention, and that to humilitate me. These men knew that I was not to be admitted to the High School. I had been brought here as a move to settle my Aunt. She would receive a letter to say that, after having interviewed me, they had found me wanting, not suitable to take advantage of the place I had won. Their decision, the letter would state, was not based on my parents' absence, but on my own unsuitability. What other explanation could justify a question such as this? I was to be intimidated and put out of my stride. All this passed through my head in a timeless second. I answered him.

'You mean, sir, that herrings are fourpence each so that four would cost one and fourpence. But herrings are not that price. My Aunt buys them every week from Mrs Mansfield in Corporation Road. A long time ago, they were two a penny, then they went up to a penny each and now they're twopence each and that's more than most people can afford. Mrs Mansfield could not sell a herring for fourpence and she would never sell half of one.'

A stir rustled along the table top. Some of the men picked up papers and put them back again. One removed his spectacles, wiped them and clipped them back on his nose. The man who had asked the question said, 'My dear girl, the question was hypothetical. I was merely testing your aptitude in mental arithmetic.'

Then a man in the centre spoke.

'Your parents live in the United States of America, I understand?'

'Yes, sir.'

'And when did you last see them?'

'On my eighth birthday. The day they left.'

'Can you tell us why they left you behind?'

'I don't think they left me, sir. I wanted to stay. With my grandmother.'

'Your grandmother?' He looked down at the paper on his bit of table. 'But you live with your Aunt. Where is your grandmother?'

'She died.'

That seemed to satisfy him, and another man continued.

'What we should like to know is why your parents have not sent for you. A child's place is with its parents. Are they not thinking of sending for you?'

'I don't know what they are thinking, sir. I only know that my father will not become an American citizen. He is still British and he wants me to be educated here. He thinks it's better here, for education.' (I withheld my mother's views on the subject. My father's, I sensed, were useful.)

After a silence which gave this man time to write on his paper, another man spoke in a high, clipped voice, a little nervously, it struck me, as though he knew he should

250

make a contribution but had difficulty in knowing what it ought to be.

'Well, you're still very young, but what are your own views on the subject of your education?'

He received a surprised stare from the man in the centre which, I felt sure, meant that his contribution was anything but the right one. As far as I was concerned, it was all right. I had plenty of views on that subject.

'I want to go to the High School, sir. In fact, I had made up my mind to go there if I could pass the examination. I wrote and told my parents so. I told them I would not go to America. I should like, above everything, to go to the High School and then to become a teacher.'

The nervous man nodded his head twice, but wrote nothing down. I took it that this information was not worth recording. Another man, the second from the end on my left, then spoke.

'I see that a medical certificate was sent to absolve you from taking stage one of the examination. Your Aunt's letters say nothing about illness. Have you been ill for long?'

This was a tricky question and I knew it. During the commotion at home I heard people tell Auntie not to mention my illness in any of her letters. A mention of this would not operate in my favour; just the reverse. But these men knew of my illness through that certificate. And what about the school registers and Sister Storey? What could she write except about illness? My answer must reduce the illness to its lowest common denominator. My brain worked furiously. The rest of me felt weak as water and longed for a chair arm to grip.

'A little while, sir. But it was due to the removal of my tonsil.'

'Your tonsil? Surely you mean tonsils. Tonsils, plural, you know.'

'No, only one, and not even a whole one. Only half. Our doctor says it was fortunate for me they only got half because tonsils are the first line of resistance against infection. With only one tonsil working, my body gave way to infection. But I'm having treatment, and the tonsil they damaged is growing again. So I'm all right now.'

I felt anything but all right. Interviews went on far too

long. Then a man at the end of the row to my right whose back was to the window and his face in shadow spoke.

'And what happened to those pet mice, Martha?'

It startled me and everyone else. We all stared at him as if we had misheard. He rose, brought over his chair and told me to sit on it.

'She had begun an exciting essay in school one day. I wish I had seen the end. Did you intend the wanderer to return?'

'It did return, sir. We caught it and put it back in the hutch. Then the others lynched it.'

Afterwards I realised how I had gradually grown to understand that if you said something unexpected, then these men were not quite sure how to take it or how to answer you. By this time, though, I wondered how long I could keep it up. As it transpired, there was no need to worry because this man, after a pause, said, 'Oh, what a sad ending. I'm sorry. However, you wrote well on coal, too. I read that and really, I'd never thought there could be so much wrapped up in a common or garden piece of coal.'

The gathering together and straightening up of papers pointed, I thought, to an end and in another minute or two, the man in the middle said that was all, thank you. The inspector asked me if I felt all right. An interview was always an ordeal. Was my Aunt waiting outside for me? I told him no, I had asked her not to come; I could get home all right alone. He actually patted my shoulder and said yes, he thought so too.

Chapter Twenty-Two

Why did she have to make the blouses like that, fastening down the back instead of the front and causing the collar to be in two halves thus exposing a section of the striped tie at the back. I couldn't see it, but I was forever putting a hand to the back of my neck to feel it, looking so silly to the girl sitting behind me. I failed to understand it, seeing that Auntie was so good at cutting out from patterns. Why could she not have bought a blouse pattern and made a blouse that looked like all the others, fastening down the front? Nor was this the only difference. Why, oh why was the blouse not white? All the others were white and the paper had said so — three white blouses. Was she blind to colour?

'But the material is not white,' I had argued when I'd seen it on the table fresh in its folding from Newhouses. 'It isn't white. It's a dirty sort of colour.'

'The material is unbleached. It will whiten with washing and boiling. All white material is unbleached to start with. They use strong bleaches to whiten it and take out all the body so that there's very little wear left in it. I cannot afford new material again in a hurry. Your blouses will have to last until you outgrow them.'

'How many boilings will be needed to turn it white?'

'How do I know? I've never counted the boilings when I've washed unbleached sheets.'

'And is that why the material's so thick and ridgy? Will the ridges wash out? Margaret's blouses are not thick like that. The material's thin and smooth.'

'This is poplin, not cotton. It's warmer and wears better.'

She was determined that they should be warm. She lined them with material of the same colour but with a satin finish, the sort in use these days for lining curtains. I was inclined to blame these blouses for the relapse into another bout of illness within a few weeks after entering the High School. It was all very well taking into account her struggle to buy all the items listed under Compulsory Uniform Regulations. I had gone with her to Newhouses and tried on the gymn tunic, blazer, winter coat and matching cap shaped like a pork pie. The summer hat, it stated, could be purchased next term. I did not try on the tie nor the navy blue knickers about which there was that terrible scene.

'Can anyone tell me,' she asked in her ringing voice, 'why High School girls have to have special knickers?'

No wonder the assistant looked startled and customers found time to stand and stare. After all, she seemed to have addressed the entire department. The assistant said, 'I don't really know, madam, but it could be for doing gymnastics.' 'I thought,' said my Aunt, 'that that was the purpose of the gymn tunic,' She paid over the counter three pound notes and received a piece of paper, folded, placed in an envelope and handed over with the words, 'Your account, madam.' and I knew, by various indications, that she felt diminished. She had been silent while the items where packed and said no more than 'Thank you,' between tight lips. And that same tautness was in her body and the set of her head; a kind of mask.

'What's in that paper she gave you?' I asked, linking it with her demeanour.

'Nothing much. It's the way I'm paying the rest of the bill, bit by bit. Newhouses know they will get their money, but it's the first time I've had to do this.'

So, if we had to be different in the way it was paid for, why did she need to increase the difference in the blouse material and style?

Differences were thrust upon you within the first half hour of entering the High School. We were assembled in rows in a vast hall containing no desks. At the back were very tall girls and the height decreased towards the high platform at the front. I stood more or less below it, no one having told me where to stand. Hymn books were distributed and we sang a hymn I had never heard before, 'Lord, behold us with thy blessing'. A tall thin teacher with straight grey hair read some prayers, then her place at the stand was taken by a short, stocky woman wearing spectacles and an even more severe hair style. After a short speech, she told everyone to dismiss to their classrooms except the new girls who must await instructions. I saw no one I knew, but a girl on my right suddenly spoke to me.

'Isn't it awful?' and when I nodded, she said, 'Let's stick together, shall we? My name's Doreen. . . .'

I don't remember her last name and, although I recall perfectly her round face, short bobbed hair, worried, spectacled eyes, I have no recollection of seeing her again. Within minutes we newcomers were segregated into groups called Forms 2A, 2B, and 2C. I quickly absorbed this differentiation which extended into the playground, and, more gradually, the fact that 2C, consisting of the scholarship pupils, was at the bottom of the scale, the underlings. Two other factors marked me off as different — I was absent Monday and Thursday afternoons and was forbidden by a medical certificate to take part in physical training or games. So, when the rest removed their gymn tunics and tucked their blouses into their knickers — as the shop assistant had guessed — and were scrambling up wall bars or vaulting a thing called a horse, I was in our classroom doing homework, or prep, as it must now be termed.

I was there one Friday afternoon about a month into term with a book of ballads lying open before me. Outside, netball was in progress and, as I had watched the game practised during afternoon breaks, I could follow it by the sounds. It was a second storey window open at the top. I heard the thump of the ball caught and passed, the running thudding feet, the sudden hush while the shooter was aiming, the bounce through the goal net and the whistle, 'Well-played! Two–one, Reds.'

My throat hurt, my head ached and I knew I was hot. I did not even hear the door open, only the voice, 'Oh, I'm so sorry. I thought this classroom was empty. Is something wrong? Are you not feeling well?'

A tutor! But this approach marked her as different from the ones who had taught me. Different altogether, from anyone. How did I see her, at that moment? As someone perplexed, but striving to deal with her perplexity; to get at the meaning of things; her exceptionally wide mouth

255

letting words go reluctantly, thinking about them. High colour in her face, high cheek bones — high enough to support a pair of rimless lenses — and a quantity of short, black hair tousled as if she'd just come in from the wind. A touch of diffidence clung to her, standing there just within the door, pushing the fingers of one hand into her hair making it stand up, fine and wiry.

'Shall I bring the sal-volatile?'

I said no, thank you, having never heard of that, then told her I was listening to the netball.

'You've not been sent in?'

'No, I'm excused.'

Her finger tips pressed her brow as if she were trying to deal with the problem. She said, 'But you can't be more than eleven?' and I told her I was not. She registered concern. 'Oh dear, you're young to have started with that. Never mind, only once a month.'

'Once a . . . No. I'm not allowed to play games at all. It's doctor's orders.'

Her skin flamed. She pressed a bit of hair into some sort of wave. We stared. Her face puckered as though trying to come to terms with something. I longed to say, 'Don't worry. Please don't worry. But oh, how glad I am you're here.' Of course I said nothing at all. The ball hit the window. The whistle blew. I was back in 2C classroom.

'I'm sorry. Sorry you can't play games. Do you mind if I sit here to mark some work?'

I couldn't believe my ears, but managed to say, 'Of course not.' I didn't know her name and we had been told not to address a tutor as just Miss. She had opened her first book and used her fountain pen two or three times when she looked up. 'What is that you're studying?'

'The Armada. At least I'm learning it.'

'What, all of it?'

'Well, it's fairly easy to learn. I've done half.'

'Good gracious! Do you really like it?'

'Not much. Except the bit about the beacons.'

'It isn't poetry, of course. Do you like real poetry?'

'Some of the poems we learned at Victoria Road I loved. Some not so much. I like Shakespeare's sonnets.'

'Good gracious!' She learned over, fumbled in her bag

256

and brought out a slim book with a dull green back.

'Here's a book of modern poetry. *Poems of Today.* Perhaps you'd like to try some of those?'

'Thank you. But I have to learn this for homework. Prep, I mean.'

'Of course. You're new this term, I gather. What is your name?'

I told her and she said, flicking through the pages, 'There's a poem in here called 'Martha'. By Walter de la Mare. Here it is. Would you like to read it?'

I took the book and read the poem and, when she asked me, I said yes, it was beautiful though not a bit like me. I had been in a hazel wood once, but never in a hazel glen. And I had no children to tell stories to. At that she laughed and said, 'All the same, I think there's a resemblance. You can borrow the book, if you like. It's my own. Let me have it back some time.'

Then she got up, said she must go, and left without marking so much as another book.

That was my last day at the High School for a long time. As my muscles smouldered with pain and my temperature soared, so, to redress the balance, my spirits sank. The word 'depression' was not in common use then except for a shallow concavity in the ground. You were in either low spirits or the slough of despond, the origin of which was still known to many. When Doctor Macphail resumed his visits, his own lack of despondency enraged me, especially his silly pun about my being back to the front again.

'Why don't you say I'm back where I started? What's been the use of it all?

'Is she delirious, Doctor? I don't think she's aware of what she's saying or she would never speak to you like that. '

'Don't worry, Miss Drinkhall. She's in full possession of her senses.'

'Of course I am. I'm just sick of being ill. It's no use telling me this time that I won't forget things. What about the ones I haven't learnt like French and Latin and Maths?'

'You'll catch up. This is only a temporary set back, another bout of rheumatic fever which tends to return. Your body's claiming a chance to fight it. You've a set of excitable glands, a blessing in disguise, perhaps, for when you're grown up. This world will never be free of disease; as one is overcome, another will take its place. It's the resistance built in childhood that counts.'

What did I want with these prophetic utterances? 'What's the use of talking about when I'm grown up? I don't want to grow up. I should have died before, and I want to die now. So there!'

'How dare you talk so in front of the doctor? You're a naughty girl with your peculiar moods and Mrs Burt is quite right about you. You've always had a naughty streak. You're a bit like your mother.'

'Now, now, now,' the doctor interposed, 'Leave out family matters. I'd rather have a patient in this mood than one who refuses to speak at all,' and that silenced me. 'It's all a question of patience, and when you're feeling a little better, there's no reason why you shouldn't have some of your friends in to see you. There's no risk of infection and they'll do you good. And back for your hospital treatment as soon as possible.'

The Burts had moved to a new house near North Ormesby but they arranged with Auntie to give me a Christmas Party in the bedroom, an innovation indeed since ordinary parties, as distinct from family gatherings, were little known in our social setting and earnest parents were just having to admit them into their children's lives. A bedroom party, as Mrs Burt said, was quite something, and Laura was bringing the two children of some close friends of theirs, the Swinnertons. Cyril slung some paper streamers round the picture moulding, there being no space for a tree or even a mistletoe what with the double bed and all the funiture. We played guessing games such as Animal, Vegetable or Mineral, and games with pencil and paper, the outstanding one being Consequences suggested by Kathleen, a tall fourteen-year-old. At first I was all against this 'what happens when boy meets girl' game, but found myself laughing as the absurd and unconnected sequence of events was read aloud from each paper at the end. 'He turned her over his knee and spanked her' was a consequence which I suspected came from Laura; it was so like her. My suggestion of whist was turned down by three non-players who had seen only Happy Families in the card line.

At tea-time there was constant traffic on the stairs with both sets of parents and Auntie clattering up and down with tea, sandwiches, cakes, jellies and tinned pears – the only tinned fruit I would eat – and finally the Christmas Cake. This was cut on the commode, decorously concealed beneath an embroidered cloth and, for this event all the adults crowded into the room so that there was not an empty square on the patchwork quilt and little air left to breathe. Laura said that a bedroom party was fun and was told by her father to remember this one since he hoped it would be her first and last. Auntie said we had Mrs Burt to thank and I supported this by saying, 'It's a lovely party, Mrs Burt. Thank you,' thus closing a door on all criticisms and resentments. As the Christmas Cake was handed round, my Aunt said, 'I didn't send one to America this year. I thought they would be here.' And Mrs Burt asked, 'Is there still no word of them coming?' She was as critical, I knew, of my mother's behaviour as she had been of mine, having often remarked that she was no mother, leaving her child like that.

'It's postponed almost month by month. I don't know when they'll come and, really, I see no point in it. With Martha at the High School, she'll not be going back with them,' and in the silence which followed, we each pursued our own thoughts, or none at all.

Such thoughts, unspoken, tend to weigh on the air so that, when everything had been cleared away and everyone had gone, the words that Mrs Burt had sound reason for saying and which I could read in her expression came knocking on my consciousness and had no trouble in gaining admittance. What good *had* come of my getting into the High School? I had nothing but *Poems of Today* to remind me of a brief month in that building, the building which, from the night of the Felix Corbett concert, I had imagined to be the Palace Beautiful. The book had been returned to school by my Aunt who had seen no one but Miss Bedford. Then, in some obscure manner, it had come back. This had occurred during the first days of high fever and afterwards the only fact I could extract from her was that it had been sent as a gift from the school. I was chilled and baffled.

'Didn't you ever discover her name — the one who gave it to me?' I pestered again and again.

'No. How many times have I to tell you? Miss Bedford asked me to wait in her room. When she returned, she said she was sorry you were ill and perhaps you'd like to keep the book as a gift from the school. If you liked poetry, you would probably enjoy it.'

'But she said it was *her* book, the teacher who lent it to me. Her own, not the school's, and she asked me to return it to her.'

'Well, that's all I can tell you. You probably misunderstood, what with your temperature and your headache. In any case, why are you making such a fuss? It's very nice of the school to give you a book. You should be grateful. I told Miss Bedford, as I've said dozens of times, that you would write to say thank you, but she said no, she would rather you didn't. The matter was closed, and I had to tell you so.'

She had told me so, and, however much I tried, I could not alter that end. I reached over to the wash stand, picked up the book and drew it to my chest. The matter was closed. Not a 'matter' and not 'closed'. A thing of beauty which she'd destroyed, or tried to. Well, I still had the book; hers, not the school's, and already much of it was in my head. So different from anything I'd heard before. A whole new world. I opened the front of my nightgown and pushed the roughish surface inside against my skin, and something bordering on ecstasy was released as words proceeded in their customary manner through my head:

> Hers the kiss of Mother Mary,
> The long hair is on her face;
> Still she goes with footsteps wary,
> Full of earth's old, timid grace.

I didn't know whether it was she or the earth. They were one and the same, and no one could destroy that moment. It was, is, and will ever be.

Chapter Twenty-Three

The reason for my parents' return and their subsequent stay for the better part of a year has always remained unclear. For people in our walk of life, the Atlantic was not an ocean one whimsically crossed and recrossed with no set intent. It was as much as you could do to find the fare for the initial voyage westward and very rarely did you return within a decade. My cousin had returned in less than two years ostensibly to take back Doris Mould, my Aunt and I knowing she would never go, and I believe he knew it too, at heart. He came for a month just after the General Strike of 1926 and found the town in worse shape than when he'd left it, the Strike having managed to throw three thousand more men into the ranks of the unemployed. Being money conscious, I saw then his visit as a quixotic way of spending his hard-earned savings. 'Please go back and find a nice American girl,' I had urged him, but, even before he left us, according to Auntie, he had his sights set on a Model T Ford. I also thought that if my mother was determined that I should join them, then why had she not arranged for me to return with Bob. It would have saved a lot of money. Moreover, it was known for children to cross the Atlantic on their own in the care of the shipping company and under the watchful eyes of the purser and other officers. And why, in 1927, must my entire family come for me, thus spending so much that they could not afford? The purpose of this interlude always remained vague, unstated, undefined, although it may have had its own obscure consequences. For one thing, it turned my world upside down; at an age when I should have been putting away childish things, I suddenly reverted to childhood, or into those carefree imaginings for which that stage of life is said to cater.

'She doesn't look anything like as poorly as I'd expected.' These are the first words I actually recall my mother saying, and I was not concerned with how she saw

me healthwise, only with how she viewed my extraordinary position and appearance. A great girl of twelve seated
on her Aunt's lap and with a number of corkscrew curls
twitching about with every move of her head. What my
mother was seeing was not *me*; an unpleasant fact for
which I could see no immediate remedy. Never before had
my hair been twisted for a whole night in ten rags, and
twisted so effectively that I had been unable to brush out
the corkscrews. Moreover in the undimmed recollections
of my childhood, there had been but one lap-sitting
session and that on the knees of a Sunday School teacher
when I was six. My Aunt and I had always been too busy
to indulge in nursing in this particular sense; and my
mother, I remembered, eyeing her now, had never been
given to such demonstrations of maternal care. At this
moment, without creating a scene, I saw no way of
removing myself because, after having cleared the table
and washed up, Auntie had pulled me onto her lap and was
holding me there by force. Was she, I wondered, making
quite sure that I didn't land on my Mother's?

Mother was seated on a chair brought in from the front
room. My sisters, Bessie aged ten and Monica, seven,
were planted more securely than I, each on one end of the
fender, their hair in short, straight bobs and fringes, one
dark, one fair. My father was missing. He had some work
to complete, and would follow, we were told, in the late
summer. So here they were at last, and, on the fringe of
my own painful self-consciousness, there hovered a
twinge of curiosity about my mother's feelings after four
years absence from the house that had been her home but
had now lost its homemaker. Grannie had not been
mentioned as we had eaten the excellent supper of ham and
egg pie with sliced potatoes crisped up in the frying pan.
My sisters had used forks only and Mother had cut up
their pie into small pieces. Despite this, a lot had been left
on their plates, likewise small chunks of queen cakes and
almond tarts which they were prepared to accept when
offered, but not prepared to clean up.

'Don't you like your cake?' Auntie asked. They seemed
surprised. Bessie nodded and Monica said, 'Yeth thank
you, Auntie,' but neither did anything about the left-overs

which would do, my mother said, to feed the swans on the park lake if they were still there.

Cyril and Mr Gendall — Tom was still boarding at Minnie's — had eaten their suppers earlier, for the train had been late and we had suffered an hour's harrowing apprehension before the motor cab had finally drawn up at the door. The cases had been taken upstairs to the room I'd always thought of as Mother's, and here we were, after Auntie had washed up with Mother drying, all sitting in a rather awkward silence which had been broken by my mother's remark. It was well and truly broken because, in the ensuing minutes, all that Auntie had written to Mother regarding my condition was now reproduced verbally. I do not suppose for one moment that Mother's initial remark had been intended to inflame her sister. It might have been an expression of genuine relief at finding me not lying prone, but upright, becurled and able to tuck into food better than my sisters. But, whatever its intent, I'm sure Auntie saw it as a spurt of gunfire to be immediately countered by a prolonged volley of ammunition.

When she paused for breath, Mother suggested that they make for bed. The liner had lain outside the river from two in the morning awaiting the tide and no one had had much sleep. Then there had been the long wait in Liverpool for the train, so they were all pretty tired.

'I was up myself soon after four,' my Aunt replied. 'The bed to change and Mr Gendall's belongings to move again. It only seems like yesterday since he moved back into his own bedroom.'

'Last June,' I specified. Being now the end of April, I felt that Ralph had enjoyed a reasonable spell of viewing the grounds of the Nurses' Home and there was no need for such commiseration. He and Cyril were in the front room singing and playing a latest song hit, 'Me and my shadow strolling down the avenue', one line of which, 'By twelve o'clock we climb the stairs', seemed singularly appropriate as Mother, followed by my sisters, did so. Auntie looked in to tell them that was enough, we were all dead beat and needed a long night's sleep. But, before I went upstairs, she had enough energy left to remark on the peculiar clothes the children wore — those extraordinary jackets tied round their bottoms and those stockings, well, she couldn't believe it. One pair bright red, and other bright blue and *rolled down below their knees!*

A few mornings later, when Monica asked for a bag of bits to feed the swans, Auntie said, 'You're going now?' and gave one of her penetrating looks at Mother who answered it with, 'Yes, it's somewhere for them to go while I tidy up the bedroom and give it a clean.'

Already there had been words about clothes left lying on the bed and floor although drawers and the wardrobe had been emptied to accommodate all their garments.

'What a mess your bedroom was in! I've folded all those clothes and put them away or hung them up.'

'But Blanche, I don't know why you need to go into the room.'

'Because I've always done so. To make the bed, tidy up and clean it.'

'But that was for your lodger. Surely you don't regard us as lodgers!'

I think this was something Auntie had not considered. She thought it was beside the point, and said so. 'I like to know that all the rooms in my house are clean and tidy. And it's bad training for the children, never teaching them to fold away their clothes.'

'I'm not going to natter at them. They've had to largely bring themselves up when I've been out working, and they've managed. I wanted this to be a holiday for them.'

There was a break in her voice and I think Auntie heard it. What she replied was perhaps the obvious reply in the circumstances, but it did nothing to ease the tension between them.

'You'd have been better staying in England and letting Harry work for you.'

This morning she said, 'You can leave the bedroom if you want to go to the park. They can't go there on their own.'

'Why ever not?'

'Because only a month ago Martha was molested by a man in that Park.'

'Molested?'

So everything had to wait for a re-telling of my molestation. I was sick of it. I wished for the hundredth time that I

264

hadn't been so stupid. I had let a man persuade me into having a ride on his bicycle and the ride took us up a steep little hill rutted with tree roots and overhung with tree foliage. His hand fumbling under my coat that overlapped the saddle had meant nothing to me but, when I dismounted and that same hand fumbling in his pocket had drawn out a green boiled sweet and offered it to me, I took it that poison was intended. I flew and reached home in a state of near collapse. The fuss had been inordinate. A policeman − not Constable Allinson − had arrived and refused to believe that all the man had done was offer me a sweet.

Mother said, 'You can't be serious forbidding the three of them to go to the park together?' and she laughed. 'It's the only place round here for them to play and I've talked about it for long enough − the lake, the ducks, the swans. There might be some young ones and the daisies should soon be out. That's what I've longed to see, the park grass strewn with daisies. Give them the bag of scraps, Blanche, and take your ball. I suppose you'd better keep to the paths. You can't be under our feet all day. Next week I must get them into school.'

She did, but really to no one's satisfaction. As she had battled in Lawrence, Massachusetts, to get her children accepted as English speaking − not German, Italian or Greek − so now she struggled with Miss Bailey who said they were 'so far behind' in everything but reading that she did not know where to place them. Since they had no knowledge of pounds, shillings and pence, they ought really to be in the Infant Department. My mother, I discovered, was hot-tempered with teachers, and the fact that Bessie's teacher disposed of her by standing her for most of the time behind the blackboard, did not tend to cool her temper and caused her, I think, to pass disparaging remarks about the uniform in which, she said, I paraded. All American children wore what they liked to school. Uniform was a waste of money, encouraged class distinction and destroyed individuality.

The few weeks I was back at school before we went to Danby were not easy for me, either, being lost regarding French and Latin. It was decided that I must drop

Latin after the summer holiday and do Physics instead, a decision which I suppose was necessary, but which I have regretted all my life. Apparently it was impossible for me to re-live the lost year in 2C. I must move up with the rest.

At the start of the summer holiday we were whisked off to Danby to stay with Emily Cook, a woman who had known the family long before they had come to Middlesbrough and who knew Cousin Liz. Auntie had protested strongly about my going; I must not miss my treatment days. 'There are plenty of trains,' Mother had pointed out. 'She can use them.'

We children did not sit around listening to what Mother had to tell Emily Cook. I woke very early every morning, and very early had my sisters out either sailing paper boats on the rivulet at the bottom of Emily's hill, guiding them round the little boulders, pushing them through when the stream dipped underground; quinquereme of Nineveh to me, Laconia, Samaria to them; or sprawled on the edge of the moor that rose sheer above Emily's cottage. There they were a sufficient, if mind-wandering, audience for my cosmic discourses.

'It's not true that God made man in a moment of time.' They were pulling stubborn rushes from damp earth. 'Because, you see, the world was millions of years old before there were any men.'

'Or women,' Bessie elaborated.

'It was a beautiful empty world, like that,' and I drew an arc with my arm to indicate the moor.

'But sheep,' said Monica as a black faced one approached. 'I do wish I had some licorice all-sorts.'

'Why?'

'I gave a sheep one when we came. It liked it.'

'I don't think you should feed sheep licorice all-sorts. It's not part of their diet.'

'I can't give them any more. We haven't had any sweets since.'

This was true, but not a subject on which I then wished to dwell. It boiled down to money again.

'Anyway, when animals came, they weren't a bit like simple sheep. They were hundreds of times larger with extraordinary shapes and names. They all died out and no one knows why.' I was glad they took it solemnly, because the fate of these creatures was not only sad, but important.

'But some small creatures like monkeys survived and men came from them.'

'Women too?' asked Bessie.

It was useless to say anything. Her ignorance of 'men' as the collective noun for mankind just had to be endured.

'I'd like to have a little monkey,' said Monica, 'and watch it turn into a man.'

I was staggered by her lack of understanding. Yet how could I clarify the process. I didn't understand it myself, though aware of its overriding importance in my thinking.

'And some day all men, and women,' I emphasized for Bessie's sake, 'will die out and something else will take their place.'

'Children,' suggested Monica. 'Nothing but children. Children will not be wiped out.'

'Children too. It will be the end of the world as we know it, but it won't happen in a moment of time, as the Bible says, but in millions of years. That's what the Bible really means.' They had heard as much as they wanted to and said they were hungry.

The morning we set off to walk to Huck-a-Back, I believe my Mother was hoping for eggs, bacon and griddle cakes. We'd had bread scalded with Oxo for breakfast and I knew why. I heard Emily tell her she would find a great change in Lizzie who would now be seventy-eight. 'You'll not be welcomed by the couple who've gone in to take over the farm. I've heard the woman has no patience with the poor old soul. Folks say she'd be better off gone.' But Mother went her own way which was, that morning, towards Huck-a-Back. Until she was stopped by the storm. Just past Castleton Bridge, as we began the rise up to the village, a few raindrops fell, large as bullets and thunder growled in the hills. 'We'd better turn back,' said Mother. 'A storm's brewing and Huck-a-Back's too far.' I was relieved, having never forgotten how lightning viewed Huck-a-Back as a target. The storm took no time to brew. We had just re-crossed the bridge when the sky formed a black backcloth for patterns of lightning like tree roots. Thunder crackled and exploded and a torrent of rain made a mockery of our clothes. In a lull, as the noise rolled away, we were aware of another sound, a car coming down the hill making towards Danby. Mother drew us nearer the bank where we waited in the downpour. It came slowly, took the bend, approached us, then passed, a large pale gold shape with only the driver inside. It took the next bend and was out of sight.

'I could not believe it,' we children heard many times before reaching Emily's. 'Absolutely typical of England! A woman and three children out in a storm like this, and a car with room for at least five people passes them by. Such a thing would never, never have happened in America.'

Chapter Twenty-Four

Castleton, Commomdale, Kildale, Battersby, change. Great Ayton, Nunthorpe, Ormesby, Middlesbrough. Every station diminishing the certainty with which I had set out that a letter from my father must be waiting. An envelope, a page with something written on it, it didn't matter what, but enclosed in the folded page some money. At every stop the certainty had decreased, turning gradually into a cruel hope. Emily's bread and oxo could not last forever. Mother, I understood, need pay nothing for our lodging, but Emily had had to ask her to help provide our food. I carried a library book which Hannah had sent for Mother who was now returning it. Trying to read it was useless; I read the first four lines over and over again. They began and ended with the word 'hole'. Well, the hole in which Mr Polly found himself could be no worse than our hole if there should be no money from Father. As I alighted at Middlesbrough station and handed in my ticket, a thought struck me. From where would I have got the money for the fare if I had had no return ticket? Because Mother hadn't a penny. I couldn't have come for the Thursday treatment and we'd have had Auntie taking the next train to Danby.

Down the steps, along Albert Road, across the square to Southfield Road, down Woodlands Road to Park Lane and number 85. Through the door, the hall, and so to Auntie in the scullery and the smell, the mouth-watering smell of baking.

'What now?' She kisses me on both cheeks. 'You're early. You've been running.'

I flop onto the wooden chair by the deal table where she is crumbling fat with flour for pastry. Afraid to ask, afraid to hear the word No, prolonging the hope as I used to do when we were very poor with no lodgers, choking on shredded wheat, listening for the postman's rap.

'Hullo, Auntie. Is there a letter from Father?' There, I've said it.

'Yes, it's on the kitchen desk.'

The tension draining from every pore in my skin. The indescribable quiet within me. The welcome weakness.

'When did it come?'

'Tuesday. I saw no point in sending it on when you were coming today. You don't look well. There, drink up.'

Beef tea. Real beef tea. Heavenly, and a fresh baked cottage loaf.

'But Tuesday! If you'd sent it, it would have been there yesterday.'

'Goodness me, what difference does that make? What does it matter?'

Matter? Why do small things like this matter as much as if the world had come to an end?

'Because she has no money. Had no money after Monday. We had nothing to eat yesterday. At least nothing but oxo. Father's last letter came two weeks ago. The fare cost a lot, and my fare back and forth.' My Aunt throws the pastry onto the board and kneads it. Quite unlike her because that's not the way to treat pastry. Light handling is what is requires, as she has often told me. Her cheeks and ear turn an angry red.

'Can you credit it? There's no wonder you're upset. She comes back here to a good home where I do my best for you all. Give you good food and not ask for a penny. Then suddenly she up and takes off to Danby without giving me one good reason. And expects you all to live on fresh air and water.'

'She did say she thought it was too much for you, all us four here.'

'So she goes to Danby with no money to make it too much for Emily Cook. Where's the sense in that?'

I shook my head, spooned up the soaked bread speedily and asked for more.

'Don't spoil your appetite for your dinner. Rabbit pie. Ready in an hour.'

'I won't. Beef tea gives you an appetite. Not like oxo which is too salty.' So I was tucking into a second mugful when she said, 'Your Mother is beyond all understanding. I gather they've had to work like slaves over there to keep the four of them housed, fed and clothed. How have they managed to save the money to come back here? And why has she come?'

These two questions had plagued me from time to time.

'I suppose she was worried. You worried her about me.'

'She had a right to be worried. Was I supposed to keep everything from her until the time came when I must tell her you were dead? But now you're better, what good is she doing here, penniless and unable to feed you?'

There was no reply to that. She was voicing my own uncertainties about my mother's obscure intentions which had never, in my hearing, been expressed in words. As far as I could tell, Mother lived from day to day. Auntie had rolled out the pastry and was fitting a strip round the edge of a pie dish filled with pieces of rabbit and gravy.

'The trouble with your Mother is, she doesn't know what she wants.' I sat drinking and considering. Was that her trouble? But why shouldn't she know, at her age? By devious means I had calculated this to be thirty-six. If you didn't know what you wanted at thirty-six, then when were you likely to know?

Auntie attached the pastry lid, then, balancing the enamel dish on the palm of her left hand, she deftly shaved off bits of surplus pastry.

'Let me have the bits, please. I'll do a rabbit to decorate the middle.' Usually she planted there a few strips haphazardly. The rabbit might serve to change the subject, I thought. It did so.

'And how's Emily Cook?'

'Emily? Oh, she's all right. Lovely eyes. Bluish-black, the way I remember Cousin Lizzie's, but much larger. Her hair's dark and straight and her skin's beautiful, smooth and creamy with no spots or pimples like most people have.' (I was getting them myself and my Mother had dabbed them with the primrose coloured lotion that the chemist made up from a prescription for her own face. The stuff dried and caked leaving yellow blotches that brought to mind the stone head in Guisborough Priory.)

'Emily does nothing with her skin except wash it in rain

271

water. We have to wash in rain water anyway, and drink water from a pump.'

'I know. I know Emily Cook, too. Have known her for years. She was a bonnie girl. It was her undoing.'

My mind had left Emily and was toying with the problem of discovering how much money Father had sent before I gave the letter to Mother. I had heard of steaming open envelopes but it struck me as tricky and risky. Something in the nature of an X-ray should be invented to use in circumstances such as these. Auntie's strange remark interrupted my speculations.

'What do you mean, undoing?'

'Her good looks landed her with two children to bring up. Susan and Stanley. They're still there, aren't they?'

'Oh yes. I don't know how old they are. Older than I am. I think their father's dead.'

'He's not dead. They have no father.'

'But everyone has a father, some time.'

'Not always. I must say I got on well with Emily. She was good to Robbie's mother. But I could not understand her. I suppose you can make allowances for one fatherless child, but for a second one in a couple of years. And totally devoid of shame. How she's managed to bring them up I don't know, but I do know she can't keep you four as well. Wash your hands and set the table. You mustn't be late at the Infirmary.'

'Now Martha, bend over, touch your toes, straighten your knees. Come on now, absolutely straight, no cheating, and bring your heels closer to the wall. Unbend very slowly, feel every bone in your spine touch the wall in turn. No, that won't do. I can get my hand between your spine and the wall just in one place — the place that matters. That's better. Pull in your stomach. That's good. Right, now you can relax and get under your lamp for a few minutes. Your last X-ray was very good. Just a bit of growth lost in your right leg, but who knows, it may still catch up. It's amazing how bodies adjust.'

I thought about it on the way back. (I had been coming alone for treatment for some time.) My spine was straightening, my leg would grow. I wished my head would make the same progress. All was not straight inside it; nothing was making sense. Not for the first time I wished it were possible to run away from adults — to be free of them. If only you knew how to find the next meal. It was all very well for R.L. Stevenson to talk about making your kitchen where 'white flows the river and bright blows the broom'. A pretty piece of fancy, I thought, which gave no suggestion about where you'd pick up something to cook in your kitchen. I did not believe he had ever been without food. Really hungry people did not crave crusts dipped in the river. Crusts dipped in oxo were bad enough. I felt disillusioned with poetry as I crossed Victoria Square.

At home was this enormous basket sitting on a chair. Like a washing basket with a handle. Like the one Cousin Lizzie used to bring filled with butter and eggs for Middlesbrough market. This one was partially filled with packets, tins, plates and basins covered with grease-proof paper. A pure white tea-towel hung over one side, ready, I thought, to be laid over the top when the time came.

'What's that for?'

'For you to take. Something to feed you, just in case. I'll see you to the station and you've no distance to walk with it at Danby. If it's too heavy, leave it with the station master for your Mother to collect. There's enough of one thing and another to keep body and soul together at least for a few days. The letter is at the bottom. (Had she suspected my intentions?) It's safer there because I don't see how you can lose that basket. Hannah lent it. She happened to pop in.'

'Did you give her Mr Polly?'

'Yes. She says your Mother's a bit like the man in that book, just wanting to escape from things for a while. Perhaps from her family, she suggests. Hannah and her books! They'll turn her head one of these days! She believes books dictate everything we ever do.'

'Not dictate, Auntie. Reflect,' a remark which she disregarded.

'Anyway, Hannah thinks that when your father gets back, things will sort themselves out.'

I am sure my Aunt could not have had X-ray eyes or any less sinister method of seeing inside that envelope. I must give her the benefit of the doubt and put it down to intuition or simply a knowledge of my parents' mercurial behaviour. As it transpired, the basket's contents — meat pie, sausages, bacon, eggs, home-baked bread, teacakes, fruitloaf, a packet of tea, a tin of cocoa, a jar of Bovril and a packet of shredded wheat really saved our lives, which was the way I put it to my Mother who first told me not to be ridiculous and then added, inconsistently, 'I don't quite know where we would be without your Aunt.' Where we would have been I do not know either, because the envelope contained no more than a letter indicating that the money we needed was still beyond our reach, being attached to my father's person as, at that very moment, he was walking the decks of the *Antonia* in mid-Atlantic. The boat was expected to dock early Monday morning and, since Auntie had bought me a return ticket, there I would be that morning, travelling at a leisurely pace along the Whitby to Middlesbrough line while my father was speeding thence on an express train from Liverpool.

Emily Cook was unable to accommodate all five of us. Our bedroom, which we all shared, had no room for more than the double and single bed. Mother had occupied the latter, we three the former, while Emily slept on the kitchen sofa. To go to Lizzie's was out of the question, Emily had said, but there was Cockerill's farm in a fold of the hill just beneath Huck-a-Back and there, as a result of my Mother's arrangements, we were to gather as a family reunited soon after seven on Monday night. My father and I with his luggage would reach the farm in style, driven the mile and a half from Castleton station in Mr Cockerill's trap.

On my return from the Infirmary that afternoon, I found him eating a plateful of bacon and eggs and Auntie in an excellent mood.

'Here he is,' she informed me, 'really enjoying his meal. He hasn't had a taste of proper bacon since he left here four years ago. Would you believe it, there's nothing but thin, streaky stuff over there, and it tastes *sweet*. How can anyone imagine bacon tasting sweet?'

He paused in his eating to greet me with a kiss on the

cheek and a pat on the shoulder. 'Hullo there! My, how you've grown! Quite a young lady.' He then sat down to resume his meal but, while dipping a forkful of bacon into the egg yolk (and I noticed that he had not dispensed with a knife; his fork was in his left hand), he added, 'I've been hearing about all your troubles. It has been a worry, but your Aunt pulled you through and now you're all set to go places.'

His hearing about the troubles did not surprise me but I wished he would elaborate on the places to which I was bound, be more specific than my Mother had been. The subject might be broached by saying, 'Well, I got to the High School,' which I did say.

He glanced up at me, very lean and very brown, with plenty of thoughts behind his eyes even if they were not put into words.

'Yes, you did very well. We're proud of you. And I've heard of your Auntie's battle with the powers that be. If she hadn't won I think we would have had to come back here to settle, if only to pay borough rates! It's a mad world.'

He was right about that. But what he said about coming back was disturbing. Could it be possible that their destiny, my parents' and sisters', had rested on the outcome of that battle, not to mention my own tussle with the Board? Had Auntie and I failed, would they have come back to stay? But, as it was, they might not stay? I disliked the idea that so much had depended on me. And what about Auntie? What would govern her decision about Ayton? It was all a muddle and I wished one thing might be decided so as to set something else in motion and let us get on. I should never escape Miss Gibson's training — direction and a goal. Living from day to day was impossible.

He was certainly eating with a relish. Had he too been hungry? On the boat?

'What was the voyage like?'

'Oh, so so. A squall in mid-Atlantic and a swell for a couple of days. She's a small vessel, the *Antonia*, and carrying hardly any cargo, the steward said. For ballast, so she pitched a lot. The *Cunard* saved on food! I understand they're intending to fit the larger boats with stabilizers. I suppose it's a good idea, but they'd be more sensible preparing them for troop ships.'

'Whatever do you mean?' my Aunt demanded.

'Just that there will have to be another war. Look at the recovery in Germany. No strikes there!'

'Were you sea-sick?' I asked.

'No. I'm not subject to that affliction. I ate everything put in front of me.'

Auntie was not to be diverted. 'I don't like this talk of war, Harry. We've had quite enough. What did the millions die for? It was a war to end wars, you know that.'

My father laughed. 'So you'll see to it that there'll be no more?'

'Yes. With a lot more people, I will.'

'The will of the people!' He was tucking into apple pie swathed in Brunton's cream. 'Not a reliable thing. It vacillates. What do most people care about? Feathering their own nests, lining their own pockets, and if munition factories help them to do that, they'll make munitions. They don't stop to think where it's all leading,' and her reply was, 'Everyone knows where life leads in the end. But there's the time between. Now you'll have to hurry, or you'll not catch that six o'clock train.'

His luggage had been left at the station, so he and I walked there together. My feelings troubled me, being not the way I thought they should be. This was my father, a man specially belonging to *me*, not just another man like those amongst whom I had spent the last four years. I knew how to regard a grandfather, a grown cousin, an uncle, a doctor. I was versed in the infinite variety that existed amongst lodgers. In an odd way I accepted my Mother as a substitute for my Aunt. There should, I assumed, be something special in the way a girl regards her father, and vice versa. Once I had known what it was. But now the only sentiment I could pin-point was a satisfaction that he should see me wearing the blazer and banded panama hat of the High School. He had stated his pride, that once, and told me that, though the bicycle had not yet materialised, it was on its way. Up to now, he supposed, I must have had little chance to use it. Nevertheless, as I tried with my slight limp to keep up with him

276

along Albert Road, with this tall, lean, brown, black-haired man carrying the replenished food basket, I had to keep reminding myself that I was walking beside my father, as if the relationship must be clung to, or it would easily slip away.

Chapter Twenty-Five

Had it not been for an abiding pre-occupation with money, or the lack of it, I doubt whether we children would have 'prospected for gold' as we did in the locality of Baysdale Beck. These activities and what followed there put a stamp on the rest of my life, confirming the six-year-old experience in a bedroom at Huck-a-Back as a church confirmation stamps the early baptism, so that the region has remained an Eldorado though different in nature from the one for which I searched at the age of twelve. It also provided that means of mental escape mentioned to my Aunt by Hannah Kneeshaw. Hannah, though lacking the practical insight and drive of my Aunt, drew on a fund of book wisdom. She had seen Mr Polly as a man struggling to understand his own mind and had immediately seen my mother in Mr Polly. I do not know whether she stretched the analogy to my father and myself, but she could well have done so. An escape was what we all needed, to take our bearings, decide whither we were bound and head in that direction.

At Cockerill's farm, with Huck-a-Back on a shoulder of moor above it, my Mother released us for this experience by refusing to be concerned with where we were or what we did. Three in number ensured safety in her view and we would turn up when we were hungry. The farm had no regular mealtimes; food was, as they say, on tap. Mother placed herself alongside the large, placid Mrs Cookerill and helped with the ceaseless succession of jobs falling to a moorland farmer's wife. My father was released to range himself with the farm workers and found an abundance of odd jobs. As a family we were together only during the night — the five of us slept in one bedroom occupying two double beds and we all slept well. So, if we three children could be bunched together as one, then I would say that each entity of our family led very private lives during those summer weeks of 1927 which justified the outlay of money spent on this visit to England.

How I could hold the view that R.L. Stevenson was an impractical ingenue ranting about green days in forest and blue days at sea, yet at the same time believe that a real version of his treasure island lay on a small area of exposed earth and tree roots where Baysdale Beck runs into the Esk, is difficult to understand. This irrationality might have been the norm for a twelve-year-old of my time.

'I know those flat stones are not natural,' I told my sisters, and it was true that most of the stones on that small island were rounded.

They were rounded by the action of water racing over them for two-thirds of the year as beach pebbles are rounded by the tide. Here and there, however, lay a flat angular stone impervious, it appeared, to natural forces and I drew the conclusion that it had been manhandled into place and for what other reason than to conceal a metal box of coins, a treasure trove? The recovery of this would put an end forever to our penurious condition.

Billy Cockerill, a younger son of the household, willingly produced the necessaries for the dislodgement of stones, flat or otherwise. This was an everyday procedure on a moorland farm. So we procured a cheerful rusty-red spade with a blade worked well away from its original shape, a fork with two of the five prongs missing, a trowel, some lengths of iron bars and an ancient hammer that took me all my time to lift. It purpose was obscure but I was too proud to show my ignorance and ask. With one or other of these we set to work, digging, levering, heaving at these eccentric 'flatties' which, for the most part, resisted our attempts and stayed put. But one, I remember, we managed to move, then raise, panting, to an upright position and allow to drop, with relief, upside down. The soggy surface thus exposed was alive with strange forms of life. They squirmed, twisted or scattered and while, into my head sailed Simon Peter's sheet, knotted at four corners and filled with unclean creeping things, my team were expressing disgust in sounds not classed as speech. We were not biologists and I put an end to this.

'We must dig,' I rallied them, 'and dig deep. This stone has not been placed here for nothing.'

With broken spade and fork we undermined the home of earth worms, thread worms, slugs, wood lice, centipedes, silverfish and beetles all of which must previously have existed in the happiest harmony under their tombstone. We delved until the extreme depth of the hole became exciting and took precedence for a while over the nature of our quest.

'It's like a rabbit hole,' said Monica, 'going down and down and down. Where will it end?'

That became apparent as each trowel of earth grew wetter until finally it was wallowing in water.

'Look,' cried Monica, 'we can't go any further. It fills up, like at the seaside.' To the right and left of us the beck sang and laughed.

How long it was before I brought reason to bear on our persistent excavation of this small island, I do not know. We spent each day there except my two Middlesbrough days, slaking our thirst with handfuls of brown water, eating bacon sandwiches and rock buns and ignoring time. Each morning we arrived there with hope renewed until at last I could bear no longer the mocking song of the beck.

'We've been wasting precious time,' I exclaimed. 'Who would hide a fortune in a place open to all passers-by?' and I indicated the bridge over which had crossed at rare intervals a member of the Cockerill family and no one else. 'We must travel upstream, away from all civilized life,' and this we did, starting off in the beck itself with shoes and stockings slung across our shoulders.

The current was strong. 'Why can't we turn round and go the other way?' urged my sisters.

'Because,' I explained carefully, 'it isn't Baysdale Beck that way. It's the Esk River and flows where everyone can see it right up to Castleton Bridge. No one would hide a fortune in a place as easy to reach as that,' and I felt that the chance of finding it was in direct proportion to the effort exerted. Fortunes were not won by meandering in a field on the banks of a wide river.

As we struggled with the current, the beck increased its pace and grew deeper thus compelling us to take to dry land. This was a conglomerate of large boulders, alder stems and roots, high bracken and sturdy rushes and while we battled with these, the beck rollicked by in exultant mood.

'Look,' said Monica, 'look at those paper flowers.'

The drive for money deadens the senses. I had not noticed the bell heather springing in clumps behind a boulder, erupting in patches from the slope above our heads. The ground coverage of ordinary heather, or ling, was still in the pale bud stage, but the bell heather's crisp papery bells were the colour of Auntie's piece of puce velvet. Monica reached to pick some and pulled at it in vain, scattering the tiny flowers as they detached themselves.

'That's not the way,' I told her. 'You bend back a stalk, press it hard against the lower stalk and it breaks.' The memory of how to do this came from long ago. I picked her a few sprigs which she clasped tightly while I dropped back into the beck. It frothed angrily at my knees as I felt into rocky cavities and drew out nothing but wet moss.

'If we gave up now,' I called, 'the very next hole would be the one.'

'Which one?' asked Bessie, bending over a boulder to see.

'The one with the treasure in it. The one we're looking for.'

'But how would we know, if we'd given up before?'

This was a good question and proved that Bessie could reason if she chose to do so. It was not an easy question to answer.

'I suppose we wouldn't. But it's that fear of just losing it that keeps you searching. Just in case. You've heard people say, "Keep going. It will be just round the next bend."'

Apparently she had not and chose to withdraw from my world into hers. As I climbed out of the beck, I saw her on top of the rock under which I'd been bent double. She was turning in a slow pirouette and throwing heads of bell heather into imaginary laps. She had never relinquished the 'crazy habit' as my Father called it of jigging about and throwing out her arms. Who does she think she is now, I wondered, Ophelia?

I spurred them on until we reached a place where the beck takes one of its elbow bends and encloses a deep pool.

Here the current slowed its pace and the bright brown of the water darkened. Sandy banks shelved round it and, from our side, alder trunks reached over and alder branches formed a knotty woven roof. I remembered.

'It's the sheep dip where Cousin Lizzie pushed in the sheep to clean their coats. There's the bank they climbed up!'

And where I fell asleep and heard her calling me. Here I should like to have stayed for a while but felt that that would be fatal. I knew now that we were well beyond Huck-a-Back and must press on.

The distance between Dibble Bridge and the ford at Elbow Field is not far by road, but following the snaking course of the beck more than doubles the distance. Still, we cannot have been far from the ford when we found the coin and it was Bessie who spotted it.

'We've found it,' I heard her announce, as I strove to stay upright on a wobbling boulder. It was that stretch of beck which flows through a fairly steep and narrow gorge.

'Found what?'

'The treasure,' called back Bessie's voice. Then Monica's elaborated.

'It's a coin.'

'What, one coin?'

I lurched to the bank and climbed by clutching at bracken. The three of us stared at it.

It lay in the centre of a flat outcrop of rock exactly as though it had been placed there. It was the colour of the beck but glinted in the sun's rays that speared a young birch and reminded me that the sun itself was westering. It was a coin, and it looked like a gold one. It might have value, might even be treasure. But why was it not hidden? Why be placed where all the world might see, to draw attention to itself? Elder knots and rowan branches and migrating geese and Huck-a-Back six years ago and now a coin laid purposely for us to grab! All the superstition, unreason of my childhood, a childhood which ought to be behind me, rose up and said, 'Do not touch that coin. It has been put there to tempt you. You do not know the consequences. Leave it alone. '

Bessie stretched out her arm and picked it up.

'Here,' she said, 'put it in your knicker pocket. I'm going back.' And, since no bolt from the evening sky struck us down, I took it and examined it.

A man's head was on the face and a name round the edge, Isaac Newton. On the back was an intricate design, an eagle with wings outstretched perched on a pole round which were entwined two serpents. There was a scattering of leaves and a woven uptipped basket holding fruit which did not fall out. Round the upper edge I read HALF-PENNY and at the bottom a date − 1793.

You could hardly call it treasure trove, but I felt we must call it a day. The sun was far lower than it should have been, having refused to stand still. 'We must cross the beck,' I said 'and get to the road.' We did this with difficulty, Monica on my back, her legs round my waist. She clung on, but lost a shoe, and on the other bank we looked hopelessly into the swirling waters. The shoe might be found, hooked on an alder branch but in another time, by other children.

We reached the road to see half of a blood red sun behind the hill where Baysdale Beck must rise. Around it the sky was ruffled, grey and purple, frowning at us. Monica walked the sandy road with a shoe on one foot and a stocking on the other until there was no sole left and her foot was a blistered mess. We employed various means of carriage for her but the progress was slow. I bathed her foot under the spring outside the farm and at night applied some ointment from a tin Mother kept for her hands. We did not mention the matter.

Father showed some interest in the coin.

'It's old,' he said, 'but Isaac Newton did not die then. He'd been dead for years. You know who he was?'

'Yes, I read it in the Encyclopedia. An apple fell, he wondered why and decided that the earth pulled it down. The law of gravity and a lot about the moon and the planets. But what has he to do with a halfpenny?'

'It's to commemorate him. A commemorative coin. Not much is it, poor chap? A halfpenny!' He laughed, then added, 'Even so, better than spending thousands on war memorials.' He handed me the coin. 'Put it away. When you're old it might be worth something, who knows?'

'It's really Bessie's. She found it.'

'Can I spend it?' Bessie asked, and when she was told not, she said what would she want with the silly thing?

Mrs Cockerill was disinclined to view it with either curiosity or awe, and certainly saw nothing supernatural about its lying where we had found it, on a slab of rock like an altar, as I told her, at the same time wondering if she knew what an altar was.

'Nay,' she said, 't'farm workers cart a lot of aud rubbish around in their pockets. Someone rounding up t'sheep has pulled out a kerchief and yon aud coin with it. Reckon it's bin in his pocket for years.'

'Over a hundred and thirty, if he got it new,' I said, and everyone laughed.

That night my sisters were asleep before I was. Monica's lost shoe bothered me, but compared with my anguished guilt over the matter of my Grandmother's broken umbrella, this worry was as nothing. We had not told Mother and we were not intending to do so. Monica need not go barefooted; she had another pair of shoes. The shoe had lost itself as my sisters' clothing often seemed to do. Mother would search high and low, and then forget it. It was the same as a lie, I thought. You had to acknowledge that. For a while a niggling doubt squirmed in my mind, like one of those wire worms we had uncovered. Was I farther off from heaven than when I was eight? I consoled myself by reciting mentally that poem, 'I remember, I remember,' which we had learnt at Victoria Road School. I got as far as, 'And thought the air must rush as fresh as swallows on the wing,' and then I slept.

Chapter Twenty-Six

The sun cannot always have shone while we were at Castleton, but no time, except for eating and sleeping, did we spend in the house itself. We played in barns where the hay was replenished in August. I can see that hay cart now, rumbling ponderously back to the farm from the meadow below Dibble Bridge with three girls and one large boy a-top the high load. Dusk had fallen and an out-sized paper moon, painted orange, hung low over Castleton Village. The slow beat of the cart-horses' hooves and the rattle of harness mingled with shouts of, 'Get off, get off, Billy Cockerill. You're smothering me.' Our lungs were filled with the smouldering scent of sun-baked hay, hallucinatory, I imagine, for at one point I seemed to be disembodied, floating level with the top of the load and close beside it. I sailed past the tips of beech branches on the farm side of Dibble Bridge and saw them snatch at my sisters' hair. 'Just stop it, Billy Cockerill, you crazy boy. Stop pulling my hair!'

Queenie, a donkey from the sands at Whitby, came to the farm in late August. To be fostered, we understood, for the winter. With no sandy beat along which to plod back and forth, back and forth, and no thumping stick on her hide to remind her of what life was about, the poor creature was confused and disorientated. She threw Monica within a minute of getting her straddled over the bare bony back. My sister was bruised and sore but forgave the animal when I insisted that, smitten with remorse, it had squeezed three tears out of its eye. I saw this moisture as I clutched its mane and spoke soothing words into one ear. There may have been moisture from the other eye also. I could not be sure of that.

The next day Billy saddled her.

'I've a few jobs to do in Castleton. Do you lot want to come along? You can take turns riding her there. She'll have a sack of hen corn to carry coming back.'

I rode her first to take the less steep half of the hill. The donkey and Billy had fair shares of obstinacy, a quality, I suppose, needed equally for life on the sands or the moor. Queenie took the first few yards of the bank and stopped. After the fifth stubborn halt, Billy grew savage with his whip and his language.

'Please don't hurt her,' I beseeched him. 'She's not used to hills.'

'She'll get used to them.' he shouted, 'in a place where there's nowt but hills. She's not cropping our grass all t'winter for nowt.'

It takes a few minutes to climb on foot to the crossroads. Queenie did it in an hour and then, before anyone could sense her intention, she swerved right. She had seen a steeper hill ahead, but a level bit of road to the right and this she took at a pace one does not associate with a donkey. Having demonstrated this speed, she then decided to unload herself. I was thankful that she threw me on the soft grass verge. By the time I had manoeuvred myself into a sitting position, she was out of sight. I recall waiting till the others reached me, giving me time to think confused thoughts about the ways of donkeys and how best to treat such creatures.

On Mondays and Thursdays I took the basket back to Middlesbrough, had my treatment, had time to struggle with a march by Handel on the organ and returned sometimes as late as the six o'clock train from Middlesbrough. Each time Auntie asked me my parents' intentions and received no information. I learned that Great-Uncle Watson had been.

'He's pestering me again about going to Ayton.'

'Why? Has his wife died?'

'No, but I gather that the gap between life and death is narrowing. I told him it was doing that for all of us, himself included. But if your mother and father don't come home soon, you'll have to come anyway, to start school. You can't be missing your second year at the High School.'

'Will you go to Ayton if she dies?' I asked.

'I've told him straight that I'm not going without you.

He'll have to get used to it, that's all.'

My Aunt found the Cockerills vexatious in so far as they had their own produce. They had potatoes, mutton, ham, bacon, chickens, rabbits, eggs, gooseberries, raspberries, blackcurrants and all the pastry things associated with these and the basket carried townwards always had a small supply of one or more of these commodities. At first my Aunt had been at a loss what to send farmwards. It was not in her nature to feel beholden to anyone, but what was the use of sending cakes to Mrs Cockerill? Mrs Cockerill's cakes, I told her, were enormous, about the size of Auntie's Christmas cakes, and the flat tins in which she baked gingerbread and such like would hardly sit on our bentwood table. This posed a real dilemma but not for long because I hadn't mentioned fish. Did they have any fish, she asked me, and I could safely say that I had never tasted fish at the farm. And that was why the basket I carried away from Castleton station contained three layers of herrings, boned, rolled and oven cooked in vinegar. This was not the first time I had carried such a shoal concealed under grease proof paper and a starched white cloth. As I climbed the station hill, I saw them in my mind's eye, lying side by side, each one shining black in the middle and shading to a dark then lighter grey towards the curled up edges, and in the centre of every one a little black fin protruding like a decoration.

I wondered again what would be their ultimate destination. My Father would eat one or two but only under duress. He had always held that mackerel was the only fish with any flavour. I would eat some, but my sisters had to be forced into picking about with one, mostly extracting bones so fine that I was struck by their marvellous eyesight. The Cockerills were conservative about fish. If there were fish in the Esk, the men had no time to spend catching them. I heard Mrs Cockerill tell Mother that they made a point of having fish pie on Good Friday but, apart from that, they were not really fish people.

How could I suggest to Auntie, I wondered, that she sent too many herrings too often? She asked me every time if there had been enough for so large a number of people and every time I assured her that there had been more than enough. She refused to take this in its literal sense and I was burdened with the twice weekly embarrassment of carrying herrings to people who did not want them. The predicament was occupying my mind afresh as I dropped the basket a few yards beyond the crest of the station hill. It was not heavy, but awkward, and my legs were afflicted with a curious inertia which I put down to our tussles with the donkey.

It was a rare evening. No wind, not even a stirring of air. No cloud, just a blueness sealed up above which merged towards Westerdale with a fanned out flame of colour that was sunset. A scrap of a poem came into my head, one I'd copied from a school library book during a gymn session.

> Its edges foamed with amethyst and gold
>   Withers once more the old blue flower of day.

The slow, deliberate curve of long vowel sounds caught me up like one of those Atlantic breakers I had heard so much about. Then, as I stood facing the sunset, with no one else in sight across the miles of moor, it happened again, the thing that had happened in the Huck-a-Back bedroom six years before, the flowing into my body of something from around me and a dissolving out of all the rest.

I cannot say what time elapsed before I felt again the deadened, weighted legs, before I noticed the hat held by its elastic in my left hand. Thought focused on the hat with its striped band. It told me I must have moved on since I was six. Yet I felt that was not so. It's a problem, I sensed, more vital than surplus herrings. It's a problem with an answer that I ought to know, but don't. It's like the spinning top and the dead still lake. How to be alive and at one with the universe without the need to be always moving on. At that moment, to move on was the last thing I desired. The moment was enough, and ought to be the End.

I stooped to pick up the basket and saw the bumble bee, a huge one, settled on the cloth. I lifted the cloth and shook it but the bee clung there like a clump of striped brown moss grown on the white surface. I tore off a corner of grease proof paper, folded it and tried to lever the creature away. It legs seemed glued to the cloth. The hat brim would be stronger so I got that inserted under the legs which seemed as lethargic as my own. Surely, surely it wants to fly! But when at last I detached it, it fell upside down on the track and waved its legs at me. It's dying, I thought, but hated to leave it there on that hard and gritty surface. So I turned it back onto the hat brim and carefully manoeuvred it off with the wedge of paper to lie right way up in the heather. I returned to the basket to cover its contents and the fishy, vinegary smell of pickled herrings rose into my nostrils.

When I say that the following day the pain struck me, I don't really mean that. Anything that strikes you comes from outside. This came from inside, from a part of me that I had never known to exist, had never imagined. Having been taught nothing about the human interior, I gave no credence to such a thing. My body was composed of, working from the outside, skin, veins, flesh, muscles and bones; and apart from the heart which made strange movements and noises, the inside was empty. Of course I was familiar with pain, in legs, arms, neck, chest, back. You grew used to it. But to this pain I should never grow accustomed. From the moment it uncoiled itself from this unimagined place between stomach and back, then proceeded to twist, grip, squeeze, rack and spread an agony through all parts below my waist, I knew that never, never should I grow used to it.

I was perched on one of the two holes in the seat of Cockerill's earth closet when it began. I clutched the rounded edge of the wood, bent in a spasm towards the floor and retched. I hung there for probably a minute which seemed hours before the pain lessened, then I straightened up and hit the white-washed wall behind me with my head. I thought, when such a thing as this happens, there are only two worlds, pain and relief from pain. But, even as the thought crystallized, the pain struck again. I fell off the seat on to my knees and vomited into the hole, vomited for the first time in my life, as far as I knew.

A smell of excrement and ashes filled my nose. The pit needed emptying, but Mrs Cockerill's daily nagging failed to turn the men from haymaking to a job which Mr Cockerill thought could wait. The smell was familiar but that morning different, being the smell of fish. Not easy to explain, since all food remains went to the cats. I knelt there till a fresh onslaught of pain subsided. Like waves, I thought, and rested a clammy forehead on my palms in a position of prayer. It was then, when the pain had receded almost to a point of comfort, that I grew aware of a wetness between my thighs. I pulled a square of newspaper from the hook, wiped myself underneath and was about to drop it into the hole when I saw the blood, in patches with one thick trickle tracing a way down.

Through the garth and the kitchen I managed to move with legs pressed tightly together, each foot planted in front of the other and the rest of me following with a sideways wobble.

'Hi,' called Monica, 'you've been ages. Come on.'

'Where's Mother?'

'Collecting eggs with Mrs Cockerill.'

'You two go and play. I have a pain. I'm going to bed.'

I knew her mouth was agape at this strange news, also her eyes as she watched my equally strange progress. She followed me into the little passage and watched me all the way as I dragged upstairs the legs which I did not dare to separate. At last I was on the bed. Nothing mattered now but willingness to accept. Whatever might be happening, acceptance was all. Another spasm corkscrewed through me. I clamped my lower half to the bed, flung the rest about and felt my forehead lather with sweat.

I did not hear any footsteps on the stone stairs, only my Mother's voice say, 'Now then, what's wrong?'

'A dreadful pain.'

'Where? In your chest?' Despite the pain, I was aware of an odd note in her voice. A note of anxiety?

'No. Not in my chest. It's below. In my stomach and back. And down into my legs.'

'What have you been eating? Surely not unripe brambles or green apples. If so, you ought to know better.'

'I haven't.' I flung away from her. 'It's not anything I've eaten. I want Auntie. I want to go home.'

To portray my Mother as insensitive or unsympathetic

would be wrong. She was not. She had the qualities of a normal, caring mother and, while living with her at Danby and then at Castleton, I had appreciated a relationship with an adult which was wholly satisfying. My mother was undemanding. She neither fussed, nor fretted, nor sought on our part any display of affection or even acknowledgment of her motherhood. Thus, she set us free of obligations to her and I knew that I was happier getting along with her in the background than with my Aunt whose personality was so intrusive. In my sisters' language, which I did not absorb, I would have said Mother was OK.

At this moment, however, I was ill or more than ill, I believed, and my Aunt was the one to deal with illness as well as with other trials and tribulations which had beset us. She was strong, and the place to be at the moment was in her bed. When I cried out, 'I want Auntie,' I did not realise that I had struck my Mother where she was weakest; nor could I understand the violence of her reaction.

'Don't be so ridiculous. The trouble with you is you've been thoroughly spoilt. Ruined, in fact. I should never have left you. I know that now. I don't know what I was thinking of to let you have your own way and, this time, if we go back, you're coming too. Here you are with a bit of a stomach ache and you think you're dying.'

'I am, this time. I'm bleeding to death.'

'You're what?'

'I'm bleeding to death underneath.'

She investigated. Then laughed.

'Calm yourself, I ought to have known. There's nothing wrong with you. Just stay as you are until I get you something to put on. For goodness sake don't mess up the quilt.'

She rummaged in a drawer and returned with a small square towel, a narrow kind of belt and some safety pins. She folded the square and placed it between my legs.

'Hold it there,' she said. 'Now stand up and I'll get you fixed.' But the pain racked me again.

'I can't. It's too bad. I'm going to be sick. I was sick in the closet.

'Well, I'm afraid you'll have to get used to it, like every

291

other woman. Because for the next thirty to forty years you'll have this every month with perhaps the odd spell in between when you'll have worse than this to go through.'

I couldn't take that in. The present was too urgent.

'But what is it? Why am I bleeding?'

'You're bleeding because you have grown up. As far as women are concerned, that means you can have a baby.'

I eyed my mother with suspicion. Crippled with pain as I was, I could still spare a thought for her. I did not want to see her taken to an asylum.

'What, have a baby now? Any time?'

'Why must you be so very stupid, Martha? I don't think your sisters will ask me such silly questions when their turn comes. You won't have a baby until you're married. And that will be some time yet. You can forget about that side of it.'

She had half-pulled, half-lifted me from the bed, and when, to use her own phrase, she had got me fixed with this towel underneath, I was less aware of the trickling blood. I was able to think again.

'But don't women have them when they're not married? Like Emily Cook?'

'Oh, so your precious Aunt's been talking to you about Emily, has she? I thought she might have held her tongue. But no. She never could see beyond her own limited horizons. Anyway, as far as you're concerned, you can stop worrying on that score. I don't think you're the sort who will go in for having babies before you're married. I'll get you a Beecham's Powder from Mrs Cockerill. That will take care of your pain although you might bleed for a few days. It's nothing to worry about. You'll feel better afterwards. In fact it might take care of a lot of your aches and pains. You really are a bit like your Aunt Blanche.'

There were many questions I could have asked in order to find answers to some of the things I ought to have known but didn't. It is hard to say why I was silent except that the pain still ravaged me and she was wrong in her assertion that the powder would take care of it. It continued at intervals through the weekend and again on Monday when I went to Middlesbrough feeling decidedly weak. Auntie seemed not to notice and I didn't mention it.

But when the hospital Sister saw the state of the affairs, she told me not to come in future when I was menstruating. That was my first hearing of this word and I asked her to repeat it. She eyed me with some surprise and said, 'Has no one told you about it?' When I said not really, only that it was how you started having babies, she looked nonplussed. After a few seconds of consideration, she said,

'Well, my dear, it's not my job, you see, and I don't want to get into any trouble. It's your Aunt's or your Mother's, whichever woman is responsible for you.'

I wasn't quite sure on whose shoulders this load rested.

'I saw Elizabeth Watson only once during our stay at Cockerill's, and it was the last time I should ever see her. It was also, as far as I can recall, the only occasion when we went anywhere with my mother and there seemed to be a crowd of us — Mrs Cockerill, her daughter, the woman who was then at Huck-a-Back supposed to be 'seeing to Lizzie' but, according to popular report, treating her abominably. There were also some Davisons from Middlesbrough who, my Mother said, were as nearly related to Lizzie as we were and would be keeping in touch with her now that she was failing. I asked what she meant and was told that naturally Lizzie could not be expected to live forever and there would be at least the furniture. (She kept them waiting for six more years.) Then there were four of us and Cousin Lizzie herself. It was a strictly female party, as such parties were in those days, and each of us carried a basket. We were going blueberry picking above Elbow Field and these berries, I understood, were picked once or twice in the season for pies, bottling or making into jam.

We waited by the gate below Huck-a-Back and watched the two women come down the hill, one using a stick. When they reached us, I was shocked to see Cousin Lizzie shorter than myself. I remembered her as being tall and very upright. Now she was small, shrivelled and stooped over a stick. Her clothes seemed the same except that the ample skirt was trailing the ground. My Mother greeted her and asked how she was.

'You remember me, don't you, Lizzie? I'm Monica, Annie's girl.'

293

Lizzie had straightened a little and was peering into my Mother's face.

'Annie died, didn't she? Both of them died.'

'Yes.'

'Aye. There be a time tae die,' and she turned along the sandy road, mingling with the rest. This meeting troubled me. If she did not know Mother, then how could I expect her to know me? Soon she fell back from the rest and I, too, slackened my pace and walked beside her.

'May I carry your basket please?'

She gave me a glance and inclined her head. So old, I thought. Much older than Grannie ever looked. Yet she's only seventy-eight and Granny was seventy-five when she died. Do three years make such a difference? Her stick struck the ground, then skidded an inch or so before being lifted, and she kept her eyes on the road. I remembered how, six years ago, they had seen where mine could not, her dog stirring the sheep on the far horizon.

'What has that woman done to you?' I cried inwardly and with anger, ready to blame anything but the years for this terrible change.

'Where is Lad?' I asked, and had to ask again and explain.

'Oh ay, Lad. He's gone. They've twea young dogs now.'

'Don't you round up the sheep, as you used to do?'

'Nay, not ony more. There's a man on t'farm now.'

'What about the cats? There must be some cats?'

'Cats? Oh aye, there's allus cats about.'

'And do they cover you at night on the kitchen sofa?'

She made a funny noise in her throat that might have been a laugh.

'Nay. I gan upstairs tae bed. Thoo gans up to bed, doesn't tha?'

I realised, for the very first time, that, when we had stayed there, she had slept on the sofa in order that we four might have the two bedrooms. How odd, I thought, that you don't work such things out when you are six. I had connected her with that black sofa, seen her covered with cats as if she'd spent every night of her life there. To me she had been a sofa-sleeping person. She had slept on our kitchen sofa at home.

The two Davison women now dropped back and positioned themselves on either side of her. Sensing that I wasn't wanted, I joined the rest just as they turned left down a track much steeper than the top half of Castleton Hill, and there, below us, lay this spectacular place.

At this point in its meandering course, Baysdale Beck makes its most dramatic right-angled bend with the moor rising vertically from one bank to an immense height. Heather, birch, boulders, bracken all cling to this vertiginous elevation which faces the steep hill we were now preparing to descend by means of a narrow, snaking track. Between these two heights, level with the beck and cradled in its elbow is a wide, flat expanse of bright green, closely shaven turf.

Nowadays, because it makes an ideal playground for children and picnic ground for adults, Elbow Field is rutted and marred by the action of cars. But then, only farmers or shepherds passed by and no one paid it a visit except the locals for berry picking, as we were doing. Seen from the hill top that day, the perfect turf glowed like an emerald in an ornate setting of purple and many shades of green. For the real heather had come into bloom and its purple was patched with the green of the blueberry plant, the bracken and the yellowing birch.

Some ten feet from the bottom of our track was a rowan tree and here the picnic contents of baskets were carefully arranged with thermos flasks propped up against protruding boulders. The women fanned out up the bank to our left and were soon at work. My sisters and I went to look at the berries. Their slender stems, as much as a foot in height, carried an abundance of small moist leaves which you lifted to find the round berries of a uniquely velvet blue, the riper ones shining black. We crammed our mouths with them, then marvelled to see our lips and chins stained blue, an obstinate dye, difficult to remove even when scrubbed hard with handkerchiefs wetted in the beck.

'Don't eat them all,' called our mother, as if we could! 'You can pick some to take home for your Auntie. She used to love blueberry pie.'

'Afterward,' I called back, and heard an answering echo

from the opposite hill. My sisters were beside the ford where the beck slides smoothly over flat stones certainly laid by men. They are evenly spaced and, when extreme drought occurs, are usually renewed. Across the ford the steep road rises like a narrow ribbon bound over the brow of the moor.

I left my sisters to their safe and easy doings in an inch of water and made for the rowan tree. Nothing is left now but a stump protruding from the bank. It was then a large and shapely tree and, on that day in late August, its polished clusters of scarlet berries gleamed amongst the unpolished modest leaves. It made you catch your breath to look at it. I caught mine and stopped in my tracks. To paint, to paint was the thing! To be an artist. To paint this explosion of colour — sky blue, grass green, heather purple, beck brown and berries flaming red. To splash those colours all over a space as large as the chapel wall! To capture it and to hold it forever, with the humps of women's bottoms rising out of the moor, two children playing by the ford and the figure in black under the rowan tree. I would be an artist. I would have every detail of this in my mind, and one day I would paint it on some enormous canvas for all the world to see!

Cousin Lizzie was sitting at one end of a long, flat stone. A sheep with a black head and curled horns cropped beside her, its dun coloured coat pressed against her skirt.

'Does it know you?' I asked.

'Aye. It were a weakling brought up on t'bottle.'

I made to sit down, but she held me off and brushed from the stone a handful of sheep droppings, round and hard like tiny marbles, only black. They scattered over the turf.

'Has it been here long, Cousin Lizzie? This stone, I mean.'

'As long as Ah can recollect.'

Were we, I wondered, to sit in silence? In the essential silence of R.L. Stevenson? The silence of mightier movement, of winds and rivers, of life and death? *Poems of Today* was now as much in my thinking as once the Bible had been. Perhaps still was. I shook my head to clear it. I ought, I supposed, to be picking blueberries for Auntie.

'How long has this rowan tree been here?'

'As lang as that, too. Me Mither and Grandmither came here to berry pick.'

The sheep, still chewing slantwise, rested its head on her lap and went on chewing.

'It's a beautiful tree,' I said. 'The storms won't blow it over, will they?'

'Nay, not with them deep roots.'

We sat, ruminating. Then, 'Once a lassie asked me t'same thing aboot them rowans back home.'

Eagerly I took it up. 'It was me. I asked you when I was six. Martha. You remember?'

She *must* remember. Not be like Grannie who went without knowing me. Suddenly, it was imperative that Elizabeth Watson of Huck-a-Back should recognize and then remember me. Otherwise, who would I be? I would not be myself.

'Nay, Annie lost Martha. The little lass died.'

'No, no. Not that one. She was my Grandmother. She had Monica — Monnie, remember? Then Monica had me.' (So Abraham begat Isaac, and Isaac begat Jacob.) 'And we stayed with you at Huck-a-Back. Remember?'

'Aye. She went away. Her last one.'

'But I didn't. I stayed.'

Then, when she turned and looked at me, I knew it was my face, or something of me, that she was taking in. 'You're the lass that stayed put?'

'That's me,' I cried with a wonderful gladness. Then saw, propped upright by its boulder, Mrs Cockerill's bulky thermos flask.

'Cousin Lizzie, would you like a cup of tea?'

She smiled. Toothless, skeletal, immeasurably old. 'Aye, that'd be nice, lass. What, out o' that thing?' as I tried to twist off the cap. 'It'll not taste t'same as frae t'aud brown pot at home.'

Epilogue

Just after my thirteenth birthday when, Auntie told me, the bluebells on the wooded slopes of Roseberry were in bud and a clump of rare white bluebells which he'd uprooted from there were budding too in Great-Uncle Watson's garden, his wife, Ellen died. She died the day before my father, mother and sisters left Liverpool on the *Carinthia*. And shortly afterwards, my Aunt gave a special polish to Mother's bedroom suite, her own brass bedstead, her dining table and six chairs, and, of course, the slender Georgian table and the small round bentwood one. She packed the old china with expert care and filled another crate with bits and pieces. She and her uncle had had their second fight. The first had been to do with me, the second to do with the organ. But removal day saw that instrument strapped to the inside of the van and presiding over the rest. The van left, and later in the day Auntie followed by train with me and my books in tow. I refused to have them put in the van, it was too risky.

I travelled to school by train. A mile along the lane to Great Ayton station, then Nunthorpe, Ormesby, Middlesbrough, and down the long flight of steps to Albert Road. From there you could see before you, at the far end, the High School clock tower. I was correctly shod, stockinged, blazered, hatted and gloved, and my satchel was set at the proper angle across my shoulders. If the shade of a younger girl had just slunk into a shop doorway and waited there until I passed, I failed to notice her, my thoughts being now on other matters. I had turned my back on a belated childhood, though not without some deep embedded sadness. But I was on the move. Goodbyes had been uttered — some for a long time, some forever, as with Minnie's husband. But Minnie still had Tom to see to, and Hannah her mother, for many years to come. Cyril and Ralph, I'd heard, were actually chasing girls instead of merely viewing them from afar;

and, as for the Park Lane house, Auntie continued to draw rent for it until, in the not so distant future, Uncle Watson let fall his spade and, without reflection or fuss, his hold on life. Then Gertrude claimed the house.

Auntie had her uncle to tend in more ways than one. When the cooking, feeding, washing, ironing and cleaning were done, there came the evenings when she had to play Ludo with him and contrive to let him win. How she continued to manage this I could never understand, because once or twice she turned the job over to me and I found I had neither the ingenuity nor the inclination to cheat in order to lose. He sulked outrageously when I won and I refused to play again. We never took to each other and, to save him the pain of seeing me wasting time, I always used the bedroom for my homework, the room I still had to share with my Aunt.

At school I recognised that there had been some truth in Mr Rouney's summing up. The C, or scholarship, forms were often in trouble and people tended to say what else could one expect? We would never be quite what we had wished to be. But then, at thirteen, I was content with the way things were. We had been studying the Essays of Elia and something, though by no means all, of the life of Charles Lamb and his poor demented sister, Mary. Now we were to act a play based on this, a play called, if memory hasn't failed me, *The Quaker Girl*. Charles, it seemed, had been in love but could not marry. When it came to casting the parts, she had said, holding on to the words as if they were too important to let slip carelessly away, finger tips ruffling further her unruly hair, 'Martha, would you like to be Hester, the Quaker girl? I think the part would suit you.' And, for the time being, that sufficed.